S0-BFB-190

River of Fear

Rod Davis

Morningstar
Communications LLC

River of Fear
Copyright © 2003
by Roderick C. Davis
All Rights Reserved.

Printed in the United States of America.
No part of this book may be reproduced without
written permission from the publisher, except for brief
quotations embodied in literary articles or reviews.

www.riveroffear.com

Edited by: Suzanne Anderson
　　　　　　Maurissa Morningstar

Published by
Morningstar Communications LLC
P.O. Box 5740
Pagosa Springs, CO 81147
(970) 731-9055
www.morcom.info

ISBN 1-880047-96-9

Foreword

River of Fear is a fascinating, intriguing, mysterious suspense novel. The author, Rod Davis, has a knack of making what seems to be unbelievable, very believable. As reviewers say, "It's a real page turner!" ... a great read that makes it hard to put the book down even for a few minutes.

The best thing about this book is that it is not the last but the first of the River of Fear trilogy. Davis is a first time novelist, but most readers we have talked to nearly all rate this book a 9 or 10. I agree.

River of Fear is set in the mountainous northwest woods of Maine in the middle of winter - not an unfamiliar place to author Rod Davis. As a former Mainer and avid snowmobiler (who now lives in Las Vegas, NV), Rod knows the scenery, the people and the unexplainable phenomena very well.

His characters ring true and events in the book grab you and shake your realities hard. This book has other worldly experiences, encounters with a powerful, shimmering light circle, magnetic pulsations, run-ins with mysterious strangers, disappearing animals and snowmobiles! His easy, matter of fact style lets the reader journey through the paranormal phenomena. Mainers agree that the story is pretty close to being true - it's about things that really DO happen in the Maine woods!

Davis creates suspense and action from the very first chapter and he maintains it throughout the book, dropping hints to the reader about what might be going on but never giving the story away until the end. He leaves you wanting more, and we will get more with the next two books. Yet, the first book ends in a complete way. It is a delicate matter, these continuing stories ... not to cheat the reader of the satisfaction of a good book, yet, leave them ready and hungry for more.

Stephen King and Dean Koontz, move over and make way for another weaver of suspense and intrigue, Rod Davis! Days after traveling down the River of Fear in the Maine woods, I can still feel the chill of the air, feel the rush of the icy river and the fear that the characters confront in this exciting novel. The second and third books in the River of Fear trilogy will be released soon. The author and the publisher have done something unique. You can be among the first to get a copy - or even a sneak preview - by registering at the website: www.riveroffear.com.

Jerry Pippin, Host of his own Internet Radio Show
at www.jerrypippin.com

Praise for *River of Fear*

Rod Davis is able to make the unbelievable, believable! *River of Fear* reminded me of a Stephen King or Dean Koontz novel. I was immediately able to see what was happening and have feeling for the characters.

Mary Kilts
Manager, AmeriSuites
Shelton, CT

"This book is a mystery action thriller that keeps the reader involved with much descriptive detail as he travels through the many miles of trails and backroads of Maine on snowmobiles. The characters and the reader encounter powerful, unexplainable forces, eerie sounds, magnetic pulsations and some very strange people! The author's writing style makes the reader feel that they are there and involved with the story as it unfolds around them. *River of Fear* is well written and keeps the reader wondering why, and wanting more in the way of thrills and action-packed adventure of the unknown forces they encounter."

John J. Stein
Polk City, FL

River of Fear is a fascinating mystery set in the Maine woods. The story line keeps you on your toes - I couldn't put the book down because the book keeps you guessing about what is going to happen next. The mystery revolves around the paranormal - maybe UFOs, maybe spirits, maybe a mirror world to ours. You, along with the characters, just don't know until the end. This is one of the best books I've read - I loved it! I can't wait to read the next two books and find out what REALLY is going on!

Albert Barrios
Las Vegas, NV

What an intriguing, mysterious suspense novel! I'm not a reader; however, *River of Fear* is a book I couldn't put down! The characters were true to life, just like real people I know who live in the Maine woods. The paranormal, ESP experiences and ET encounters the main characters have in this story held my attention - I've had experiences like this myself!

Marnie Souza
Cape Elizabeth, ME

River of Fear creates excitement and anticipation - a real page-turner. Rod Davis is able to engage the reader to the extent that you feel like you're participating in what is happening. I couldn't put the book down. I believe you have a winner ... and I need the next book!

Robert Yorks
Union, ME

I enjoyed this unique blending of the accurate description and atmosphere of our winter Maine woods with the paranormal and "other worlds" experience. *River of Fear* contains true-to-life stories about things that really do happen in the Maine woods! Rod Davis is able to create and maintain suspense, dropping hints about what's really going on but never letting the characters "get it" until the end. I can't wait to see how the story continues in the next two books.

Sandi Ingro
White Wolf Restaurant
Stratton, ME

River of Fear is pretty close to being a true story. It may be written as a novel, but I'll tell you there's a lot of truth in it. I know, because I live in the Maine woods. Read it and find out for yourself what it's like to experience things that you just can't explain!

Rick Day
Porter, ME

River of Fear is one of the most interesting and imaginative books I have ever read. It kept my attention so well I lost all track of time and could not put it down. I especially liked the mysteriousness of the character Zen and the "Circle of Shimmering Air."

James Lavin
Stratford, CT

Attention High Adventurers! This is a great book for anyone who enjoys intrigue and mystery. The characters are true to backwoods Maine – I could really relate to the places and the Mainers. And, as a pilot, I liked that the book was realistic in that respect, as well as the many accurate descriptions of snowmobiling. I was enthused by *River of Fear* and would definitely give it high marks and recommend it to young - or young at heart - readers.

John Karchenes
(Chief Cochese)
Coplin Plantation, ME

"This is a very different kind of book and it really kept my interest. The author has great imagination. The characters in *River of Fear* are very intriguing. Rod Davis creates a lot of anticipation and suspense in the story, especially when mysterious thing happen to certain important characters"

June Kovalsky
Stratford, CT

"*River of Fear* is an interesting science-fiction or paranormal mystery story. It held my interest - I kept waiting for the other shoe to fall, and of course, it did. The author uses descriptive narrative that really brings you into the scene to experience what the characters are going through. You can feel the eerie silence and the reactions of the people in the story."

Kenneth Warbrick
Las Vegas, NV

Dedication

This book is dedicated to: My wife for the countless hours of support and her on going encouragement that was invaluable to me during the writing of this book; To my son for providing me with the inspiration; and to my daughter for being one of the most giving persons I have ever known.

Acknowledgments

I would like to thank: Wes Bateman for the many interesting and inspiring hours that I spent with him; Chester Hataburda for his technical advice; Pat Sabattis, who was reluctant to meet, but proud to share some of his heritage as a member of the Passamaquoddy Indian Tribe of Maine; and James Fedak for sharing an experience that I shall never forget.

Also, my thanks to the many other people who agreed to be interviewed ... I am grateful to all.

It was mid January, and a perfect Monday morning. The sun was shining so brightly that the freshly fallen snow was sparkling with tints of reds, yellows, and blues. The tracks of deer, coyotes, rabbits and squirrels could be seen everywhere winding in and out of the bushes and trees. The air was so cold that it froze the inside of your nose every time you took a breath. The sky was a deep blue color and there were gentle gusts of wind that made the trees creak in protest causing little puffs of snow to fall from their branches. Rob Day and his old friend Rudy were taking their usual daybreak walk one mile down a snowmobile trail to a beaver pond. Rudy was an eleven-year old basset hound that Rob affectionately calls Toot-man, or Toot, depending on whatever comes to his mind at the time, and Rudy answers to both of them.

Rudy loved the morning walks and was acting like a typical basset hound in the powdery new snow. Every track was something new and exciting to investigate, and he went at it with all the enthusiasm of a six-month old puppy. Rob totally loved walking with his old friend and watching his canine antics. He was always amused when he saw Rudy after he had buried his head in the snow to check out a particularly interesting scent. His furry face would be covered with snow and his long ears, that he so often stepped on, would look like they had been dipped in flour. Rudy respected the fresh fallen snow and he did not wander far away from the snowmobile trail. Being two dogs long and a half a dog high, he had learned his limitations long ago when it came to soft deep snow. Rob guessed that at Rudy's ripe old age, if the scent was not seriously enticing, he was not really interested in doing the dog stroke through the soft snow in order to check it out.

The snowmobile trail they were walking on was actually an old logging road, and all the locals referred to it as the Harris Pasture Road. The road winds its way along the base of East Kennebago Mountain for a mile and a half before it begins its gentle rise to a clearing that overlooks Flagstaff Lake. East Kennebago Mountain is a part of the Longfellow Mountain Range that stretches from South to North along Maine's western border. Rob's mind began to drift as he was admiring the spectacular view of East Kennebago Mountain, enjoying the early morning sun reflecting off the snow on the southeastern slope. He thought about how fortunate he was to be able to come up to camp just about anytime he and Eileen felt the desire.

He had spent four years in the Air Force, and during that time he learned that working for a large corporation, or even a small company for that matter, did not mesh with what he wanted out of life. He did not like the idea that his earning potential would always have a defined parameter, and the possibility of ending up in a dead end position was even *more* unappealing. After much soul searching, he decided that being an entrepreneur was his best choice. He knew that he did not want to operate a business that constantly required him to be in one location, such as operating a restaurant or a gas station. As far as he was concerned, that was akin to being married both to Eileen *and* to a business. Each could be demanding, but the business would be unforgiving if it did not get the full time attention that it required.

He had diligently explored many business opportunities, and it was several years before he found a niche that gave him everything that he was looking for, and it came quite by accident. During a luncheon meeting with a business associate, the main topic of discussion was about a competitor in a neighboring town that was about to lose everything he had worked for over the past fifteen years. The man's business had grown in leaps and bounds during the first seven years, and it was still expanding, but his profit margin was shrinking faster than the business was growing. After lunch Rob called the man to compliment him on the growth of his business, and suggested that they meet for lunch on the premise that Rob wanted to learn his formula for success.

That lunch meeting launched a new business for Rob, and he became a turnaround consultant. That was more than ten years ago. He was able to work from his home in Cape Elizabeth, Maine, and also maintain a working office in his camp, allowing him freedom to work when and where he wished.

His relaxed mood came to a sudden halt when he and Rudy crested a hill overlooking a long deserted beaver pond. The moment that they topped the rise he looked down at the pond to see if he could spot any wild life, and he stopped short in his tracks. Above the center of the snow covered pond, imprisoned in winter's frigid grip, a sphere of distorted air suddenly appeared. It was about twenty feet in diameter and approximately twenty feet above the surface of the pond. As the distortion appeared, everything became stone quiet. The sounds of birds chirping, woodpeckers pecking on trees, crows cawing in the distance, and the chattering squirrels all stopped. It was as if someone had pulled the plug on Mother Nature's sound system. The surface of the shimmering air reminded him of the way heat radiates off a tar road on a very hot summer day. A mirage forms in the distance that looks like the road has water on it. Then a closer view turns it into vertical shimmering waves reaching towards the sky. He was puzzling about it when he heard a noise that sounded much like a TV sounds when the station goes off the air. The sound immediately intensified as though someone was turning up the volume. The sphere got somewhat larger, and then there was a noise that sounded like a drawn out *PHIIIIP* ... and it was gone.

The silence hung heavily as though everything had been suspended in time, and as abruptly as they had ceased, the familiar forest noises returned. When Rob looked at the beaver pond he expected to see the heat-like waves hovering over the snow again, however everything appeared to be perfectly normal. He looked down at Rudy and saw that his buddy was shaking, which was highly unusual. Rob felt a quick chill and he knew that it was not the cold that had caused it. Based on past experience he knew that his sixth sense had just kicked into high gear. He reached down to scratch Rudy behind the ears, and then patted him on the side, which seemed to comfort him, but he could not shake his own uneasy feeling. He had spent a lot of time in the Maine forests and felt very much at home there. He had a deep respect and a great love of the woods, and whenever he was out in nature, he was at peace. Never before did he feel as uncomfortable as he did now, and that feeling was very disturbing.

He stood up and said to Rudy, "Toot-man, what d' ya think that was all about?" He stood looking at Rudy like he actually thought that he would get an answer. Rudy raised his ears, cocked his head to the right and gave Rob a quizzical look that could only be interpreted to say, "You're asking me?"

"Come on, Toot! Let's mosey on down to the beaver pond and see if we can figure out what might have caused that circle of distorted air." Rudy took a couple of unsure steps, appearing to be uncertain about going with him. He momentarily paused, put his head up to sniff the air around him, and deciding it checked out OK, began following Rob down the trail. As they were walking toward the beaver pond, Rob's senses were unusually alert and he felt like he was trying to look everywhere at once. They were about fifty feet from the pond when a tree branch snapped. Rudy's ears perked up and he exhibited a degree of caution as he stopped to sniff the air all around him. Rob also stopped. All of his senses came alive. Before taking another step he carefully scanned the tree line where the sound had come from, but other than the snow ladened branches of the trees bordering the swampy meadow around the western edge of the beaver pond, there was nothing to see.

Rob continued walking down the snowmobile trail toward a bridge spanning a brook at the east side of the beaver pond. When he was about twenty feet from the bridge he could see animal tracks that began at the woods and crossed over the beaver pond, but they did not continue all the way across. He was studying them when Rudy came up alongside and nuzzled his leg. "Whatcha up to, Toot?" Rudy looked up at Rob with his basset hound happy face, gave a soft bark and started down the trail toward the bridge. Rob continued down the trail, walking in Rudy's paw prints as he approached the bridge, all the while looking out at the tracks on the beaver pond. By the time he reached the bridge where Rudy was waiting for him, Rob was so focused on the pond that he had almost stepped on his old friend. Rudy gave a sharp bark to get his attention.

Rob stopped as soon as Rudy let loose his sharp yip, but he did not take his eyes off the tracks on the beaver pond. Talking aloud to himself, he said, "I can't see any tracks going back into the woods, and not only that, I can't see anything that indicates that the animal turned around. Could it be that the animal walked backwards in its own tracks to get off the pond?" Feeling more than just a little ridiculous about talking to himself he said, "I'll tell you what, Toot-man, if that animal walked backwards in his owns tracks, it would be a miracle!"

"Come on, Toot! Let's take a walk out there." Rudy was less than anxious to venture into the deep snow, and after a couple of steps Rob thought better of it too. "Toot, this snow is just way too deep to walk out there without snowshoes. Let's go back to camp, get the snowshoes and something to eat. This can wait for a bit."

* * *

The walk back to camp seemed to happen in an instant. Rob was so deep in thought about the goings-on at the beaver pond that he did not remember any part of it, and did not realize that Rudy wasn't with him. He called out to him a few times, and when he did not show up right away, Rob went into the camp. He wasn't a bit concerned because it was not unusual for Rudy to find an interesting scent and spend some time checking it out.

He walked into the camp and a mouthwatering smell of freshly brewed coffee and frying bacon wafted across his frosty nose. "Mmmmm, mmm! Eileen, that sure smells good, and man am I hungry!" Turning to look at him she said, "Well, while I'm finishing up the eggs and bacon why don't you set the table and pour the coffee?"

Rob muttered under his breath, "O.K. I'll play your silly little game of why don't I!"

Either she didn't hear him or she chose to play *his* game and ignore him, because the usual word game stayed put. Eileen is Rob's Gal Friday. Even while raising their two children, she was the backbone of the inner workings of his office. Unlike all their friends, they started their family right away, and there was a well thought-out reason for that. They wanted to have their children while they were young and hoped their children would follow suit. The idea behind that philosophy was the fact that there wouldn't be a huge generation gap between them and their grandchildren, giving them the opportunity to enjoy them even more.

* * *

Rob was setting the table and pouring the coffee while Garth Brooks sang about friends in lowly places, which Eileen said he really related to. He liked almost everybody that he met, and had friends and acquaintances from all walks of life. Some she approved of, some she tolerated, and some she'd have nothing to do with. While he was setting the table he told Eileen about the tracks that he saw on the beaver pond. "When we're done eating, I'm going to get my snowshoes and take the Skidoo back to the pond to check them out. I've *got* to satisfy my curiosity."

"Well don't take too long. Thad is going to be here at 11:00 AM for our trailside cookout, and he's always very punctual."

"Oh yeah, that's right! I'll make sure I'm back in plenty of time."

Just as he finished his sentence, Rudy made it known that he was at the front door, ready to come in. Rob walked over to the door, and as soon as he had it open enough for Rudy to squeeze through, he bounded in, making a beeline to his food dish. Rob got a smile on his face and said, "We don't have to guess *if* he smelled the bacon while he was doing his *I wanna come in* routine at the door."

Rudy gave his food dish a brief sniff, and then turned his attention to Eileen, imparting to her his best sad basset hound look that usually got immediate results, but this time it was not the results that he was looking for. She yelled at him to go lie down, and as if he could really understand, she told him that his turn would come. While he was dejectedly walking over to his bed by the fireplace and while Rob was pouring a second cup of coffee, the phone rang. Eileen answered it and told Rob that it was Thad. He took the phone from her and said "Thad, mind if I call you back? Eileen's just putting breakfast on the table."

"Don't have to ... just reminding you that we're going to eat out on the trail today, or did you forget?"

"No sir! I wouldn't forget that for a flatlander minute." According to Thad, a flatlander minute was about as long as a mountain-man's memory, and Rob didn't know if that was good or bad, so he never asked. "I've been looking forward to it for over a week now!"

He could hear Thad's voice brighten as he said, "All right, see you at 11:00 A.M"

"Hey, Thad, hold on a sec. You're coming here, right?"

"Yup."

"All right, see you then."

* * *

When breakfast was finished, Rob grabbed his snowshoes from the basement and went out to the shed to warm up his Skidoo Formula Deluxe. The snowmobile looked just like the day it did when he took it out of the showroom, because he not only believed in keeping the sled in showroom condition, he also followed a strict preventative maintenance program. Even though it was still fifteen degrees below zero, three pumps on the primer and one turn of the key caused the engine to purr to life. Rob heard Rudy's barking over the sound of the snowmobile engine and knew what that was all about. Rudy wanted to go for a ride. He looked so sorrowful each time he saw Eileen and Rob getting ready to go for a ride on their sleds, because he knew from experience that they would be gone for the day. To help soften his obvious disappointment, Rob had gotten into the habit of taking Rudy for his own ride just before they left. Eileen called it Rob's guilty conscience bribe.

He went back to the camp and let Rudy out, and true to form, he immediately ran over to the sled. Whenever Rob started the sleds after they had been sitting overnight, if it was a windless day, a cloud of exhaust fumes would linger until they were fully warmed up. Either because he was overly anxious or hardheaded, Rudy hadn't learned his lesson and invariably ran right into the cloud of fumes. As soon as he got one whiff he would quickly bury his nose into the snow, rubbing it this way and that to eliminate what had to be a very irritating sensation.

While the snowmobile was warming up, Rob lashed his snowshoes onto the rack on the back, along with a hatchet and small hand saw for good measure. By the time everything was tightly secured to the rack, the engine was good and warm and it had finished puffing plumes of oil-laden, grayish-white exhaust. Before leaning over to pick up Rudy and put him on his lap, he gave the throttle a few quick bursts to clear any oil from the plugs. Rudy knew Rob's routine very well, and as soon as he heard him clear the engine he stood up and placed his paws on Rob's leg, making sure that he wouldn't leave without him. Leaning over, he put his hand under Rudy's rump, lifted him onto his lap and then looked over at the living room picture window to wave to Eileen in case she was watching. But she was nowhere to be seen and he felt a little pang of disappointment. "OK, Toot-man, we're ready to roll."

The moment that they turned onto the Harris Pasture Road, Rob squeezed the thumb throttle and didn't ease off of it until they were doing forty miles per hour. Rudy's ears were flying out from his head like limp wings, and the powdery snow spraying out from the sides of the snowmobile created such a huge cloud that everything behind them was left in a total whiteout. The walk to the beaver pond had taken them almost twenty minutes, but the ride took them less than four.

Rob stopped his Formula on the bridge by the beaver pond and let it idle for a minute while he looked over the area. It did not appear that anything had changed since he had left, less than an hour before.

When he shut off the machine Rudy struggled to get off his lap and the scene, less than graceful, was almost laughable when he slipped off Rob's lap, his body twisting back and forth like a fish out of water as he fell into the snow. Three shakes from head to tail and he was off at a trot up the track that they had just made.. While getting the snowshoes from the back of the sled Rob momentarily wondered why Rudy was in such a rush. As he strapped on his snowshoes, he felt the dead silence. No sound came from the breeze as it worked its way through the branches of the trees. Nor could he hear the plane above, or the musical sound of the birds calling out to each other. There were no sounds at all. The dead silence made him feel like he was in a vacuum, but none of this sank in. He was too focused on those tracks on the pond.

He called to Rudy and started down the bank to the beaver pond. When he was about twenty-five feet out on the pond, Rudy came bounding down the bank in Rob's snowshoe tracks. Rob went straight to the end of the animal tracks that he had seen earlier, which were about 150 feet from where he left the snowmobile. As he was approaching them he thought that they looked like stick holes in the snow, but after an up-close careful examination he could see that they belonged to a large deer. He also saw where its belly had rubbed the snow between the tracks. He walked alongside the tracks to where they emerged from the pine trees and he could easily see a deer run just inside the perimeter.

It was so well used that it led him to believe that this was probably the edge of the deer wintering yard, but he could not see or detect anything unusual. He slowly retraced his steps back along the tracks, all the while trying to see if there was any sign that the deer had walked backwards in its own tracks, thinking that was absolutely out of the question, but was just making sure. When he reached the spot where the tracks ended he was totally convinced that all of them were made in a forward motion. He stood there for almost fifteen minutes while he thoroughly studied the surrounding area to see if the deer could have possibly jumped straight up out of its tracks and landed some distance from where he was standing. He thought that that possibility was as far fetched as changing his occupation to writing fairy tales. But still, he had to satisfy his curiosity.

Everywhere he looked there was nothing but unspoiled snow, except for a spot about six feet to the left at the 11:00 o'clock position. That one spot looked like a round depression about two inches deep and about a foot and a half in diameter. Scratching the back of his head, he muttered, "This is beyond me," and headed back toward his snowmobile. It suddenly occurred to him that Rudy was not with him and he called for him to "come" several times, getting louder each time. He began to wonder where in the heck he had gotten off to, and then thought that it certainly couldn't be too far in the soft deep snow.

When he got back to the bridge he took off the snowshoes, tied them back on the sled, and then sat sidesaddle while he waited for Rudy. He was just about to call out to him again when he saw him running on the Harris Pasture Road, at the top of the hill overlooking the beaver pond. "I don't know how you got up there, Toot, but I'm glad you're back." Then he thought for a couple of seconds and said, "Where the heck did you get off to?"

He was about to pick Rudy up and put him in his lap when he heard the static-type hissing noise again. He looked down at Toot, and saw that the hair on his neck and back was standing straight up. Looking over toward the beaver pond where he had just been, he felt a chill shoot up and down his back as his eyes settled on the circle of distorted air. Only this time it appeared to be pulsating. Then he noticed a hawk making lazy circles in the sky about one hundred feet off to the left of the distorted air. It must have spotted a mouse or some other choice tidbit because it suddenly slowed its forward motion and started making very tight circles. Rob had seen this behavior many times and made the assumption that it was trying to zero in on whatever caught its attention below.

The static-type hissing noise ended as suddenly as it had started and Rob looked back at the circular distorted air. It was no longer pulsating. It was just hovering in one position, and then unlike the last time when it made its noisy exit, it simply faded from view. Rob looked back at the hawk and it was once again making its lazy circles, which were getting closer and closer to the perimeter of the beaver pond.

He started the Formula and looked back at the pond over his left shoulder. Everything appeared to be normal. Just as he turned his head to start across the bridge, he saw out of the corner of his eye that the circle of distorted air had reappeared, and when he turned around and looked directly at it, he saw that this time it was about ten feet in diameter. The hawk, now only twenty feet away, appeared to be wobbling its wings side to side, the way a pilot waves his wings to say good-by after performing in an air show. Suddenly, the hawk let out a screech as it shot into the circle of shimmering air. It reminded Rob of a piece of paper being sucked into a very powerful vacuum cleaner. He heard that PHIIIIIP sound again as the hawk hit the surface, and his mouth dropped open when the hawk and the circle of air simultaneously disappeared.

Rob's mouth was still wide open in surprise. He did not believe what he had just seen, and was having trouble coming to grips with the whirlwind in his mind. Then he felt Rudy shaking and that brought him out of his mental state. He squeezed the throttle to head back to camp, and went up the trail about 250 feet to a large area where he could turn around without using reverse. Using reverse in this deep soft snow could mean a walk instead of a ride back to camp.

When Rob reached the bridge by the beaver pond, he slowed down to a crawl, looking over the whole area. He shut down the engine and waited and listened to see if anything else would happen. After twenty minutes passed, the only noises that he heard were the chirping of birds and the occasional sound of snow as it fell off a tree branch. Rudy started to fidget and when Rob looked at his watch he saw that it was 10:15. He gave Rudy a couple of pats on the head and said, "We'd better get back to camp."

While heading up the trail to camp, Rob recalled the first time that he had seen a strange circular object. He and Eileen were dating at the time, and had gone to their favorite passion pit in Roosevelt Forest on a hot and humid summer evening. They had been parked for over thirty minutes that particular night with the windows open, and it was highly unusual that they could keep them open that long. The area in which they had parked bordered a large swamp and in warm weather the mosquitoes were always as thick as the humid night air. Another characteristic was the loud music of hundreds of frogs peeping and croaking in search of a mate. But on this specific night there were no sounds at all. Both of them had just remarked about how quiet it was and the fact that there were no mosquitoes. Then Rob looked out his side window. He saw a light about twenty feet away that was about the size of a medium beach ball. The light, which appeared more like a glow than a light, was steadily pulsing from a very dim light to a brighter dim light. He could not believe his eyes and thought that he was probably seeing things. He turned away from the circular light four different times for several seconds, but each time that he looked back the light was still there doing its fading in and out routine. Finally, Eileen asked him what he was so preoccupied with, and he clearly remembered her comment when she looked over his shoulder and confirmed that he wasn't hallucinating. It was simple and to the point, "I think that we should leave."

He was in the mood for more time in the passion pit, and had no desire whatsoever to leave so early. He was convinced that if they stayed that he had a real good chance of getting lucky that night, but then again he always had that feeling when they were there. Somehow the lucky part never materialized, but he did develop a very good understanding of what "Lover's Nuts" was all about.

In the past, he had seen phosphorous glow on rotting logs at night in the woods, but this light was different. His curiosity got the best of him and he got out of the car to take a closer look. He wanted to know what was causing it. As he walked toward the light he kept wondering what kind of phosphorus could create this type of pulsation. His thought process came to a screeching halt as a bolt of fear shot through him. He saw three round lights about the size of a quarter emerge from the pulsating light. They were in a perfect triangular formation that was about the size of a pool table rack, and the urge to pee in his pants became overpowering, as they started moving slowly but steadily toward him. He stopped in mid step, freezing in his tracks, just staring and not believing what was happening in front of him. Eileen had slid across the front seat to look out the driver's side window. She saw Rob standing in mid-step and wondered why. She looked past him and saw the three small circles of light moving across the ground toward him. As soon as her mind registered the scene in front of her, she let out a blood-curdling scream, which was all the catalyst needed to break his paralytic state of mind. His survival instincts promptly took over as he twisted around and bolted to the car like he had wings on his feet.

The dirt road going into Roosevelt Forest was a maze of boulders jutting up here and there, and Rob always had to carefully pick his way up the road. After he turned the ignition key and the engine roared to life, he did not bother negotiating the humps and bumps on the way out. Sparks flew every which way as he left his entire exhaust system behind.

The ride to Eileen's house would have been quiet if it weren't for the blaring noise of the exhaust from his 59 Ford Fairlane 500 Retractable Hardtop Convertible. They were on a section of road that was very dark, and seldom traveled at this time of the evening. Their adrenalin was thrown into a gushing turmoil once again when the beach ball size light suddenly appeared right in front of the windshield and Eileen let out another blood-curdling scream.

* * *

Rob was still deep in thought about the ride from Roosevelt Forest to Eileen's house when he found himself pulling into his driveway. The first thought to pop into his mind was that again he did not remember driving back to camp. He parked his sled next to Eileen's and put his snowshoes in the shed. When he walked into camp he was mentally immersed in the events at the beaver pond and plopped down in his chair, totally unaware of his surroundings. He was taking off his boots when the phone started to ring. Rob finally noticed that Eileen was nowhere to be seen, so he reached over and answered it in his normal jovial way, "Top of the morning!" ... really expecting it to be his friend Thad calling again. Of course, the person calling was a stranger and did not quite know how to respond to Rob's unconventional way of answering the phone. After a few moments of hesitation, a female voice that seemed unfamiliar to him asked if Mrs. Day was at home. In an attempt to hide his embarrassment Rob enthusiastically answered, "Sure, hold on a sec."

Eileen picked up the phone as Rob headed down into the basement to stoke the wood furnace, which he had dubbed "The Monster!" When it is really cold, like -25° F to -50° F, he can load it with three two-foot logs that are nine inches each in diameter. That single load of logs will maintain the camp at a comfortable 70° F for ten hours. He had learned the hard way that the logs need to be significantly smaller when the temperature is above 0° F, otherwise the camp turns into what Thad Cook calls 'tee-shirt weather' real quick!

When he came back upstairs Eileen was still talking to the caller, so he heated his coffee cup with hot water and poured his third cup of the day. Heating the cup with hot water was a cold weather trick that he learned from Jack King, an old hunting buddy who knew a lot about keeping his coffee warm, but who seemed to lack much in the way of personal hygiene.

About ten years back, Rob and Jack had gone on a Mule deer hunting trip in Utah with two of their friends, Josh Randall and Phil Bennett. They rode with a local rancher in his Ford Bronco to a remote area. He had given them the nickel tour of the immediate camp site to familiarize them with the conveniences, which consisted of a ten by twenty one room cabin with three double bunk beds, a table with two benches, three oil lanterns, a sink, wood furnace and wood stove, and a three-holer outhouse which was about fifty feet from the cabin. The minute the nickel tour was done, and without any fanfare at all, he left them on their own for the next seven days. Early in the morning on the fifth day, Josh brought down an eight pointer that dressed out at 265 pounds. He and Phil were not really experienced hunters like Rob and Jack, and when Josh yelled for help, Jack was the first to arrive. He found Josh standing there with his foot on the big buck, and he wore a huge toothy victory grin that seemed to cover his entire face. Jack asked him what he was waiting for, which brought a blank stare from Josh.

"What d'ya mean?"

Jack responded, "You can't just leave a deer like that, you have to dress it out, so get to dressin'."

"I ain't never dressed no deer before. You're the great white hunter, how about some help?" Jack pulled his buck knife from a leather sheath that was hanging from his seriously worn belt. Whenever anyone asked him when he was going to buy a new belt, his standard answer was, "This one's barely broken in."

He made a few skillful cuts that would have impressed a surgeon, stepped back and said, "The rest is yours." For a moment Josh looked like he was going to lose his breakfast, then set his jaw hard and went to work. He knew that if he didn't, the never-ending ribbing back at camp would be unbearable.

That night it was Jack's turn to cook and he pulled out his trusty buck knife to cut apart the chicken that he was getting ready to prepare. Josh happened to look over and nonchalantly said, "Hey, Jack, did you wash that knife?"

"Nope!"

Josh's face paled like it did that morning when Jack went to work on his deer and said, "What d'ya mean, nope?! Isn't that the knife that you used on my deer this mornin'?"

"Yeah, what of it?"

Josh muttered some remark that no one could hear and Jack just said in a conversational way, "You think that's something? I've been here five days, taken at least that many dumps and haven't washed my hands yet!"

* * *

Rob's mind journey ended when he heard Eileen yell at the top of her lungs "Oh fuck you!" – and then heard her slam the phone down on its cradle.

"Wow! What was that all about?"

"It's getting so that I can't stand phone solicitors!"

"Why, what's wrong?"

"They just won't accept 'no' for an answer. The girl that just called was selling magazine subscriptions. I was very polite and said; thank you for the call, but I'm not interested."

"I hate to tell you, Eileen, but that's not what it sounded like to me!"

"Well you didn't let me finish. This phone solicitor just wouldn't stop. She kept saying, 'let me just confirm your address', and I kept saying, 'I'm not interested.' Finally I did explode and hung up on her."

"Hung up on her! I've never heard you like that before." She gave him her 'that is enough' look, and he took the hint and went about his business.

Just at that moment, and only for that moment he was tempted to tell her about the phenomenon at the beaver pond, but he decided to keep it to himself. She and Rob had experienced several unexplainable events over the years, which always happened when they were together. The only witness to this event other than Rob was Rudy, and Rudy wasn't talking, so Rob figured he'd better not either.

* * *

With his fourth steaming cup of coffee in hand he reached up to get Eileen's snowmobile boots from their convenient drying place on the overhead support beam between the kitchen and the living room. The camp was only a shell when they had bought it from the Niles, and they, along with their children and Rob's best friend Shane DeLong, spent many long hours painstakingly finishing it off on the inside. The objective was to make the camp rustic, but homey. The walls were finished with rough-cut shiplap pine boards in varied 6, 8 and 10-inch widths that were nailed vertically on inside walls, and at a 45° angle on the outside walls, all with the unfinished side facing out. The ceiling was left open to give it that "campy" feeling.

Because Rob was 6'2", he had no trouble reaching the boots. His dark brown eyes were sparkling as he tossed the boots over to the couch where Eileen was sitting. She jumped at the loud thump the boots made when they hit the floor, and because they landed rather close to her feet she shouted a few remarks at him which he conveniently (his standard operating procedure) failed to acknowledge. He decided that his absence was the better part of valor at that moment and reached back up on the support beam to get his knit hat. He brushed back his thinning hair as he put the hat on and quickly walked to the hall closet for a broom to sweep last night's powdery snow off the front porch. His ever-increasing scalp visibility frequently prompted more than just a little kidding by friends and family, but he always took the kidding well. He had to because he frequently dished it out.

* * *

Rob and Eileen had met at a church youth dance during the summer school break in 1968, and had become high school sweethearts. Those that knew them said that they seemed to be inseparable. Rob still wonders after twenty-plus years of marriage exactly what it was that drew him so strongly to her. She loved to dance and was very good at it, while he could care less about dancing, which came through loud and clear when he was on the dance floor. She was only five feet tall, and he often kidded her by saying that he thought that she was still growing when they got married. When he thought long and hard about it, the only thing that made sense to him was that in addition to her beauty and stunning figure, which was accentuated by her long, flowing, auburn hair and hazel eyes, she had a personality that radiated across the dance floor. The magnetism that brought them together turned out to be a home run. While a lot of their friends' marriages had floundered and eventually failed for one reason or another, Rob and Eileen's marriage, though not totally smooth (they definitely had their moments), had flourished. They were pretty much on the same mental wavelength and often they would come up with, and sometimes verbalize, the same thought at the same time.

* * *

Thad Cook was a very good friend of Rob's. He was one of Baldwin Plantation's old-timers, and anyone could sit and listen to him tell stories about days gone by and never tire of it. He stood about six foot three inches tall and had a pair of feet that would support a man twice his size. At seventy-six years old he still enjoyed riding his snowmobile, four-wheeler, and paddling his canoe across lakes, ponds and down rivers. For many years, and at his own expense, Thad had been maintaining the trails and bridges around the immediate area that are used by the snowmobile and ATV riders. He seldom got any thanks for it, and never any money. He mentioned a few times that some younger person needed to take over, and Rob thought that he was hinting for him to do it. Rob would help out if he could, but unlike Thad, he didn't have a lot of extra time on his hands.

Thad's camp, which was located at the beginning of Big Foot Hollow Road, was about a mile from Rob's, and everyone around, including Thad, said that he had a million dollar view. From his front porch you could see Bigelow Mountain, Sugarloaf Mountain, East Kennebago Mountain, and the entire valley area. It is a breathtaking view that one never tires of, especially in the fall when the leaves change color. Thad had a CB in his camp, and when some other CB'er would yell for "Bigfoot," Thad would reach for the mike and the chatter would banter back and forth for quite sometime about the big doings of the day, or perhaps the night before. In Rob's opinion, Thad's CB was a local gossip line. According to Thad, sometimes the gossip got "pretty juicy," to use his expression, especially when they told him about a local waitress that spent, on the Q-T, a long evening (actually all night) with a temporary resident. A temporary resident is also known as a weekend-warrior or a flatlander camp owner. Supposedly the waitress was hired to do some work at the flatlander's camp, but when she was there all night, the second-guessing really went wild.

Thad's camp-mate was a golden retriever named Ginger. Ginger was a great lover of dog biscuits and almost any other doggie treat. Rob never saw her turn her nose up at anything, and her canine figure definitely showed it. Her days of jumping into Thad's pick up truck were definitely on the wane, because in addition to her abundance of fur and flesh, like Rudy, she was on in years.

Ginger was showing lots of gray on her snout and face, but true to the breed, she still loved to play. Years back Thad had bought Ginger a Frisbee, and to this day she would walk around outside the camp with it hanging out of her mouth, sporting that goofy "I dare you to take it away from me" look on her furry face. If anyone managed to wrestle it away from her, she would get all perky and do her high step while waiting for you to do the inevitable, and once the Frisbee is in the air, she would do a fast waddle to retrieve it.

Rob thought it was really neat the way Ginger would strut around with her Frisbee in her mouth, so he bought one for Rudy hoping he would do the same. Of course Rudy had a little difficulty carrying it since he's so short. Anyway, Rob's vision went up in flames as soon as Rudy decided to eat it, and that was the end of that.

* * *

While Rob was getting all their snowmobile gear together, Eileen finished up the breakfast dishes. The smell of bacon still lingered in the camp and Rudy went to his dish to check it out again. Once he determined that there was still no bacon in it, he gave Rob his best "I'm really disappointed" look. Rudy learned that unlike Eileen, Rob was a major soft touch, a real sucker for the "sad look." He saw Rudy's look and like a perfectly programmed android, he went directly to Rudy's favorite cabinet and fetched up a large meat flavored dog biscuit.

Sitting up to beg is not part of a basset hound's repertoire, so Rob never made a fuss when giving Rudy his treats. Rudy could be very affectionate, but when it came to food he had the manners of an aggressive kennel dog. He snatched the biscuit from Rob's hand just missing his long bony fingers, and instantly was at a trot to his favorite eating spot, the living room rug.

Rudy usually missed Rob's fingers, but on one occasion Eileen was not so fortunate. When that happened, Rudy had instantly known that he had goofed. His first clue was Eileen's scream of pain. His second clue was the sound of her stomping foot, and at that point Rudy's distinctive character came shining through, demonstrating an uncharacteristic canine trait. He dropped his biscuit down on the floor, which *had* to be very difficult for him because he was salivating before he even took it, and he put his nose close to Eileen's leg while looking up at her with an obviously concerned look on his sad furry face. Rob was convinced that he was trying to say that he was sorry, and Rudy stayed there until he received a forgiving pat on the head. So it came to pass that when Eileen gave Rudy a biscuit, she would simply toss it to his favorite eating spot.

* * *

With Eileen's blessing, Thad Cook and Rob had decided that today would be the day that the snowmobile trip would be to nowhere in particular, and wherever and whenever the spirit moved them, they would stop and have a trail side cookout. Thad called again at 10:40 hours, just as Eileen was hanging up the dish towel. It was obvious that he was anxious to get going, so Rob went out to get the snowmobiles ready.

When he stepped out on the front porch he checked the outdoor thermometer that was hanging on a huge red pine. The thermometer has a picture on its face of a deer jumping over a fallen log, and the needle was laying right over its nose, pointing to the 10° F mark. Rob said more to himself than anything else, "I guess the weather man's going to be right, 20° F for a high today. That'll be perfect for the cookout."

* * *

Eileen was a warm-weather girl and was clearly happy about the fact that the temperature was expected to go all the way up to twenty. When they were riding their snowmobiles she seldom complained when she got cold, but she would make it *known* and that meant a homeward bound direction was the next item on the agenda. Rob did not have a clue as to how they were connected, but when Eileen's nose got cold, so did her hands and feet.

The sleds' gas tanks and injector oil tanks were topped off and Rob was just heading back into the camp for his helmet and gloves when Eileen came out and insisted that he put the handlebar mitts on her Skidoo. He said, "For crying out loud, Eileen, it's going to be warm today ... why in the hell do you want those on? You have heated handlebar grips and thumb throttle, why do you need those things, too?"

She didn't say a word. She just tossed the mitts down on the snow in front of Rob and went back into the camp. He yelled, "Fine! I'll put the damn things on!" All the while muttering to himself, "Give the little lady what she wants."

* * *

Whenever Eileen asked him to do something for her that he thought was contrary, he'd always remember the day when he took her shopping to get a steak to cook over a red-hot charcoal fire on the outdoor grill. On that particular day, as far as he was concerned there were several nice looking steaks in the meat display case. Nonetheless, she didn't see one that met her requirements, and the meat cutter that was waiting on her obviously did not want to cut another steak. He wanted to sell what was already on display. While being very polite, he persistently and diligently tried to convince her to select one of the steaks from the meat case. The storeowner, or maybe he was the manager, overheard the conversation and said, "Give the little lady what she wants." Rob saw the smug look on her face and decided that within reason, he would always try to give her what she wanted when the circumstances dictated that it was the wise thing to do.

Rob and Eileen were watching a couple of deer walking through their back yard when they heard Thad Cook's snowmobile coming down the road. The sound of his machine was unmistakable and it made such a racket that it scared the deer. They both admired how graceful they were as they went bounding for the safety of a thick stand of pines just across a brook that meandered through their back yard.

No one around had a snowmobile that sounded like Thad's. They did at one time, but no more. Thad would never say die when it comes to keeping one of his toys going. His sled, a 1965 Arctic Cat Panther, sounds like a lawn mower that has been modified to accept a super charger. However the sound is very deceiving because when it says that he must be doing about 70 miles per hour, he is actually putting along at 15.

About ten years back, he had built a small storage shed to keep his Panther out of nature's elements, and he usually doesn't keep the sled in there unless there's no snow on the ground. Two days ago Rob went to visit Thad and when he didn't see the Artic Cat he asked him where it was. He nonchalantly responded by simply stating, "In the Cat House ... had some work to do on it, and just haven't taken the ol' girl out yet." It wasn't the first time that he heard Thad call it the "Cat House", and he still wasn't sure if Thad was putting him on or not.

Thad came down the driveway with his feet propped on the hood and tunnel rails where the hood ties down. His felt lined snowmobile boots made his feet look much larger than his size 13. As a matter of fact Rob thought that they sort of looked like clown shoes, and he almost expected to see the top half of Thad's feet flop forward as he brought his snowmobile to a stop. He didn't have his face shield down and when Rob went out to greet him, Thad's eyes and nose were dripping and his nose looked like he could give Rudolph some competition. Rob tried to come up with some smart remark, but all he could think of to say was, "Cold, ain't it?"

Thad's cryptic reply was,"It's 'snot' bad at all."

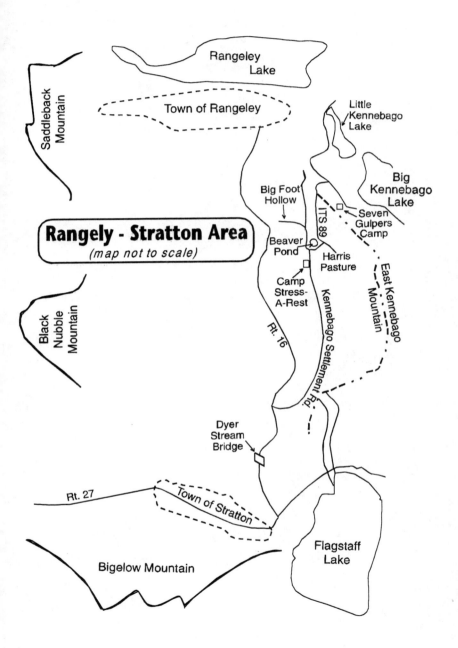

Rangely - Stratton Area
(map not to scale)

Rangeley Lake

Town of Rangeley

Saddleback Mountain

Little Kennebago Lake

Big Kennebago Lake

Big Foot Hollow

ITS 89

Seven Gulpers Camp

Beaver Pond

Harris Pasture

Camp Stress-A-Rest

Kennebago Settlement Rd.

East Kennebago Mountain

Black Nubble Mountain

Rt. 16

Dyer Stream Bridge

Rt. 27

Town of Stratton

Bigelow Mountain

Flagstaff Lake

2

Thad led the way, turning left out of the driveway onto Kennebago Settlement Road. Eileen and Rob followed him for about two hundred feet before he made a right turn to head toward the beaver pond and ITS 89, the same trail that Rob and Rudy had gone down earlier that morning. As they approached the beaver pond, Rob slowed down and carefully looked over the area. Everything appeared to be the same as it was earlier when they had left after the hawk had disappeared. Rob was convinced that the phenomenon he had seen earlier would not soon be forgotten, if ever, but he hoped that whatever it was that had happened was over for good. He pressed the thumb throttle on his liquid-cooled Skidoo Formula 500 Deluxe, slowly picking up speed at first, while taking several quick looks to his left, scanning the entire pond. After he crossed the bridge bordering the eastern edge of the pond, he increased his speed to catch up with Thad and Eileen. As he was leaving, he failed to notice that the sphere of shimmering air appeared and established a hovering position over the western edge of the pond.

He went about a half a mile before hitting the ITS 89 Snowmobile Trail, and when he looked to the left he spotted Thad and Eileen just topping a hill in the distance. The Arnold Trail Snowmobile Club maintains this section of ITS 89, and as Rob and Thad anticipated, the trail had just been groomed. It was as smooth as a newly tarred highway. The only snowmobile tracks on the trail were those made by Thad and Eileen. After turning onto ITS 89 he quickly accelerated up to 40 miles an hour, wanting to catch up with them as fast as possible. As he crested the hill he suddenly had to hit the brake. Thad and Eileen were sitting alongside the trail and appeared to be admiring the view of Saddleback Mountain and all the ski trails that meandered down its northeastern side.

Rob brought his sled to a skidding stop and walked over to "chew the fat" with Thad. As he approached him he noticed that he had a far away look on his face, like he was in the middle of some intense daydream. "Hey, Big Foot! Whatchya so intent on?" Thad's return look was something that he had never seen on his face before.

"You OK, Thad?"

"I think so. Age must really be catching up to me 'cause I don't remember a thing since I went over the beaver pond bridge. It's like one second I'm crossing the bridge, and the next second I'm sitting here on the side of the trail looking at you talking to me. You want to know what's really weird?"

"What's that?"

"At first I see your lips moving, but I don't hear your voice. Then as I'm about to tell you to stop playing games with me, because I know I'm not deaf, it was like you finally decided to put sound to your lip movement. You trying to mess with my mind or somethin'?"

"Thad, I like to bust your chops, but I wasn't bustin'. My lips weren't just moving, I was talking all the time, trying to find out what you were concentrating so hard on. Do you want to head back to camp and make this trip another day?"

"No. I'm all right. Let's go. By the way, I'm going to stop at the Seven Gulpers for a break and we can check the camp. That OK with you?"

"Sure, lead the way."

* * *

When Thad reached the Seven Gulpers he pulled off the trail and parked his Panther right in front of the camp. The camp was about five miles in the woods and about half way up East Kennebago Mountain. It sits in a one-acre clearing, and although it has a great view of the valley and lakes below, it does not begin to measure up to the view that Thad has from his camp.

Rob and Thad always stopped to check on the Seven Gulpers camp when they were in the area, acting as sort of a backwoods

Neighborhood Watch, similar to what they have in the suburban areas to keep crime down. Only here it is intended to make sure that Mother Nature's elements do not cause additional damage after evidence of a break-in is found. The locals and temporary residents automatically keep a vigil making sure that all is OK when they are in the vicinity of an unoccupied camp.

On more than one occasion Thad had found something amiss at the Seven Gulpers' camp, and he took the necessary steps to temporarily fix the problem. And once he got back to camp he always called his buddy, John Spencer, to let him know what he had found, and what he did to help out. John and six of his friends had built the camp sometime after the Korean conflict. Whenever the group got together at their camp, they put away a serious amount of beer while playing poker or pinochle, or just plain "chewing the fat". A few of the locals that joined them in their festivities from time to time dubbed them the Seven Gulpers. John and his friends liked the name so much that they painted it onto a sign and nailed it to the front of their camp.

Whenever Thad called John about a problem that he had found at their camp, he would always chat some about the new areas that were being logged, and all the locations where different companies had removed their logging equipment, not to mention all the juicy gossip being passed between and amongst the Baldwin Plantation and Stratton local residents. Without exception, he covered all those subjects before he got around to telling him the reason he called. Of course, that drove John crazy because the only times Thad called him was to deliver bad news about the camp. So whenever he picked up the phone and heard Thad's voice, his stomach would start churning in anticipation of the news that he was about to receive. He really didn't want to hear stories regarding Baldwin plantation gossip, or anything else for that matter. He just wanted to get the bad news over with. But that idea never occurred to Thad. He did the chitchat thing so as to help soften the news.

One of his calls to Spencer had been to tell him about a bear that had literally busted into their camp, making splinters out of the front door. John was really pleased when Thad described in brutal detail the incredible mess that it had left behind.

As usual, Thad checked the front entrance to make sure that everything was secure, while Rob took a stroll through the soft snow around the entire camp. As he worked his way down the opposite side of the camp he almost tripped over a cable that was buried in the snow. One end of the half-inch thick cable was attached to the floor joists under the camp, and the other end was anchored to a huge pine tree. Over the years the camp started to slip as the footings settled into the ground on the downhill side. John and his buddies were at a point in life that camp time meant playtime, which never left any time for any major camp repairs, and leveling the camp would be a major project. The tilt did not bother them, so as long as the pine tree was alive and well, which they figured would certainly outlast them, that was good enough.

* * *

Once they deemed that the camp was OK, Rob suggested that a ride to the top of East Kennebago Mountain was in order. Thad looked like he may have some other spot in mind so Rob piped up, "It's as clear a day as I've seen in a long time. You can literally see forever. Come on, Thad, you know that you like the peace and quiet up there. Besides, whenever we go snowmobiling in January, how many days do we get like this with such a clear view?"

Thad grunted his agreement, started his snowmobile, and without hesitation pulled back onto the trail. Eileen pulled out right behind him, and Rob brought up the rear. Single file they worked their way up the steep and twisting trail to the top of the mountain. The ride was spectacular with the fresh fallen snow weighing down the pine tree branches on both sides of the trail. Most of the way up the mountain, the sun was in the right position to reflect miniature rainbows here and there off the snow-laden branches.

As they entered the clearing on the top of the Kennebago, Rob pulled around Thad and parked his snowmobile on the highest spot, which is his favorite vantage point to take in the awesome view. The three of them simply sat on their snowmobiles for nearly ten minutes without talking, just absorbing the peace and quiet while enjoying the panoramic view. The beauty of the valley below could only be described as awe-inspiring. The distant mountains were shrouded in shades of blue, shadowed here and there by scattered white puffy clouds that looked like giant cotton balls floating overhead. They had been quietly sitting there, deep in their own thoughts, when a fox walked out from the low pine trees just to the right of Rob, and stopped not more than five feet from him. Its thick winter coat was a mixture of various shades of rust brown, with a blending of black here and there, and it had such a luster to it that it looked like it had just bathed in a rich shampoo. Rob wasn't surprised to see the fox come so close, as this was not the first time that this had happened. During hunting season a couple of years back, he was sitting quietly on a camouflaged folding stool about fifty feet from a deer run, when a fox came by and stopped right next to him. It stood there for about a minute before realizing that Rob was there beside him. In fact the fox was so close that he could have reached out and touched it just by moving his arm. However, when the fox noticed him sitting within accurate spitting distance, he made a very hasty retreat, while a smile worked its way onto Rob's face. The critter had reminded him of a cartoon character trying to make its getaway. Its legs seemed as though they were going like crazy for a second or two, before it got traction and quickly disappeared.

However this fox was different. When he casually looked over at them sitting on their snowmobiles, he made no attempt to run away. After a moment or two, Rob decided the fox was studying them. He was very surprised when it took some free-and-easy steps forward, and nonchalantly sat down. It seemed as though the fox was taking in, and enjoying the same view as they did. After five minutes went by he was beginning to think that the fox was mimicking them, but then he thought to himself, "Man! That's really far out! My imagination is in overdrive today!"

When the fox took a long slow look over its shoulder at Rob, a strange feeling came over him. This animal did not act like any fox that he had ever seen before. His sixth sense slipped into high gear and he began watching the fox very closely, looking for signs that the fox could have a loose screw, or worse yet, rabies, although that was not very likely this time of year. This past fall he had heard on the Bangor Country Western station that rabies was running rampant in Maine. However the fox did not act or appear to be sick. Just the same, it was disconcerting it did not seem to be afraid.

The fox sat and blinked in the bright sunlight for at least ten minutes, then he slowly hunched, doing a stretching exercise, and lazily scratched his left shoulder. Once he had apparently satisfied his itch, he looked back over his shoulder at the group, then nonchalantly stood up and slowly walked around the clearing, stopping here and there to sniff whatever interested him. A downy woodpecker landed on a nearby tree that obviously had been dead a long time. The sparse stubby branches on the dead tree gave it the appearance that it would make a good prop in a horror movie. Almost in unison, Rob, Eileen and Thad turned their attention to the busy bird. It was doing its sporadic skip up the tree looking for something tempting to eat, and after the woodpecker flew off in its continuing search for food, Rob remembered the fox and decided to see what it was doing. It was now sitting about ten feet away from them, with its tongue hanging out, and looking very perky. He could almost swear that it had a canine grin pasted on its face, just like he was watching a funny scene in a sitcom.

Rob decided that the fox was not sick, nor a threat, and turned his attention to pulling a candy bar out of the rear compartment of his snowmobile. As he started to tear the Mounds bar wrapper open, he noticed that the fox was paying very close attention to him. As he made the first tear in the wrapper the fox stood up and trotted over to him, just like Rudy did when he knew that food was at hand. The fox covered most of the distance to the back of Rob's snowmobile before it sat down, and at that point only five feet separated them. His ears were fully perked up as he stared at Rob with a happy, expectant look on his face as if to say, well it's about time you brought out the goodies!

"I'll be darned, he's a moocher! That's why he's been hangin' around."

Rob broke off a piece of the candy bar and tossed it toward the foxy critter, no pun intended, and it landed about one foot in front of an inquisitive nose that did not waste much time checking it out. The fox quickly picked up the succulent morsel, pointed his snout toward the sky and after chewing it four times, swallowed, looking back at Rob like he was expecting more. Just like Rudy! Rob couldn't resist the fox's charm, and he carefully tossed it another piece. As soon as the candy left his hand it looked like it had wings, and floated toward the fox in slow motion. It looked as if it was going to bounce right off the fox's nose, and in fact, if the fox had his mouth open the candy would have dropped right in. Rob at first thought the fox may have been a mooch that was not afraid of humans, and furthermore, he now demonstrated that he was not stupid. As the piece of candy neared his nose, he moved his snout slightly to one side and let it drop onto the snow. He gave it a quick sniff to make sure that it was what he expected, and it too disappeared. The fox finished swallowing the last piece then he sat down like a well-trained dog, and gave Rob another expectant look.

Eileen spotted the look, and knowing full well that Rob was a soft touch, she piped up and said, "Hey! That's my candy bar, and I want the rest!"

Rob could hear Thad chuckling as he turned to the fox and said, "Sorry, pal, you lose." The fox continued to watch Rob intently as he picked up the candy bar, folded the wrapper over and put it into a zip-lock bag. He looked over at the fox as he opened his snowmobile compartment to place the bag inside. He realized he had more than just a little feeling of empathy for the fox. The snow was soft and deep and the fox would have a lot of difficulty hunting for food. It did not soothe his guilty feeling when he saw that the fox's ears were drooping. It reminded him of Rudy when he was being scolded for doing something wrong. The fox had the same look of betrayal.

He looked over at Thad and said, "You have anything that we can feed this guy?"

"Maybe, let me check." As Thad turned around to look in the cooler that he had mounted to a rack on the back of his sled, the fox ran to the center of the clearing and began to growl as if trying to warn something off.

They were watching in stunned silence when it suddenly yipped and jumped like it had been dealt a blow.

Rob looked at Thad and said, "What the heck do you suppose that was all about?" Before Thad could answer, the fox start to growl louder and slowly moved backward into a crouching position.

Rob yelled to Thad and Eileen, "Start your sleds! This fox might be sick after all!"

By this time the fox was running in circles like it was chasing its tail, but the circles were larger than that. Rob yelled to Thad, "Maybe this fox is schizophrenic. Its acting like it's chasing a phantom. Let's get the hell out of here before it turns on us!"

* * *

Rob took the lead as they headed to the trail on the opposite side of the clearing, and as they were negotiating the steep descending trail as it twisted its way down the mountain, he thought of a good spot for their cookout. Once they were back onto ITS 89, he turned to the right onto an obscure trail that was about three quarters of a mile from the Seven Gulpers. The trail was short, seldom used, and led to a camp that was built by one of Thad's friends. The first time that Thad had brought Rob here to see the view, he told him that a buddy of his by the name of Fred Powers owned the place. Rob knew that in this particular case, saying that Fred *owned* the camp was not true in the strictest sense, because the camp sat on land that had to be leased from the Mead Paper Company. But leased land or not, as far as Rob was concerned, Fred had made a great choice. The camp overlooked the Little Kennebago Lake from the northwest side of East Kennebago Mountain. If you looked due West past the Little Kennebago Lake you could see the distant mountains in New Hampshire.

Fred Powers, now a retired high school English teacher, had built the camp about thirty years before and it looked like it took more determination than skill in order to get the structure up. The camp was about thirty feet long and fifteen feet wide. The roof and sides were covered with rolled roofing that was as unsightly as acne. Fred periodically had a problem with hikers breaking a window to get inside, but more than likely it was because they needed to get out of some bad weather. They didn't cause any damage other than the broken window and they never took anything. But Fred wanted to bring the problem to a screeching halt, so he built a multifunctional wooden shutter for each window. The shutter was not typical by any means. It was fastened to the top of the window casing with inside hinges rather than being mounted in pairs on each side of the window. He had to use different lengths of hooks to hold up the shutter. He used the short shank hook when he wanted to let in the daylight, and the very long shank hook when he wanted to have a full view of the outside, and depending upon where he was standing or sitting at the time, he could include a view of the distant mountains in New Hampshire. When he dropped the shutters down and hooked them from the inside, the camp was break-in proof (to a certain extent). But according to Thad, with all the light shut out, the camp became a serious mouse haven.

As Rob approached the clearing surrounding Fred's camp, he pointed the nose of his snowmobile toward the front door, and turned to the left as he neared the snow covered steps. The snow was soft, and if they were going to walk around without sinking out of sight, it would have to be packed down. Rob continued making circles in the clearing in front of the camp to pack down an area for them to walk in.

Thad and Eileen had no way of knowing that Rob had made an executive decision to have their trail-side cookout here. They didn't realize the real reason he had taken the Mounds bar out while they were on the top of the mountain. He was famished, and if that fox hadn't come along, that candy bar would have been history. Eileen would never have had a chance to say it was hers. Just as he was completing his second circle Rob saw Thad and Eileen coming up the camp trail. They both quickly put two and two together and joined him in the parade. After a couple more passes each, the surrounding area was sufficiently packed down to support them while they walked about.

* * *

Rob parked his snowmobile at the mouth of the trail exiting the clearing, and set the brake. Thad and Eileen had just shut their engines down as Rob was taking his camera out of the back compartment of his snowmobile. "Hey, you guys, stand fast a moment. I want to get a picture of you with the view of the lake and mountains in the background."

Thad got a deep scowl between his eyes and Rob knew why. He was never very happy about having his picture taken. Rob was a camera bug and loved taking pictures, and Thad always resisted being part of them. Rob usually countered Thad's negative feelings by saying, "Just think about all the fond memories that we'll be able to talk about, sometime in the future, while we're looking at these pictures during happy hour." In fact, once, out of exasperation Rob just blurted out, "What's the matter, Thad? Do you believe in that old Indian tale ... that part of your spirit is lost to the picture?" That statement had flashed into Rob's mind because in the past he and Thad had many discussions about the spirit world while sipping on a favorite cocktail during their happy hour ritual.

Thad was not a great believer in the teachings of the church. As a matter of fact he was not much of a churchgoer at all. He claimed that his last recollection of being in church was when he was baptized a few months after being born, and that happened only because his mother, a very good and God loving person, insisted upon it. Rob always took a firm stand that there was no way that Thad could possibly recall his baptism. He told Thad that he had probably seen pictures that were taken by some family member during the baptismal ceremony, and maybe also some pictures that were taken at the usual family gathering afterwards, so that is what he truly recalls. However, Thad always insisted that neither his parents, nor any other family member for that matter, even knew that cameras existed at that time.

Thad loved to reminisce during their happy hours, and one day he told Rob about a particularly nasty session that he had in the hospital, and how it changed his philosophy regarding the spirit world and the hereafter. About six years before, Thad had part of his colon removed due to cancer, and once a year he needed to go into the hospital for a colon exam to make sure that no new polyps had surfaced. He claimed that his beliefs regarding the spirit world all stemmed from a colonoscopy exam that he had about four years back. The doctor who had performed the colon surgery on Thad had moved out of the area shortly after the operation, and Thad asked his family doctor to recommend a specialist for his yearly check ups. Dr. Claymore, who according to Thad is so old, that he must have driven a tin lizzy, recommended a Dr. Rebecca Rosen. Thad was up in his years, but he wasn't beyond modesty, even when it came to a physician. So when Dr. Claymore recommended a female physician, Thad fought him hard and long for another recommendation, still, Dr. Claymore convinced him that she was the best.

Dr. Rosen found several polyps during the colonoscopy and snipped them off. Thad thought she snipped them a little too close because he bled a lot. In fact he continued to bleed for several days after the polyps were removed. He refused to stay in the hospital, and against his doctor's orders, signed himself out. He told her that he could convalesce better back at camp than he could with some busybody nurses fussing over him and interrupting his sleep during all hours of the night.

Late one night, about two weeks after he had signed himself out of the hospital, Thad had a real bad spell. He woke up from a deep sleep completely disoriented and very dizzy. On nights when there is no moon to cast shadows in Baldwin Plantation, especially if it is overcast, it is impossible to see without a light. As a matter of fact, you can put your hands right in front of your eyes and not even be able to see a silhouette of them. There was electricity in the area at that time, but Central Maine Power had not yet run their power lines as far as Thad's camp, and he had to depend upon a generator. This particular night was not only moonless, it was also overcast, which blocked out the dim, but helpful light from the stars. Thad fought a psychological battle for a few minutes, just trying to piece together where the heck he was. He finally began to put things in their proper place, and realized that he was in his camp. He carefully groped around in the pitch-black darkness to find the phone that he kept on a nightstand next to his bed. When he found it he almost knocked it to the floor and just barely caught it in time. Thad had thought ahead about dark nights and the fact that he may have to make an emergency call, and had bought a phone with a large dial pad. He felt for the numbers and dialed 911.

* * *

Alan Hanbury was on duty when Thad's call came in. He had known Thad for many years and he had been to his camp several times before. As a matter of fact, his last trip to Thad's wasn't very long ago. His shift was just ending the day that Thad called 911 after a heavy piece of angle iron had fallen off a shelf in the Cat House and hit him in the temple. Thad told him that he had just regained consciousness, but felt like he was going to black out again. Alan was very concerned, and he made short work of getting to Thad's. As a matter of fact, it took him about thirty-two minutes to cover the distance of twenty-four miles of a miserable road with more curves in it than a slow moving river flowing through a level valley.

Alan's adrenalin was still in high gear when he arrived at Thad's that night. Moose were plentiful in the area, and just after he crossed the Dyer Stream Bridge he almost had an intimate relationship with a cow and two of her calves. The three of them were taking up almost the entire road, and he quickly decided that he would hit the calves, because they would cause the least amount of damage, and just maybe he'd be able to continue on his way to Thad's. Fate, luck, providence, or whatever you want to call it, was Alan's best friend that dark night. Right at the moment when he thought it was inevitable that he was going to hit them, the group parted, with the calves to the right and the cow to the left, just in the nick of time. Alan's eyes were wide and his heart was pounding as he quickly turned the wheel to the left and went whizzing right between them.

* * *

However, this trip to Thad's was not made at breakneck speed. He just didn't sense the urgency in Thad's voice this time. But when he drove into Thad's driveway he felt a shiver go up his spine and he became very concerned. There were no lights on inside. Both he and Jimmy Grant grabbed their flashlights and the medical kit and took off at a run to the front door. Ginger was right there to greet them, whining and obviously very nervous, giving Alan even more reason for concern. While he went over to the bed with his medical kit to check on Thad, Jimmy lit the gas lamps, and as soon as three of them were burning brightly, he joined his partner.

Alan quickly looked at him and said, "He's unconscious and his vital signs are pretty weak. Get the gurney, we need to get him to the hospital fast!"

* * *

When the emergency staff at the Farmington Hospital checked his blood pressure, they found that it was very low. High blood pressure was his *usual* problem. According to Thad, they needed to put four pints of blood into him when all was said and done. He said that after he dialed 911 he must have blacked out again because the next thing that he knew, he was freezing and being hurled down the inside of a swirling tunnel of trillions and trillions upon trillions of tiny little lights. They were whirlpooling around and around like they were in a tornado. He said that the tunnel was pretty big, but he had no recollection of how much room he was taking up in it. He said that he saw one steady light in the center of the tunnel, which he thought might be at the end of it, and it kept getting bigger and bigger and bigger. As he got closer to the steady light he felt warmer, and warmer, and he had a feeling of being very glad, and then he changed his mind and said it was a happy-time feeling. He had difficulty in describing it. But the feeling kept getting stronger and stronger. Then all of a sudden he was at the end of the tunnel, and the light that he had been looking at was just everywhere. He felt like he was being absorbed, or that he was being sucked into it, again having difficulty describing exactly what was happening. Then he said it was right then that he had a feeling that he equated to a sexual climax, but he went on to say much more than that, more like the greatest sexual climax ever. Then he felt that he could describe it even better by saying, "but multiply the intensity of that feeling times a million". He went on to say the next thing that happened, "I began hearing words telling me something, and it was like the answer to life. It explained why everything is the way it is." Most of all, he remembered saying to himself, "Boy, do I gotta remember that! That is *so* simple!" Then, the next thing he knew, he was back in the tunnel again, hurtling at a tremendous rate of speed.

Then he kind of paused, like he was vividly remembering the experience, and Rob finally asked, "What happened next?"

He didn't look at Rob, or anything else for that matter. He was just staring into space and said, "Bam! I'm in a bed freezing cold, shivering. Standing all around me were men and women dressed in green and white. At first I thought that I must have finally 'bought the farm', and the good and the bad must be arguing over who will get me. But then I thought, the bad guys wear either black or red as far I can remember. Where in the hell does the green and white come in?"

Thad went on to say, "Little by little my focus and reasoning came back, and I realized that I was lying in a hospital emergency room with doctors and nurses looking over me. One of the doctors leaned over and asked me how I felt.

"I told him that I wasn't sure if I was disappointed or relieved; and Dr. Chan did not exactly know how he should reply to that statement, so he chose to ignore it. He told me that I gave them quite a hard time, and that he thought they had lost me for a while there.

"I asked him what happened and he told me that I had some internal bleeding and lost a lot of blood. He said that in addition to four pints of blood, the nurses administered some blood coagulants to stop the bleeding, and if that didn't work he would have to operate.

"Just about then, a burst of light went off in my mind like a flash bulb in an old-time camera, and I told Dr. Chan that I had a colonoscopy two weeks ago and there was internal bleeding after Dr. Rosen snipped off some polyps. I told him that I had been taking it easy and I thought it should've gone away.

"He told me that he would check that out. He said he wasn't sure if it did go away. Anyway, I spent a few days there while they tried to determine what was wrong."

Because of that episode, Thad was a beaten man. His pride had been shattered. His woman doctor was right and he was wrong. That did not compute in his way of thinking, and he was having an extremely difficult time accepting it. But he also had another startling thought. Dr. Chan had said that he had thought that they had lost him. Thad began to wonder what he had meant by that. Little by little he recalled that he had heard voices as he was hurtling toward a light, which he had found extremely soothing and comforting.

Then he felt a sense of loss as he fully remembered and realized that he did not quite make it to that soothing light, the light that gave him comfort in a way that he had never felt before. And the knowledge! But as hard as he tried, he couldn't remember the answer to life and why everything is the way it is. He could only remember that he knew. Now he fully understood why he was both disappointed and relieved when he first woke up.

From then on Thad was firmly convinced that life goes on after the body gives up its will to live, and he would share that information with anyone willing to listen to him.

Thad was not a well-educated man in the academic sense, but he was a well-read man. More than once he told Rob that there is an energy source inside our bodies, and that when we die that energy source goes into another dimension. He also believes that sometimes a person's energy does not quite make it into the other dimension, and when that happens, some spiritually sensitive people may have a ghostly experience.

And Rob did not disagree with him. One day after Thad had finished pontificating about life and the other dimension, he said, "Thad, I think that this is purgatory that we're in now and the past deeds that an individual has to atone for determines how long that individual stays here."

Thad took a long look at Rob and said, "How did you come up with a bright idea like that?"

"Well, Thad, how many people do you know on this earth that don't have any problems at all?"

"None."

"That's my point exactly. No matter who you are, no matter how much money and influence you have, you still have problems to contend with."

* * *

Rob walked over to the stone fireplace overlooking the Little Kennebago Lake. Fred had also built the fireplace, but it was a masterpiece compared to the camp. According to Thad, one of Fred's buddies who was a stonemason built it to Fred's specs, but Fred still took the credit for building it. Thad thinks that when he had it built he was actually more interested in sitting in front of it on a starlit night than cooking the occasional steak, pork chop, hamburger or hotdog on it. He loves to watch the flames licking at the frosty night air while listening to the logs as they snap, crackle, and pop their hypnotic tune. The mesmerizing flickering of the flames, commingled with the different noises of the burning logs and East Kennebago night sounds, always succeeded in putting Fred into a euphoric state of mind unmatched by anything else he had ever experienced. If the truth were known, Fred used the fireplace much more for relaxation than cooking. Adding to the mystique of the fire is the panoramic view of the night sky that houses the Milky Way and sheds an occasional dying meteor. The air up on the East Kennebago is so clear that on a cloudless night, at first glance, the Milky Way almost looks like haze way up in the night sky. Then as your eyes adjust you can see, or maybe it is just your imagination, the billions of individual stars.

* * *

Rob brushed the snow off the fireplace while Eileen and Thad unloaded the burgers, fixings, kindling and That Stuff™ from her sled. By the time Thad had walked over with the load of goodies from Eileen's sled, Rob had walked (actually waded) down a path in the deep fluffy snow to the fireplace. He had just placed tinfoil on the packed snow in the pit of the fireplace when Thad set part of their lunch and some other items down on the left wall. Rob watched as Thad reached deep into his coat pockets and produced two frosty Buds. His face lit up like a five hundred watt bulb and he said, "Buddy, I can really count on you to think of everything!"

Eileen never understood how they could enjoy a cold drink when, as far as she was concerned, it was freezing out.

Rob took That Stuff™ from amongst the items that Thad had set down on top of the fireplace wall and placed a handful of it in the middle of the tinfoil. Then he piled the kindling on top of That Stuff™, and within just a few minutes of lighting the match, the fire started spewing forth yellow and blue flickering flames. Once it was burning freely he leaned over and picked up his beer from the snow alongside his left foot. He took several slow swallows, savoring the flavor of the barley and hops as he casually stood back up.

Eileen interrupted his enjoyment saying, "I'm so hungry that I feel like I could eat enough for two people," as she handed him the grate and burgers. He gave her an ear-to-ear grin that said, "OK." He placed the grate on the fire, then adjusted it so that it was supported on all sides and as level as possible. Next, he grabbed the burgers and laid them side-by-side on the grate. After he picked up his "King," he turned to Thad as he was getting ready to take another sip and said, "What d'yah think about that business with the fox?"

"It's funny you should ask. Just as we were leaving, I looked back at the fox and it looked like he was jumping up in the air to catch a bird that just took to flight. Only there was nothing that I could see right off that the fox could have been jumping at, so I stopped to get a better look."

And that was it. Thad just stood there sipping his beer and casually looking around like he was taking in the view. Rob could not believe that was the end of the conversation. "Yo! Thad! So what did you see?"

"Well, actually I was trying to figure whether I should tell you the truth or make it up as I went along."

"Thad, I've never heard you talk in riddles before. What gives?"

"I've never seen the likes of it, Rob. It was like the fox had reached around and somehow grabbed himself by the neck! It looked like he was pulling himself up and down. I may be on the long side of my sunset years, but my elevator isn't skipping floors yet. I thought long and hard deciding whether I should tell you about this or not, but that feeling that I had ... I just had to tell someone. Even if they did think that I was flipping out."

"Tell me about that feeling that you had, Thad."

"I felt like time stopped. I felt like the only thing in the whole world was me watching that fox do his crazy aerobics."

For a moment, Rob teetered on the brink of telling Thad what happened at the beaver pond that morning but quickly decided that he should keep it to himself.

* * *

The burgers were a savory fond memory when they threw snow over the last of the glowing embers in the fireplace. Rob watched the steam rise a short way up into the air before it quickly dissipated. He wrapped up the tin foil and, as he headed over to his snowmobile, he saw that Thad was tying the knapsack and grate onto the back of Eileen's sled. "Hey, Thad, thanks for that!"

Rob stepped up on the tunnel rail of his Formula, swung his leg over and sat down on the soft cushiony seat. One pump on the primer and the sled started right up, making that 'Bombardier' hum that he loved to hear. He was switching the hand warmers and thumb warmer to high to take the chill out of his gloves when he heard Thad yell for him to take the lead. He nodded his acknowledgment and started to head down Fred Powers' three hundred foot driveway, if you could call what looked like an old skidder trail a driveway. The driveway was fairly straight and Rob kicked his Formula up to thirty miles per hour in what seemed like the blink of an eye. When he reached the end, he checked his mirrors to see if Eileen and Thad were right behind him, but there was no sign of them. He figured that they were just taking their time. He hooked a right onto ITS 89 heading toward the Seven Gulpers and the trip down the East Kennebago.

He did not pay much attention to any of the scenery on the way back because his mind was wrestling with the strange events of the day. In all his life, he had never experienced more than one unusual episode in one year, let alone in one morning. He wondered what in the name of Sam Hill was going on? First the distorted air over the beaver pond, and the stone silence for no reason, followed by the static hissing noise and the feeling that time stood still while he was looking at the vertical, shimmering air. Coupling that scenario with the fact that Thad also had the feeling that time was standing still while the fox was doing what seemed to be the impossible, Rob knew that he would not quickly forget this day.

The upside to his thought process was that Eileen was none the wiser as to what was going on. That was good because she had an over active imagination anyway, and hearaing about these events would likely shift it into overdrive.

* * *

Rob was so engrossed in thought that he had reached the bottom of the mountain and had gone about half way through a mile long straightaway before he thought of checking his rear view mirrors for Thad and Eileen. They were nowhere to be seen. Feeling a little bit uncomfortable that they weren't behind him, he decided to pull over to the side of the trail and wait. It wasn't the first time that he'd had to wait for them, but recent events made today a whole lot different. He knew that they sometimes rode the trail slowly while trying to spot a moose or deer that might be foraging in the woods, and of course, if they did spot one or the other they would stop to watch the animal until it was out of sight. If it was a deer, it was usually history pretty quickly. On the other hand, moose are not typically afraid and take their sweet time about whatever they are doing. He always told Eileen that the reason that moose are so slow is because they were dealt a short hand when it came to brains.

Of course he also liked to stop and watch a deer or moose, or the occasional fisher that he might see while riding, but sometimes he liked the thrill of pushing his sled hard, especially on a weekday when there are very few other riders on the trail. But today he did not think that he had been pushing his sled hard at all and he assumed that Thad and Eileen must have stopped to watch a moose or a deer. He really could not remember whether or not he had hustled down the mountain. His mind was reviewing the crazy events of the day, so he had no recollection of the trip down.

Five minutes went by and they still had not shown up. Now he was positive that they must be watching a moose taking its time eating some branches off a tree, so he turned off his sled to enjoy the peace and quiet while he waited. Another ten minutes passed and he still could not hear their sleds in the distance. Everything was stone quiet with the exception of the chattering of a red squirrel that sounded very upset. But he did not give it much thought because unhappy squirrels are not uncommon in the Maine woods, especially when some venturous rodent invades its neighbor's territory.

After another ten minutes went by and he still could not hear the sound of Thad's super charged Panther screaming along at fifteen miles an hour, he started getting very uneasy. Finally he decided that he had better head back up the trail to find out what was wrong. Maybe Thad's vintage sled had decided to give him some grief and Eileen was sticking by until Mister-Fix-It solved the problem.

He fired up his sled, popped it in reverse and did a u-ee. As soon as he had his machine headed toward East Kennebago Mountain, he put the throttle to the handle bar and was doing sixty in the blink of an eye, or at least it seemed that way. When the trail curved and started winding its way up the mountain, he backed off on the throttle, but only enough to maintain control of the sled as he used the weight of his body, leaning this way and that to work the sled over bumps and around the curves. His adrenalin was pumping hard and he could feel it so he knew that it was not just the thrill of the ride, but it was his growing fear of something worse than just Thad's sled breaking down.

* * *

Thad had started out behind Rob as they were leaving the clearing in front of Fred Powers' camp. However when they hit the main trail, instead of following Rob toward the Seven Gulpers, he made a left and headed back to the top of East Kennebago Mountain. Eileen did not see that Rob had turned right and she followed Thad, thinking all the time that they were following Rob.

When they got to the top of the mountain Eileen was surprised that Rob was nowhere to be seen and she turned to Thad to ask where he was, but stopped short. Thad was sitting on his machine with his helmet in his hands and his eyes had a blank look to them, like he was in a trance. Eileen put her mitten-covered hand on his arm and softly said, "Thad?"

No response. She started getting a little frightened and said louder, "Thad!"

He looked at her, but still said nothing. Then again, you could not say that he really looked at her. It was more like he looked through her. She shouted his name this time, "Thad!"

Slowly, recognition began to show in his eyes and he stood up to look around and then developed a very surprised look on his face. "How in the hell did we get back here? And where's Rob?"

"You're kidding me, right, Thad?"

"I'm not kidding at all. The last thing that I remember, Rob had just put out the fire, we packed the sleds and I told Rob to take the lead. What're we doing back here? And where's Rob?"

Eileen took a very close look at Thad to see if he had a smirk on his face, but there was none. He appeared to be dead serious. She asked him again, "Thad? You're putting me on, right?"

He could see that Eileen was concerned and was just making sure that he was OK, but now *he* began to get an uneasy feeling. This was the second time in one day that he had CRS (Can't Remember Shit). If he was a young fella just coming off a bender he could understand a loss of memory. But up until that day he had experienced no recall problem. He was having difficulty coming to grips with these recent befuddling events.

"Maybe I had best make an appointment with Dr. Claymore to see what's wrong. If one of you guys weren't with me when I decided to kick my brain into neutral, I wonder what would have happened to me?"

Eileen looked past Thad's left shoulder and saw something that looked like a fur stole hanging over a stubby branch of the dead tree where they had seen the woodpecker earlier. She started walking over toward it, and as she drew closer she could see that it looked just like the fox that Rob had been feeding.

Thad said: "Is that the fox that we saw this morning?"

"Yes, I think so."

"Is it alive?" He started walking toward the tree to get a closer look when the fox suddenly rolled to its left and fell off the stubby branch, dropping to the snow below. After a few seconds went by it looked over at them, and it had a look about it, as if it wanted help, then it sank into a sitting position. After a few seconds, and with what looked like a tremendous exertion, it struggled to stand back up. They could see that its hind legs were shaking with the effort that it took, and all the while the fox was looking intently at them. Once it was standing on all fours it shook itself off, and suddenly Thad's entire body began to tingle with a nervous type sensation that kicks in when your sixth sense slips into high gear.

The sensation started in his toes, quickly traveling up his spine and all the way to his head. He could count on one hand the number of times in his life that had happened and he quickly grabbed Eileen's arm and said, "Let's move slowly over to our machines, but try to do it as naturally as possible."

"Why? What's wrong, Thad?"

"I don't know. But something sure doesn't feel right."

They continued to casually talk as they walked toward their sleds. They had gone about ten feet when Thad looked back to see what the fox was doing. It was nowhere to be seen, and that suited him just fine.

* * *

The snowmobiles were warm and purred to life as soon as the starter was engaged. Thad took the lead as they drove their sleds slowly toward the trail at the far end of the clearing. All of a sudden Thad's taillight flashed bright red and Eileen watched as the rear end of his machine slipped around to the right. When he came to a full stop, he jumped off his sled and came on a trot back to her.

"What's wrong, Thad?"

"Listen, that fox just ran across the clearing, jumped in front of my sled and sat up like Ginger does when she wants a treat. I ain't never seen no fox do that before, and moocher or not, it just ain't right!"

"Where's the fox now?"

"He ran off into the woods when I stood up. I'm headin' down that mountain and I ain't stoppin' for nothin'. You stay right behind me and do the same."

"Now you're scaring me, Thad."

"Look, this ol' sled of mine isn't very fast, but that thing you're ridin' is a rocket, and I know that you can really make that machine talk when you want to. If I start doing strange things, stick your thumb throttle to the handlebar and don't slow down until you get back to camp, and make damned sure that you don't stop for nuthin'."

"Thad, if you stop, I stop. I'm not gonna leave you behind."

"Listen, if you do have to leave me and I don't catch up after a short while, have Rob call the game warden to get some help to look for me. The two of them would be of more help to me than you. No disrespect."

"None taken."

"Remember, you kick that sled of yours if I start actin' funny."

"OK, but I still don't like the idea."

* * *

Rob was absolutely cooking up the trail when he saw snowmobile headlights ahead, and instantly backed off the throttle. At a quick glance it looked to him like Thad was in the lead. He pulled off to the side of the trail and was stepping off his sled when Thad blew right by him without even slowing down and Rob was perplexed because he acted like he didn't even see him.

"Hey, Thad!" Rob yelled as he went by, and thought, "Yeah! Right! Like he can hear me over the screaming of his Cat."

Eileen stopped on the trail opposite Rob and met him half way across it.

"Hey, Eileen, what's up with Thad? Does he have the shits or something?"

"Rob, I'm worried. Thad had another memory blackout session a little while ago."

"Another one? Where did it happen ... back at Fred's camp?"

"No, back up on top of the Kennebago, and don't you give me that look! I thought that Thad was following you, and I went along for the ride. When we got there I walked over to him to find out where you were and how come we went back up the mountain. I'll tell you what, Rob, he didn't *know* why we were there, and I got a little scared because he really looked spaced out."

"Welllllll, it's a good thing that you followed him instead of me."

"You mean it's a good thing that I didn't see which way you turned, because if I did I would have followed you, and if that happened ... who knows what would have happened to Thad."

"Hey! We'd better haul ass and catch up to him. The way that he went by me, he could be having another one of his mini fugues."

By the time that he had turned his sled around, she was already a quarter of a mile down the trail, kicking up a cloud of snow. She must have really been moving, because after five minutes had gone by he still couldn't catch a glimpse of her.

Rob's machine was purring at forty-five miles an hour when he reached the bottom of the mountain where the trail made a sharp right turn before leveling out. He saw the spot where he had pulled over to wait for Thad and Eileen and at that point he expected to be able to see her somewhere up ahead on the one mile straightaway. But she was nowhere to be seen, not even a cloud of snow.

"Man! I must be taking a Sunday drive compared to her!" Then his mind shifted gears and he wondered to himself why she was going so fast. At their normal speed of thirty-five to forty miles per hour, they would quickly catch up with Thad. He felt the beginnings of an uneasy feeling spread throughout his body as he put the thumb throttle to the handle bar. His sled catapulted forward and almost instantly he was going so fast that it seemed like he was skipping from the top of one mogul to the top of the next, and his Formula performed just like it was normal business. He had never pushed his sled like this before, and his body was vibrating with an adrenalin rush, the likes of which he hadn't experienced since the time that he almost fell off a 500-foot cliff.

At the end of the one-mile straight away the trail made almost a complete U-turn to the left, crossing Delaney Brook, and twisting its way back toward the base of East Kennebago. The trail remained level for about two miles before starting an ascent up the southwest side of the mountain. Thad and Eileen were sitting off to the right side of the trail just past the Delaney Brook bridge, and appeared to be having a normal friendly chat as Rob pulled up.

Trying to make light of the way that he really felt, Rob yelled over to Thad, "Hey! How come you just blew right by me back there? You becoming anti-social all of a sudden?"

"Nope. I just wasn't ready to stop. Besides, I knew that you would catch up right quick."

Rob looked at Eileen and said, "I'll tell you what, you really kicked that machine of yours, huh?"

"You might say so." And being more than just a little coy said, "Why, did you find it hard keeping up?"

"Nope." Rob's macho was about to come through loud and clear when he thought better of it and said, "I just found it hard to believe."

Then he looked at Thad saying, "What happened up on top of the mountain?"

"Not much to talk about. Catch you later." Thad started his machine and he was gone ... just like that.

Turning to Eileen, Rob said, "Did I do something wrong?"

"I don't think so. I think Thad has a lot on his mind with what happened to him today, not to mention how the fox spooked him."

"What happened?"

"I've got to pee and it's not as easy for me as it is for you out here on the trail. So let's get going and I'll tell you when we get back to camp."

* * *

Before he knew it they were at the Harris Pasture Road turn-off. They made the turn and had gone about a half a mile when Rob slowed down to a crawl as he approached the bridge by the beaver pond. Off to his right he could see a faint circle of distorted air, which was not nearly as pronounced as it had been when he had seen it earlier. Actually the circle of shimmering distorted air seemed to be drifting toward him, as if blown by a gentle breeze, but there was no breeze at all. The air was very still.

He was tempted to stop and see if anything would happen this time, similar to what happened with the hawk this morning. But when he thought about Eileen being in back of him, and the fact that she had to pee, he changed his mind. After going about two hundred feet he saw a deer run across the trail in a panic, its eyes looked like they were wild with fright. He didn't think that he could have scared the deer that badly. The snowmobile trail passed alongside the deer's wintering yard, and they had to be used to hearing and seeing snowmobiles, so he slowed back down to a crawl and looked around to see if he could spot what could have terrorized it. His first thought was that it might be coyotes because there were lots of their tracks everywhere in the new snow from last night. The heavy concentration of tracks was a strong indicator that they were probably hunting in this area, so he expected to see a couple of them run across the trail in hot pursuit of the deer. However nothing showed up, so he motioned to Eileen to take the lead, and as she got alongside of him he jammed the throttle to the handlebar. The race was on!

Unbeknownst to Rob, the shimmering air had started moving quickly toward them just as their machines shot forward with each of them jockeying to get the lead.

* * *

Thad did his best to keep Harris Pasture Road as smooth as ITS 89, but it was almost impossible. Harris Pasture Road was heavily traveled by the weekend temporary residents that came up to the mountains for a getaway, distancing themselves from the rat race, taking mind and body off the stress machine, as well as enjoying some great riding. To groom the trail, Thad towed a homemade drag behind him that he had made from an old steel boxspring, and he had to go slow to make sure the holes in the trail would get filled in as much as possible with the loosened snow. On the other hand, the Arnold Trail Snowmobile Club equipment was state of the art and the trail that it left behind was smoother than most highways.

Racing on a trail groomed by Thad was a real challenge. As a matter of fact, just staying on the snowmobile was a challenge. Harris Pasture Road empties into, or starts from, an open field that borders Kennebago Settlement Road, depending upon who is describing it. The wind coming down off the East Kennebago whips the loose snow along the curving tree line and creates a large snowdrift right at the entrance to Harris Pasture Road. With all the snowmobile traffic going to and from ITS 89, that drift gets firmly packed, and at this particular time of year it is a bump to reckon with. Rob and Eileen came shooting out of the road from the beaver pond and when they hit the snowdrift, they went sailing through the air for about twenty feet before touching down. As they went across the road to their camp, Rob thought that it was a good thing that Thad did not witness this stunt, because if he had he would have called them a lot more descriptive names than just flatlanders.

They parked their snowmobiles in front of the shed and Rob went to get the gas cans to top them off while Eileen, doing the pee pee dance, brought the grate and empty knapsack into the camp. She opened the front door and as she stepped in, Rudy was standing right there with his tail wagging so hard that his whole body was moving from side to side. Eileen reached down to pet him on the head, and she just barely touched him when he bolted for the front door. It was obvious that he too had to go very badly or maybe he was just overly anxious to greet Rob. "OK, Rudy, hold your horses. I'll let you out!" Eileen had hardly opened the door two inches when Rudy jammed his nose into the opening and charged forward with so much force that it tore the door out of her hand.

The gas was gurgling out of the five-gallon can into Eileen's gas tank when Rudy ran up to Rob carrying on like he had not seen him in a week. "Hey, Toot-man! Really happy to see me huh?" Rob set the gas can down as he bent over to scratch Rudy behind both ears at the same time. Rudy let out a grunt of satisfaction and immediately sat down as if he expected this to go on for quite a while.

The loud crack of a dry and brittle branch, as if it was being snapped off a pine tree, echoed in the woods just behind Rob. Rudy let out a soft "woof" and took off at a trot down the snowmobile track that Rob had made earlier. He reached the edge of the woods in short order and raised up his nose as high as he could, all the while sniffing the air in all different directions, looking for a scent. Rob gave a casual look around the immediate area and saw nothing. Evidently Rudy didn't pick up a disturbing scent because he was doing the typical laid-back trot back to Rob for more scratching, his ears swaying side to side, sweeping the trail with each step. When he sat down next to Rob with that expectant look on his furry face, Rob said, "Sorry, pal. I'll take care of you later. Right now I want to finish topping off these sleds."

It was early in the afternoon and, as far as Rob was concerned, one of the ten best days of winter. He really didn't want to quit riding just yet, and was trying to decide whether to cover the sleds and get caught up on some paper work, or go for a ride to Flagstaff Lake to pick up the newspaper at the Pines Market. He was so wrapped up in his thoughts that he did not notice everything turning stone quiet. He looked over at Rudy when he heard a whine that ended abruptly, and that's when the same static noise that he had heard at the beaver pond filled the air.

3

Both Rob and Rudy stood very still while trying to see in all directions at the same time. He glanced down at his old friend and saw that he was shaking again. He leaned over and put his hand on Rudy's head and gave him several reassuring pats. After a few seconds he started to look up in the air for any sign of the distorted air, the same as, or similar to what he had seen at the beaver pond. But there wasn't anything that resembled that picture, which was very unsettling because he could still hear the static hissing noise.

"Toot-man, let's take a walk into the woods and have a look around." Rob walked past the shed to get his snowshoes that were sticking up out of the snow next to their four hundred-gallon propane tank. The tank had been casting a shadow over them, and even though the temperature had risen considerably from what it had been before when he and Rudy took their walk on the beaver pond, the neoprene bindings were still pretty stiff. The moment that Rudy saw Rob grab his snowshoes he came bounding over with his basset hound happiest sad face and stood right beside him. It looked like his whole body was wagging his tail.

As soon as his snowshoe bindings were good and tight he said, "OK, Toot-man, let's take a look-see!" They climbed up over the snow bank that had been left by the snowplow alongside the shed, and headed toward the woods. Rudy zigzagged from one snowshoe track to another as Rob broke the trail.

He was heading toward a break in the wall of pine trees that was actually a well-travelled deer trail. It was one of many that twisted and wound its way through and along the edge of the deer's wintering area, where they forage throughout the cold and snowy months. The pine trees in this area were about ten feet tall and stood very close together, providing great cover for both rabbits and deer.

Once they reached the tree line, Rob paused to see if he could still hear the static noise, and Rudy stood patiently behind him sniffing the air all around. He didn't know if it was his imagination but the static hissing noise seemed to be coming from every direction. He turned around and looked back across the clearing, all the way to the woods on the other side of Kennebago Settlement Road. He could see the trees gently swaying from side to side and that indicated that there was a breeze. Yet, he could not feel any movement of the air where he was standing. He was looking to see if any of the dead leaves remaining on the nearby poplar trees were moving when everything went stone silent and he immediately felt the sensation of being in a vacuum.

He started to move into the pines along the deer run, and after going about twenty feet he started to feel something like a tingling sensation over his entire body and he stopped short. The sensation did not go away but it did not change either. He looked behind him to see how Rudy was doing but the only evidence that his dog had been behind him was his tracks. Suddenly the tingling sensation was gone and Rob felt a gentle breeze. He looked down at Rudy's tracks again because something stuck in his mind about the way they had looked.

On closer examination, the tracks looked exactly like Rudy's normal walk and they just ended right behind him without any indication that he had come to a stop. Rob unbuckled his snowshoes and slowly turned around on them, being extra careful not to disturb anything. He squatted down to look under the low branches of the pines to see if somehow his old friend had managed a jump to the side to investigate some interesting scent, but the tracks did not show any sign of a kickout that would be made if Rudy had pushed hard with his legs to make the jump. It is no secret that a basset hound does not have the ability to jump very far to the side from a walking stance, but Rob still checked the entire area around where Rudy could have possibly landed, and then even further. But the only tracks that he could see were snowshoe rabbit tracks that wound their way in and around the base of the short pine trees.

"Hey, Toot-man! Where are ya!?" Rob listened to see if he could hear Rudy working his way back to him, but there were none of the usual telltale sounds.

"Hey, Toot! Come on boy!" Still nothing, and that was not like Rudy, unless he was on a hot rabbit track. If he were, everyone for a mile around would know it.

"This is impossible!" Rob said to himself. He stepped off his snowshoes to the right, and started crawling in a semicircle through the powdery snow, working his way back to the clearing near the shed. When he got to the edge of the clearing he let out a low groan. Working his way through the low hanging branches, had allowed the fresh powdery snow to frequently fall down his neck, soaking him all the way down his back. And to add insult to injury, along with the melting snow, tiny little dead pine needles also managed to find their way inside his shirt.

* * *

Just as he reached the clearing, Eileen walked past the corner of the shed looking for him. He did not notice her standing there and he was a sight to behold as he performed various gymnastic maneuvers in an attempt to stop any additional snow from melting down his back. His gyrations were even more exaggerated by the fact that he was trying to keep the pine needles that were inside his shirt from causing additional discomfort. He stopped his outlandish movements when he heard Eileen laughing and he slowly turned around to see where she was.

Still laughing out load she said, "Rob, just what in the heck are you doing? Are you trying to invent some kind of new exercise to limber up?"

"Very funny! Rudy disappeared. He was behind me one minute and gone the next. I've called and called him, but there's not even a hint of him being around, so I decided to crawl through these stupid pines to see if I could find any of his tracks. And if I didn't find any, then I wanted to at least follow his tracks from the beginning of the pines to see if I can figure out where he went. And I'll tell you what! Unless he's developed a new talent and learned how to walk backwards, step for step, retracing his steps without disturbing any of the tracks that he had made during his forward motion, he's done the impossible and disappeared right into thin air. What-da-ya think about that!?"

"I think I'm going to go back into the camp, sip some Swiss Miss and work on my puzzle. That's what *I* think!" Then she looked over at the snowmobiles and said, "I see that you still haven't covered the sleds. Are you going to go back out again? 'Cause if you are, it's a beautiful day and I'd like to go to. Just so long as you don't stay out too late."

"Yeah, I was plannin' on it. I thought that maybe we'd take a ride to Flagstaff Lake, but I want to find Toot-man first, and I also want to know what happened with you and Thad on top of the Kennebago after we left Fred Powers' place."

"OK. I'll wait inside for you, and I hope you find Rudy soon."

"Yeah, me too."

* * *

Still not wanting to disturb any of the tracks that he and Rudy had made as they walked through the clearing and into the pine trees, Rob waded through the snow alongside of them. It became much more difficult when he reached the pines. He continued calling for Rudy, but there was still no sound or sight of his furry friend by the time he reached the spot where he had left his snowshoes. He strapped them back on and started to painstakingly recheck the area immediately around him. He took his time, inch by inch, looking for any clue at all that Rudy had backtracked. Quite frankly, he thought that scenario was totally impossible. But still, he had to check, because as far as he could determine, that was the only option.

It took him much longer than he thought to reach the end of Rudy's tracks, which is actually where they started when he and Rudy had climbed over the snow bank to walk out to the pines, and he didn't see any clue that he had hoped for. Each and every one of Rudy's tracks had a little tuft of snow sticking up on the backside, and four depressions in the front where his toe nails had dug into the hard packed lower layer indicating only forward movement, no back stepping. Even though the idea was totally unappealing, he decided to crawl under and through the pine trees one more time. He just had to be one hundred percent sure. Unfortunately, when all was said and done, he was not only thoroughly soaked and itchy again, he ended up with the same unknowns.

At times like this he would always talk himself through a routine to find a solution. "I must have missed somethin'. Logic tells me that he couldn't have just plain disappeared. I think I need to poke around some more. I've already made a semicircle to the right. Making a semicircle to the left makes sense, and I'll keep expanding the circle on both sides until I find some sign of Rudy."

He completed the circle and expanded it several times. After a little more than thirty minutes he had managed to work his way beyond the thick growth of short pine trees and was in a stand of hardwood trees that had recently been logged. He stood at the edge of the hardwood growth, scanning the area for any sign of Rudy when he spotted what looked like a circular depression in the snow. The terrain sloped upward at about a thirty-degree angle, and he had a view that allowed him to see that the imprint was about twenty feet in diameter. It was like someone had decided to set a huge ball down in that spot. But what he found extremely strange was that the depression did not vary from its concave appearance even where there were small trees (which were left as seeders by the logging company for new growth) within the depression.

He walked up to the edge of the circular depression and continued around its entire perimeter. The snow was soft at the edge but was rather loosely packed inside the imprint. Other than the occasional rabbit track and bird track, he could see no other disturbances in the new snow cover surrounding the circular depression. While slowly looking all around and then up toward the sky, he recalled all the strange events of the day and muttered to himself, "And the day isn't over yet!" He felt somewhat overwhelmed and that is a feeling that, until that day, had been totally alien to him. More to himself than anyone else, he muttered, "What in the hell is going on around here?"

Whenever he had reached the end of his rope in the past, he would experience a sensation not unlike a small charge of electricity that traveled through his body, starting at the tip of his toes and continuing all the way to the top of his head. Suddenly he felt that same sensation, but he could not fathom why! He didn't feel like he was frustrated, it was more like being confused. He made up his mind that he had used up all his options, and said to himself, "I think I'll head back to camp. Maybe Rudy'll be there asleep on the rug and this will all seem like a weird dream."

* * *

Once again, before he knew it he was back at the camp. Like the other times, he was so deep in thought about the day's events that he didn't remember the walk back. He took off his snowshoes and stood still for a few minutes and if anyone had seen him they would have probably thought that he was in a trance. Finally he set his snowshoes behind the propane tank and headed for the front door expecting to hear Rudy bark a greeting but there was only silence when he opened the door.

He stepped in and placed his gloves on the end table as he said to Eileen, "Rudy's not here?"

"Nope. Did you see any sign of him?"

"No, I didn't, and that's got me real worried."

"Rob, Rudy's probably gone off on a rabbit track. He's done that before and we didn't see him for a few hours. He'll be back soon."

"I don't think so, Eileen. I couldn't find any sign of him at all, and what's more, if he was out there working a rabbit, we'd hear him baying from time to time. I was out there for more than thirty minutes looking for him and I didn't hear him once. That wouldn't bother me if there was a strong wind that could drown out his baying, but the wind is calm. Nah, as strange as this may sound, based upon everything that I could see when checking Rudy's backtrack, he just flat ass disappeared into thin air. And I'll tell you something else, I kept expanding my circles looking for some sign of him, and you know where the thick stand of pines ends near the stone wall, and the hardwood growth starts?"

"Sure."

"When I reached the clearing there was a about a twenty-foot circular depression in the snow. I walked around the whole thing and what I found really strange was that the angle of the depression was constant, even around the trees in the imprint. It was like somebody had set down a huge Wiffle Ball, and the holes lined up just right to fit around the trees. Eileen, up until today I could always rationalize my way through almost anything, but when I think about the way that Thad acted today, that crazy fox, and now this! I've run out of rationalization. I think it's a first for me.

I don't have any answers that make any sense. There's something else. I didn't tell you about what happened when Rudy and I took our walk this morning."

"Why, what happened?"

* * *

Rob filled her in on everything that had happened that morning when he and Rudy had taken their walk, including the static-like noise around the camp and the strange tingling sensation that he felt just before Rudy disappeared. Then he said, "What happened to Thad up on the Kennebago? You still have to tell me about that! And my instincts tell me that it's gonna be weird. Even if it isn't, when you put all this crap together in one day, how could anyone in their right mind rationalize it?"

Eileen was quiet and appeared to be deep in thought, so Rob said: "What are ya thinkin' about?"

"I was just trying to think of something that might make sense, but nothing comes to mind except that I think that we should pack up and go home."

"I might agree with you if I had found Rudy, but since I haven't, it's not an option. I can't just abandon him. He may love to chase rabbits and be woods-wise, but he certainly doesn't have the ability to survive on his own. An animal not only has to have cunning to survive in these Maine woods, it also has to have speed, and speed is not Rudy's forte. Before we do anything, I need to get a hold of Thad and Jack King and tell them about everything that's happened, and get their feedback. You know, I'm goin' to have to be very diplomatic when I present this information, especially to Jack. It seems so far fetched even to me, that it's likely that neither one of them will believe me. As a matter of fact, now that I think about it, I don't believe me!"

He was quiet for a few moments before saying, "I'm going to take my sled up to Thad's. Do you mind staying here in case Rudy shows up?"

"No, that'll be fine. I've got my puzzle to keep me busy and my Swiss Miss to keep me warm. Don't be gone too long though, I know how you and Thad like to talk, and with what you want to talk about, it could go on forever." Then as if someone had secretly reminded her she said, "Furthermore, with what you just told me,

I certainly don't want to be here by myself any longer than I have to."

He was about to reassure her that nothing would happen but a feeling of foreboding made him change his mind. Instead he said, "Trust me, it won't be that long. I'm not only concerned about Rudy, I'm also worried about you, and I want to get back as quickly as I can." Rob grabbed his helmet and gloves and headed for the door.

* * *

The key was still in the Formula's ignition and he turned it to the start position, pulled up the kill button and pressed the primer three times. As soon as he turned the key to engage the starter, the engine came to life with its deep throaty purr that he loved to hear.

He did not like to ride his sled down Kennebago Settlement Road once the snow had melted on it, so he made a snowmobile trail that went through the woods to the right of the camp. The trail, only about five hundred feet long, emptied into a three hundred fifty-acre field that butted up to Thad's property, which was a little more than a mile away. When he rode his snowmobile to Thad's he preferred to make the trip across the field rather than use the road. And especially today, he felt that the field was the way to go. He hoped that by skirting the woods all the way he had a chance of spotting Rudy.

He finished putting his helmet and gloves on and gave the Formula some throttle. As he went by the camp he saw Eileen watching him through the living room picture window. She waved to him just as he squeezed the throttle and shot forward toward the end of the house. He stood up a few inches off the seat and leaned forward as he rapidly approached the snow bank. He was airborne for a short distance and out of sight in the blink of an eye. Eileen smiled as she thought to herself, "Boys remain boys".

* * *

He came out of the woods behind Bill James' camp and headed off to the left to skirt the forest along the edge of the field. If he took a straight shot it was a little over a mile to Thad's, but following along the tree line as it curves in and out of the field adds another half mile, and he intended to keep looking into the woods all the way. However, was he being realistic with himself? Did he *really* expect to see Rudy? He could not fathom why such a dreadful thought popped into his head, and he pushed it aside.

He slowly made his way along the tree line, following it as it made a sharp curve to the left, bringing him into an area that reminded him of a mammoth cul-de-sac about the size of a baseball field. When he was about a quarter of the way through it he looked up ahead and followed the tree line as it curved back to the right, hoping to catch a glimpse of Rudy, but disappointment continued to reign king. He stopped periodically and shut off his machine to see if he could hear him baying in the pursuit of a rabbit, but no such luck. As he approached the opposite end of the field where Thad's camp was, he could see here and there the tips of fence posts sticking a couple of inches out of the wind-blown snow. The fence marked the boundary between a string of camps on Bigfoot Hollow Road and the old Nile Homestead. Thad must have just thrown some more fuel into his wood stove because Rob could see a thick column of smoke billowing up from the chimney long before he could see the camp on the opposite side of a small rise.

* * *

Thad was standing in the front doorway of his camp watching Rob as he rounded the turn into his driveway. His land has four buildings on it; the camp, the outhouse, the cat house/workshop, and a shed that is filled to the brim with all types of items that you'd find in lumber, electrical and plumbing supply stores. One of his favorite pastimes was going to garage sales, and invariably he returned to camp with something that he was sure would come in very handy at some point in time, usually when he decided to tackle a project around camp that tickled his fancy. God help him if Murphy's Law reared its ugly head turning his small project into a major problem. In the past, Rob had been there when he ran into a problem and decided to look through the pile for the part that he needed, and luckily he had found it. According to Thad, the part would usually be on the bottom of the pile. As far as Rob was concerned, all that effort wasn't worth it. When he took into consideration: (i) all the time that it takes to dig out the part from the pile, assuming that you find what you need; (ii) all the time that it takes to put everything back; and (iii) placing a value on your time . . . it's absolutely cheaper and quicker to go into town and buy the part!

* * *

Rob parked his sled next to Thad's big blue three-quarter-ton Ford pickup truck, and Ginger immediately did her happy face waddle over to greet him. He reached over and gave her a friendly scratch behind the ears and a rub under her chin, and it soon became apparent that Ginger was definitely in the mood for affection. She wasn't ready to move out of the way so he could get off his sled, and the moment that he stopped petting her, she'd use her nose to nudge him with canine authority, letting him know that as far as she was concerned, the job wasn't finished yet.

Thad already knew that Ginger was in the mood for attention because she had not left him alone since he returned from his trailside lunch. So he stepped down the two steps from his porch and walked over to the sled to talk. By this time Rob was scratching the full length of her back all the way from her head to her tail, back and forth, and Ginger made sure that she got the maximum benefit that she could by stretching her skin taut in the area where Rob was scratching.

* * *

"What're you doing here? I thought that you and your better half would be back on your machines for a ride to Flagstaff Lake. You'd make good time without having to stop and wait for the ol' man now and then."

In spite of his effort to stop it, a big smile crept onto his face as he said, "Yeah, I know, we were going to, but Rudy's missing and I'm totally baffled as to where he could be." He brought Thad up to date with everything that had recently happened back at his camp and when he was finished Thad lifted his hat to scratch the back of his bald head as he said, "There's been a lot of strange things goin' on today, not to mention my brain taking a hike into neutral periodically. As a matter of fact I just got off the phone from talking with my doctor. After I told him what had happened to me he scheduled an appointment on Wednesday for an EEG. I guess he wants to see if there's anything wrong between my ears, and after what's gone on with me today, maybe there is!"

"Welllllll, it's not a bad idea to get yourself checked out." He paused for a few seconds, trying to think of the right words to say, and then just blurted out, "Thad, I need to ask a favor. Would you mind bringing Ginger down to my camp? I'd like her to kind of wander around with me in the area where I last saw Rudy. Maybe she might pick up his scent and help me find him." He waited several seconds for an answer, and when Thad still had said nothing, he continued by saying, "You know as well as I do that if she picked up his scent that she'd go looking for him, and besides, she can get around under those low pine tree branches a hell of a lot easier than I can."

"Sure, I'll be happy to bring her down. Why don't you head back to camp and tell Eileen to put on a pot of coffee. I'll chew the fat with her while you and Ginger go out looking for Rudy."

"Ya got a deal, Thad! See ya back at camp in a short short."

As Thad headed back into his camp to get his coat and truck keys, Rob cranked up his machine and maneuvered it back into the tracks that he had just made. He figured that one more look along the treeline was worth a try.

* * *

He was just walking into his camp as Thad approached the driveway. He stuck his head in the door and saw that Eileen was sitting on the couch, hands in her lap just looking straight ahead at the TV, but the TV wasn't on. As a matter of fact, neither was the radio. The camp was stone silent and the only noise that Rob could hear was the sound of Thad's truck turning into the driveway.

"Eileen, you okay?"

She looked over at him with what he interpreted as a blank look in her eyes, the same blank look that Thad had earlier in the day. Then her lips started working like she was trying to say a word, but instead her face screwed up into the type of face a woman gets when they are about to cry. Then the flood began. It had been so many years since he had seen her cry that he could not imagine what had brought on this outburst.

He walked over to the couch and sat down next to her and didn't take his eyes off her as he took off his gloves and helmet. It was warm in the camp and he was already starting to break a sweat, so he started working at the zipper on his coat while he put his other arm around her.

"What's the matter, hon?"

She brought her crying under control and said between her hiccupping sobs, "I don't know, Rob, I just don't know. I was sitting here thinking about Thad and Rudy when you came through the door and all of a sudden I just started crying. I don't understand what brought it on."

"Well, that's just another thing in the list of weird for today. You okay now?"

"Yes."

Just then Thad knocked on the door, and it was no surprise when Ginger was the first one in. She immediately went over to Rudy's dish to see if it held any goodies. One quick sniff was all it took and she walked the other way when she discovered it was empty. Just like Rudy, the next place she headed was the cabinet where the dog biscuits were kept and unceremoniously parked herself in front of it.

Rob said a little facetiously, "Now I know why you're so thin Ginger," as he got off the couch and started to head over to the cabinet. Stopping short he turned to Eileen and said, "I'm going to take Ginger over to where I last saw Rudy. Wanna put on a pot of coffee? Thad would like to have a cup while he's chewing the fat with you."

"Sure. Thad, how many cups do you want?"

"Two's good for me."

"Rob, do you want me to make any for you?"

"Sure, I'll have a cup when I get back in."

* * *

He nudged Ginger aside with his right knee so he could open the cabinet door to get the box of dog biscuits. At the same time he also snapped a piece of paper towel off the roll to wipe Ginger's saliva off the floor. "Guess you really want this biscuit, huh, Ginger?"

Holding the biscuit in front of her, like the proverbial carrot hanging out in front of the donkey, they headed to the front door. As he opened it he said, "See you guys in a little bit."

Once they had gone down the steps, Rob gave Ginger the biscuit and, standing alongside of her, looked all around, wanting very badly to see Rudy running up to greet them. But that was a pipe dream and the sound of Ginger crunching and savoring her biscuit drowned out any further thoughts.

He gave her a few moments to diligently check the entire area around her for some tiny remaining morsels that might have escaped the trip to her gullet. When it looked like she was ready to give up, he said, "Come on, Ginger, time to find Rudy." They both started walking over toward the tracks that he and Rudy had made to the woods and, once they reached the snowbank, he stepped aside and said, "Go ahead girl, go find Rudy!"

He did not really expect much from her but still he was rather disappointed when Ginger just walked nonchalantly in front of him, casually sniffing here and there. Of course, if he had really stretched his imagination, he could interpret that movement as a halfhearted attempt to check things out. But, at least she got the hint and went first.

Patiently, Rob followed her as she ambled slowly along the trail. Just as she paused to check out what Rob had assumed to be an interesting scent, he heard a chickadee in the pine trees up ahead make its chicka-dee-dee call. A split second later, the static noise began. Ginger's head snapped up with her ears fully alert, listening intently while she tilted her head from side to side. Both of them were looking in every direction around them when Rob heard a sound that resembled a soft "whump" that could be best described as a muffled thump. Then there was silence. The static noise was gone.

Ginger took a couple of hesitant steps toward the direction of the "whump", then quickly picked up her pace, which exploded into a run. Rob didn't want her to get out of his sight since he still didn't know what had happened to Rudy, and he called to Ginger to come back. But she would have none of that and kept charging forward, full speed ahead. She did not slow down one iota when coming to the pine trees, and in the blink of an eye she disappeared among them, running full speed on the track that Rob had made earlier. He had not seen Ginger move so fast in at least five years. He took a couple of steps and thought briefly about getting his snowshoes, but he did not want Ginger to get too far out in front of him. Even though he had already broken the trail, the snow was not firm enough to support his weight, so he had to do a hopping-like run through the deep snow to get to the pines.

When he reached the treeline, he held his hands out in front of him, sweeping the pine branches out of his way as he ran, while constantly keeping a vigilant eye out for Ginger. The last thing that he wanted to do was to trip over her. She just might stop to check something out. When he came to the backside of the pines where the hardwood growth began, he saw just twenty feet away, Ginger and Rudy, sniffing each other all over.

Rob was overjoyed. He yelled, "Rudy, Ginger, come!"

Rudy looked over at him and immediately started bounding over. Actually, it was more like he was swimming through the snow, adding a hop here and there. Ginger, on the other hand, just stood where she was, head up, sniffing the air in every direction. He yelled, "Ginger, come!"

This time she looked back at him and started slowly working her way over toward him, wading through the tracks that Rudy had just made. Rob became curious, wondering why she frequently looked behind her while she made her way over, so he took a long, hard look at the spot where she and Rudy had met. This whole scene just didn't make sense to him. He wondered where Rudy had been all this time, and made up his mind that snowmobiling this afternoon was out. He decided to take both dogs back to camp, and then come back to thoroughly check the area. He wanted to figure out where Rudy had been.

* * *

Thad and Eileen were sitting at the kitchen table sipping the remains of their coffee. The empty paper plates that were in front of them told Rob that a snack was also involved. Eileen saw Rudy and jumped up from the table to greet him. Rudy felt, as well as saw, her eagerness, and he quickened his pace to meet her, and then sat down when she started to caress him. She looked at him momentarily, just to make sure that he was OK, and then gave Rudy a big hug and said, "Where'd you find him?"

"Actually, Ginger found him about fifty feet from where I last saw him. It's really kind of weird. I looked everywhere, and I mean everywhere in that area. I didn't see one thing that could have given me the slightest clue that he was still there. I mean I was convinced that he had just disappeared into thin air. I couldn't find a sign of any kind that he had wandered away".

Thad piped in and said, "I know you well enough and I've seen how good you are at tracking. I don't think that you missed anything. As a matter of fact, some times I think that you are part Native American Indian."

"Guess what Thad? I *am* part Indian. According to my Grandmother before she passed away, one of her descendants was a Passamaquoddy, but we never really checked it out."

Rubbing the back of his bald head, sort of like he was trying to bring it back to life, Thad said, "Just add this to the next chapter in the 'Book of Weird' for today."

Eileen decided to put in her two cents and said, "You had to miss something, Rob. Things just don't disappear into thin air, except through an illusion at a magic show, or in the movies."

"You're right. I'm going to head back out there, but I'm leaving the dogs here. I want to do a thorough check before it gets dark."

Eileen looked at Thad and said, "Would you mind staying with me until he gets back?"

"Sure. Just make some more of those delicious biscuits and some coffee and I'd be happy to stay and chat some more."

"That's a deal. Rob, make sure you're back before dark. I don't like what's been going on today."

"Neither do I. Don't worry, I'll head back as soon as I see the sun go down behind the Kennebago. Thanks for stayin', Thad."

He nodded an acknowledgment and Rob headed out the door.

* * *

The warmth of the day was waning and Rob felt the air bite his nostrils as he breathed in. He also felt a little bit of a chill from leaving the warmth of the camp. He strapped on his snowshoes and followed his tracks back out to the pine trees, and in less than five minutes he reached the far side.

When he emerged from the pine trees, he stopped and stood in the clearing close to the area where Ginger had found Rudy, trying to decide if he was going to make another attempt to locate any tracks that Rudy had to have left behind when he disappeared. Finally, he made up his mind and he was about to carefully check both sides of the trail that he and Rudy had made earlier. But then his rationalization mode kicked in. He was fighting with his emotions when his mind started telling him that he was only trying to convince himself that he must have missed the spot where Rudy had jumped to the side. He was beginning to think that it wasn't even likely, but still, he had to make the effort, because it was the only thing that seemed logical. After all, Rudy did show up in the area where he should have been all along. But, if Rudy had been there all along, then his tracks should be all over the place, including near the area where Ginger had found him. As soon as that thought hit his conscious mind he said, "That's it! That's the smart thing to do. I should've thought of that before. I'll find Rudy's tracks where Ginger found him and back track on them. Why do it the hard way?"

Rob slowly walked the twenty feet from the pines to where Rudy and Ginger had been eagerly sniffing at each other, his snowshoes making a crunchy sound with each step. The afternoon warmth had made the very top of the powdery snow from last night a little wet, and it was starting to freeze. As he slowly walked the twenty feet, he kept looking as far as he could to either side, but there was nothing in the snow that looked like tracks that could have been made by Rudy. He stopped and stood in the very spot where he first saw Ginger and Rudy together, and slowly scanned the area around him as far as possible, a full three hundred and sixty degrees. He had just finished his scan when he began to feel the same vacuum sensation as he had felt earlier. All his senses jumped into high gear, waiting for the static hissing noise to begin. But there was nothing, just that feeling.

He started rationalizing, which conjured up the same logic as before, that the only possibility left was that he missed something earlier. Rudy simply had to have made his way out here in the track where he had just walked. But if so, where was Rudy when he was looking and calling for him? He started another scan around him, shifting his eyes back and forth about fifteen degrees each time before continuing to the next segment that he had mentally marked out. The sun had shifted somewhat and now he could make out what appeared to be another round concave area in the snow about twenty-five or thirty feet away. It was similar to the depression that he had seen earlier, and he looked over to that area just to confirm whether it was in fact in the same location that he remembered. He could make out a small area of the depression. So he was right! This was another imprint. What could have made such an imprint? Had it been there before? Had he missed seeing it? Possibly, but he didn't think so.

Walking backwards in snowshoes was not something that he had mastered, so he did his best to turn around without disturbing too much of the snow at the spot where he stood in case he wanted to come back and have another look. Once turned around, he walked back to the edge of the pines and followed the track that he had made earlier when he saw the first depression in the snow. As he followed his track he kept looking for any sign that Rudy had walked in his tracks. Nothing.

He reached what he had labeled the "Wiffle Ball" depression. Nothing had changed ... except for a new rabbit track going through it, and a few bird tracks that, judging from the size, must have been made by a ruffled grouse or a raven. He looked in the direction of the other depression but he couldn't see any of it from where he was standing. While he was doing a three sixty and keeping his scan to a fifteen degree sweep again, he noticed that he no longer felt the vacuum sensation and wondered when it had stopped. And then a realization hit him. The sun was much lower in the sky than it had been a few minutes ago, or *was* it just a few minutes ago? He looked at his watch and it had been an hour and a half since he had left Thad and Eileen. He could not have spent more than fifteen minutes to complete everything that he had done since he had left camp. Even if he allowed thirty minutes, how could he possibly account for the other hour? There just wasn't that much ground to cover. It didn't make any sense. As a matter of fact, this *day* didn't make any sense. A sense of fear came over him.

He checked his watch again to see if it could be running fast, but based upon the fact that the sun was so low in the sky, the time lapse had to be right. Talking to himself, he said, "Maybe it skipped ahead. Yeah, that's probably what happened. I'd better get it checked when we get back to Portland." But he knew where the sun was, and instantly came to the realization that his rationalization could not shake off the creepy feeling in the pit of his stomach.

Giving one more quick check of the area around the "Wiffle Ball" depression, he headed back down his track and walked over to what he had labeled depression number three. It was just like the "Wiffle Ball" depression, except no trees were in the concave area, and there were no tracks around it anywhere.

He made another quick visual check of the area and then made a circular sweep about fifteen feet from the perimeter. Not one sign of a track that could have been made by Rudy. The sun was dipping behind the Kennebago, leaving the whole area in its shadow. Exasperated, he headed back to camp but he was discouraged. He had no answers, only questions, and that was not a note that he liked to quit on.

* * *

When he walked into the camp Ginger immediately greeted him but Rudy didn't budge from the spot where he was lying. As a matter of fact, he didn't even raise his head to give Rob a visual greeting. He just opened his eyes for a moment and went right back to sleep. Rob thought that was highly unusual and Thad, still sitting at the kitchen table said, "Either Rudy's in total La La Land, or you just got the cold shoulder. Either way, that's something *I've* never seen him do before."

"You got that right, Thad! Hey, Toot-man, what's up?"

Rudy did not budge. Rob went over to him and gave him a gentle pat on the back of his head and a scratch behind his ear. Still no response ... not even a grunt of pleasure. He didn't even attempt to open his eyes.

"I've never seen you like this, Toot! Not even after a long hunt. I'll tell you what, you guys, wherever he was, and whatever he was doing must've really knocked him for a loop."

Finally Eileen chimed in saying, "You know you're probably right. I don't remember seeing him move at all since you went back out. What about you, Thad?"

"Nope!"

Rob studied his old friend for a few seconds and said, trying hard to be cheerful, "I'm sure that he'll be himself by tomorrow morning."

Just then Eileen remembered that Rob's friend had called while he was out back and said, "By the way, Jack King called while you were out."

"What did you tell him?"

"I told him that you were out taking a walk and that I'd have you call him when you got back in."

"That's it?"

"No. He asked if we were going to be here for the weekend, and I told him that I wasn't sure."

"OK. I'll give him a call in a few minutes." And with that Thad said, "Well, I guess that it's time to get back to camp and start supper."

Rob looked at him and said, "What'chya havin', Thad?"

"I've got all my leftovers since Friday that I'm gonna throw into a pot. It's an easy night for cookin'."

"That doesn't sound very appetizing to me, Thad. Ya want to have supper with us?"

"I'd really like to, but I should get to those leftovers before they become Ginger food."

Eileen knew how to convince him to stay and said, "Thad, I called Tommy Lemieux yesterday and he is delivering some lobsters a little later. If I call right away I can probably catch him and have him deliver a couple more. What d'ya think?"

"Eileen, deal! As far as I'm concerned those leftovers just became Ginger's."

"Fine, I'll call Tommy now."

* * *

As soon as she got off the phone she looked at Rob and said, "I want to give you my two cents before you call Jack. You found Rudy and I don't want to stay here another day, let alone over the weekend. I'd be much happier if you called Frank Lovett and told him that we're heading back to Portland. If he's busy, he and Lindsey can always pick up the Explorer at the Rangeley Airport any time before it snows, and put it in the garage. He doesn't have to drive us there."

"Listen. If you want to go home ... fine. But I'm just gonna turn around and come right back. I have no desire to leave until I understand what's going on around here. Besides, desire has nothing to do with it. I wouldn't be able to concentrate on *anything* with the events of this day still burnin' a hole in my mind. I need to understand what's goin' on."

"All right, I'll stay, but on one condition. I do not want to be here by myself, especially after dark!"

"No problem. I wouldn't feel very comfortable leaving you here alone anyway. Where I go, you go. Fair enough?"

"Not really, but OK."

"Thad, you mind if I call Jack King right now?"

"Help yourself. Mind if I turn on the TV and watch the news while you're chatting?"

"You know how to operate the TV and the antenna. Help yourself."

Just as Rob reached for the phone, it rang. "Hello. Hey, Jack! I was just gettin' ready to call you!"

"Yeah, sure. And the IRS is refunding all income taxes that everyone paid over the past ten years too!"

"Hey, Eileen! Wasn't I just picking up the phone to call Jack when it rang?"

She yelled back, loud enough to be sure that he could hear her, "That's right Jack!"

"Yeah, yeah, yeah. You lie and she swears to it."

"Quit bustin' my balls, Jack! I've had one of those days."

"Sorry, buddy. What's goin' on?"

He told Jack about the distorted circle of air, including the static noise at the beaver pond and out behind the house, and all the other details that went along with it.

When he finished, Jack was silent for a while, let out a soft whistle and said, "Sounds like I should come up now and not wait for the weekend. The women can keep each other company while you and I check things out. That sound good to you?"

"Sure, as long as you can take the time away from your business."

"No problem. Actually I really wanted to head up in the morning anyway, and not this weekend, but I didn't want to be pushy and interfere with any plans that you and Eileen might've had."

"When it comes to you and Nancy, there's *never* a question. We all like to do the same things, and as usual, you'd just blend into whatever we're doing."

"Fine. You want to meet me at the Rangeley Airport in the morning?"

"Sure, what time?"

"Nancy and I'll go to the airport now and get the Cherokee ready so all that's left is the morning preflight. We should get to Rangeley Airport at about 08:00 hours. I'm going to stop at the shop and pick up some of my electronic equipment to load on. Maybe we can get a feel for what that static noise is that you been hearin'."

"08:00 hours is fine. I'll clear the snow from the space next to my Cessna, and get the tiedowns and chocks ready for you."

"OK, buddy, thanks for that. See you in the morning!"

Rob hung up the phone and remained sitting on the loveseat for a few seconds thinking about an agenda to follow after Jack and Nancy arrived. Thad was buried in the news and had no clue that Rob had finished his conversation, and Eileen was talking to herself in the kitchen, a thing Rob never understood. It totally escaped him how people could have a full-blown conversation with themselves. He just sat there for a few minutes letting his mind adjust to the possibilities that the new day could bring, and the longer he thought about them, they seemed endless. If he didn't bring his thinking under control, he wouldn't be getting much sleep. Before getting off the loveseat he said to himself, "Tomorrow's not going to be *just* another day."

4

The lobsters were a fond memory by the time Thad decided that he and Ginger should head back to camp. "Camp's gonna be pretty cool. I bet the wood stove and cook stove burned out at least a couple of hours ago", he said, as he got ready to leave.

To most people that would not be a concern because their camp is insulated and holds the heat fairly well. However, Thad's camp had *no* insulation and when you get close to the eaves you can see daylight along all of the edges.

Rob yelled after him, "Careful going down those steps, there may be some ice on them. See ya tomorrow."

"Ayuh. Eileen. Thanks for the meal. It was delicious."

"You're welcome, Thad. Have a good one!"

Thad was just pulling out of the driveway when Rob said to Eileen, "Man! Was he in a mood to talk or what! I'm so tired I can hardly keep my eyes open. I hope Thad didn't see me doing my mini nod-offs periodically, 'cause every now and then he gets kind of sensitive and he'd probably think that I was bored with his story telling."

"As a matter of fact, one of your so called mini nod-offs wasn't so mini. When you let out the beginning of a snore, Thad got a serious look on his face and said that his company must bore you. Who knows what tomorrow will bring."

"And I thought that it was just my imagination that he was a little cool towards me as he was leaving. Well, I'm going to bed. I've had it. See you in the morning."

Eileen was putting some things away in the kitchen and said, "I'll be there in a couple of minutes. Rudy hasn't moved a muscle ever since you came in. Hope he's OK tomorrow."

"I'm sure he'll be himself when I get up. Good night."

She intercepted him half way across the living room floor, gave him a kiss on the cheek and said, "Love you."

* * *

Rob looked at the clock as his head hit the pillow, noting that it was 23:15 hours, and the next thing that he knew, it was 04:15 Tuesday morning. He knew instantly that sleep was at an end for the night. He was wide-awake and he felt like he had slept much longer than five hours. His mind jumped into high gear, mostly thinking about Jack King and his extensive electronic knowledge.

He had met Jack when he was stationed at Chanute Air Force Base in Rantoul, Illinois. Jack was a lean and mean six feet tall with the thickest head of curly black hair that Rob had ever seen. He and Jack had gone to the YMCA to do laps in the pool one day after work, and Rob was still doing his stretching exercises to limber up when Jack dove into the pool. When he surfaced Rob saw that his hair looked exactly the same as it did before he dove in. He jokingly yelled to Jack, "Sure you don't have some black blood in ya somewhere down the line?" Jack threw him the birdie and started doing his laps.

They were both on temporary duty at Chanute, and one day Rob's assignment was to critique an electronics class that Jack was conducting. He was demonstrating how electricity flowed on an oversized circuit board, and unbeknownst to him someone had failed to perform an assigned task, so the circuitry on the board was live. When he touched one of the components on the board he got one hell of a jolt and went down. Rob yelled for someone to dial 911 as he ran over to him to administer CPR. The ambulance and medics were there in what seemed like the blink of an eye, but everyone attributed Jack's survival to Rob's quick actions. When he visited Jack at the hospital the next day, Jack was fully aware of what had happened and the fact that Rob had probably saved his life. A strong bond developed between the two of them and it didn't matter how much distance separated them, they stayed in touch.

* * *

Still lying under the covers, not quite ready to get up yet, Rob was trying to figure out what Jack might have in mind when he said that he was going to bring some electronic equipment with him. That thought came to a screeching halt when several coyotes started howling in the forest behind the camp, breaking the early morning tranquility. For a moment, he thought that they sounded somewhat different from other times when he'd heard them hot and heavy on the trail of their prey. The howling sounded like it was coming from the clear-cut where Ginger had found Rudy, and he surmised that they were after a deer. As suddenly as it started, the music of the hunt abruptly stopped.

He was thinking to himself that they must have made the kill when suddenly the phone started ringing. The sky was turning pale shades of gray. He was stunned. He felt like he had just been thinking about the kill, and that was at 04:30 hours, but now the clock said it was 06:15 hours.

He reached over, grabbed the phone on the nightstand and spoke a foggy, "Hello?"

"Hey, Rob! Jack! What'd I do, wake you up?"

"I was awake at 04:15 hours and I guess I dozed back off, although I don't have a clue as to why. I felt wide awake and was ready to get up." He paused for a second, gathering his thoughts and said, "You at the airport already?"

"No. I was just calling to let you know that we won't be there until about 10:00 hours. Murphy's Law, don't you know."

"OK, good enough. I'll still have everything ready for you. See you then."

Rob looked at the clock again to make sure that he had read the time correctly. It read 06:17 hours, no mistake. He sat up on the edge of the bed to put his socks and underwear on, then paused. Suddenly he felt like he hadn't slept in a week. "Man, what the hell happened? Two and a half hours ago I was ready to get up and set the world on fire. Now I feel like I just finished running the boot-camp obstacle course ten times in a row. Wow! What is going on?" He looked over at Eileen and she was still sound asleep.

He got up and went into the kitchen to make the coffee. After turning off the nightlight, he filled the Krups coffee maker with water and was putting the Gevalia Stockholm Roast into it when, as usual, he casually looked out the window to see if there were any deer around. He didn't have to look very long before seeing about fifteen of them standing among the birch trees, and almost all of them were looking through the window at him. He got a big smile on his face and said, "Feeding time at the zoo! OK, guys, as soon as I get the coffee goin', you're next."

He reached under the sink, grabbed the handle of a three-gallon bucket and headed down into the basement. The wood furnace kept the basement nice and warm but it felt a little cool so he thought that he'd better check the fire. He opened the back and front drafts of the furnace before opening the firebox door. There was a nice bed of glowing red-hot coals. Taking the poker off the hook over his head he spread them evenly around the firebox and put in three more logs, closed the door and the drafts and headed over to the bag of Course 14 Blue Seal feed that he gave to the deer each morning. He set the bucket on a four by four sheet of plastic that caught any overspill and went to pick up the fifty-pound bag of feed that was three quarters full. He had one hand on the top of the bag and one on the bottom, and went to stand up like he normally did, but he kind of stalled and the bag never left the floor. He let go of it and stood up slowly as if he were a ninety-year old man. "What the hell!" He looked down at the bag and felt himself breaking out in a cold sweat. "Damn! I must be coming down with the flu."

He walked over to his workbench and sat down on the stool, bending forward and placing his chin in his hands. He sat there for a while letting his body adjust and then went over to the bag again. He studied it in the same manner that a weight lifter studies the bar and weights that he is about to press, kind of willing himself to do it. He bent over, grabbed the bag, gave a grunt and stood up with what seemed to be no effort at all. "Just like old times," Rob thought, "That's more like it." And what never dawned on him was the fact that he felt "just like old times" the rest of the day. The incident totally left his mind.

He went back upstairs and walked right in front of Rudy with the bucket of feed in his hand. That act normally would've brought Rudy eagerly to his heels, but not this morning. He was still in a deep-breathing sleep. When he let the storm door go, it slapped against the jamb with its normal bang and that was the breakfast bell for the deer. He saw several of them run across the road from the woods on the opposite side, and by the time he got to where he had seen them standing in the birches, he figured that there must be forty or more deer waiting to be fed. He knew that they were anxious to eat but he took his time putting the feed down. He learned some time ago that it was best to make a lot of small piles of feed, rather than a few large ones. When he had made the few large piles in the past, the competition between the deer got pretty nasty.

By this time of year the deer had lost much of their memory of the terror that they had experienced during the hunting season, and quite often they got so close to him while he was putting down the feed he could reach out and touch them. But even though it was a temptation, he never did, because he didn't want to spook them, and this morning was no exception. He turned around to look at the pile that he just poured onto the snow, and a deer already had its nose into it. He realized why it was willing to take a chance on being close to him. It wanted to make sure that it got its share before the competition joined in, which usually happened very quickly after their benefactor left the immediate area.

He had just finished pouring the last pile when he recalled that he had heard the coyotes early this morning. He also remembered that in the past whenever the coyotes hunted deer near the camp, the deer were spooked and did not come near him for a day or so 'till they got over it.' He was pondering what made today so different from the other times when a Kamikaze Blue Jay, wanting to share in the deer's food, almost flew into the side of his head. "Not *too* hungry, are ya pal?"

* * *

He opened the front door and started to step into the camp, but he had to stop short. Rudy was sitting right there with what appeared to be a hurt look on his furry face. "Hey, Toot! Good to see you up, ol' Buddy!"

Eileen was sitting on the couch with a cup of coffee in her hand, and she had been studying the puzzle in front of her. She looked up and said, "He's been sitting there whining for about five minutes, but I didn't want to let him out with all those deer around."

"He doesn't bother the deer. All he does is sit up on the snow bank watching me, and if he thinks the deer are getting a little too close he lets out a soft bark to warn them off, but that's about it."

"I see. I poured your coffee. It's on the kitchen table."

"Thanks. I think I'm gonna take a walk down to the beaver pond with the Toot-man."

She looked up at him saying, "Don't we have to get to the airport to pick up Jack and Nancy?"

"No. Jack called earlier. You were sound asleep and never heard the phone ring. He told me that they weren't goin' to get here until 10:00 hours. He said something about Murphy's Law ruling."

* * *

Rob had finished his coffee and was standing at the front door, coat and hat on and ready to go. He called for Rudy to come several times, and wondered what was taking him so long. "Hey, Eileen, do you see where Rudy's at?"

"No. Hold on a sec, I'll go and check the bedroom." After about a half a minute she said, "He's sleeping on our bed."

"You've got to be joking! He's gotten a ton of sleep. He must not be feelin' good," and then Rob remembered how he felt when *he* woke up, and also the scene when he tried to lift the bag of deer feed. "You know, maybe there's a bug goin' around. How do you feel?"

"More tired than usual, but other than that, just fine."

Rob walked into the bedroom and gave Rudy a few shakes as he said, "Come on, Toot, its 07:30 hours! You ain't gonna sleep your life away. Common Toot! Let's go!" Rudy gave him one of those "you've got to be kidding" looks and grudgingly got off the bed. When they went out the front door Rob got the impression that he slithered down the steps rather than walking down them.

* * *

Eileen sipped her coffee as she looked out the living room window, watching Rob and Rudy walk side by side down Kennebago Settlement Road. She could see the steam shooting forth from each of them as they breathed, and thought to herself, "I'm glad that's not me out there!"

When they were completely out of sight she picked up her puzzle board and sat down on the couch. Reaching for her coffee she stared at the partially completed puzzle and the pieces that she had arranged at different sections on the board where they matched the pattern of the scene. Setting her coffee down she started to absent mindedly stir the puzzle pieces that were still in the box, just as a woman grabs several strands of her hair to twirl them in her fingers when she is in the midst of a daydream or perhaps deep in thought. But she wasn't deep in thought. As a matter of fact she wasn't thinking at all. Her mind was completely blank. After a minute or so, she said to herself, "I guess the puzzle isn't my thing this morning." She picked up the puzzle board and box and placed them back on the bed in the guest bedroom, which could not really be called the guest room any longer because Rob had commandeered it as his office.

He had verbally rationalized his action to Eileen by stating, "All of our friends and family would prefer the privacy of the upstairs anyway."

She had finished her coffee and was in the bathroom brushing her teeth when she heard a faint static noise, and at the same time felt her nightgown and bathrobe start to cling to her. She made a mental note to start using more Bounce this time of year to stop the static cling. But when she felt the hair on her head starting to move, like it was being drawn away from her, she froze. The toothbrush was still in her mouth against her teeth but not moving. She held her breath while she rolled her eyes in all directions, looking to both sides and any place that she could see behind her in the mirror. She saw nothing that gave her concern.

Finally she took the toothbrush out of her mouth and dropped it in the sink, walked over to the bathroom window and looked out into the backyard. There were no birds, which was extremely unusual for this time of the morning. In fact she couldn't remember a time when there weren't numerous chickadees and nuthatches, gold finches and other members of the finch family, grosbeaks and a sundry of other birds flitting from feeder to feeder. They would fly to the nearby trees after grabbing the oil sunflower seed of their choice. But not one bird was to be seen. No red squirrels, and no deer. The deer would often come back during the morning hours to see if they had missed any flavorful morsels of oats, corn and molasses. The back yard was deserted, and that just didn't happen this time of year, especially during this time of the morning when food was around.

The static noise was getting louder and it seemed to be coming from the front part of the house. Just as she stepped from the bathroom door, the noise quit and so did the static cling. Her nightgown and bathrobe drifted away from her body and her hair fell back to her shoulders. She stepped into the living room just in time to see someone walk past the right side of the picture window, and it looked like he was heading toward the front door steps. She ran over to the couch, and while kneeling on the cushions she slowly leaned toward the window, looking as far as she could to the right.

She saw a man standing about ten feet from the front door steps, and the fact that she saw him was not nearly as disturbing as the way he was dressed. The clothes that he had on were similar to the styles that were popular in the 80's. And what made it even more unusual was that at about two below zero, this man wasn't wearing a hat and overcoat. Stranger still, he was wearing what appeared to be dress shoes. Nobody dressed like that around here, not even in the warm weather! He was tall, maybe about six-foot two or three, and it didn't look like he had an ounce of fat on him. His hair was all wonky, sort of like Rod Stewart's style, and not one thing about him fit into Baldwin Plantation, nor this era.

Eileen watched the man intently as he stood there looking around in different directions, and she couldn't decide if he was trying to figure out where he was, or if he was trying to see if anyone was around. Suddenly his head snapped around and she found herself looking him directly in the eye, and she felt a river of fear rushing through her whole body with a force like she had never felt before. She tried to scream but no sound would come out of her mouth. Maybe it was her subconscious self-preservation system that activated the suppression mode. Then, as her conscious mind took over she thought, I won't make any noise ... maybe I won't be seen. But she instantly realized that was ludicrous because he was already looking at her. However, she began to think that he wasn't just looking *at* her. She had an unmistakable feeling that he was probing her inner thoughts.

Her heart, already pounding in her chest, started to beat more wildly, and she felt herself getting faint. She quickly put her hand on the back of the couch to stop herself from falling into the window, and when she did, out of the corner of her eye she thought that she saw the man take some steps in her direction. But when she regained her composure and looked back out the window she saw him going in the direction of the front porch. That was the straw that broke the camel's back, and her fear turned into unadulterated panic. But at least she had enough wits about her to realize that she had to get a grip on herself if she was going to have a fighting chance to survive. She knew that she had to do something quickly to find a way to defend herself. Suddenly, like someone had popped a flash card into her mind, she remembered that Rob had a shotgun and ammo upstairs. She was forcing herself to get off the couch to go upstairs when she saw the knob to the front door turning. That sight broke her paralytic fear and she bolted for the door, snapping the deadbolt into the jamb, and in that instant of time she wondered why she hadn't heard the storm door opening. She always knew when Rob was coming into the house because the door return was ancient and she could hear its plunger groan in protest each time the door was opened or closed.

With the deadbolt secured, she immediately spun on her heel and broke into a sprint for the stairs. She took them two at a time and had the shotgun in her hands so quickly that it all seemed like it had happened in a split second. She grabbed the shotgun shells and shoved two of them into the magazine, pumped the Remington 870 once to chamber a shell and rapidly shoved another shell into the magazine. Her confidence began to build now that she had a fully loaded weapon to use as a persuader. But as quickly as her confidence had started to build, it began to wane upon hearing the static noise once again, and feeling her nightclothes start to lightly cling to her. She thought to herself, "This is different. Before they stuck to me like plastic wrap clings to itself." Her breath came gushing out when the static noise quit after a few seconds and her nightclothes dropped away from her body. She raised her eyebrows in an expression of surprise because she hadn't realized that she had been holding her breath.

Sweat was streaming off her forehead and down her back. She willed her heart to slow down; she didn't want the pounding in her ears to drown out any of the sounds that may betray the location of the intruder, but everything was still and stone quiet. Her senses were totally alert and she stayed at the top of the stairs with the shotgun at the ready, waiting. "But waiting for what?" she thought to herself. The door was bolted shut, and unless that guy had a key, he'd have to bust his way in, and she didn't hear the telltale sound of splintering wood. Maybe he went away ...

maybe. She started slowly down the stairs, trying not to make any noise at all.

* * *

The walk to the beaver pond was pathetically slow and uneventful. They stood on the bridge and casually looked over the entire area. All the time Rob was hoping that nothing would spoil the calming effects that the peace and tranquility were having on him. The walk back to camp took even longer than the walk to the pond. Rudy found every scent exceptionally interesting, requiring a long, leisurely sniff and a few dots of yellow in the snow to state to the animal world that he had been there.

Rob looked at his watch as they were walking down the driveway to Camp Stress-A-Rest and said, "Toot, we've been gone almost an hour and a half. We could've crawled to the beaver pond and back in that amount of time." He was just starting up the steps to the front door when Rudy suddenly came to life and starting sniffing the driveway in a frenzy just like he did when he found a fresh rabbit track. He stepped down off the porch to see what it was all about just as Rudy started to expand his search in small circles looking to strike the scent again. Rob looked everywhere for a rabbit track, but there were none. Then he saw footprints that were totally out of place. He could make out several of those tracks that headed in the direction of the front door and he could see where the person had stopped and stood in one place before going to the steps. He looked back in the opposite direction and saw that the tracks had come through the deep snow in the clearing between his camp and the road. While he was walking over to the edge of the driveway he wondered why someone would walk through the snow rather than going a little further down the road to walk where it had been plowed. And he also wondered why he was wearing shoes instead of boots. No one he knew did that around here this time of year.

He reached the edge of the driveway and was mystified at what he saw. The tracks started in the middle of the clearing, which meant that the person had to make more than a twenty-foot jump from the edge of the road to reach that spot. And what was even more curious was the fact that it looked like the first step was part of a normal stride and not the usual impression you would expect to see at the end of such a long jump. He stepped over the edge of the plowed driveway and walked along the tracks, examining them very closely. The depth of the snow made the task somewhat difficult, but he was able to determine that each track was a single step. He could not make any sense out of what his eyes were telling him and decided to have a look from Kennebago Settlement Road. He turned around, walking in his own trail back to the driveway, and headed for the road. He wanted to see what the tracks up there could tell him, but when he got there, there were no tracks except for those that had been made by Rudy and himself. He pulled off his wool cap and scratched the back of his head the way Thad always did out of habit. After a few seconds, his mind changed gears and he wondered what Rudy was doing and, looking over at the front porch, he saw him sitting there simply staring at the door.

* * *

When he unlocked the front door, he couldn't get in. The dead bolt was also in the locked position and he wondered why. As soon as he unlocked the deadbolt and had the door open a few inches, Rudy tried to force his way through, making a huge racket. Rob made a serious effort to get in before Rudy. Stopping short, he found himself staring down the barrel of a shotgun. He'd never admit it to anyone, but he almost pissed in his pants.

Eileen just stood there staring back at him with fire in her eyes. They were speechless and motionless for a few seconds, both of them in shock. She finally broke the silence and yelled, "You son of a bitch! I want to go home, NOW!"

He slowly brought up his arm and gently directed the shotgun away from his face, gingerly stepping forward, and taking it from her. Maintaining a great deal of self-restraint he said, "What's goin' on, hon?"

"I need a drink," and with that statement she headed over to the liquor cabinet, took out the Canadian Club, picked up a six-ounce on-the-rocks glass and poured it full. Still mentally numb from having a shotgun stuck in his face, Rob just stood there watching her. She set the bottle down and didn't bother putting the cap back on. Without any fanfare at all she simply picked up the glass and drained every last drop without coming up for a breath. Then she defiantly looked over at him with tears in her eyes from the burn of the whisky and poured another full glass.

This time when she set the bottle down, she screwed the cap back on, but she opted not to put it away.

She took another look at Rob, picked up her glass and carefully walked over to the couch, and less than gracefully plopped down on it. He assumed that she had walked the way she did because the whisky was already having an effect. But for the life of him he couldn't figure out how she didn't spill some of her drink when she flumped herself onto the couch. He was still standing in the same position holding the shotgun when she began telling him what had happened. She was talking so fast that he had to stop her several times just to make sure that he had correctly heard what she said.

Once she had finished, he finally moved, and only then did he realize that he was still holding the shotgun. He stood it up against the wall and sat next to Eileen on the couch, and absentmindedly reached for her glass and took a sip, which he instantly regretted. He had lost his taste for whisky a long time ago.

After sitting next to each other quietly for a few minutes he said, "I know that you're upset and probably still scared shitless, but Jack's gonna be here later this morning, and we're forgetting one thing."

"What's that"?

"Yesterday you said that you didn't want to be left alone, and I did just that. I'm sure that if I had been here everything would've been just fine."

Eileen started to object, but stopped short and gasped when she looked at the kitchen clock.

"What's the matter, hon?"

"My senses tell me that it's only been a short time since you left, but almost two hours have gone by. I don't understand it."

Rob thought to himself, "Well, that's just peachy. I lost more than an hour yesterday and now she loses almost two." He quickly figured that he'd better change the subject if he didn't want the conversation to go from bad to worse and said, "I promise that I won't leave you alone. OK?"

"No! I really want to leave this place, now!"

"Look, leaving is not gonna solve anything. Staying and solving it is actually what we need to do. I can't leave without understanding what's goin' on. We have to take the bull by the horns and do what we have to do to figure this stuff out. We have to put a stop to it. OK?"

"All right, but don't you dare leave me alone for one second!"

"No problem." Trying to lighten the mood he said, "Well, I don't have to go to the bathroom with you, do I?"

"Don't be a smart ass!"

* * *

He had started to walk over to the sink to get a glass of water to rinse the whisky taste out of his mouth when the phone rang. He answered it and Jack King was on the other end moaning about Murphy's Law still kicking him in the ass. "OKaay ... so what time do you think you'll get here now?"

"I'm not going to have these problems wrapped up until late tonight, so I'll be there at 08:00 hours Wednesday morning. That OK with you?"

Rob wondered if he should tell Jack about the stranger and his attempt to come into the camp, but decided not to because Jack seemed to be in a big hurry. He also didn't want to say anything that Jack could interpret as twisting his arm. He knew that Jack wanted to come and if he could possibly do that without jeopardizing his business he'd do it. In his mental debate he remembered his promise to Eileen and figured that he could handle this new situation without upsetting her, so he said, "Yeah, that's fine Jack. I'll see you then."

He put the phone on its cradle and said to Eileen, "Why don't you finish brushing your teeth and what not while I uncover the sleds?"

"Aren't we going to the airport to get Jack and Nancy?"

"Not until tomorrow morning. Jack still has some problems that he's working through."

"You mean that we're goin' to be here *alone*?"

"Hey, I'm a big boy. Have you ever seen me in a situation that I couldn't handle?"

"Boy is right! You've always handled things in the past but we've never been in a situation like this before."

"True. Brush your teeth and get dressed. We'll take a ride to Oquossoc for lunch and get away from this stuff for a while." With that said, he quickly stepped out the door without waiting for her to answer.

As he went down the front porch steps he thought to himself, "Either she forgot or else doesn't mind being by herself in the house while I'm outside. He stopped at the bottom of the stairs and looked to see which direction the shoe tracks went from the porch, but there were no other tracks to be seen. He examined everything in the entire area, paying very close attention to each minute detail. After finishing his close examination of the tracks, he assumed that he and Rudy had obliterated the other tracks when coming back from their walk.

While he walked over to the snowmobiles he again looked in all directions to see if there was something that he might have missed. He felt edgy and his senses were on red alert. After he put the snowmobile covers in the shed he thought that he'd better call Thad and let him know about the stranger that Eileen had seen. As he started to head back to the house, he remembered that he wanted to top off the bird feeders.

He strapped on his snowshoes and climbed over the snowbank, and as he rounded the back corner of the house a number of different birds took to flight, all except the chickadees and nuthatches. He lifted the closest feeder off its hook; a two-liter Pepsi bottle with a metal perch and seed dispenser attached to it. Just as he turned around to go back to the shed, he noticed that there were still some small piles of feed that the deer had not yet cleaned up. He automatically looked at his watch, and wondered why. Normally by this time of the morning the piles of feed were history.

Once all the feeders were filled he went inside to stoke the furnace and as he walked by the kitchen he began thinking about his empty stomach. The moment that thought took over, his mouth watered as he pictured toasted waffles slathered with Skippy peanut butter. Eileen had just placed all their snowmobile gear in the living room, hers on the couch and his on the loveseat. He went down into the basement and quickly took care of the furnace and as soon as he went back upstairs he sat down on the loveseat next to his snowmobile coat and pants to call Thad. The phone just rang and rang. "He must be in the outhouse. I'll call back in a few minutes," he thought to himself.

Thad didn't waste a lot of time in the outhouse this time of year. He made things a little more comfortable for himself by keeping his toilet seat in the camp, to keep it nice and warm. But that was not sufficient to heat the frosty air around him. Rob took the waffles from the freezer and the peanut butter from the pantry, and brought them over to the counter by the sink. As he set them down next to the toaster he looked over at Eileen and asked her if she wanted any. She replied, "No, I'm planning on a fattening lunch so I'll behave for now."

Rob tried calling Thad a few more times but still no answer. He started feeling concerned and said to Eileen, "I'm going to swing by Thad's on the way to Oquossoc and we'll take the County Road to Brochu's landing instead of taking the Harris Pasture Road."

"Doesn't matter to me."

But it mattered to Rob. He wanted to avoid going near the beaver pond today. He had to avoid exposing Eileen to the possibility of strange events, and he didn't want a battle on his hands about going home. The odds were better than even that the beaver pond was not a long shot for shit happening. He quickly finished his breakfast, picked up his vitamins and washed them down with some orange juice, took the snowmobile keys off the hook and went out to warm them up. As soon as he stepped out the door he had the sensation of being in a vacuum, and he could feel the hair on his head begin to rise, as if it was being pulled up by static electricity. The sensation was forgotten when he heard a faint static hissing noise. He stopped in his tracks halfway out of the door, and as soon as he did, Rudy started barking.

Without thinking, he began to step back into the house, and he was almost all of the way in when the static noise stopped. At the same time, the vacuum feeling went away, and Rudy stopped barking. The incident immediately forgotten, he came over to Rob's side, tail wagging like crazy, looking longingly up at him. "No ride today, Toot-man. Sorry. I can't leave Eileen alone."

She had been standing near him and said, "Why don't you take him for a short ride in the field and I'll go with you. At least that way he won't give us attitude when we get back."

"Yeah, OK. I don't need a basset hound with attitude today."

Rudy shot out the door, almost tripping Rob in the process, running over to the sleds, and then sitting on his haunches facing them. There was no mistaking the expectant look on his furry face. "Yeah, yeah, Toot, you're going for a ride." He started the sleds and chuckled while he watched Rudy going through his usual routine of rubbing his snout in the snow trying to fix whatever effects the fumes had on his delicate sniffer.

Once the sleds were running smoothly, he headed back into the camp to put on his snowmobile gear. Eileen opened the door just as he was about to turn the knob. She had her gloves under her arm and her helmet in her hand. "I'll wait for you out here, and don't close the door! I want you to be able to see me while you change."

"Fair enough."

* * *

They headed in the direction of the trail that Rob had made through the woods. Only this time, as he approached the snow bank that he had used as a jump when going to visit Thad, he went considerably slower so Rudy wouldn't get thrown for a loop. He followed the same trail that he used the previous day, which bordered the tree line, and it was obvious that Rudy was extremely happy. Once he was about half the distance to Thad's, he cut across the field toward Kennebago Settlement Road. Six deer had just run across it heading in the direction of Camp Stress-A-Rest, and he figured that those remaining piles of feed would be gone in short order.

Halfway across the field he turned right and headed back toward the camp. Rudy gave him a knowing look and promptly dropped his head and ears in a blatant display of disappointment. Rob felt a pang of remorse in his heart because he knew that his old friend really enjoyed these rides, but he rationalized that he would make it up to the Toot-man when they got back. Just as he drove over the snow bank back at camp a couple of deer ran from behind the house to the safety of the woods across the road. Curious, he thought. Safety was much closer in the opposite direction.

He left his snowmobile running while he dragged an unwilling basset hound into the camp, and locked the door behind him. Both he and Eileen were oblivious to the static hissing noise that had terrified the deer, making them run for safety, because the noise from their engines had drowned it out.

* * *

They pulled into Thad's driveway, maneuvered their sleds around his truck, and parked next to his Artic Cat. Eileen stayed on her machine while Rob walked over to the camp wondering all the while why Thad hadn't already come out the door to greet them. After all, that was S.O.P. for him. He walked up the steps and knocked hard on the door three times while leaning over to look through the window. He could hear the chatter on Thad's CB, but neither Thad nor Ginger were anywhere to be seen. Thinking that they had to be around somewhere, he walked back down the steps and over towards the outhouse, stopping by the old granite hitching post that Thad used as a urinal. "Thad! Where are ya?" No answer. The only sound that he heard was made by some chickadees that were flitting back and forth from the nearby birch tree to the bird feeder.

He walked back to his sled and said, "Someone must've come by and taken Thad into town for breakfast." Then he recalled that he always left a pad of paper and pencil by his door so that a passing visitor could leave him a message. "Wait a minute, Eileen ... I want to leave a note for Thad. I'll be right back."

He found the paper and pencil just where they'd always been and he was half way through writing the message when the pencil broke and there was no way to sharpen it. Looking at the broken pencil he said, "Ah shit! At least he'll know that I was here. I'll call him when we get to Oquossoc." He checked Thad's door to make sure that it was locked, just in case that stranger might have still been around.

* * *

They were halfway down the County Road when Rob saw three coyotes running across an old clear-cut. He had seen coyotes in this area several times before, but what caught his attention was the fact that their tongues were hanging out of their mouths. Whenever he had seen coyotes on the run this time of year, with the temperature in the single digits like it was that day, he had never seen their tongues hanging out. He recalled a typical cold day in January last year, around the same time of the month when the temperature was also in the single digits. He and Eileen had been riding their snowmobiles West on ITS 89 along the south side of East Kennebago Mountain. He had been in the lead and came upon two coyotes as he rounded a sharp left hand turn. As soon as they saw him, they had started running as fast as they could in the opposite direction. The snow was soft and very deep on either side of the trail and they weren't very willing to leave the easy running that they had had on the hard packed snow. They had continued to run side-by-side following the trail up the mountain. He had stayed about four feet behind them for over a mile, maintaining a speed that varied between thirty to forty miles per hour. Finally, the coyote to the starboard side had swerved to the right and jumped off the snowmobile trail into the soft snow, making a great effort to leap and bound down the mountain. About one hundred feet later, the remaining coyote had made a move that amazed Rob. He had thrown his body to the left and jumped off the trail heading up the mountain.

As far as Rob was concerned, that coyote had picked a lousy spot to make its exit, because as soon as it had landed, it sank so deep in the snow that all he could see was its back popping up from time to time as it struggled to get its footing to head up the mountain. He hadn't noticed if the first coyote's tongue was hanging out, but he got a real good look at number two. In fact, he stopped right beside it (and to this day he doesn't understand what possessed him) but he dove off his snowmobile directly at the coyote and grabbed its tail just as it got its footing. Luckily for Rob, when it had lunged forward its tail slipped out of his grip. At least he had had the common sense to keep his eye on the coyote's face the whole time. He figured that if it had made a move to come back at him, he would have had the reaction time to avoid the attack. But the real reason that he remembered the incident to begin with was the fact that he had clearly seen that the coyote's tongue was *not* hanging out its mouth. At the time, he had wondered why when it had obviously been pushing itself to the limit to get away.

Eileen had been behind him the whole time, and when she had seen him dive off his snowmobile after the coyote she had yelled, "You stupid asshole!"

Of course he had never heard her over the roar of the snowmobile engine, but he had had no trouble hearing her later. When they got back to camp she had ranted and raved about the fact that if he had gotten into trouble just how in the hell did he expect her to help him? He had no answer for that question and said a little contritely, "I just got caught up in the thrill of the chase and reacted without thinking. All I wanted to do was to let the coyote know what a deer must feel like when it gets brought down at the end of a chase."

* * *

Shortly after passing through Brochu's Landing they took a left on ITS 89 and headed towards the Seven Gulpers camp. He slowed down as they approached it but he decided not to stop when he saw that there were no new tracks since the previous day when they had been there with Thad. After they passed the camp they came to a fork in the trail. They had taken the right fork the day before when they went to the top of East Kennebago Mountain. This time he took the left fork and followed ITS 89 down the northwest side of the Kennebago, making his way towards Oquossoc. They had gone about a mile when the trail made a sharp turn to the left. As soon as they completed the turn the trail got very narrow and they had to negotiate several hairpin turns. As they approached the third hairpin turn, a blind curve, Rob was going very slowly because he didn't like this section of the trail. It was notorious for accidents. As he entered the beginning of the turn he leaned forward, craning his neck out as far as possible to see if there was anything coming from the opposite direction. Suddenly, at the far side of the turn, a rider appeared. His sled was out of control and was slipping into the snowbank left by the trail groomer. The rider was going so fast that when his sled glanced off the snow bank it looked like a ricochet rocket coming directly at Rob. He had only one choice and immediately took it. He jammed the throttle to the handle bar and aimed his snowmobile straight ahead, crashing through the snowbank and into the woods like a shot, instantly getting buried in the deep soft snow. Rob didn't quite make it out of harm's way in time because the oncoming rider's left ski caught and tore his rear flap.

Just after contact was made, the rider was able to slow down enough to regain control of his sled and complete the turn to the right. He continued on for about fifteen feet before stopping alongside of Eileen. She was surprised at first because she had the feeling that the rider was going to just keep on going. One quick look told her that the rider was a young male and she instantly labeled him a yahoo. The rider never once turned to look back at Rob. He simply remained sitting on his sled with his head now drooping down upon his chest.

Rob took one look at the guy slumped over on his machine and figured that he was recovering from the panic that he must have just felt. After a few seconds he started paying attention to his own situation and took a look at how badly he was buried, which was bad. He cursed under his breath and began to calculate what he needed to do to maneuver a five hundred pound sled from its snowy quagmire. One thing for sure, it wasn't going to be an easy task when he took into consideration the help that he had at hand. The rider that had just run him off the trail looked like a ninety-pound weakling and while Eileen had a strong mind, she definitely wasn't Wonder Woman. He was becoming extremely frustrated and was giving serious consideration to slapping the crap out of "Evel Knievel", when the runt was saved as six snowmobilers came riding up the trail.

Each of the riders looked Rob over as they went by and all the time he was wondering if they were going to stop. His question was quickly answered when the lead rider stopped a short distance behind the character parked next to Eileen. It soon became obvious that they knew him. As it turned out, he was part of their group. As Rob found out from one of the guys that helped him get his sled back on the trail, "Evel" loved to go fast and was always leading the pack. It was quite a lead at that. Rob estimated that he had to be a full five minutes in front of the rest of them.

Four of the six riders were guys and they all came over to give Rob a hand in order to get his sled back onto the trail. After about three or four minutes of grunting and struggling, they had it sitting back on the hard packed snow pointing down the mountain. He barely got a chance to thank them for their help when they were gone.

"Speedy" was still sitting on his sled next to Eileen and neither one of them had moved a muscle as far as Rob could tell. Rob had a burning desire to go verbally ream out the inconsiderate son-of-a-bitch, and started to walk toward him to do just that. Eileen must have read his intentions because she subtly shook her head from side to side. He brought his hands up in a questioning gesture and that only brought a very firm shake of her head, and he knew that meant a real big no. He stood there for a few seconds contemplating whether he should heed her warning, and with his mind made up he finally started walking back to his sled to continue his run on down the mountain.

* * *

They had gone about three miles when they came to a wide spot in the trail and he decided to pull off to the side. Now he wanted to find out why Eileen had stopped him from giving that bastard a tongue-lashing. He got off his sled and opened the back storage compartment and took out his flask of Southern Comfort. Normally he kept it in there to take the chill off on extremely cold days, but his nervous system was still in reaction mode and he wanted to take the edge off, and also try to relax. As soon as he took the cap off the flask, he offered it to Eileen. Without hesitating she raised the shield on her helmet, took a sip and handed it back to him. Out of habit more than anything else, he wiped the opening clean before taking a big swallow and as he was putting the flask back into the compartment he said, "Eileen, why'd you stop me from giving that jerk a good piece of my mind?"

"Because I thought that he was weird and the only thing that I wanted to do was to get away from him. Besides, I knew what you wanted to do and I didn't think it would have fazed him one little bit! In my opinion you'd have wasted your breath."

"Yeah? Well, I sure would have felt a whole lot better by getting it off my chest! So why were you in such a hurry to get away from him?"

"Well, try this on for size. That guy never got off his sled to help and I couldn't understand a word of what his friends said when they were talkin' to him. For some reason they were talking very softly. But just the same, I was listening very closely because I wanted to know what they were saying to him. I heard some of the words they said, but they weren't English, French or Spanish. I don't know what they were. That rider never said a word back to them, or to me for that matter. He just sat there with his head hanging down the whole time. He didn't do anything at all, and I thought *that* was very strange."

Rob thought for a few moments and said, "You know what? I think that you're overreacting because of what happened this morning."

"Whatever! I know what I felt and I didn't like it."

"OK. OK. Don't get all worked up! It just isn't worth it. Would you like to ride to Oquossoc over the Rangeley Lake, or do you want to take the long way and go down the old Narrow Gauge Railroad track?"

She didn't hesitate for one second to give him her opinion and said, "You *know* I don't like going on the lake, shorter or not."

"That's fine with me. Next stop is the Four Seasons. OK?"

"You got it!"

* * *

He was getting ready to put on his helmet when he heard a big commotion in the woods off to his right. He motioned to Eileen to look in the direction of the noise because he thought that it was probably a moose, and he had the feeling that it might show itself any moment. He leaned back and sat sideways on his machine, facing the direction of all the commotion. Suddenly everything went quiet, and it stayed that way for a while. Then the crashing noises began again, only this time they were immediately followed by a faint, static hissing noise.

"Damn, Eileen, let's sit tight. I want to see what's goin' to happen." He no sooner got the words out of his mouth than he heard her machine cranking over. He looked back at her and motioned her to stay put. She shook her head "no" and brought her sled right alongside of his and stopped.

"You want to stay put, fine. But I'm going to be *real* close to you."

The static noise started getting somewhat louder and he decided to check his watch. He was beginning to suspect that the loss of time had something to do with the static. It was 10:15. The thrashing around in the woods seemed to get more intense as the static noise got louder. Suddenly a moose came bursting through the tree line heading right for them. It had the same look of terror in its eyes that the deer had the day before as they ran in front of him on Harris Pasture Road. There were fewer than twenty feet separating them from the moose when it crashed its way out of the woods, and Rob didn't think that it had a clue that they were in its path.

He instantly got a bad feeling in his gut. He turned to Eileen and yelled, "Get down in the snow close to your sled, QUICK!" He turned his head back just in time to see a massive brown wall right in front of him. He let his legs and body go limp and fell to the snow alongside his machine. Out of the corner of his eye he saw the moose sailing through the air over him and he prayed that it had enough steam behind it to get past Eileen.

Because of his grave concern for his wife, adrenalin was surging through his entire system as he scrambled to stand up, turning quickly to see what had happened and feeling all the time like his heart had leapt into his mouth. The static noise was gone and the moose was already in the woods on the opposite side of the trail. He could not believe his eyes when he saw where the moose had landed. The tracks were well past Eileen almost in the middle of the groomed snowmobile trail that was about thirty feet wide. He looked back to where the moose began its jump and he estimated that it had cleared the better part of twenty feet. Right then he noticed that his hands were trembling a little, and instantly assumed that Eileen would be absolutely vibrating. And that assumption begat another thought. He needed to get her mind off the fear factor fast and he blurted out, "That's impossible! I've never seen a moose jump before, let alone a jump like this! Have you?"

He checked his watch to see how much time had elapsed as he said, "Eileen?" But she still didn't answer. He walked around to the other side of her sled, and became somewhat concerned when he saw that she was just lying there with her eyes and mouth wide open. He reached down, took a hold of her hand and started to help her up, but she just hung there like dead weight.

Finally, she looked at him and said, "I've had enough of this crap! Can't we please go back to camp, pack up and go home?"

He didn't know what to say, but he sure didn't want to go back to camp, let alone go home. Not now. Saying the first thing that came to his mind, "Listen, we both know that a moose's elevator skips floors most of the time. You remember that bull moose standing on the side of the road last October? He must have been at least fifteen hundred pounds. As I recall it was about 05:30 hours and we were on the way to the airport, remember?"

"Yeah. So what?"

"I was doing about fifty miles an hour, and as we got closer to the moose he turned and charged us, remember?"

"Yeah?"

"Well doesn't that prove to you that moose don't have all their marbles in the right order?"

"Yeah?"

"How many times has something like this happened?"

"On a snowmobile, once."

"Fine, I rest my case. As far as I'm concerned this is akin to getting hit by lightning, and your chance of getting hit by lightning is one in nine thousand. I figure that the chance of this happening again is just about zero."

"Yeah? Well, as far as I'm concerned that is a bunch of baloney. With what has been going on since yesterday, I don't trust *anything*. I'll stay with you and you won't hear me gripe anymore, but I'm not happy about it at all. Right now you've kind of got me over a barrel, and I'm not about to forget this crap that you're pulling on me. Just remember, when I'm not happy it usually goes that you're not going to be happy. You want to settle for that?"

He didn't take any time to think and replied, "I'll take my chances. Let's go." But as soon as he got the words out of his mouth he began to have second thoughts. However, realizing that second thoughts would go totally against the grain, he let his mind change gears and looked at his watch for the second time. Unfortunately there were no revelations. He could account for all the time that had elapsed.

5

They were cruising at 40 miles per hour down a trail known as Flat Iron Finger, their first leg in the trail system to the Four Seasons. Rob wasn't concentrating on the trail so much as he was playing devil's advocate with himself. He was trying to shoot holes in his theory that the distorted circle of air/static noise phenomenon could be the basis for the loss of time that both Eileen and he had experienced. He finally decided that the best way to prove his theory was to see if he could find a pattern. Maybe, once he did, it would lead him to an answer. He started focusing on the first time that he heard the static noise, which was when he and Rudy were on their way to the beaver pond. He could vividly recall seeing the circle of vertical shimmering air and he had no trouble remembering the strange feeling that he had when everything turned stone quiet just before the silence was broken by the static sound. But was there anything else? And he concluded that the final answer to that question was no. He didn't recall any physical sensations, just a strange feeling, and though he could not totally recall the walk back to camp, it did not matter because the entire walk took the usual amount of time. But then he remembered something else. When Rudy and he had gone back to the beaver pond for another look at the deer tracks that went out onto it from the pine trees, he saw a small circular depression in the snow, which was about six feet from where the tracks had ended.

He tucked that information in the back of his mind and started thinking about the second time that he had heard the static noise. That was when he and Rudy went back to the beaver pond after breakfast. Once more the circle of distorted air appeared first, and then everything turned very quiet just before the hissing noise filled his ears. In his mind he could clearly see the hawk being propelled into the circle of shimmering air, but he had no recollection of any kind of physical sensations. And once again the amount of time that had lapsed while Rudy and he were gone could be accounted for.

Now he focused his attention on the next time that he had heard the static noise. After a minute or so of mentally recreating the sequence of events after leaving the beaver pond, he could not recollect hearing the crackling noise again until he was topping off the snowmobile gas tanks, which was after Eileen and he had gotten back from their trailside lunch. He was concentrating so hard on this scene that he could vividly see himself strapping on his snowshoes and walking over to the stand of pine trees where the static seemed to be coming from, with Rudy trailing right behind. He didn't see a circle of distorted air, but he remembered feeling a tingling sensation all over his body, and that was when Rudy disappeared. Try as he would, he could not remember if there was any time that he could not account for. However a significant factor crept into Rob's conscious mind. The Wiffle ball depression! That's depression number two. Was there any connection to the static noise and the circular depressions in the snow? Maybe, or maybe not.

It didn't take any effort at all for him to think of the fourth time that he heard the hissing sound. It was instantly there just like somebody had written it on a Post-It and pasted it to his forehead. It was when Ginger and he had gone out behind the camp to look for Rudy. He didn't remember feeling any sensations when they heard the static noise. But he did remember hearing the soft "whump" shortly before Ginger ran into the pine trees and found Rudy in the clearing on the other side. And that is when he saw depression number three, which was about seven feet from where Ginger had found Rudy. Then he began to wonder if the "whump" that he heard had anything to do with Rudy's sudden appearance. Apparently the "whump" had something to do with it because not one of Rudy's tracks could be found anywhere after he disappeared. It was almost as if he was dropped there and that could account for the "whump" sound. Furthermore, he had carefully checked the entire clear-cut where Ginger had found him, and he was still unable to find *any* tracks leading to that spot, let alone some of Rudy's. So the only logical conclusion is that the static noise and tingling sensation must have had something to do with Rudy's disappearance, and probably his reappearance.

Suddenly, slamming right square into the middle of his thoughts, a sequence of events that were tied together came to him. His body tingled with excitement and he blurted out loud, "YEAH!" Each time that he saw tracks that either began from nothing, or ended into nothing, there was a circular depression in the snow nearby. But there was one exception, and that was where the stranger's tracks began in the clearing in front of the camp. But then he thought, "Maybe I just didn't pay close enough attention to detail. I'll take a closer look when I get back." Then his mind jumped to Rudy's disappearance and he thought, "There's another time that tracks just ended. That's another area that I'd better check when I get back. If I find circular depressions in those two areas then there's a pattern developing that can possibly help Jack and me make sense of everything that's been goin' on." He then brought his mind back to the time factor. "Did I lose any time when Rudy disappeared?" After pondering that question for a minute or so, still talking out loud to himself he said, "Not that I can recall."

So far he was coming up with a big fat zero in his effort to try to determine what had caused Eileen to lose time when the stranger appeared in front of their camp, and what caused him to lose time when he was checking the depressions in the clearing after Ginger found Rudy. He could not make any connections to any specific event and the loss of time but he felt that the circular depressions in the snow were definitely connected to the disappearing tracks. That was something solid he could hang his hat on. He was convinced that somehow they were connected to the static noise and the circles of vertical shimmering air. In the sequence of events since Monday morning the first time that he could recall any loss of time was when he had gone back out to the clearing after Ginger had found Rudy. But during that time he did not hear the static noise and he couldn't remember experiencing any sensations whatsoever.

Eileen certainly felt sensations when she heard the static noise while brushing her teeth and that is when the stranger appeared. She lost time during that episode but there was no logical direct link to the static noise that he could think of.

The last incident of hissing noise was still fresh in his mind. One question kept looming out at him and it didn't involve the loss of time factor. What was it about the crackling noise that terrified that moose so much that it was able to make that unbelievable jump? And that question begat another question. What made Eileen feel the way she did about the rider that had run him off the trail? He had to agree with her one hundred percent that something was terribly wrong with that whole scenario. However he couldn't think of one reason that would've been enough of a motivational factor to vacate the area. Yes, people that were the cause of an accident just didn't normally act the way that he did. Their usual reaction was one of being contrite, and was almost always coupled with a genuine desire to help the person that was wronged. He muttered under his breath, "That's just another chapter in the 'Book of Weird' for this week."

* * *

He backed off the throttle as they neared the turnoff to a narrow trail that winds its way up a steep mountain, which was barely wide enough to let two snowmobiles going in opposite directions pass by each other. After his earlier encounter with "Evel Knievel" he was still a little gun-shy, and his pace going up the mountain was slower than normal. But his conservative speed was also because of a little superstition. He really didn't subscribe to the karma theory but he decided that today wasn't a time to tempt fate since the next intersection they were heading toward was called Crash Corner.

When they arrived at Crash Corner there must have been twenty-five snowmobilers parked there taking a break. Rob didn't know if they were going to head down to Flat Iron Finger or not but he was happy that he didn't have to pass all those sleds going in the opposite direction while he was climbing that narrow section of the trail. He really liked the scenery in that area and would have missed it if he had to concentrate on hugging the edge. He paused briefly at Crash Corner and then took a right, the beginning of a nine-mile stretch, which was the next to the last leg of their trip to Oquossoc. Rob had never seen a name on any map for this section of the trail system, but it is wide, fairly straight and usually well groomed.

They made good time getting to the end of No Name trail, and to Rob's surprise, they rode the whole length of it without coming across any other riders. As they approached the end of the trail they had to slow down to almost a crawl because it made a ninety-degree left-hand turn dumping them onto what used to be a rail bed for the Narrow Gauge Railroad. As you would expect, this section of the trail system was level and straight as an arrow, and stays that way for seven miles. It was about 20 feet wide and you can see riders coming from the opposite direction at least a mile away. It was the main trail from Oquossoc that connects to trails leading to Eustis, Stratton and the non-lake route to Rangeley, including a trail that ends up in Pittsburgh, New Hampshire. As a main feeder trail it had a lot of snowmobile traffic and this day was no exception. Rob saw a long line of riders approaching from the opposite direction, and even though the trail is plenty wide enough for snowmobiles to easily pass by each other, he elected to back down from 40 mph to 30 mph. The first few sleds that went by were going so fast that he had the temporary sensation of standing still and he decided to back down another ten just to be safe.

* * *

When they pulled into the Four Seasons Restaurant parking lot there were so many snowmobiles that they had a difficult time finding a place to park. Considering it was only Tuesday, which is usually a very slow time of the week, Rob was absolutely amazed at the number of sleds there. Checking his watch he saw that it was 12:15 hours and immediately assumed that the majority of the riders out and about today had decided to come to this particular restaurant for lunch. He turned to Eileen and said, "It's gonna be a long wait before we get to eat. You want to stay here or do you want to go to the Oquossoc House where there are probably fewer people?"

"Let's stay here. I'm not sure that my bladder can last long enough to make the trip over to the Oquossoc House."

As they walked up to the busy restaurant they elected to go through the front door rather than the side door and when they walked in they saw nothing but wall-to-wall people. The only two seats available were at the bar and Rob made a beeline toward them. Placing his gloves in his helmet, he set them both on the chair while he took off his coat. Eileen came up alongside of him and said, "I don't want to eat at the bar so let's have a drink and wait for a table to open up."

"Fair enough. Give me yer coat and helmet and I'll place them over on the rack."

He had just gotten back to the bar and was sitting down when the barmaid came over to take their order. He knew what he wanted but could see that Eileen was trying to make up her mind. Taking the lead he said to the barmaid, "While she's making up her mind give me a bottle of Corona and a shot of Jose Cuervo Gold and two pieces of lime. Oh yeah, and also some salt, please."

The barmaid began to write down his order when she paused and said, "We're having a special on the Jose Cuervo 1800 today. It's a lot smoother and it's the same price as the Jose Cuervo Gold during the special."

Smiling, he said, "Thanks, I really appreciate that information, but I like the bite of the Gold."

She gave him a funny look and seeing that Eileen had made up her mind she turned her attention to her saying, "And what can I get for you?"

Eileen hesitated, and then quickly deciding against whatever she was considering, said, "I'd like a hot chocolate."

"You want whipped cream on that?"

"Yes, please, and would you please get a table for us when one comes open?"

"Sure."

As the barmaid walked away, Rob saw an opportunity to "bust them off" on Eileen, which he really enjoyed doing from time to time, and started to shake his head in mock disbelief as he said, "Nice of you to finally make up your mind. For a minute there I thought that it had boarded the slow boat to China!"

She looked at him and paused just for a second before saying an emphatic, "Very funny!" She immediately knew that she had 'been had' once again when she saw the victorious smirk taking shape at the corners of his mouth.

* * *

Rob was looking around at the different people in the restaurant to see if there was anybody that he knew when Eileen poked him in the ribs. As soon as she was sure that she had his attention she leaned forward and whispered in his ear, "You should listen to what the people are talking about at the table right next to us."

Six snowmobilers were sitting there and they were having a very animated conversation. Rob could not make out what they were saying and asked Eileen what she had heard. Leaning closer to him she softly said, "They're talking about some static noise that they heard and I know that you'll really love this. They also saw two deer running in a panic at the same time."

"Right! How could they hear the static noise over the sound of their machines?"

"Don't ask me! Ask them!"

Not being able to resist the bait he walked over to the table, put a smile on his face and said, "Howdy. How's the riding been?"

They were still talking in an animated fashion when he interrupted their conversation. The guy sitting at the opposite end of the table started to stand up like he was in the mood for trouble. He was a "big mother" and Rob figured that he was about fifty pounds overweight. He had arms on him like a gorilla and as soon as he was standing tall, Rob estimated that he was about six-foot five. He had a Harley bandanna tied on his head and Rob's mouth involuntarily dropped open when the guy expanded his chest so the first thought that came to his mind was, "Holy moly! Just like they do in the animal world to intimidate an intruder."

"Whoa, big fella! I'm just being friendly. My wife heard someone in your group talking about static noise and a couple of scared deer."

The gorilla's face softened a little as he said, "Yeah? What of it?"

"Well, we had a similar experience and I just wanted to talk about it. My name's Rob and my wife's name is Eileen."

She had been watching and listening to what was going on and when she heard her name she promptly walked over to help keep the peace. One of the women at the table stood up, stuck her hand out to Eileen and said, "Hi. My name is Mindy."

"Hi, Mindy, nice to meet you. I wasn't trying to eavesdrop on your conversation but when I happened to hear one of the people in your party say "static noise," it caught my attention. My husband and I heard static noise on the way here and that's why I asked Rob to come over and talk to you."

After taking a hard look at Eileen, wondering if her leg was being pulled Mindy said, "Where did you guys hear the static noise?"

"Do you know where Black Cat Hollow is?"

"Sure, we take that trail when we go up to the top of East Kennebago Mountain."

"Good, so you'll know where I'm going to be talking about. We have a camp over on Kennebago Settlement Road. Do you know where that is?"

"Sure. The Dead River goes under it right by Barry Pendleton's farm, right?"

"That's the road. We left camp to come here for lunch and decided to stop and take a break once we passed through Black Cat Hollow. You know where the trail gets somewhat wider just as you get to the bottom of the mountain?"

"Sure."

"Well not too far from the bottom of the mountain there's a real wide spot and I think that's where the guys that groom the trails take a break."

Mindy cut in, saying, "I know the exact place that you're talkin' about."

"That's where we stopped for our break, and *that's* where we heard the hissing noise."

"Really! We heard it near the big split rock. You know where that is?"

"Sure."

"We were on our way here from Eustis and had to stop for a break because big boy Bubba sittin' over there had coffee bladder. Do you know where the turnoff to Stratton is, just before the split rock?"

"Absolutely. We've been down that trail many times."

"Well, we were somewhere in between the cut off to Stratton and the split rock and we were there for about two or three minutes when this crackling noise began. All of a sudden two deer jumped over a blowdown about 15 feet in front of us and I could swear that they had panic in their eyes."

Bubba, who is almost as big as the Harley bandanna dude, piped up, "I live in Eustis and I hunt these woods all the time and I ain't never seen no deer in that area before."

About that time the Harley bandanna guy started walking over to Rob, putting out a huge hand on the way and said, "My name's Stormin."

"Stormin! That's a real unusual name there, Stormin."

"Well my nickname is Stormin Norman but everyone just calls me Stormin. Did you guys see anything when you heard the static noise?"

A smile busted out that covered his whole face as he said, "I guess the hell we did! A moose came crashin' out of the woods, headin' right at us, and I'm pretty sure that this moose was also in a panic because it jumped right over us *and* our sleds, and that's sayin' somethin' 'cause our sleds were parked side-by-side. I ain't never seen no moose jump like a fucking gazelle before, have you?"

Rob looked over at Eileen and she was giving him one of those "watch yer mouth" looks. He had a habit of mimicking and blending in with the type of person that he was talking to, and that annoyed her to no end.

"No man! As a matter-of-fact I ain't never seen no moose jump, period. And another thing, pal, I think you're shittin' me. Like I said, moose don't jump, especially like that."

Stormin looked at the other guys sitting at the table and shrugged his shoulders in a questioning manner as if to say, am I right or wrong? They all paused just to bust his balls, and then shook their heads in agreement.

Switching back to a more sophisticated mode, Rob said, "Gentlemen, I do not have any reason to kid you. It happened just like I said. Have any of you heard this static noise anywhere else?"

They all gave each other an inquisitive look and shook their heads no.

Taking a very professional posture he said, "I'd like to ask you all a favor. I'll give you my phone number and if you hear the static noise again, would you please give me a call and tell me where you heard it?"

The third guy, who had said nothing up to this point, said with a real suspicious look on his face, "Why do you want us to do that?"

"Because my wife and I have heard the static noise several times in a few different places, and I'm trying to figure out if this noise is confined to a certain area or if it's everywhere."

Stormin got a much more friendly look about him and said, "No sweat, man, we're glad to help if we can. What's your number?"

Rob went over to the bar, picked up a pen and a few drink napkins, wrote his number on three of them, and then handed one to each woman sitting at the table. He tried to maintain a serious look on his face but the smirk gave away the lighter side of his intent as he said, "If your husbands are anything like me, they have a good chance of misplacing this napkin but, from experience, I know that women are much better at holding onto things." He turned to the guys and said "Thanks. I appreciate your willingness to help me." Then he motioned to the barmaid to send a waitress over to the table as he said, "What are you people drinking?" And he knew immediately that he would get their cooperation when he saw the beaming smiles on Stormin and Bubba's faces.

While everybody's drink orders were being taken, Rob went over to the bar to get his and Eileen's drinks. The waitress met him when she was half way back to the bar with the drink orders and said, "This one's gonna cost you dearly, big boy! *These* people know how to drink!"

He looked over at her and said, "It's just what I expected, Kathy. How've you been?"

"I've been behaving myself. Can't you tell? I've lost about thirty pounds!"

Rob made a show of looking her up and down and said, "Not bad at all," and quickening his pace he added, "When're you gonna lose the next thirty?"

She took a fast look around to see if anyone was watching before flipping him the birdie.

Eileen and Rob had known Kathy for years. Part of the standing ritual each time they meet is to find a way to get in a verbal jab or two just for fun, sort of like one-upmanship. But anyone around who didn't know better would think that big trouble was on the way.

While walking the rest of the way back to the table, he made up his mind that he wanted to get to know the quiet guy and held his hand out as he walked up to him saying, "I didn't get your name."

As he stood up to shake Rob's hand he said, "My name's Len." The guy was lean and clean-cut and did not look like he belonged with the other two guys, kind of like a fine wineglass sitting between two everyday beer glasses.

Rob took an obvious close look at him and said, "Are you from around here?"

Len paused just a moment before saying, "No, I'm from Boston. I'm just visiting for a few days."

Rob studied him for a little while longer before it finally got the best of him and he said, "What do you do for a living in Boston?"

"I'm a litigation attorney." And when he saw Rob's questioning look, he knew all too well what the look was about; what's this guy doing hanging around with the likes of them? Without waiting for the obvious and sometimes unspoken question to surface in some delicately engineered manner he said, "Bubba is my cousin. In the spring we fish together, in the fall we hunt together, and in the winter we snowmobile together."

A smile worked its way onto Rob's face and he was getting ready to say something that he hoped would be witty when the waitress came to the table with a tray full of drinks. As soon as all the drinks had been set on the table he asked Kathy to add it to his tab. As she walked away the six snowmobilers raised their drinks in a toast to Rob. "My pleasure. Glad to meet ya, and don't forget to give me a call if you hear that static noise again."

Bubba was the first to answer and said, "No problem, man. You and your ol' lady have a good ride this afternoon."

"Thanks, Bubba. You too."

* * *

Just as they sat down back at the bar Kathy came over and said that she had a table for them. Rob smiled saying, "Thanks for the speedy service. That was much quicker than I thought it would be."

She looked over her shoulder as she led the way to the table and said, "You just got lucky."

They grabbed their drinks and followed her to a table that just happened to be right alongside the wood stove. The waitress put a menu in front of each of them and said, "I'll be back in a few minutes."

He thanked Kathy and as soon as she left he turned to Eileen and said, "We've got the hottest seat in the house."

"Brilliant deduction, Sherlock! And I'd love it if I could take off my sweater, long underwear and snowmobile pants."

Smiling the whole time, he said, "Hey! You're the one that's always complaining that you're cold so I don't want to hear you moan about the heat now." And as soon as he finished his remark he heard the guy at the table next to them start to chuckle. When he turned his head to see who it was, he found himself looking at a round-faced guy with laughter in his eyes. Rob took a quick look at Mr. Smiley's companion and didn't see *any* laughter on her face. At that point he wasn't sure if the guy was laughing at what he had said to Eileen or if he was laughing at the expense of the woman sitting in front of him. Ultimately he decided that the wisest thing to do was mind his own business.

Almost the instant that he turned his attention back to Eileen he felt a tap on his shoulder. When he turned his head to look back at the round-faced guy, he saw the same twinkle in his eyes and heard him say, "Hi. Name's Matt. Didn't mean to butt in on ya, but I couldn't help laughin' at whatchya said to yer lady friend. My wife and I go through the same crap all the time."

Reaching over to shake his hand he said, "Glad to meet ya, Matt. My name's Rob and my wife's name is Eileen."

"Stone-face sittin' in front of me there is Gloria," and with that they both simply stood up and slid their table next to Rob's, immediately starting a conversation as if they had known each other forever.

Taking an instant liking to Matt he said a little facetiously, "Glad you accepted my invitation to move your table next to ours."

Matt chuckled and said, "I saw some common ground and figured that we ought to get to know each other. Besides, I knew you wouldn't object when I told you that we heard static noise also."

He suddenly had Rob's undivided attention. Matt's table was at least six tables from where they were seated at the bar and at least seven tables away from Bubba and party. He was trying to figure out just how Matt knew that Eileen and he had heard static noise. Matt must have read the questioning expression on his face and said, "I heard you talking with those people at the table by the bar when I was on my way back from the men's room. I heard you say static noise and it caught my attention so I listened in on your conversation for a little bit."

Eileen sent a quick and knowing look to Rob and then turned to Gloria saying, "Where did you hear the static noise?"

"I don't know exactly where we were when we heard the noise. We were on our way from Stratton to Rangeley and we had stopped to take a break just past a bridge that crosses over a brook."

Rob thought for a few seconds and said, "There are a few bridges that cross over a brook on that trail. Do you remember if there were any trail markers near that bridge?"

At that point Matt jumped back into the conversation and said, "We had just left the groomed trail to cross over a plowed logging road and we hadn't gone twenty feet before we came to the bridge."

"I know exactly where you're talking about. That plowed logging road comes in from Route 16 in Baldwin Plantation. That's taking a very long way to get here. What'd you do, get up at two in the morning to make the trip here for lunch?"

"No, this wasn't today, this was yesterday."

"I see. Was there anything else besides the static noise?"

Matt and Gloria just looked at each other for a few moments, as if they were trying to see the answer in each other's eyes. Rob kept his mouth shut and so did Eileen. Whatever was going on between them, they did not want to interrupt it. Finally Gloria looked at Eileen and sheepishly said, "I saw a man standing near the plowed road in what looked like a leisure suit. At first Matt was in denial and told me that I was crazy. He said that I've been fasting too long and that I'm beginning to see things. But ever since yesterday I've felt a need to eat my regular meals again "

Matt jumped back into the conversation saying, "Yeah. And she's one hundred percent easier to live with now!"

Rob had been looking intently at Gloria and she must have felt his stare because she turned to him and said, "What?"

"Look, let me set the record straight. Eileen and I just had a couple of days that haven't made much sense at all, and what we heard you say, we can believe, but I'm trying to understand how it fits in the overall picture. First, tell me more about this guy wearing a leisure suit."

Both were quiet and did the looking at each other routine again before Gloria took the initiative to take up the slack in the conversation. "I know that this is going to sound like something out of this world, but here goes. Both of us were staring at this guy and when we discussed it later we found out that we both were trying to make sure that we weren't seeing things. This weirdo was looking in the opposite direction from where we were standing and it seemed like he was fixating on something. We both were staring at him for a minute or so when suddenly his head just snapped around and he looked right at us. But what was really weird, I had the feeling that he was looking directly at me. I could feel the force of his eyes locked onto mine. However, that in itself isn't weird. What's really strange in this whole scenario is that Matt had the exact same feeling as me ... at the exact same time."

Rob was not sure that he truly understood what she was trying to tell him, so he cut in asking, "What makes you so sure that he was looking at both of you at the same time?"

Matt answered saying, "Because, at most he was only looking at us for five seconds when the static noise got louder and, well, it looked like he was sucked away at this incredible speed. Bingo, he was gone!"

There was another short pause and Gloria picked it up saying, "There just wasn't enough time for him to try to get that mind-lock on each of us."

That statement got Eileen's interest and she said, "Gloria, what do you mean by mind-lock? A moment ago I thought that I heard you say that you felt him lock onto your eyes."

She paused before answering and looked at Matt like she wanted him to take over but he just sat there looking back at her. Starting slowly at first, she said, "I really didn't want to say what we really felt. It just sounds so theatrical."

Rob lost his patience and said, "Damit, Gloria, just spit the words out, will ya!"

Eileen immediately came to her defense saying, "Don't listen to that jerk! He doesn't have any couth. Calm down and take your time and just tell it like it was. Don't leave anything out."

She let out a big sigh and said, "There's really not much more to tell. When Matt and I talked later it finally came out that we both felt like he was probing our minds. I can't explain why we felt that way, we just did!"

Matt had been sipping his coffee from time to time, but mostly he had his elbows resting on the table with his chin in his hands, while his eyes went back and forth between Gloria, Rob, and Eileen, depending upon who was talking. When there was a lull in the conversation he said, "Somethin' else happened today that I thought was just as weird. I wake up early, see, and this morning I wanted to take a walk before Gloria made breakfast. I decided to walk toward an old survival school and I was about halfway there when I spotted this rabbit doing a real fast hop down the side of the road." Pausing for a moment to make sure that he said it right, he continued, "I remember that I was wondering why this rabbit was out in the open in broad daylight when all of a sudden it just disappeared. How do ya like that as somethin' for weird?"

That really got his curiosity in high gear and Rob asked, "Where was that?"

"Do you know where Kennebago Settlement Road is?"

"Sure. Where on Kennebago Settlement Road?"

"Just past Darryl Wayde's place headin' toward Bonnie Brook."

"I thought I knew everyone that lives down that way. Where do you live?"

"I don't own the place, it belongs to a friend of mine, and he's kind enough to let us use it from time to time."

Wanting to know exactly which camp it was, Rob asked, "Is there a name on the camp?"

"Sure," and he paused like he was trying to remember it and finally said, "It's Better-n-Nothing."

"Okay. I know just where you were at. Did you hear any static noise or see anything strange when the rabbit disappeared?"

"Not a thing."

Turning to Eileen, Rob said, "We've talked to two groups of people since we got here and so far we are batting a thousand. I wonder if the average would remain the same if I had an opportunity to talk with everybody that was having lunch here?"

Everyone had already decided what they were going to eat by the time Kathy came back to take their orders. As soon as she was gone, they continued talking about the different things that had happened to them over the past couple of days that they found hard to explain. Most of what Gloria and Matt had experienced was similar to what Eileen and Rob went through, the only difference being that Rob had not told Eileen about the hawk disappearing into the circle of vertical shimmering air.

Gloria, Matt and Eileen wanted to enjoy their meal without the threat of indigestion and changed the focus of their discussion to delicious meals that they had at several different restaurants in the Rangeley Lakes area during the last year. Rob on the other hand was quiet and deep in thought, mentally plotting each of the locations of static noise heard by the snowmobilers that he had talked to. So far the greatest distance from the beaver pond that the static noise had been heard is about five miles as the crow flies and only two of those instances could be considered near the five-mile mark. The first time was when the moose jumped over them and their sleds, and the second time was when Gloria and Matt had stopped by the bridge. And as he thought more about the distance, he figured it was more like three miles than five miles. But what he found most interesting of all is that all the other times that the static noise was heard, it was in a tight two-mile radius around the beaver pond.

* * *

When they were almost finished eating, Rob gave his phone number to Matt and told him to give them a call that night, suggesting that a few games of cribbage might be fun. He wasn't really in the mood for card games; what he really wanted was the company. Matt and Gloria got up to get their snowmobile paraphernalia on and Rob told Eileen to order another hot chocolate. He decided that he needed to chat with some of the other people in the restaurant. She said, "Listen, I don't want to sit here like a bump on a log while I'm waiting for you, so if you're going to go chat, I'm going with you."

"Fine, hold on a second." Rob got Kathy's attention and motioned for her to come over. As soon as she walked up to the table he wasted no time in asking her to bring him a Corona with a piece of lime and a "hot chocolate for the missus." As soon as she brought them their drinks, he paid her and they started mixing among the other people in the restaurant. Most of the people were friendly, however some were distantly so. Of the eleven other groups of people that they talked with, only four had an experience or two that they were willing to admit they could not easily explain, and all of those experiences happened within two miles or less of the beaver pond. When he had finished talking to two elderly people that were part of a large group of snowmobilers sitting at a long table in the back, he nonchalantly glanced at the clock and saw that it was almost 14:45 hours. The first thought that popped into his mind was that they'd better hit the trail. All the strange events of the past couple of days were working feverishly in the back of his mind, and he wanted to check certain areas around camp for circular depressions in the snow. It was the third time that day he had felt a burning desire. He wanted to get back to camp with plenty of daylight to spare. Looking at the opposite end of the table he saw that Eileen was still having an animated conversation with two of the women. Catching her attention he pointed to his watch and gave her the high sign that he was going to the men's room. She nodded an acknowledgment to him, said her good-byes and was a few steps behind him on her way to the ladies' room. As they approached the doors to their respective bathrooms he said to her, "I'll meet you over by the coat rack."

* * *

He was standing by the coat rack, his coat unzipped and his helmet in his hand when he remembered that he wanted to call Thad. He set his helmet back on the rack and walked over to the pay phone, fished a quarter out of his pocket, dropped it in and dialed Thad's number. He stood there listening to it just ring and ring. He was hoping Thad was in the out house and taking his time to answer the phone, so he let it ring about fifteen times before placing the handset back on its receiver. With that, he was more concerned than before yet was making a conscious effort to look like "business as usual" as he walked back over to the coat rack. He hoped that by just being himself he wouldn't attract a barrage of questions from Eilene who was rapidly becoming a nervous ninny.

She had just finished strapping on her helmet and was all set to go as he walked up. She looked at him and whispered, "Where were you?"

"I remembered that I wanted to give Thad a call but he still wasn't home." He felt very satisfied with himself when there was no further conversation and thought, "This is one of the few times that I successfully hid the fact that something was bothering me."

* * *

While the snowmobiles were warming up, Rob walked over to Eileen and asked her if the two women that she was talking with had anything to say about strange phenomenon. She thought for a moment before answering and said, "They were very pleasant to talk to and we discussed quite a few different things that they thought were strange but none of them fit into the scenario that we're looking for. I got the feeling that they had overactive imaginations and they were the kind of people that are very polite, but I think that they were just trying to make things fit so that we could have a longer conversation."

"How many people do you think were in that restaurant?"

"I'm just guessing, but I would think that there were about sixty people in there."

"I'd say that you're pretty close to being right on target. So, out of all the people that we talked with, there were six groups that heard the static noise and/or saw something that they couldn't explain." He paused for a bit to gather his thoughts and said, "Based on what everyone has told us, they all covered a serious amount of real estate between yesterday and today. So maybe these strange phenomenon are not as widespread as we thought because the heaviest concentration seems to have been within a five mile radius of the beaver pond."

"Rob, I don't want to say that you're jumping to conclusions, but in a scientific sense we haven't even scratched the surface yet. I don't think that we've talked to enough people to have that degree of certainty. Don't you agree?"

"There's some merit to what you're saying, but my gut tells me that I'm pretty close to being right. Look, it's 15:10 and if we don't dilly-dally and take any breaks along the way, we can be back to camp by 16:20 hours."

"What's the rush?"

"I have a hunch, and I want to take a real close look at a couple of areas around the camp while we still have some daylight, and believe me when I tell you, I *need* to satisfy my curiosity or I won't get any sleep tonight."

* * *

They had just finished parking their snowmobiles in front of the shed when Rob checked his watch and yelled, "Hey Eileen it's 16:19 hours, how's that for calling it right?"

"What do you mean?"

"Remember? At the Four Seasons I said that if we didn't stop and dilly-dally along the way that we'd be here by 16:20 hours." Rob looked at his watch again and said, "It just turned 16:20 hours."

Not impressed at all she said, "Yeah, yeah, yeah, I'm so proud of you."

He put a hurt look on his face as he said, "You're all heart!"

* * *

They both got to the door at the same time and as he was unlocking it he could hear Rudy whining on the other side. "I bet that his bladder's talking to him, 'cause he doesn't normally whine at the door when we get back unless he's close to going beyond capacity."

He was one hundred percent correct. As quickly as he opened the door Rudy rushed through the opening, literally flying across the front porch, zipping down the steps and dashing directly to a big clump of snow at the other side of the driveway. When he lifted his leg Rob could swear that he heard him grunt a moan of relief. Eileen had an issue of her own and stepped around him, quickly disappearing into the camp.

He had mentally filed away the two areas around camp that he wanted to check for circular concave depressions in the snow, and was anxious to get started. Letting the door go, he decided not to waste any time and started to walk over to the clearing where the stranger's footsteps began. He was carefully scanning the entire area when he felt Rudy nudge his leg. "Hey, Toot! How's it going, buddy?"

Rudy stood there looking up at him while wagging his tail with serious enthusiasm. "Okay, Toot, I'll take you for a ride in a few minutes." With that Rudy trotted over to the snowmobiles and sat down. It was almost as if he had understood exactly what Rob had said.

The moment that Rudy left his side he started scanning the area beyond the footprints again. He thought he saw a depression in the snow located between the beginning of footprints and the snowbank at the side of the road. But due to the angle of the sun at that time of day it was hard to tell for sure, so he walked up the driveway and out onto Kennebago Settlement Road to get another look from a different angle. At first the view wasn't much better than from the driveway, but as he walked further down the road he could clearly see a circular concave depression in the snow. It was about three to four inches deep and about five feet in diameter. He stood there for a moment with his hands on his hips, just pondering how something like this could be possible.

He heard Rudy make a quiet "woof" and that reminded him that he also wanted to check the area where he felt the tingling sensation when Rudy disappeared. He walked back toward the driveway and as he approached it, Rudy came up to meet him. His ears were perked up and he still had an expectant look on his furry face. Rob reached down and gave him a pat on the head as he walked by, and as though someone had thrown a switch, Rudy's tail stopped wagging and his ears drooped down as he watched him continue on his way past the snowmobiles. He didn't understand that Rob had a mission, but just like the faithful companion that he always was, he reluctantly followed his master. Anybody watching Rudy as he followed Rob over to the trail that they had made the day before when they walked out to the thick stand of pine trees would have sworn that he had lost his best friend. His head was hanging down and his tail was almost dragging in the snow. Perhaps if Rob turned around and had seen this open display of overwhelming disappointment, he would have taken pity on his old friend and postponed his mission until the next morning.

As soon as he started up over the snowbank he thought better of it. The hard crust of the morning was gone and he did not feel like wading through the soft snow. He strapped on his snowshoes and headed back up over the snow bank. Once again Rudy started to follow him and it was still very obvious that his heart wasn't in it. When Rob noticed that Rudy was following him his first reaction was to tell him to go back, but he quickly recognized that his basic protective instincts had brought on that emotion. He knew that it was because the last time that he and Rudy had walked down this trail, Rudy had disappeared. However, he was determined not to fall into the trap of being overprotective. When he reached the place where he had last seen Rudy behind him, he stopped and scanned the whole area within a ten-foot radius from where he was standing. He could see absolutely nothing that looked like a circular depression in the snow, so he crouched down to a lower position and scanned the entire section again. This time he did see something that looked like a small concave depression about five to six feet away from him. He looked over at Rudy and told him to stay, hoping that his basset hound stubbornness would not step up to the plate and take a swing. After taking three or four steps he glanced behind him, fully expecting to see Rudy right there, and he was very surprised when he saw that he had stayed, very alert, in the same spot.

When he reached the circular concave depression he made sure that he did not disturb any of the snow surrounding it but he wanted to get close enough to make sure that it was a perfect circle and not a depression made by snow falling from the tree branches above. After carefully examining the entire depression, there was no doubt about it. It was perfectly round and absolutely symmetrical. Talking to himself he said, "Well, this is certainly following the path of consistency. I wonder if I could find a circular depression in the snow near where the two deer mysteriously appeared, which according to Bubba, 'deer ain't never in that area' ... and it would be a significant pattern in the puzzle if I found a depression in the snow near where Matt saw the rabbit disappear. I'll have to ask him to come with me so he can show me exactly where he saw that happen, 'cause I don't think any of its tracks would be left on the road. However, I'm positive that I won't have any trouble finding the deer tracks between the big split rock and the trail going to Stratton."

He looked at his watch. It was almost 17:00 hours. "Man! Time sure does fly. I'd better take Toot-man for his ride before it gets totally dark. He thought for a couple of seconds and said out loud, "I know just where I'll take him for a ride. Up to Thad's to see if he's back."

* * *

Rudy's ears were floating in the breeze as they headed across the field toward Thad's. The sun was casting a beautiful red hue in the sky just past East Kennebago Mountain. Rob thought to himself, "What a beautiful time of the day." But his low-keyed euphoria didn't last very long. When he pulled into Thad's driveway it was readily obvious that no one was at home. Rudy jumped down off his lap and started giving the entire area a thorough sniffing and Rob assumed that he was looking for some sign of Ginger.

He walked up the two steps and into Thad's front enclosed porch. The note that he had left for Thad that morning was untouched, and the proof was the broken pencil, still in the same position. As far as he could tell, no one had been there since he had. When he stepped back outside and looked at Thad's truck he thought that perhaps it would be parked in a different position than it had been in the morning. But after walking over and taking a closer look, he could see the snowmobile tracks that he and Eileen had made when they drove behind the truck and parked next to Thad's Arctic Cat. The tracks had not been disturbed and Thad would have had to drive over them in order to back out of his driveway.

There was nothing more to do there, so he went over to his machine and started it up. It's a good thing that Rudy came running over when he heard the snowmobile purr to life because when he put his paws up on Rob's leg to be lifted up onto his lap, Rob said, "Toot! I almost forgot ya, ol' buddy." Giving one more look at the camp as if expecting Thad's face to appear in the window by the sink, he pressed the thumb throttle and they started on their way back through the field to camp.

* * *

Out of the corner of her eye, Eileen saw Rob and Rudy going past the living room picture window as they headed toward the shed. She later wondered why she did not hear Rob's snowmobile until after she saw him go by, because normally she could hear him at least a quarter of a mile away, and sometimes more, depending on the weather and the direction of the wind at the time. But she finally rationalized that she must have been concentrating so hard on whatever she was doing that the sound didn't make it through to her conscious mind.

She headed to the front door and when she stepped out onto the porch Rob was already coming out of the shed with his snowmobile cover in his arms. She yelled over to him, "Thad called while you were out giving Rudy a ride. Come in as quick as you can and change because we need to go get him and Ginger."

"Why? Where are they, and is he OK?"

"He's fine, but hurry up and I'll give you all the details when you get in here."

Rob must've really gotten himself into high gear because he was in the camp in what seemed like no time at all. While he was taking off and putting away his snowmobile gear, Eileen told him that the conversation that she had with Thad was short and sweet. Then she went on to say, "The only thing he told me was that he and Ginger were at the Farmington Hospital and then he asked if we could give them a ride home. I asked him what had happened, but he never said a word. So after a few seconds, I told him that you were giving Rudy a ride and that you'd be back shortly. Before I said good-bye I told him that we'd probably be on our way within a half an hour."

"What time did Thad call?"

"It was somewhere around 5:15, so it was about ten minutes ago."

"Don't you mean 17:15 hours? Because 5:15 could either mean 5:15 in the morning or 5:15 in the afternoon."

Getting a little red in the face she said, "You tell time the way you want, and I'll tell time the way I want!"

* * *

It was almost 19:00 hours by the time they pulled into the Farmington Hospital parking lot. Thad was sitting in the lobby and Ginger was lying at his feet. He was holding a bag in his lap and the top was open. His head was in the downward position like he was looking in the bag, but when Rob walked up and said, "Hello there, Big Foot," only Ginger looked up. Thad was sound asleep. Rob reached over and gently shook his shoulder and it seemed like it took forever for him to wake up. When he first opened his eyes and looked up at him, Rob had the feeling that he was seeing the exact same empty look that Thad had in his eyes when they were riding the trails on Monday.

"Thad? Are you okay?"

"Yep! I guess I just nodded off for a bit. I was in the middle of a dream when you woke me. And I know that I was enjoying it, but damned if I can remember what it was about."

"You ready to leave yet?"

"Sure, but watch Ginger for a minute while I go to the bathroom, and then I'll be ready to go."

"Tell you what, Thad, while you're in the bathroom I'll take Ginger out and give her an opportunity to go also."

"Thanks. I'll see you out there. Where are you parked?"

"Straight out, and to the left, in the second row."

Eileen chimed in and said, "I'll keep the Explorer warm while you walk Ginger."

"Good idea, be there in a minute or two, or maybe longer. She may take a little time to find the right spot to relieve herself in a strange place."

* * *

Thad was uncharacteristically quiet as Rob drove the first few miles toward downtown Farmington where they would pick up Route 4 towards Rangeley. He wasn't sure if it was because Thad was tired, or because he was still under the effect of some drug they had given him while he was in the hospital. He made up his mind that the only way to find out was to jump-start him into a conversation. "How're you doing, Thad?"

After a short pause, he said, "I'm doing OK."

"How'd you end up in the hospital?"

There was a long pause before he finally answered saying, "Just as it was getting to be daylight, I heard a static noise, and at the same time I got a funny kind of lightheaded feeling that I've never had before. At my age a symptom like that could be a pretty strong warning sign that something's about to happen, so I called the emergency rescue people and they sent out an ambulance to get me."

"How did Ginger get down to the hospital?"

"Mostly because it was my buddy, Alan Hanbury, that was driving the ambulance and he knows that Ginger is a very well behaved dog."

"I didn't know that behavior had anything to do with it. I was under the impression that an ambulance had to remain fairly sterile. Isn't there some type of a regulation that prevents the paramedics from allowing an animal in the ambulance?"

"I think that there probably is, because at first Alan did not want to let Ginger in the ambulance. But I told him that Ginger is much cleaner than some of the drunk derelicts that he has to pick up and take to the hospital and he couldn't find a good argument to that one so he put Ginger in with me."

"Well, I have to admit that's an argument that I would not have thought of. What about when you got to the hospital?"

He started to liven up and kind of chuckled as he said, "The paramedic with Alan wanted to tie Ginger to a tree while I was in the hospital. I told him *like hell* he was and that she was coming into the hospital with me. He tried to tell me that animals weren't allowed in the hospital and I quickly pointed out to him that I've been in the hospital when people brought a patient's pet into their hospital room for a visit. The paramedic had nothing more to say and I held Ginger's leash while they wheeled me into the ER."

"For an old codger you're pretty doggone sharp! What did they do to you while you were in the hospital?"

"Well first a nurse listened to my ticker and checked my blood pressure, then she took some blood and left me alone for a while. When she came back she said that my doctor would be in soon and that he would take over. That got me a little concerned so I asked her how my heart sounded and I also asked if my blood pressure was high as usual. She said that my heartbeat was strong and steady and that my blood pressure was normal. Normal for me is around 210/140 ... but when I asked what normal meant, she said it was 110/80. You know what, Rob?"

"What's that, Thad?"

"For as long as I can remember, my blood pressure has never been that low, and what's more, I haven't taken my blood pressure pills in four or five days."

"What're you doing different that's brought your blood pressure down? Have you changed something in your diet, or have you started exercising?"

"Nothing that I know of, unless it could be because I started walking everyday to limber up my knee."

"It could be that the walking is what's doing it. How far are you walking?"

"Well, let me see here. I walk all the way to the old survival school and back. That's about a mile each way."

"Yeah, I agree. That's a pretty good distance. That could be a big part of whatever's helping you. So what happened when your doctor came in?"

"He checked me over and told me the same thing that the nurse had said. Then he said that since I was here that he would go ahead and do the EEG now instead of making me come back again tomorrow. Before I could say Jack Shit they wheeled this machine into the room and hooked up a bunch of wires to my head. Dr. Claymore stood there the whole time looking at this tape as it came out of the machine, and I just happen to have a copy of it in this here bag."

"What did Dr. Claymore have to say after he read the tape?"

"Well, when I asked him how it looked, he got this silly ass grin on his face and said that knowing me as well as he did, as far as he was concerned it looked normal. I was watching him as the grin turned into a smile on his face and I said, so what's that statement supposed to mean? He chuckled some and said that it was just fine. Dr. Claymore and I go way back and he likes to kid with me occasionally."

"Well, as long as you're feeling fine, that's the most important thing to me."

* * *

Just as they were turning off Route 4 onto Route 27, heading to Kingfield, Rob looked at Thad in the rear view mirror and said, "When you heard the static noise, did it last a long time?"

"I don't really remember, why do you ask?"

"Actually, there's something that I haven't told you yet. Remember when Rudy was walking with me out to the stand of pines near our camp?"

Thad responded with a questioning, "Yeah?"

"Well just before Rudy disappeared, I heard some static noise and I felt a tingling sensation." It took almost the whole ride back to Baldwin Plantation to bring Thad up to date with the incidents that he could immediately recall, including the conversations that he had with the other snowmobilers at the Four Seasons. He finished the last of his briefing just as they crossed over the Dyer Stream Bridge on Route 16, and there was cold silence in the Explorer until they turned onto Kennebago Settlement Road.

Rob looked at the clock on the dash as they turned onto the camp road. It was 20:20 hours, and according to the outside temperature display, it was 10°F. His mind quickly switched gears and he thought about how cold Thad's camp was going to be, and he did not think that it was a good idea for him to hang around in that cold temperature while his camp was warming up. Looking at Thad in the rear view mirror he said, "Why don't I drop you at our camp with Eileen while I go up and start your fires? She'll put on a pot of coffee and we can chat for a bit while your camp heats up. How's that sound?"

"Sounds pretty good to me. But I bet Ginger is starved. How about bringing back some of her food with you?"

"Sure. You want me to bring the bag of food or do you want me to pour some in her bowl and bring that." He thought for a moment and said, "For that matter, she can have some of Rudy's food. I've never known her to be fussy."

"Since you offered, and I was hoping that you would, that's fine with me. I just didn't want to be too forward by *asking*."

Giving him a bit of a sarcastic jab, Rob said, "You must be turning over a new leaf. I've never known you to be bashful."

* * *

Both fires at Thad's camp had been started and he was just walking back into Camp Stress-A-Rest when he heard the phone ringing. Eileen yelled to Rob, "Jack King had called earlier and that's probably him calling again." He picked up the phone and said, "Joe's Morgue, you stab-em, we slab-em." There was silence on the other end of the line for several seconds, and then the person that had called hung up without saying a word. With an incredulous tone in his voice Rob said, "Well, whoever called can't take a joke, or that call just wasn't that important."

Eileen was a little more than irritated with his arrogant attitude and said, "Aren't you ever going to grow up?"

"Hey! If what I just said isn't grown up, then the answer's no." Looking over at Thad he said, "I made a fire in both the woodstove and your cook-stove. Your camp should be nice and roasty-toasty when you get back there."

Thad didn't look at him or acknowledge his statement, so he assumed that he was preoccupied with whatever was being said by the news commentator on 20/20. Rob figured it would be a good time to call Jack King. His spirits lifted considerably when Jack answered the phone and he said, "Hey, buddy! How're they hanging?"

Jack was quick to retort and said, "Side-by-side, man, side-by-side. How're ya doing?"

"Great! I've got a lot to share with you, but I'll wait 'til I see you tomorrow. Are you still planning on getting into the Rangeley Airport by 08:00 hours?"

"Unfortunately, it's going to be more like 13:00 hours but that's a lock. I've taken care of all the problems that had reared their ugly heads but Nancy has some shopping to do before we can leave."

"That's cool. If there's a change just give us a call and leave a message on the answering machine. I'm planning on being out early in the morning to check on a few things."

"Will do, but I see absolutely no changes. See ya tomorrow."

"Looking forward to it. Take care." He hung up the phone and Thad was still focused on 20/20. Turning his attention to Ginger he noticed that she looked like she was still hungry so he gave her some more food, which was devoured in no time.

Of course, as soon as Rudy heard Ginger crunching on the food he quickly came to life and let it be known that he was hungry too. As soon as both dogs were satiated, he poured some Gentlemen Jack on the rocks and savored a few tiny sips as he walked over to the loveseat. He set his drink down next to the phone and gently lowered himself into the seat. After moving this way and that a few times to get into the right position, he just sat there and occasionally sipped his Gentleman Jack while he mentally planned what he was going to do in the morning. Suddenly, out of nowhere he remembered that he had asked Gloria and Matt to give him a call.

"Eileen!"

"What?"

"Did Gloria or Matt call and leave a message?"

"The only message was from Jack."

Thad had memorized the phone number for every camp in the entire area, so Rob said, "Thad, do you have the phone number for the Better-n-Nothing camp?"

"I can't tell you what it is because I only remember a number as I'm dialing it. You want me to dial it for you?"

"Yeah, I'd appreciate that."

Thad ambled over to the loveseat, dialed the number and handed the phone back to Rob. The phone rang only once before it was answered. "Hi, Matt, this is Rob. How're you doing?"

"Gloria and I are just lounging around. Actually, we're beat after all the riding that we did yesterday and today. What can I do for you?"

"Would you mind meeting me tomorrow morning? I'd like you to show me the spot where the rabbit disappeared."

"Why?"

"I have a hunch that I might see something that will explain how it happened."

"Sure. What time do you want me to meet you?"

"I'll pick you up at your camp at 07:30 hours, or is that too early for you?"

"That's just fine for me, I'm an early riser, remember?"

"Sure I remember, because I'm an early riser also. But I thought that maybe because you're so tired today that you might want to sleep in tomorrow."

"07:30 hours is fine. See you then."

"Looking forward to it, Matt. Thanks, and take care."

It was 05:30 hours and still very dark and very cold when Rob strapped his snowshoes onto the Formula and started it up. While the sled was warming up he went back into the camp to finish his coffee and exchange his gloves for mittens. Mittens kept his hands much warmer than his gloves did when the temperature was below -20°F. Neither Eileen nor Rudy were up and about, so he double-checked to make sure that the door was securely locked on his way out. He needed to get an early start because he figured that by the time he got over to where Gloria and Matt had seen the stranger on the plowed logging road, it would be pretty close to sunup. And he also knew that after he succeeded or failed, and he preferred not to consider the latter, it would take him the better part of an hour to get over to where Bubba and party had seen the deer near the big split rock. Thinking optimistically if he really hustled he would be able to be back to camp by 07:15 hours and then he would have plenty of time to meet Matt by 07:30 hours.

He barely put any pressure on the thumb throttle and went slowly out the driveway to keep the noise down as much as possible. At the end of his driveway he turned left on Kennebago Settlement Road and the moment that he passed the Harris Pasture turnoff he put the throttle to the handlebar and started making some time. He knew some shortcuts to get over to Davis Plantation where he had to cross over Route 16 to intercept the Stratton/Rangeley trail. The handle grips and thumb throttle heaters were on high, but when coupling -25°F with the 40 to 50 mph wind chill factor, the combination made it so cold that his hands and thumb were still extremely uncomfortable.

The sun was just cresting Bigelow Mountain when he came to the bridge by the plowed logging road. Slowing down almost to a crawl, he drove past the bridge and down onto the road before stopping his sled. He wasn't quite sure where to begin his search because Gloria did not say exactly where she had seen the stranger standing on the road. He spent the better part of thirty minutes trying to find something that looked like it could have been a depression in the snow, and all the time wishing that he had thought to ask Gloria to explain exactly where she had seen the stranger standing. He crisscrossed the entire area several times while doing a thorough visual scan in all directions, and was just in the process of verbalizing his frustration when he heard a logging truck making its way down off the mountain. Knowing that this guy had to be loaded to the hilt and on his way to the mill, he decided that the smart thing to do was to vacate the area and give this big boy all the room that he needed. Less than a minute had passed when he found himself tooling down the groomed trail on the opposite side of the logging road, headed toward Stratton. He felt a great deal of disappointment because he had not found what he was looking for, but he was far from discouraged.

Winter sunrises in the Longfellow Mountains inspire awe in almost every person who is lucky enough to witness the reddish glow that is cast upon the vast panorama of snow covered mountains and valleys. And there are always bonuses for the patient spectator, especially on certain days when the sun brings out a rainbow of colors from the sparkling white snow. Rob had seen many of these radiant sunrises, and without fail he had always paused long enough from whatever he was doing to enjoy the majestic view. No matter how many times he had tried to capture it on film, and no matter what filter he used when he was snapping the picture, he had never been able to seize the true beauty that his eyes beheld. He was so absorbed in the changing scenery as he rode the trails that he was caught by surprise when Route 16 came looming upon him after he topped a small rise.

After bringing his sled to a stop, he checked his watch and was pleased to see that in spite of the fact that his mind was lingering on the beauty around him as he rode the trail, he had made good time. In fact, he was right on schedule. Thinking out loud he said, "If I'm lucky and there're no surprises, I'll be at the split rock in about thirty minutes."

Once across Route 16, the trail passed alongside the Stratton Town dump, and he counted seven deer walking up one of their well-packed trails for their morning feeding. The dump caretaker had a warm spot in his heart for the deer, and he bought feed for them throughout the long winter months with any extra revenue that he could generate from selling discarded treasures. That included cans and bottles that had a five-cent deposit return. About a mile past the dump the snowmobile trail got very narrow and dropped down along a slow moving river that is home to some of the largest brook trout that Rob had ever seen.

The trail along the river twisted and wound its way through towering red pine trees and there were several camps during that stretch of the ride that overlook the river. The open landscape around the camps gave the snowmobile riders a glimpse here and there of what they would soon be crossing. Rob slowed down as he approached the steep riverbank, and even though he knew that it had been well below freezing for almost five weeks and the likelihood of open water was just about nil, he still carefully checked the river from one side to the other. The slow moving water that spawned tens of thousands of annoying bloodsucking insects in the warmer months was now totally hidden by Mother Nature's icy blanket. He watched the nose of his sled rapidly drop down the four-foot riverbank to the frozen surface below. There was always a temporary feeling of relief when the sled's skis continued out on to the ice instead of piercing it to find a home in the mud below. The Formula's skis clacking on the ice while crossing the river had him semi-mesmerized, but his reverie was suddenly broken when he thought he caught a glimpse of shimmering air out the corner of his right eye. As quickly as he turned his head to look in its direction, the vision disappeared.

Once he went up the bank on the opposite side of the river, it was very slow going. Much to his dismay, the trail was just a series of one to two-foot high moguls for about a quarter of a mile. Luck wasn't with him after all, and it added another ten minutes to his estimated time to the split rock. After passing the moguls the trail came to a T, and he turned left. At that point the trail became considerably wider, and he estimated that he was about five miles from the big split rock. The wide and winding trail was well groomed and there were tracks from only two snowmobiles on it, which was a strong indicator that the groomer had been through during the night. After about two miles, the trail became straight as an arrow for as far as he could see, and he quickly kicked his speed up to 50 mph. He had gone about one mile when he *knew* that this time his eyes were not playing tricks on him. This time he was absolutely sure that he saw a circle of distorted air in the clear-cut off to his left. Without even thinking about what he was doing he brought his sled to a sliding stop. He sat there for almost a minute giving serious consideration to climbing the bank in front of him to get up into the clear-cut for a better look. Finally, with his mind made up he aimed his sled at the bank, stood up on the tunnel rails and was about to squeeze the throttle when common sense finally took over. "Man, if I do that, Murphy's Law will make sure that I'll have to slow down to get around something, and that's when I'll sink in that soft snow. Then I'll really be screwed."

Looking up the trail about one hundred feet he noticed that it became level with the clear-cut. Deciding it made much more sense to have a look from there, he slowly moved forward, keeping a vigilant eye over his left shoulder all the time. As the snowmobile trail evened out with the clear-cut, he had an unobstructed view of the shimmering air. It was about twenty feet above the snow and looked like a Christmas ornament hanging from the hook of an invisible crane.

Curiosity took over and Rob turned off his machine, deciding that he wanted to see if anything was going to happen. As soon as he did, he could hear a faint static sound, and almost simultaneously he saw the circle of wavering air start to pulsate, rather like what a frog's throat does when it is breathing. He was transfixed by what he was watching, and was totally unaware of the lone coyote out in the clear-cut that was heading directly toward the pulsating distorted air. His hypnotic stare broke when he detected movement out of the corner of his eye to his left, and when he looked in that direction he could see the coyote. Muttering the first thought that popped into his mind he said, "You don't have to be a genius to know what the pulsating air is up to."

He watched as the animal got closer, and all of a sudden it seemed to him like the circle of shimmering air began a floating descent, getting closer and closer to the snow. When the coyote was about ten feet from the pulsating air, the scene unfolding in front of Rob's unwavering gaze quickly changed. The animal suddenly appeared to have one hell of a tailwind blowing up its backside. Its long wintry coat looked like it was going to come loose and fold right over its head. For a moment the coyote just stood in one place, bracing its legs against this unbelievable tailwind. Its head dropped all the way to the snow, and it looked like it was pressing its lower jaw against its front paws. It was fighting and scratching for the best foothold that it could get when suddenly in the blink of an eye it was airborne, and almost instantly the yowling canine disappeared into the pulsating circle.

For the second time in three days he got a sensation that went from the tip of his toes to the top of his head and his adrenalin system shifted into the afterburner mode. The circle of distorted air stopped pulsating almost immediately when the coyote pierced its surface. Still sitting there and watching, Rob thought to himself, "Well, this is different from when the hawk was sucked in, because when *it* disappeared, so did the circle of shimmering air. Not willing to take his eyes off the wavering air, he reached down and felt for the key to start his machine. The moment that his hand touched it, the crackling sound intensified and the shimmering air seemed to change its angle. The longer he watched it, the more he got the feeling that it was turning to face him. He was still trying to figure out if his eyes were playing tricks on him when he saw it start to pulsate once again as it moved toward him. All at once his mind screamed to him, "Get the HELL out of here." He jammed the thumb throttle to the handlebar and was gone in a swirling cloud of snow. He never looked back until he reached the T at the Eustis/Rangeley trail. Slowing down as he approached the intersection, he looked in his rearview mirrors and over his left shoulder to see if he could see anything that resembled wavering air and when he saw no sign of it he let out a sigh of relief.

As soon as he stopped at the intersection he turned left and he started looking for deer tracks crossing the trail, although at this point he had to admit to himself that his heart wasn't really in it. What he truly wanted to do was to put all this craziness on the back burner and head back to camp, pack up, and get the hell out of there! Well, at least think about it. His body felt a little weak as the tension was draining out of him, and he had the start of a headache. However, reality quickly took over and he knew that after what had just happened, he *had* to find out what was going on. He rode slowly up the right hand side of the trail looking for a blow-down, and that is where he hoped that he would find the deer tracks that Bubba had told him about. After going about half the distance to the big split rock, he saw a blow-down about twenty feet off to the right hand side of the trail. Slowing down even more, he maneuvered his machine as far as he could to the right without going off into soft snow, and stopped. Standing up on the tunnel rails of his sled he looked toward the blow-down, and after only a few seconds he spotted what looked like stick holes in the snow heading away from it. Knowing that they were actually deer tracks he let his eyes follow the direction that they were headed, and it looked like they would cross the snowmobile trail about twenty or thirty feet further up.

He eased his way back onto the trail, inching his way up to where he thought the tracks would cross, still constantly checking the whole area to his right along the way in case the deer had changed their direction. As it turned out, his first hunch was correct. The tracks crossed the trail almost thirty feet from where he had initially stopped and it was very easy to see that it was two sets of deer tracks. While he was untying his snowshoes from the machine he looked further up the trail and he could see where it looked like several snowmobiles had pulled off to the side.

After he finished strapping on his snowshoes, he felt hesitant about taking the first step toward the blow-down. He was still unnerved by what had happened back in the clear-cut and he was not totally convinced that he was out of harm's way. His nerves were so on edge that he decided to take off his helmet, knowing full well that with it off he'd be able to hear even a faint hissing sound. He instantly wished that he could keep it on as the frosty morning air penetrated his balaclavas. However he had no trouble deciding that the cold was preferable to being surprised by the sudden appearance of distorted air. So far it had always been preceded by a total vacuum-like silence, which he was sure would be undetectable with his helmet on.

When he stepped off the groomed trail he expected that his snowshoes would sink somewhat into the soft snow. But they didn't sink at all, and after a few steps he looked back and saw that he had only left a few scratches on the surface. When he tied the snowshoes onto his machine he did not think about the fact that during the night it had gotten very cold, and that he'd have no problem walking on top of the snow. He was tempted to go back to his sled and take off the snowshoes, but decided to press on. He walked around the backside of the blow-down and had gone about fifty feet when the deer tracks ended. He stopped and started scanning the entire area for a depression in the snow. It did not take very long before he felt his body begin to tingle with excitement. There it was, about eight feet straight back from the tracks! It was about twelve feet in diameter. He walked up to the edge of the depression for a better look. It was a perfectly symmetrical concave depression that looked like it was about fifteen to eighteen inches deep in the center. Talking to himself he said, "Bingo! This is much more than coincidence. Come to think of it, I've *seen* a hawk and a coyote disappear into the circle, and I've also *see* the circle of shimmering air touch the snow. Now I know for sure why tracks just appear from out of nowhere with no logical beginning and end as though whatever had made them simply disappeared into thin air." Then he thought to himself, "Yeah, I know, but if a person hadn't seen all this happen, how could I convince them that I'm telling the truth? How could I be sure I wouldn't end up locked away in a padded room?"

His extra sensory perception was fully operational and when he felt his nervousness begin to reactivate he knew immediately that something wasn't quite right or *soon* wouldn't be. In either case the adrenalin pumping into his blood stream was providing serious motivation for him to get going and without even thinking about it he started back toward his sled. Just as he was picking his way around the blow-down something told him to look at his snowmobile. When he did, he thought that he saw someone standing near it. He started to squint to get a clearer view and as soon as he did so, he tripped over a branch sticking out from the blow down. His right arm automatically shot out and he grabbed onto a nearby tree to keep from falling. The moment that he got his balance and looked back at his machine, there was no one there. His mind was in a whirlwind and he started to feel slightly lightheaded. Being woods-wise, he knew that it could be disastrous to lose consciousness right now so he immediately squatted down on his snowshoes and put his head between his knees. About a half a minute went by and it seemed like his head was beginning to clear, and slowly he began to feel normal. However, at this point in time he was not sure what normal meant. Finally he stood up and walked over to his Skidoo, put the snowshoes on the seat and sat on top of them to keep them in place. When he reached for the key to start his Formula, it was not in the switch! He was certain that he had left it there. He *never* took it out while he was on the trail. He stared at the empty keyhole hoping that it would stir up a memory that would tell him what he had done with it and when that didn't work he started to look in the snow around his sled. Suddenly his search came to a screeching halt. The footprints all around his Formula were exactly like the prints left by the stranger in front of their camp!

Rob let the air rush out of his lungs and he was surprised to see that his hands were shaking. He knew that he had not been seeing things. Now he understood that he was *not* alone. He was beginning to understand that what he had felt as fear in the past during some scary situations was only a small exploratory step into terror. What he was feeling now was the most intense fear that he had ever known in his life. And what made this fear worse was his knowledge that he was not in control of the situation and for now, there was nothing he could do about it. He knew without a doubt he was totally terrified because he was afraid to look up and he had *never* felt that way before in his life. He mustered every bit of self-confidence possible and through sheer will power forced his head and eyes to move upwards. At first he only looked straight ahead, focusing on things he could see by just moving his eyes from side to side. He felt a flood of relief surge through his body when he didn't see the stranger standing there. He slowly sat up more erect and looked to his left and over his shoulder behind him. Then he looked back to the right and all the way behind him. He was alone. When he was stretching to look back over his left shoulder his right foot slid on the tunnel rail, and he thought that he heard a metallic scraping sound as his foot slid forward. He leaned down to the right, lifted his foot off the tunnel rail and swung it backwards. Then he saw his key lying there on the tunnel rail as plain as day.

He pulled off his mitten, reached down and picked it up as quickly as he could. In one smooth motion he brought it up, jammed it into the switch and twisted it. The Formula purred to life. He briefly wondered why it started so easily, as it had been sitting in this bitter cold for about thirty minutes, but as rapidly as the thought flashed into his mind, it was gone, and so was he.

The quickest way back to camp was to turn around and head back past where he had seen the coyote disappear into the pulsating circle of air. But short or not, he wasn't ready to have anymore of that. This section of Eustis/Rangeley trail was about ten feet wide, hilly and winding, and in spite of that he made excellent time to an old logging road that emptied into Harris Pasture. The logging road was wide and fairly straight and he was convinced that even Mario Andretti would have gotten a rush if he were riding with him. It seemed like his sled was barely touching the snow as he flew up the trail and he never felt his snowshoes cutting into his rear end and thighs every time that he hit a bump.

* * *

The moment that he pulled into the driveway he fully realized what a beating his backside had taken on the way back. Luckily the snowshoes were still snug under him but his gluteus maximus and thighs were definitely the worse for wear. Once he had parked his machine in front of the shed, he gingerly lifted himself off the snowshoes and placed them in the snow next to the four hundred-gallon propane tank. As he walked to the front door, his gait seemed a little strange with his legs spread somewhat apart, and now he knew for sure why cowboys walk the way they do. Just before he reached the door he looked at his watch and saw that it was 07:10 hours.

He opened the door and Rudy was right there to greet him. Eileen was sitting on the couch with a steaming cup of coffee sitting on the end table alongside of her and it was obvious that she was working on her puzzle. She looked up with a smile and said, "Good morning, Booby! You weren't supposed to leave me alone, remember!?"

Booby is one of Eileen's endearing terms that he really disliked because he equated it with being called a jerk. But in the early years of their marriage when he protested being called Booby, she simply chose to ignore him. After a while he decided that he would just roll with the punches and come up with an endearing term of his own, which he chose to use now.

"Good morning, 'Shrimp-o'."

Choosing to ignore her statement about being left alone, hoping that the subject would get lost in the conversation he went on to say, "Would you please get the Advil out of the medicine cabinet for me?"

"Got a headache?"

"Yeah, and I feel like I've been kicked in the derriere by a whole herd of mules."

"What happened?"

"Just please get me the Advil while I get a cup of coffee and I promise that I'll tell you while I get out of this snowmobile gear."

He had just finished putting the half and half in his coffee when Eileen handed him two Advil, which he promptly washed down his throat with the steaming hot coffee. Tears came to his eyes and rolled down his cheeks and blended right in with the sweat that was coming off his forehead. He set the coffee cup down and wrestled his boots, coat, and snow pants off as quickly as he could. All the while, Eileen was giggling like a little schoolgirl. He looked at her and said, "What in the hell is so funny!?"

"In all the years that I have known you, you have never learned to be careful with hot coffee or with *any* hot food or drink for that matter."

"I keep doing it because I know how much it amuses you." And he just barely got those words out of his mouth when the phone started to ring. Eileen walked over to the loveseat, sat down and answered it. After just a few seconds she just stuck the phone up in the air at Rob. "Who is it?"

"I think it's that lawyer from Boston. You know, Bubba's cousin."

As he took the phone from her she said, "Remember! You weren't supposed to leave me alone, and you've still got some *'splainin'* to do, Ricky!"

"Yeah, OK, Lucy!" And then turning his attention to the caller he said, "Hello?"

"Hi, Rob, I hope I'm not calling too early. This is Len Purdy, Bubba's cousin. How are you this morning?"

"Super, and no you're not calling too early. I'm an early riser. Did you guys hear or see something?"

Len could detect the excitement in Rob's voice and said, "Look, we all had a long conversation last night, and the discussion revolved around the fact that no one really wanted to call you and tell you what we saw. Even though we all *know* what we saw, when you come right down to it, we don't want to believe it. But after sleeping on it, we gave our word to you, and that means a lot to us, so I was elected to give you a call."

"I appreciate that, Len, but what's all the mystery about?"

After pausing slightly to gather his thoughts he continued, "We decided to take the Tim Pass trail back to Eustis, and when we took a break at the top of Tim Pass, Mindy heard that static sound, and as it got louder the rest of us heard it too. Everyone started looking around to see where the sound was coming from, and suddenly Stormin yelled for us to look back down the trail to the left at about the 11 o'clock position. I'll tell you something ... I've never felt such a jolt of fear before, and I think it was because I couldn't make any sense out of what I was seeing."

There was nothing but dead air on the phone for about ten or fifteen seconds while Len thought about how he should proceed, but Rob sensed that he was changing his mind about telling him anymore and decided to give him a leading question. "Did you see a circle of distorted air?"

"Yeah! But how did you know that?"

"I'll tell you in a minute, but first tell me what happened, and start from the beginning. Tell me absolutely everything that you can recall."

"Well, the first thing that I recall, and I'll never forget it, was the feeling that I had when we turned off our machines. It's kind of hard to describe, but it was like we were in the middle of total emptiness. There were no sounds whatsoever, and the air was very still, and I remember thinking that was really strange because I noticed that all the trees around us were swaying when we started working our way up to Tim Pass. My uneasiness intensified a whole bunch when I looked over to my right and saw the trees moving pretty good, but I couldn't hear or feel any wind. I just don't remember having that kind of an empty feeling before. Anyway, I had just finished making up my mind that it seemed overly quiet because we had just shut our machines down, when Stormin yelled for us to look. I couldn't believe my eyes when I saw this circle of wavering air about thirty feet off the ground."

Rob cut in saying, "That circle of air must've been pretty close."

"Why do you say that?"

"Because as I recall, the top of Tim Pass is covered with a thick growth of pine trees that are about forty to fifty feet tall."

"Well, you're wrong! That thing was about seventy to eighty feet away from us."

"How in the hell could you see that shimmering air seventy to eighty feet away?"

"Because the whole area's been logged."

"Oh, I wonder when they did that? Maybe it was this past summer."

Len quickly shot back, "No, I think it was pretty recent because the pile of logs that we saw on the side of the trail when we were working our way up the mountain didn't look that old, and besides, the equipment is still sitting near the areas that were logged. Also there was another huge clue. That road had been plowed within the last two weeks."

Wanting to get Len back on track Rob said, "Is it just the circle of shimmering air that scared you so much, or was there something else?"

"Oh yeah! There was definitely something else. It looked like that circle of air started to pulsate as it began to drift towards us, and that is when the fear of God seemed to get a grip on everyone at the same time. Bubba was the first to start his sled, and it sounded to me like everyone else immediately followed suit. Bubba may have been the first to get his machine going, but Mindy was the first to haul ass. Believe me when I tell you, we got out of there quick! I bet if someone had put a stopwatch to the whole scenario and told us to repeat the exercise, we'd never get close to that time again. But you know, for some reason I just can't forget that empty feeling that I had after the sleds were shut down. It was just a momentary feeling, at least I think it was momentary, but I just cannot shake the memory. It's always first in my thoughts, and I can't get a handle on why."

Cutting in, Rob said, "I'm sure that time will take care of that." All during the conversation, wanting to cut it short, he was hoping that Len would forget that he was supposed to tell him how he knew it was a circle of shimmering air that the group had seen. He was already late for his meeting with Matt and he prided himself on always being on time. Wanting to keep Len's mind off of the subject he said, "When are you heading back to Boston?"

"My wife and I are up for the week, so we'll be heading back sometime on Sunday."

"Len, I sincerely appreciate your taking the time to call me. I wish you and your wife a safe trip back to Boston."

"Not so fast, Rob. I want to know how you knew that it was a circle of shimmering air that we saw."

He was hooked and there was no way out without being a jerk, so he said, "Len, could you hold on a minute and I'll be right back to you?"

"Sure."

Rob momentarily pressed the hang-up button to get a dial tone and called Matt. When he answered the phone he sounded very tired and Rob said, "Did I wake you, Matt?"

"No, we just didn't sleep very well last night for some reason, and for a change I had a hard time dragging myself out of bed. I've been waiting for you. Are you getting ready to come over?"

"I'll probably be there in ten or fifteen minutes, Matt. I received an unexpected phone call and they're still on the line, but as soon as I finish I'll head right over. Is that okay with you?"

"Why don't you just make it for 8:30. Gloria's already cooking breakfast and she gets testy if I'm not here to eat it when it's ready."

"No problem. It'll give me a chance to get something to eat also. See you at 08:30 hours."

They said their good-byes and Rob got Len back on the line. "Thanks for that, Len. I was supposed to pick up a friend at 07:15 hours, and I wanted to let him know that I was going to be late."

Len wasted no time getting back to the subject at hand and said, "So, tell me how you knew that we had seen a circle of shimmering air."

Rob told Len everything that he remembered, and he made an extra effort to make sure that he did not leave out any important details. Len was quiet for the better part of thirty seconds before saying, "What do *you* make of all this?"

"I hate to admit it, but I haven't got a clue yet. The only thing that I think I've figured out is *why* tracks suddenly begin or end, but I'm absolutely mystified as to *how* it can possibly happen."

"I'm curious, Rob, you said that a friend is coming into town today to give you a hand. What's his background?"

"He is an electronics whiz."

Len paused again like he was digesting that information before saying, "Well, I wish you guys luck. If there is any way that we can be of help, call us. You want to get a pencil and write down this number?"

"Sure, hold on a sec." Rob wrote the number on a pad by the phone and thanked him for the offer. When he put the phone on its cradle, he asked Eileen what she would like for breakfast and she immediately knew what that meant.

"Ok, what would *you* like for breakfast, Rob? Bacon and eggs?"

"Yeah, that would be great. I'm starved! I'll have three eggs, four pieces of bacon and two slices of toast. Would you mind fixing that while I go out to feed the deer?"

"Now how did I know that I was going to end up cooking breakfast?"

"It must be that extraordinary clairvoyant ability that you have."

She was openly smiling as she said, "Yeah right. The malarkey is really getting deep, isn't it?"

Rob had already grabbed the bucket for the feed and was on his way down into the basement, acting as if he had not heard that last statement.

* * *

He made sure that he was right on time to pick up Matt. As he was approaching the camp he could see Matt standing on the front porch with an insulated mug up to his lips, and steam was shooting out of his nostrils. When Rob saw him give a halfhearted wave just as he pulled into the driveway, he wondered what was wrong. By the time he stopped in front of the porch Matt had walked down the steps and was standing there waiting to open up the passenger side door. As he was pulling his head inside the Explorer and closing the door he said to Rob, "I expected you to come up here on your snowmobile. You kind of surprised me."

The seats were down in the back and Rudy wasted no time making his way over to Matt. He stopped when he was a few inches away and whiffed the air around him. Whatever his sensitive nose told him, it must have been OK because he walked the rest of the way over to Matt and gave him a very thorough sniffing. Finally satisfied that this stranger was no threat, he walked back to lie down in his favorite corner in the rear of the SUV.

Rob decided to respond to Matt's statement, but he hid the real reason that he brought the Explorer. "My backside is a little sore after all the riding that my wife and I have done since Monday morning, and we're going out again today. I guess I'm getting old because my self preservation mode must have taken over and ordered me to give my butt some comfort for a little while." He wasn't very good at hiding the truth, and he had a bit of a telltale smirk on his face. He knew that he didn't get away with *anything* when out of the corner of his eye he saw Matt giving him a "you've got to be pulling my leg" look. Ultimately he decided to just leave it alone. Sometimes things are simply best unsaid.

As soon as he backed out of the driveway and had the Explorer pointed toward Darryl Wade's place he said, "Matt, how far past the Wade's do I go before I should slow down?"

"Not too far, but the moment that I see that we're getting near the spot, I'll tell you to slow down."

"I'm curious, Matt, are you absolutely positive that you didn't see or hear anything when the rabbit disappeared?"

"I've been wondering if you'd get back to that question. I really didn't want to say anything with Gloria sitting right there because it happened so close to camp. I'm pretty sure that if I told you right then and there, that she would've made me pack up and leave the moment we got back here. The answer is yes, I did hear and see something." And then, just like Len, he shut up.

Rob looked over at him wondering when he was going to start telling him more, but it didn't seem like he was going to. Finally he couldn't stand it any longer and said, "Matt?"

"Yeah, I was just trying to decide where to begin. Slowdown, we're coming to the spot now." They drove about another twenty feet and stopped directly in front of a huge apple tree. "Let's get out here and walk the rest of the away." Rob pulled out a couple of feet from the snowbank before stopping so Matt would have room to open the door, and then almost in unison all three piled out of the Explorer.

Rudy immediately started hightailing it up the road, and Rob quickly called him back because he did not want him to disturb any sign that might still be there. As soon as he was alongside of them, they continued on their way, and all the while Matt was describing what had happened when the rabbit disappeared. They had walked about fifty feet when he interrupted his story and said, "It was right here!"

Rob looked around for Rudy and was happy to see him headed to the opposite side of the road. He had his nose high up in the air above him, obviously on a mission to check something out. Satisfied that Rudy wouldn't be around to disturb any signs of what had happened, he turned his attention back to the location where Matt had seen the rabbit disappear. He looked everywhere in the immediate area and did not see a single rabbit track. But that wasn't a big surprise. He could see several snowmobile tracks going up the side of the road right where, according to Matt, the rabbit would have been doing its fast hop. Those snowmobiles had obliterated any chance of seeing the rabbit's tracks, and to top it all off, they could have been made by him and Eileen while on their way to Brochu's Landing the previous day. Finally he looked up at Matt and said, "Why are you so sure that the rabbit disappeared here?"

"You see that scrape on top of the snowbank?"

Rob walked a little bit closer to the edge of the road and could see a very pronounced furrow in the top of the snowbank where it crests. He pointed at it while looking at Matt and said, "Is that what you're talking about?"

"Yeah, that's it."

"Well you have me stumped Matt. Did you make that mark so you could find the spot again?"

"No, that was made by the rabbit."

"You saw the rabbit make it?"

Matt heard the unbelieving tone of his voice and defensively said, "Yeah! When it literally shot from the road into a pulsating circle of air that was over there, and it kind of glistened, but that word doesn't really describe it right."

Rob cut in and said, "How about shimmering? Does that work better?"

"Yeah, much better. Weird, huh?"

He really did not hear the last of the answer because he was concentrating on where Matt was pointing. He could see the tops of a few wooden stakes sticking out of the snow, but that was it. What he did not find was what he really wanted to see most of all, a depression in the snow. Looking back at Matt he said, "Did you use those stakes sticking out of the snow over there as a landmark to remember where that circle of air was?"

"Actually, I watched the rabbit as it disappeared into that pulsating circle of air, and just as it hit the surface I saw those stakes drop out. Somethin' kind of funny though, when they hit the snow they sank in slowly, and after a few seconds I got the feeling that they were melting their way in, you know, like as the snow melted they just sank further into it."

"Matt, how high was that circle of air above the snow?"

"I don't know for sure, but maybe thirty or forty or fifty feet. I've always had trouble trying to judge distance like that."

Rob took his snowshoes out of the back of his SUV and headed up over the snowbank toward the stakes. When he reached them he bent down to get a good close look at the snow around each stake, and it didn't take very long to determine that Matt had to be telling the truth. Right at the snowline each stake had a lip of ice around it that was almost a half an inch thick, and as far as Rob was concerned that totally supported Matt's story of melting the snow as they sank in. After he thoroughly studied each stake he stood up and looked all around him, using the same method as he did when he was looking for Rudy's tracks near the depression in the snow where Ginger had found him. He had a light jacket on because he did not think that he'd be spending a lot of time out in the morning cold, and now he was beginning to feel a bit of a chill. He was so excited about the significance of what he could see around him, that he put the cold out of his mind and took his time to make a second sweep. Rob estimated that he was standing in about a two thousand square foot open area, and it didn't take a rocket scientist to figure out that there was nothing else to see. As luck would have it, snowmobilers had not ridden their machines through there. Everywhere he looked the snow was undisturbed. That was disappointing, because he wanted to see another concave depression in order to plug another important piece into the puzzle. But he immediately started to reason ... should he really have expected to see one after Matt had said that the circle of shimmering air was up so high? Probably not, but then that thought brought on another; he had forgotten to ask him if he felt a vacuum-like sensation or if he heard any crackling noises.

After walking back to the Explorer, he remained quiet while taking off his snowshoes. He put them in his SUV, helped Rudy up into the back, closed the hatch and walked up to the driver's door, opened it and sat down without saying one word. Either Matt wasn't curious or else he was being very polite, because he did not utter a sound.

The second that Rob turned the ignition key, his trusty Ford started, and warm air instantly flowed from the window defroster and floor vents, or at least it felt that way to him. He turned to Matt and said, "Does Gloria know exactly what happened here yesterday, or have you kept it to yourself?"

"Hey, Rob, I'm no fool! I absolutely love this area, and I love to snowmobile here. What's more, I don't get to come here very often, and when I do I don't leave until it's time, even if the weather's lousy. If I told her about everything I saw out here, we'd have been on our way home *yesterday*. As a matter of fact, a few of the things that your wife told Gloria while we were having lunch caused me a bunch of grief. I had to do some pretty fast talking to calm her down, and if you really want to know the truth, I wasn't tired last night. But the last thing that I wanted to do was to go to your place to play cribbage and have those two broads start talking again." And then as he thought a couple of seconds about what he had just said, he continued, "Sorry, Rob, I didn't mean any harm by calling your wife a broad."

"No offense taken, Matt, I call her a broad myself from time to time. You really look dejected. Is something else bothering you?

"Well, Gloria claims that sometime before daylight this morning she heard some static, and it's got her all shook up. After talking to Eileen yesterday she's been busting my balls ever since we got up, and as my luck would have it, today she got up at the same time as I did. I had her all calmed down last night before we went to bed. But since she heard that static this morning, she keeps harping on packing up and leaving. I don't want to leave, and that's probably why I look dejected. I'm just going to have to find a way around it, that's all."

He drove the Explorer right up to the front porch and as his passenger was getting out he said, "Matt, thanks a bunch for your help. I really mean that, and I hope you find a way to stay and do some more riding." Matt reached over and shook his hand just before he shut the door, and Rob noticed that he had a small smile on his face. Rob developed a smile of his own because he felt that Matt must have come up with a solution.

* * *

Thad was at Camp Stress-A-Rest when he got back, sitting at the kitchen table with Eileen. Both were drinking coffee and eating something that looked really good. "What's that you guys are eating?"

Taking her coffee cup away from her lips she said, "Entenmann's Cheese Danish. Want some?"

"Is the Pope Catholic? And how about a favor, gorgeous? Would you please pour me a cup of coffee while I wash my hands?"

Mimicking Rob's way of responding she said, "Does a bear dump in the woods?"

Thad started laughing and said, "You guys never stop. I'm surprised that you're still married."

While heading to the bathroom and laughing out loud he said, "We wouldn't have it any other way, would we, Shrimp-o?"

Eileen looked at Thad and quietly said, "Since he likes to be such a pain in the behind, I just give it right back. It's sort of like water rolling off a duck's back."

As he walked back into the kitchen while drying his hands Rob saw that Thad had a smile on his face and was shaking his head from side to side. The moment that he looked at Eileen and saw that she had a silly smirk on her kisser too, he knew that they had to be laughing at his expense. He was tossing the paper towel into the wastebasket when he heard Rudy pushing his dish around with his nose, which was his way of saying it's chow time. Eileen saw him change directions to get Rudy's food and said, "Sit down and have your coffee and danish. I'll take care of him."

Rob smiled a thank you as he walked over to the kitchen table to put a piece of danish on a plate that he had just taken out of the dishwasher. As he sat down he looked over at Thad and said, "So what're you up to today?"

"I've already been up to somethin'. They've been logging over by Black Nubble, and I wanted to see if they're leaving a lot of tops around. Just like you, come springtime I'm goin' to need to replenish my wood supply, so there's no time like the present to scout around and get an idea of where I can get it. I'll tell yah, I was really surprised once I got up into the woods past the Stratton/Rangeley snowmobile trail, because I found that they had plowed a lot more of the logging roads in there than I thought that they would've."

"Really! Maybe we could ride them this weekend when the loggers aren't working."

Thad looked like he was considering that as an option and then continued, "It's kind of funny. Ginger didn't lay down once during the whole trip, and she hasn't done that for at least a couple of years now. As a matter of fact, most of the time she was acting as nervous as a whore in church. We've been back in on those roads so many times over the years that she knows them as well as I do. Most of the time when we go back in there I head directly to Black Nubble to see the view from up there, and I usually let Ginger out so she can explore the area while I enjoy the scenery. Once I'm good and ready, we just mosey back down the mountain, stopping here and there, or take this road and that until we're back onto Route 16."

Rob had been nodding his head up and down the whole time that Thad had been telling his story, and as soon as Thad paused he said, "Have you ever been able to do that before during this time of year?"

"Nope. This is the first time. But since they had so many of the roads plowed I decided to do some pucker brushing on the way up, don't know why, just did. The whole reason that I'm telling you all this is because when I made a turn that was not going to take me directly up to Black Nubble, Ginger started barking in my ear and turning around in circles on the front seat, and while she was doing that she was whimpering like a little puppy. What's more, I don't *ever* recollect her acting like that when we've made that trip before."

Rob looked over at Ginger. She was sprawled out on the carpet in the living room, and it looked to him as if she didn't have a care in the world. Turning back to Thad he said, "She looks fine now."

"Yep. She's been fine ever since we got back out onto Route 16. In fact she was her old self all the way into town when I went to get the newspaper and this here danish."

"I love this stuff, Thad, but do me a big favor please."

"What's that?"

"This stuff loves me too, so don't bring it here too often, okay?"

Thad took a long slow look at him and growled, "If you had less of your Corona and tequila, I'm pretty sure that *stuff* wouldn't affect you as much."

"Yeah, yeah, yeah. You're beginning to sound just like Eileen, and by the way, what is this? The pot's calling the kettle black? As I recall, my friend, it wasn't that long ago that I remember you sipping a lot more than you do right now!"

He looked down at the floor as he grumbled a little more saying, "That's different!"

Rob was about to add more fuel to the fire when he thought better of it, and decided to change the subject. "By the way, my buddy, Jack, is flying in early this afternoon and we're going to pick him up at the airport. You need anything from Rangeley while we're there?"

His mood seemed to lighten some as he said, "Nope! I appreciate the offer, but I'm going to the Farmer's Union to get some more feed for the deer, and while I'm there I'm going to call on an old friend of mine."

While Thad was talking, Rob saw a shadow swinging back and forth on the kitchen table and looked out the window to see what was causing it. The first thing that he noticed was the birdfeeder right in front of the picture window swinging in and out from the house. It hangs from a long chain that is attached to the eaves above, and as he focused on it he thought that the sight was mighty strange. Common sense told him that wind blows alongside of the camp, not in and out. He looked at the branches of the birch trees where other feeders were hanging, and then he looked at the feeders. Absolutely nothing was moving except the feeder hanging from the eaves, and as far as he was concerned it was doing the impossible. "Thad, take a look at that feeder!"

Thad looked at it but he did not seem to have a clue as to what Rob wanted him to see. Finally Rob said to him, "Don't you see how that feeder is swinging in and out from the house?"

"Sure. So?"

Now pointing out the window at the feeder he said, "Doesn't it seem a little strange to you that this thing is swinging in and out from the house, and not back and forth alongside of it?"

"Now that you mentioned it, it does seem strange. Especially since it doesn't seem to be windy."

Eileen came over to the table to see what was happening. After watching it for a little while she looked down at Rob, gave him one of those looks that is supposed to mean something, and then walked away without saying a word. He looked at Thad, shrugged his shoulders and said, "I don't know what that was all about, but I'm damn well sure it wasn't good."

Thad looked at his watch saying, "Well, it's gettin' on ten o'clock. I think I'll head back to camp and do the dishes so I can get into town."

He stood up from the table, called Ginger and was gone without so much as another word.

* * *

The second that Thad had closed the front door Rob's mind started working overtime. There certainly had been plenty of instances where people had seen the circle of distorted air, and these sightings seemed to be concentrated in a particular area. He was pretty sure that they all were within a five-mile radius of the beaver pond, but the adage has always been that a picture is worth a thousand words. With that thought in mind he went upstairs to the cedar closet and pulled out two of his topographical maps that were standing up in the corner. He brought them down to the kitchen, then went to the basement to get a roll of masking tape. Once back in the kitchen he unrolled each of the maps and taped them to the table, side by side. Then he took a black felt-tipped pen from a cup on the counter that held numerous pens and pencils, and started marking the location of each of the known sightings on the maps.

After about twenty minutes he was beginning to wonder if he had remembered all of the places where the phenomenon had made itself known. When Eileen came into the kitchen he was standing by the table just staring at the maps, hoping that by fixating on them it might trigger a memory. The moment she saw her table was almost totally covered by maps, she asked in a very bossy tone, "What are you doing?"

"I wanted to plot each of the phenomenon appearances on the map. I've been saying that all of these events happened within a five-mile radius of the beaver pond, but there's nothing like seeing and believing. The only thing is, I'm not sure that I've marked down all of the events that we were told about. Would you get me a pad of paper from my desk?"

"Sure, but why can't you use some of the scrap paper that's over by the pen and pencil cup?"

"That paper's too small, I'd prefer my yellow lined pad."

In less than a minute Eileen came back with the pad and sat in a chair next to Rob. Without looking at the map he started writing down each of the events that he could recall, and he wrote them in the order that they happened, trusting that by doing so it would help to trigger a memory of something that he might have forgotten.

Looking for all the help that he could get, he told Eileen what he was doing and the reason behind it. She moved closer to him so that she could watch as he was marking down each of the events, and it proved to be very helpful. Writing them in order helped to jog her memory about several phenomenon appearances that he had forgotten. By the time they were finished there were quite a few inserts, each of them recalling different events that had been described to them. However Rob's penmanship isn't the greatest in the world, and even he was having a difficult time reading some of the inserts. When all was said and done, they ripped off the top sheet and Eileen typed a new one.

When she was finished typing she read out loud each of the phenomenon appearances, and Rob checked the maps to make sure that each one had been clearly marked. Once they finished, it became very obvious that the highest concentration of the known events was, as the crow flies, within three miles of the beaver pond.

Rob stood there studying the maps for about fifteen minutes before he spoke. "You know, I'd like to hop into the Explorer right now and go to the airport. I want to take the Hawk XP up for a look-see around. We just have to make sure that we're back on the ground by 13:00 hours to meet Jack and Nancy. That okay with you?"

"Well it's 10:45, and by the time I fix my hair and put on my makeup, we probably won't get out of here until 11:15 or 11:30. Will that give us enough time? And keep in mind that it's pretty cold out there and you need to preheat the engine"

"We'll have plenty of time if I call Larry Williams and ask him to preheat it while we're on our way."

"Okay, you call Larry and I'll get ready."

He was lucky and caught Larry as he was heading out the door. "You're a fortunate man, Rob. I had an itch and nothing to do, so I was just getting ready to fly to Portland for a $100 hamburger." When there was no comment from Rob he went on to say, "No problem, though. I'll just leave a little later."

Just before hanging up he said to Larry, "Jack's going to be in at around 13:00 hours. Is there a spot cleared where we can tie down his Cherokee?"

"I'll check, and if there isn't, I have the plow on my truck and I'll clear a spot for him by your bird."

"Thanks, Larry. See you at the airport."

While he got ready to leave for the airport Rob thought about all the $100 hamburgers that he'd had over the years. The burger got its name from pilots that had nowhere to go and all day to do it. Most pilots aren't interested in just poking holes in the sky and normally pick a destination, which is usually a restaurant at some airport for a burger. When they add up all the expenses, which includes the wear and tear on the plane, the cost of fuel and the goodies at the airport restaurant, the cost usually tallies up to somewhere around $100.

* * *

Rob parked his Explorer next to the hanger and hooked a leash onto Rudy's collar for the walk over to their plane. Larry had already gotten all of the snow and ice off of it, and was disconnecting the heater from the engine port. He handed Larry his credit card and said, "I pumped $41.00 into the tanks when I landed Sunday afternoon, so just add that amount to what I owe you for heating the engine, and here's $20 for cleaning off the snow and ice. I really appreciate your thoughtfulness."

Larry took the credit card and had a big grin on his face as he stuck the $20 bill in his pocket. "You've never gone up for a ride around the area during snowmobile season before. What's up?"

He really did not want to tell Larry what was going on at this point in time so he said, "I saw some coyotes chasing a moose near Cherry Run where it crosses ITS 89, and I just want to check the area to see if they got it or not. If they did, I want to make sure that it's dead. You know how the coyotes are, they'll take a moose or a deer down and eat on it while it's still alive."

Larry was listening intently and cut in, saying, "Yeah. I've seen that before."

"I'll tell you what, Larry, cats aren't my favorite animals in the world, but at least they kill their prey before they eat it. Anyway, if the moose isn't dead I'll get a hold of the game warden and give him the location. Then it's up to him."

Larry seemed to be satisfied and started to walk away with the heater when he said, "You want me to leave the charge slip on the counter along with your credit card so you can sign it when you get back, or do you want me to bring it back out to you now?"

"Why don't you leave it in your cubbyhole? Just check it when you get back from Portland and you'll find your copy waiting for you."

"Sounds good to me. See you next time."

"Oh by the way, was there a spot open for Jack to park his Cherokee, or did you have to clear one?"

"If you look to the right of your Cessna you'll see tie downs and chocks. It was already cleared, I just put the ropes and blocks out there for you."

"Thanks, Larry. I owe you another one."

Larry waved as he continued on his way. Rob waved back and then bent over to lift his furry friend up into the back of the Hawk XP. Rudy is a seasoned flyer and he went right to his usual spot so Rob could secure him into his harness. In the meantime Eileen took the checklist out of the side door pocket, and as soon as Rudy was fastened in place they both started to perform a preflight on the exterior of the plane.

Rob was a stickler for proper procedure and they thoroughly checked everything as they walked around the aircraft. It didn't make any difference that he had filled the Hawk's tanks himself, he visually checked them to make sure that they were still full. When the initial walk-around was completed, Eileen went to get a paper towel while Rob checked the fuel drain ports for water contamination, and their timing was always perfect. Just as he would finish checking the last port, she would be standing by the engine cowling with the towel in her hand. He would join her by the power plant and examine the engine compartment for any signs of leaks, and then would check the engine oil while Eileen boarded the plane to get the final preparations completed in the cabin.

He was proud of their routine and told people that it was like the movements of a well-oiled machine. Last but not least, before he climbed into the Cessna he would take off the Pitot tube cover and pull the chocks out from the wheels.

After he had adjusted his seat and fastened his harness, Eileen picked up the checklist and started calling out one by one each of the cabin preflight checklist items. From the very beginning he wanted her to be familiar with the Hawk's systems and procedures, and he knew that the simplest way to accomplish that objective was to ask her to call out each item on the checklist. When she had agreed to his proposal he gave her the Hawk's Pilot Information Manual. The first thing that she had opted to do was to photocopy the checklist for each phase of flight; before, during, and after. Once that was accomplished she had laminated them in plastic.

As soon as the cabin preflight checklist was completed she proceeded with the laminated checklist for starting the engine. Both checklists took less than ten minutes to complete and while she flipped to the next list, Rob gave a visual look outside of the aircraft to make sure that no one was around the propeller before starting the engine. While it warmed up to operating temperature he checked the radio and set the instruments for flight before they taxied out to the run-up area at the departure end of the runway.

Normally he set his altimeter to the altitude of the airport that he was taking off from. But he was not sure what he would be doing once they were airborne, so he set his altimeter to zero. He wasn't going any great distance that would require an altimeter for navigation, but around here for some reason, he wanted to know the approximate level that he would be off the ground while they were checking the different areas.

The takeoff checklist items were completed and Rob keyed the microphone saying: "This is Cessna Seven Five Eight Mike Yankee taking the active runway three-two for a right turn departure to the northwest." There was no response, and before taking the active runway he gave a complete visual check of the airspace around the airport. There were no aircraft in sight, so he increased the engine's rpm's and taxied onto the runway for takeoff.

The wind was coming right down the pipe as he smoothly pushed the throttle forward until the engine had developed full power. He scanned the instrument panel one final time to make sure that everything was still reading in the green, and then looked over at Eileen to make sure that she was ready. She nodded that she was all set, so he released the brakes and when they reached 55 KIAS (knots indicated air speed) he lifted the nose wheel off the runway just as she activated the transponder.

With the wind blowing straight down the runway he quickly developed a good strong lift and climbed to 1000 feet AGL (above ground level). As soon as he had the Hawk settled, he trimmed it for level flight while Eileen called out the cruise checklist items. The visibility was unlimited, but the sun was reflecting so intensely off the snow-covered mountain in front of him that his Serengeti Aviator sunglasses couldn't totally wipe out all the glare. As soon as he reached 1000 feet AGL both of them started looking over the nose of the aircraft to get a fix on the location of the beaver pond, and she was the first to spot it. He was just changing course to go directly to it, when off to his left side he noticed something in a clear-cut that did not look quite right. He turned the aileron to the left to lower the left side of the aircraft, and at the same time stepped on the right rudder peddle to keep his direction of flight toward the beaver pond. After scanning the area twice he thought that he might have been just seeing things, and was ready to bring his left wing back up when he spotted a circle of shimmering air. From one thousand feet it looked like it was almost sitting right on the snow, but that could be an optical illusion from that altitude, so he dropped the left wing and nose of the Cessna to go down to get a closer look.

They temporarily lost sight of the circle of wavering air as they made a wide turn to the left to come back to the clear-cut, and just before he was on a direct heading to it, he leveled the aircraft out at 500 feet AGL. The approach was faster than what he wanted so he backed off on the rpm's while at the same time raising the nose of the aircraft until his air speed bled off to 90 KIAS, and then trimmed it again for level flight. Both of them were looking intently ahead and almost simultaneously spotted the circle of distorted air. As they were looking at it, they also saw a moose making its way through the clear-cut. Taking a quick glance over at his wife Rob said, "*Now* we know why that circle of shimmering air is there."

He turned the aileron to the right because he wanted to swing out far enough to make a wide turn that would put him on a heading straight back at the moose. Once he had the distance that he felt he needed, he turned the aileron back to the left. The moment he could see the moose through the spinning propeller he lowered the nose and brought the engine to full power. He quickly dropped down to about 25 feet above the snow, and as they passed over the moose he pulled the nose up and banked to the right as the altimeter needle wound its way through 100 feet AGL.

Eileen was focusing her attention out of her side window, and as they came around behind the circle of air she was astonished to see that it looked like a languid pool of water on the backside. Turning to her husband she said, "You should take a look at this!"

He was also looking out her window because he wanted to see if the moose had turned to run in the opposite direction, and soon saw that it was rapidly making tracks away from the circle of wavering air. Satisfied that his mission had been accomplished he turned his attention to the shimmering air. He let out a soft whistle of surprise that Eileen never heard because it was drowned out by the roar of the Cessna's power plant.

Maybe it was just as well that she did not hear his whistle of amazement, because he didn't want a barrage of questions that he did not know the answer to. He took another look just to make sure that his mind correctly registered the message that his eyes sent to his brain. From his aerial perspective, the circle of air looked like it was a disk. Then a thought came to his mind asking, "But how could that be? Every time that I have seen evidence of where it touched the snow, it was a circular concave impression. How could a disk leave that kind of an imprint?"

Once again his mind was in a whirlwind, and it must have been apparent because when he finally looked at his wife, he saw a very perplexed look on her face. Wanting to immediately diffuse whatever she was thinking he said, "What do you make of that?"

"I don't know, but it looks like the circle of air is facing a different direction." She paused for a moment before saying, "Now it looks like it's following us." He heard the urgency in her voice and instincts took over as he pushed the throttle to the wall, getting all the power that he could muster in an effort to quickly gain a pilot's best friend ... altitude.

* * *

Jack and Nancy fired up their Cherokee and departed Portland International airport earlier than they had originally planned. As a matter of habit, the first thing that he did in the morning whenever he was taking a trip in his Piper, was to call the closest FSS (Flight Service Station) to get a weather briefing for his intended departure time. Everything about the weather briefing was perfect with the exception of the wind. Currently the wind was out of the northwest at ten knots, but by his 11:45 hours departure time the wind was forecasted to be at 25 knots. Unfortunately, the information meant that he would be bucking a strong headwind all the way, and to make up for it he would have to leave twenty minutes earlier if he was going to get to Rangeley by 13:00 hours.

He had another issue to contend with. Whenever the wind blows out of the northwest and over the mountains, the ride gets to be pretty bumpy at the lower altitudes, so he climbed to 8000 feet before leveling off.

Right after he had the aircraft trimmed for level flight he turned on the wings-level autopilot, which rough air or not, he always did out of habit. Jack was not a lazy pilot, but he preferred to relax while he maintained his scan inside and outside of the cockpit. The sun was almost directly over their heads and they had unlimited visibility. Looking past Nancy out the right side of his plane he could see the peaks of Bigelow Mountain off in the distance. They had made this trip many times before, and Nancy was way past looking at the scenery passing by below, so to pass the time away she pulled out a John Grisham novel that she was already halfway through.

* * *

Rudy was usually sound asleep by the time they lifted off, and this day was no exception. However, at the exact moment that Eileen had said that it looked like the circle of shimmering air was following them, Rudy woke up, scrambled to a sitting position and started making a low threatening growl, which rapidly turned into a ferocious bark. Rob had not heard him sound this ferocious very often before. In fact, the only times that he could recall were always at a field trial when a bitch was in heat and male competition was close by. Shortly after Rudy began barking, Rob felt the controls become mushy, sort of like he was in slow flight. He checked his air speed to make sure that he wasn't anywhere near developing a stall, it was just fine. Suddenly Eileen broke the silence when she yelled, "Rob, that circle of distorted air is getting closer!"

Even though he was still trying to gain altitude, the altimeter was acting like it was frozen in one place at 7000 feet. Then all hell started breaking loose. The plane began to buffet like it was approaching a stall, and at the same time the stall warning horn came on. Briefly looking over at his wife he saw that she was pale and wide-eyed. He knew that he had to do something, and quick, otherwise he could potentially go into a spin. But then reason took over, telling him that when his air speed indictor is in the green he is fine, unless he suddenly flew into a wind shear, and he did not think that would be the case. Once again, instinct took over and he pushed the yoke all the way forward, and to his amazement the nose *slowly* dropped. Basic physics told him that the nose should have dropped like a rock, but he did not have time to think about that one now. The last that he could recall, the circle of distorted air was somewhere off the starboard side of the aircraft, and he quickly reacted to that information, turning the aileron to the left while simultaneously stepping on the left rudder.

As the nose dropped lower below the horizon the plane started picking up velocity, and before he knew it the air speed indicator was in the red arc. Even though he knew he was taking a big chance on airframe structural damage at this speed, he was not yet willing to change what he was doing. As the altimeter approached 3500 feet AGL he started to gently pull back on the yoke. As he expected, with gentle pressure the nose was slow to respond, but it started coming up and his airspeed began to drop when they were at about 1200 feet AGL. He watched the air speed indicator continue to drop as his air speed bled off, and as soon as he was at the bottom of the red arc he pulled the yoke back further, quickly leveling off.

His heart was pounding in his chest, sweat was coming off his forehead and he had to dry his hands on his pant legs. He checked the air space all around him, above and below and there was no sign of a circle of distorted air. Then looking over at Eileen to make sure that she was OK, he saw that she was scrambling to get a barf bag open, and that scene *really* concerned him. It wasn't just the fact that she was going to throw up. It was because he knew that as soon as he heard her doing it, and the fragrance wafted past his nose, that he was going to be retching right along with her. As luck would have it, she was just being cautious and nothing happened. Still watching her to make sure that the crisis was past he said, "I'm heading back to the airport, any objections?"

She gave him a look that seemed to scream, "You need to ask!?"

Rob looked at his altimeter and interpolated his altitude above sea level. He was about to key the mike to broadcast to the world that they were five miles northwest of the airport at 2500 feet when he heard Jack come on the Unicom saying, "This is Cherokee Two Five One Whiskey Papa, ten miles southeast of the Rangeley Airport, inbound at 6000 feet."

Rob immediately pressed his mike button and said, "This is Cessna Seven Five Eight Mike Yankee, five miles northwest of the Rangeley Airport, inbound at 2500." And without pausing he continued, "Cherokee Whiskey Papa, this is Cessna Mike Yankee. Glad to hear your voice and look forward to seeing you on the ground."

"Mike Yankee, I'll follow you in. Where do I park my bird?"

"Whiskey Papa, the tie downs and chocks are just past where I'll be parking. Give me an opportunity to push my plane back and then you can get by."

"Thanks, Mike Yankee."

As Rob approached the Rangeley Airport he dropped down to 1000 feet AGL and entered a left downwind. The wind was still coming straight down the runway as he touched down on the numbers, and it was blowing hard enough that he had a very short rollout, making it possible for him to quickly exit the active runway without having to back taxi. Much to his surprise, they already had the Hawk pushed back into its parking place by the time they heard Jack's Cherokee coming off the runway.

* * *

As quickly as they laid their eyes on them, Jack and Nancy knew that Rob and Eileen were very stressed, and they did not go through their usual greetings, which are normally jovial and very lengthy. Everyone was uncharacteristically quiet as they loaded all of the gear from the Piper into the back of the Explorer. After the last piece was put in and Rudy was snug in his normal spot, the men got into the front and the women sat in the back, which just happened to be their SOP when riding together.

They rode in silence for about five minutes, and since Jack was loaded with anticipation for information, the silence was driving him crazy. Rob sensed his fidgeting around and started to brief him on all of the events, including the conversations with the snowmobilers at the Four Seasons as well as with Len that morning. Almost as if history was repeating itself, like with Thad, he finished his story just as they were turning off Route 16 onto the Kennebago Settlement Road, and the rest of the ride to Camp Stress-A-Rest was very quiet, with each of them very deep in their own thoughts.

7

Jack and Nancy had been married for six years and had no children from that marriage. Nancy had been engaged four times before meeting Jack, but always got cold feet before going to the altar. She was never truly sure if she was getting married for the right reasons and she did not want to say, "I Do" until she was one hundred percent sure that she was making a commitment for love, and not for the sake of love. Jack, on the other hand, had been married once before for ten years, and he always said that at least he got two great children out of the mess. They were now in high school, and Jack sported a bumper sticker on his Yukon that reads: Proud Parent of a Cape Elizabeth High School Honor Student. Rob always told him that he should have two of those stickers on his car since both of his children are honor students.

It had come as a big surprise to Rob and Eileen, and most everybody else, when Jack's first marriage had exploded, and exploded is the right term to use. In fact Rob and Eileen were totally shocked. They had spent many comfortable evenings with him and Jennifer, chatting and playing either pinochle or cribbage. Nobody could believe that Jack's marriage completely disintegrated in one afternoon after he had come home unexpectedly. Jack remembered that day well.

Jack was an antique car buff and on that particular day he had planned to go to an antique car show in Concord, New Hampshire. He had asked Jennifer to come along, but she said that she had other things that she had needed to get done and told him to go by himself.

He had three antique cars, and after agonizing over the decision, he had chosen to enter his 1949 Cadillac in the show. He left at about 11:00 hours, and on this particular trip he elected to take the Maine Turnpike south, rather than taking Route 302 over to Berlin, New Hampshire. When all was said and done, he was glad that he decided to take the Turnpike, because as he went over the bridge into Portsmouth, New Hampshire, steam started gushing out from underneath the hood.

As soon as he had seen the steam billowing out, he saw his weekend plans going to hell in a hand basket. He promptly pulled over to the side of the road and quickly hopped out of the car, having only one concern: Was his pride and joy going to be an easy fix? And was he going to be fortunate enough that it would be a quick fix so that he could bring it to THE best car show of the year?

Because he was an antique car buff and had seen steam shooting out from underneath the hood before, he knew that he had to be careful. But he was too worried about losing the weekend, so without thinking about the fact that he was literally throwing caution to the wind, he had thrown open the hood. He immediately knew that he had made a bad mistake. Steam instantly enveloped his whole head, and it came very close to scalding his face.

Once all the steam cleared away, he was able to see that the top radiator hose had a split right where it joined the radiator, and he let out a sigh of relief. He had a spare hose in inventory back home, and all he had to do was to stop the leak long enough to get there. A long time ago he had learned that when you drive an antique car, you had best be prepared for the unexpected.

Fortunately, he had two items in his trunk that would solve the dilemma, a roll of duct tape and a bottle of rubbing alcohol. He cleaned all of the grease and antifreeze residue off the radiator hose, wrapped it with duct tape, filled the radiator with liquid, put the radiator cap back on loosely so there wouldn't be a big pressure buildup that could pop his temporary fix, and was on his way back home within thirty minutes.

He had gotten so filthy while repairing the hose that he had to put a blanket on the driver's seat to protect the upholstery, and he knew that he'd have to take a shower in the basement when he got home. Jack's former wife did not like him using their bedroom shower when he was covered with grease and oil, and her unrelenting verbal abuse eventually forced him to build a shower in the basement. He had told Rob that he built the damn thing, just so he wouldn't have to listen to her yap about it anymore.

As he pulled up to the garage, a stong wind was thrasing the oak trees in the back yard. He did not see any sign that Jennifer was home, so while he was walking around to the back of the house, he fished the keys to the walkout basement door out of his pocket.

After he had showered and placed his dirty greasy clothes in the hamper by the washing machine, he had wrapped a towel around his waist and headed up the stairs to their bedroom on the third floor. Jennifer would not allow him to keep a change of clean clothes in the basement. She claimed that they got a musty smell from the dampness down there, and she could not stand to be around him when he had clothes on that reeked of mold.

Since they both loved to let fresh air circulate in their bedroom, they frequently left the sliding glass doors open on warm days, even when they were not home. It was not hard to understand why they felt safe in doing so, because their bedroom was forty feet above the ground.

As he had approached the bedroom door, he first thought that it was a little strange that the door was closed almost all the way, but then he remembered that it was a windy day, and on those days the door would blow closed if they left the sliding glass doors open. When he had opened up the bedroom door he was shocked to see his wife's face buried in an Oriental woman's crotch. It is probably needless to say that Jennifer and her lover were also totally stunned.

Jack was seething with rage and screamed at Jennifer, "You scumbag bitch! So this is the real story behind you, huh?"

The Oriental woman was the first to recover her composure and said, "Why don't you take that towel off, big boy, and do both of us?"

He looked at her and said, "No! I'm not into that!"

Then all hell broke loose when she retorted, "Why, aren't you man enough?"

Those words were the catalyst that drove Jack ballistic. He ran over to the bed, grabbed the Oriental woman by the throat and yanked her out of it, almost breaking her neck in the process. He told Rob that he did not remember much after that, except the fact that Jennifer had dialed 911, and the next thing he knew the police were in the house.

Because of the business that he was in, and specifically because of the type of electronic equipment that was his specialty, Jack was friendly with most of the policemen in the department. In fact, two of the policemen in that department worked for him during their off-duty hours.

They had not put hand cuffs on him when they brought him to the police station, and when they got there they had put him in a cell without locking the door, telling him to cool off. Never once had he bragged about it, but they did not even book him because of the 911 call. However, they had not been ready to give him Carte Blanche and when suppertime rolled around, Sam Geffinger, one of the policemen that worked for him, said that he would go out and get Jack whatever he wanted to eat. Two days later, after he felt that he was in total control of his emotions, and they agreed, he left. The rest was history.

Nancy had been a blessing for Jack. While Rob and Eileen always thought that Jack's marriage to Jennifer was good, Jack appeared to be moody at times, and during those times was very argumentative. Since his marriage to Nancy, they had seen a big change in him. Once in a great while he'd fly off the handle, but for the most part he seemed as though he was totally at peace, and he always had a smile on his face. Both he and Nancy were very giving and caring people, but Jack was much more so since his marriage to her.

* * *

Eileen was taking the food out of the cooler that Jack and Nancy had brought, and was arranging it in the refrigerator. Jack and Nancy were unpacking their clothes and personal items and setting things up in the bedroom. Rob was sitting on the couch looking at the notes he had made that morning. As he read them, he referred to the exact topographic location for each of the distorted air sightings. Suddenly, he detected movement out of the corner of his right eye. Because of many past experiences, whenever that happened Rob made it a habit to concentrate on looking from his peripheral vision. Just for a moment or two he could see a fuzzy translucent form of a person in the room near him, and as always, the apparition was about three to four feet above the floor. Just like the times before, when he turned to look directly at it, he could no longer see it.

Just before he saw the shadow, he felt a tingling sensation and then he could feel the hair on his arms and legs begin to stand up. The moment that he felt his body begin to tingle he knew what to expect. There was no need for him to look. He had seen it many times before when this same event had happened. And now he could feel that all of the skin on his torso, arms, and legs was completely covered with goose bumps. The goose bumps were not there because he was cold. Quite the contrary, they were coming from within, and he had experienced that before, but the frequency of it had steadily increased over the last three years.

When it first started happening, Rob did not understand what was causing these sensations, but while attending a workshop that focused on teaching how to communicate with your Guardian Angels, he learned the answer.

Talking in a soft voice he said, "Thank you. I know that you are with me." And with that, the tingling sensation exacerbated to a high-pitched intensity. He got up from the couch and started for the front door. "Eileen, I'm going out to the shed to check the snowmobiles and I'll be back in a few minutes."

He knew that his spirit guide had been with him, and he wanted to be somewhere by himself so that he could open communications. As soon as he stepped out the front door he immediately headed to the shed. Once he stepped inside and closed the door behind him, he concentrated on emptying his mind as he relaxed his body, and then he said a prayer to summon his spirit guide into the light. After saying the prayer, he took a folding lawn chair off its hook on the wall and sat down. The moment that he had a comfortable position, he cleared his mind of everything, and in a short time he was in a trance. He had no sense of what might be going on around him. At that point he was focusing totally on raising his vibration level.

After attending the workshop, he had bought several books to learn more about channeling. Once he felt at ease with what he had learned, he asked Eileen to sit with him in the room during the first few times that he attempted to enter into a trance to communicate with his spirit guide. There were several failures before he learned how to totally open his mind. The first time that he succeeded, Eileen heard him begin to talk, and at first she did not comprehend what he was saying. She actually thought that he was giving up for that session. But that thought was fleeting, because she soon knew that he was repeating what was being said to him.

While Eileen did think to make some notes of what Rob was hearing, she was not sure that she had time to write down everything. After the first few successes, whenever he was going to enter into a trance, he had placed a voice-activated tape recorder next him.

It was cold in the shed and he had no way of knowing how much time passed before he started feeling and interpreting the vibrations from his spirit guide. As it turned out, a tape recorder was not necessary for this session. The communication was shorter than normal. His spirit guide simply told him that he had a message for him. The message was that he would soon meet some deceitful people that would tell him that they are from the other side.

As quickly as his spirit guide had made his presence known, he was gone, and Rob's mind was still whirling with questions that he had wanted to ask. He didn't understand why the connection between them broke so quickly. It never had before. He tried to bring his mind back to the light, wanting desperately to make the connection with his spirit guide once again, but after a few minutes he began to notice a sensation in his body that was different from the one that he was looking for.

* * *

The moment that Rob lost contact with his spirit guide, he began to notice the same feelings that he had experienced at the beaver pond with Rudy. Everything became very quiet, then came the feeling that he was in a vacuum. After that, the static noise began. He walked to the front of the shed and opened both of the doors. The moment that they were open he began to look in every direction to see if he could locate a circle of shimmering air. Suddenly he felt a sense of weightlessness. After a couple of seconds he fully realized that it wasn't just his imagination, because when he looked down at his feet he could see that they were a few inches off the floor. Abruptly the static noise ended and he dropped to the floor with a horrendous thud, shaking mind, body, and soul. He hit the floor with such force that he wondered why he did not go through it. The ensuing vibration rattled most everything in the shed. His mind was whirling: Why did he hit the floor so hard, when it was such a short drop? After pondering the question for a few seconds, he realized that it felt more like he was propelled to the floor, not dropped.

Shortly after the ringing in his ears quieted down, he heard the tinny sound of the storm door as it banged closed. He wondered if the static sound had quit because someone was coming out of the camp. No sooner had he finished that thought when Jack appeared in the doorway and said, "Hey buddy, why don't we take a ride on your sleds? I'd like you to show me where you saw the circles of shimmering air and those depressions in the snow."

"If it's depressions in the snow that you want to see, we can start right here. There're two out in a clearing that is beyond the stand of pine trees behind the shed, and there's another one just before the pines, and there's one more that's between our driveway and the road. Come on! Let's go over to the driveway, and when you've seen enough of what's there to satisfy your curiosity, you can go down into the basement and get the pair of snowshoes that I've got hanging on the wall. You'll need them when we go to look at the two depressions in the clear-cut out back. While you do that, I'll check the sleds to make sure that we've got enough fuel and oil."

After Jack had seen all of the depressions, he was disappointed. He did not know any more now than he did before. He was not sure what he had expected to see that would help his analytical process, but he was disappointed nonetheless. When they finally walked back into the camp it was 14:45. Eileen and Nancy were chatting over a cup of coffee at the kitchen table, and they did not pay any attention to the men as they changed into their snowmobile gear for their ride to the beaver pond.

Neither Jack nor Rob said much while changing, and said nothing at all while warming up the sleds. When they were ready to leave, Rob took the lead as they headed out of the driveway. It was 15:10 hours by the time they parked their machines on the bridge by the beaver pond.

Jack had already made up his mind that he did not need to go out onto the pond to take a look at the tracks and the depression in the snow, so they just stood on the edge of the bridge to look the area over. Jack had just turned to ask Rob a question that had occurred to him as he was looking around the perimeter of the pond when everything abruptly turned stone quiet. Rob was in the midst of pointing to the pine trees located in the left quadrant of the beaver pond, wanting to show Jack the spot where the deer tracks had emerged. Jack felt the silence envelop his senses and looked in the direction that Rob was pointing, thinking that he was trying to let him know what was causing it. When he fixed his gaze on the area that Rob was pointing to, he saw a deer come bounding out onto the pond from the pine trees. Rob saw it too and gave Jack a soft elbow in the ribs to get his attention. Leaning closer to him to whisper in his ear he said, "I think something's getting ready to happen." However, after thinking about it, he wondered why he felt it was necessary to whisper.

Rob unzipped his coat and pulled out his Sony digital zoom camera, keeping his eye on the deer all the while. He quickly got his camera ready for the action that he expected to shortly unfold before their eyes. Right after he had the camera all set he looked through the telescoping lens to make sure that he had not accidentally fogged it up with his warm breath. The lens was clear and he immediately used it to scan the beaver pond. Finding no circle of shimmering air, he concentrated his search in the sky up above him, and then started a 360° sweep around, hoping to see something that resembled the object that he was looking for.

He was beginning his second sweep when he spotted it at the two o'clock position from where he and Jack were standing. It was approximately thirty feet above the snow-covered pond, but this time it seemed to look different from the other times he had seen it. He was finally able to put his finger on why it was not nearly as distorted as the other times.

While the deer was making its way out onto the beaver pond, the circle of air started a methodical descent. With each step that the deer made toward the center of the pond, the circle of air continued descending closer and closer to the surface. During the whole time that the shimmering air was dropping further below the horizon, its appearance slowly changed. The wavering air became more distorted as it got closer to the surface of the pond.

When the deer was about twenty feet from it, it suddenly dropped the rest of the way to the surface, and the moment that the lower perimeter of the shimmering air touched the snow, the static noise began. When the hissing sound began, the deer looked like it wanted to reverse its course, and through the camera's telescope lens Rob could see the fear in its eyes. The crackling sound seemed to intensify and Jack yelled to Rob to look quick. As soon as he looked to where Jack was pointing, he saw an object come shooting out of the circle. At the rate of speed that it came out, he expected to see it zip on past him and drop somewhere in the pine trees on the far side of the pond. But as he watched, the object changed shape and its velocity seemed to drop off. Then he saw wings appear from the object, and at that point it rapidly slowed down. After a few more seconds went by, he could see that it was a hawk, and he momentarily wondered if it was the same hawk that he had watched being sucked into the circle of air on Monday morning.

Just in the nick of time he focused his attention back on the deer, and saw it being pulled toward the circle. He decided that "pulled" was correct because nothing else fit the description of what he had seen. The deer was a mere ten feet from the shimmering air as Rob brought the camera up to his eye to snap a picture. At the same moment when he pressed the shutter release on his camera, the deer literally flashed out of the viewfinder, and into the circle of air.

When Jack first looked at Rob his mouth was wide open with surprise. He quickly regained his composure and said, "If I didn't see that happen with my own eyes, I wouldn't have believed it."

"So, what you're telling me, old buddy, old pal, is that you thought I was full of it!"

"Let's just say that I was real skeptical. I actually thought that you were embellishing the truth. However, after seeing this, I don't think you have told me enough."

"I told you everything that happened, and I tried very hard not to leave anything out."

While they were talking Rob was looking all around the beaver pond for anything else that could possibly help them in their information gathering. As his eyes settled on a lone tree that made its home on a tiny island that sits almost in the center of the beaver pond, he noticed the hawk sitting on a branch that was very close to the top. It was not moving at all. In fact it was so still that Rob thought to himself, "I bet if we came out here tomorrow morning, that it would still be sitting there in that same position."

It did not take too much imagination to come to that conclusion. The recent experience with Rudy was still fresh in his mind. He remembered that Rudy was very lethargic for the better part of 24 hours after Ginger had found him. And after what he had just witnessed, he felt certain that Rudy had an experience similar to that of the hawk.

When his mind returned to his friend standing alongside of him, he heard him finishing a sentence. He had been concentrating so hard on the hawk that he didn't hear a word of what Jack had said. Rather than letting him know that he hadn't been paying attention, he said, "What do you want to do now, Jack? Do you still want to go see the other locations that I told you about?"

"No. I've seen enough. We've got some time on our hands, how about going up to the top of East Kennebago Mountain? I'm in the mood for a ride, and I'd love to see the view from up there. Besides, you haven't been up there since Thad and Eileen had their encounter with that fox, right?"

Rob did not have to think very long before answering and said, "Yeah, that's right. Okay, fair enough. Can you handle some speed, or would you like me to just cruise along?"

"Do what ever you want. It's been a while since I've been on a sled, and this one's not set up for my weight. Actually, it's probably set up for someone that's about eighty pounds lighter than me. Anyway, I want to enjoy the scenery on the way, and I also need to do some thinking."

"Do you remember how to get up there, Jack?"

"Yup. See ya there!"

They fired up their machines and neither one of them took their eyes off the beaver pond as they drove away.

* * *

After they made a left turn onto ITS 89, Jack never saw the back of Rob's sled again until he reached the top of the Kennebago. Even though he was taking his time to enjoy the scenery on the mountain and in the valley below, there is no way that he would be able to pass a quiz on what he had seen. His mind was working through everything that he had just witnessed at the beaver pond, plus all the information that Rob had shared with him. When all was said and done, he was very satisfied with the ideas that he had come up with. He now knew the exact type of tests and experiments that he wanted to conduct the next day. He felt certain that once he performed them, that he would understand enough about this phenomenon to give Rob some very sophisticated theories as to what the hell had been going on.

* * *

When Jack walked out the front door with a pair of snowshoes under his arm, Eileen and Nancy had barely acknowledged his good-bye. He looked at them as he closed the door, and he saw that their conversation was very animated. While the storm door was heading for its normal crash landing at the jamb, he was thinking to himself, "If I interrupted them and tied their hands behind their back, that conversation would never be finished. I'm totally convinced that they are incapable of talking without using their hands to clearly define the meaning of their words."

Eileen and Nancy were so involved in catching up with all the news since they had last talked, that they didn't realize the men were leaving. In fact, if it weren't for the racket that the guys had made when they went zooming out of the driveway, they wouldn't have had a clue that they left.

Rob and Jack had only been gone for about ten minutes when Eileen decided to mix some margaritas. The first one not only went down nice and smooth, it went down quickly, and they were on their second drink when they both started to feel their clothes begin to cling to their body. They instantly knew what was causing it and they froze, staring each other in the eye, each hoping to gain some strength from the other. Their intense stare simultaneously shifted to each other's hair, just as they felt their own hair begin to rise up from their neck. Their fear intensified. Eileen was the first to break the spell that seemed to be paralyzing both of them when she yelled, "Quick! Follow me upstairs!"

Eileen vividly remembered her ordeal with the stranger just a day earlier, which now seemed like only a few minutes ago. She quickly made up her mind that if this crap was going to happen again, she was going to be ready.

She flung open the door when she got to the stairway, and Nancy was close behind. She was surprised to see Eileen taking the stairs three at a time, and she thought to herself, "Maybe I shouldn't be so surprised. Fear is a great motivator."

They reached the top of the stairs in less than ten seconds, and by the time that Eileen was standing in front of the gun cabinet she could hardly catch her breath. But she didn't hesitate one second before reaching behind the cabinet to take the key from its hiding place, and in what seemed like one continuous, fluid motion, unlocked the door. The instant she had the door open, she was jamming a shotgun and a box of shells into Nancy's hands, and then rapidly swinging back around to grab a shotgun for herself. She did not bother to close the cabinet door; she just spun around on her heel and sprinted to the top of the stairway. While they were scrambling back down the stairs Eileen yelled to Nancy to load the shotgun.

By the time they thundered into the kitchen, Nancy only had one shell in the shotgun. She was very athletic and coordinated, but she still didn't find it easy to hold onto the shotgun, work a shell out of the box and shove it in the magazine while doing the quickstep down the stairs.

The box of shells tipped over when she set it on the kitchen table, the shells spilling out and rolling everywhere. Both of them started to move even faster when they heard the static noise begin. Their hands started shaking as they tried to hurry the shells into the shotgun magazine, dropping more shells than what went in. Things went from bad to worse. There were no more shells in the box or on the table, and as Nancy quickly bent over to get one that had fallen on the floor, she whacked her head on the table on the way down, and literally saw stars spinning around. She dropped to one knee as she draped her right arm on the table to keep from falling over.

Eileen finally had two shells in the shotgun and grabbed two more as she started to run toward the front door. As she started to open it she said to herself, "Rudy! Where's Rudy!"

* * *

The second that she opened the door the static noise quit, and then she felt her clothes float away from her as her hair settled back onto her head and neck. While that was happening, she heard

Rudy barking, but could not seem to determine where the sound was coming from. It was like it was coming from everywhere in the house at the same time. The hissing noise had stopped and her fear had subsided. She began to think more rationally. Before long , it flashed into her mind that she had not seen Rudy since Jack went down into the basement to get the snowshoes. Excitedly, she ran over to the basement door, and when she opened it, Rudy came thumping up the stairs.

Her body relaxed a bit and a big smile spread across her face as she watched him amble up the stairs. She leaned her shotgun against the wall, and then knelt down to give him a big hug when he got to the top. Just as she was letting him out of the bear hug, she heard him growl. Instinct kicked in and she automatically leaned back, thinking that he was growling at her. The static cling and crackling noise had begun again. She reached over and grabbed the shotgun as she was standing up, and glanced to her right as she did. Nancy was already at her side, and it was apparent that she was more than ready to use the shotgun she was holding in her hands.

"What do we do now, Eileen?"

Eileen never got a chance to answer because Rudy started barking like crazy, and then he bolted for the front door.

Turning to Nancy she said, "I'm not gonna just sit here and wait this time! Let's go!"

Eileen was right behind Rudy, and she swung the front door open so hard that the knob smashed into the wooden wall, making a dent in the process. She jammed the palm of her left hand against the storm door handle and it flew open. Rudy was gone in a flash, and both Eileen and Nancy were right behind, hot on his heels, each with their shotgun ready.

When they got to the bottom of the steps, they stopped in their tracks and watched as Rudy ran up the driveway toward a circle of pulsating air. They just stood there for several terrifying seconds while they watched it hover a few inches off Kennebago Settlement Road. Then, without even thinking about the possible consequences, they both pointed their shotgun at the circle of air and rapidly fired every single round of ammunition they had loaded into the magazine. Anyone listening from a distance would have thought that some flatlander was prematurely celebrating the 4th of July.

The circle of air simply disappeared as they fired their last rounds. Rudy put his nose to the ground and kept circling around in the area where the circle of air had been, trying his best to find a scent. Still in shock, Eileen and Nancy did not move away from the porch. They just stood there watching Rudy.

He expanded his search several times around the entire area, each circle getting a little larger, and still found nothing of interest. Finally satisfied that he had not missed anything, he lifted his nose up from the road and looked in their direction, making sure that they were still where he had last seen them. He took one more quick sniff of the road and the air in the vicinity, making sure that the danger was gone, and then he did his happy trot back down the driveway.

As he approached Nancy and Eileen he slowed to a walk, but it really could not be properly defined as just a walk. It looked like he swaggered up to where they were standing. The moment that he was between the two of them, he promptly sat down. If he was an actor in a movie, his next action would have gotten him an Oscar nomination. He innocently looked up at them with his big brown eyes, developing a very inquisitive expression on his furry face as if to nonchalantly say, "Well, where's my reward?"

Ignoring his canine plea, Nancy looked over at Eileen and said, "What should we do now? I'm not sure that I want to stick around the camp after what just happened."

Eileen thought for a few moments, weighing her limited options and said, "We can take the Explorer into town and do some shopping. I really don't know what else to do, but I agree with you. I don't want to sit around here."

The decision was made. They quickly went back into the camp and walked straight over to the kitchen table to reload the shotguns. Their half finished margaritas were still sitting on the kitchen table. Without the slightest hesitation, Eileen picked up her glass and downed the rest of it while she reached for the shaker to pour another one. Nancy followed suit and set her glass down in front of Eileen for a refill. Not bothering to coat the rims of the glasses with salt, Eileen refilled them while Nancy bent down to pick up all the shotgun shells from the floor. Just as she stood up to put them back in the box, Eileen slid her margarita across the table to her. She picked up her glass to take a sip, and as she did, she glanced toward the front picture window. She screamed as her hand involuntarily let go of the margarita, and they both heard the sound of breaking glass as it hit the kitchen table.

Rudy started barking again. Eileen looked down at him and saw that the hair running down the center of his back was standing straight up. Looking up, she saw Nancy staring at something and followed her gaze to where she was looking. Another stranger dressed in a leisure suit was boldly standing in front of the picture window, and she could see that he appeared to be studying them. As her eyes fell upon his face, she saw that he was holding his left arm up in the air in front of him. Her stare began to quickly move down his arm to his hand, and then she saw that there was something in it, and it was pointed in their direction. She screamed, "You bastard! Leave us alone!"

She had barely gotten the word, "alone" out of her mouth when there was a loud explosion in the camp. The blast was still ringing in her ears as she watched the front picture window explode outwards from its center, and the stranger disappeared. The noise had been deafening, and Eileen was still trying to figure out what had happened when she saw a trail of smoke coming out of the shotgun in Nancy's hand. She looked at the front picture window, and then back at the smoking shotgun, and as hysteria tried to take over she began laughing as she said, "Man! Rob is really going to be pissed when he sees his living room window all over the driveway!"

The combination of Eileen's statement and her laughter started Nancy laughing as well, and in short order Eileen's hysteria melted away. Their laughter quickly turned into genuine belly laughter, but both of them were still scared shitless. Finally, Eileen put her hand on Nancy's arm and said, "Let's go see if you killed that rat fink."

They had both been laughing so hard that they were wiping tears from their eyes as they went out the front door, Rudy taking the lead. Glass was all over the driveway, but no blood and no sign of the stranger. Eileen looked at Nancy and said, "Well that settles it."

"Settles what?"

"It's 12° F, and if we don't plug that pneumonia hole that you made out of our front window, it's going to be pretty cold in the camp tonight."

"That's for sure, but how're *we* going to fix it?"

"We're not! As the saying goes, I'm going to let my fingers do the walking."

* * *

They had been sitting on their sleds on top of the mountain for about ten minutes, and had already taken a couple of swigs from the Southern Comfort flask, but there was no sign of the fox. From the time that they had shut off their machines they had been alternating their gaze between Bigelow Mountain and Saddleback Mountain. Rob was in the midst of putting the flask into the back compartment of his sled when the fox came slowly walking out from the pine trees on the right side of them. It kind of meandered along until it got to be about ten feet in front of Rob, then it sat down, and it almost looked like it was insolently staring him in the eye.

Jack had been observing the whole scene and said, "Looks like your buddy may have some attitude, but at least he's here to see you." Without saying another word he reached into his pocket and pulled out a couple of large dog biscuits. As soon as the fox heard the sound of Jack's hand coming out of his pocket, he instantly forgot about Rob. Jack kept watching the fox as he gripped the biscuit with two hands to break off a piece, and the moment that the fox heard the biscuit snap, he broke into a fast trot to get closer to Jack.

Rob started laughing as he said, "Looks like you swiped a couple of Rudy's favorite treats. Now I *know* what your true mission was. You think the fox will like them as much as the Toot-man?"

"We'll soon see." He slowly lifted himself off the machine, placed a couple of the pieces of biscuit that he had broken off in the palm of his hand, bent over slightly and tossed them underhand to the fox. They landed directly in front of the critter, and it did not even have to move one inch to get them. It took a quick look at Jack and Rob to make sure that they weren't making any moves toward him, and without even bothering to sniff them as he had done when Rob tossed him the candy, he cleaned up the two pieces in a flash. As soon as they had been devoured, the fox sat back down and gave Jack an inquisitive look as if to say, "Yeah, OK, so where's some more?" Like Rob, Jack is a softy, and without hesitation he tossed it a couple more pieces, and then put the rest in his pocket.

Rob was mystified by what he saw Jack do and said, "How come you're not giving him the rest?"

"Because this is a little test. I want to see if this character does a repeat performance of what he did on Monday."

They sat there looking at the fox, and the fox sat there looking back at them. It was a stare down contest. Rob thought that the fox might finally be losing, because he could see saliva starting to hang down from the corners of its mouth. Ten minutes went by before the fox finally got up to nonchalantly sniff its way out into the center of the clearing. Both of them intently watched it to see if it would do anything out of the ordinary, as if what it had just done was not out of the ordinary. Once it reached the center of the clearing the fox just stood there with its back to them for a few moments. Then he put his nose up in the air and sniffed in all different directions around him for whatever telltale scent that he was looking for. After about a minute and a half, the fox walked to the pine trees on the opposite side and disappeared into the forest.

Jack turned to look at Rob and said, "Other than the fact that this fox does not appear to be afraid of humans, it seems to be acting pretty normal to me."

Shaking his head up and down he said, "I have to agree with you on that one." Getting up off of his sled, he walked to the back of it, opened the compartment and started to pull out the flask of Southern Comfort for another sip. But then he changed his mind and put his hand back into it, and started fishing around, looking for something else. Shortly a smile broke out on his face as he pulled out a different, but smaller flask. He twisted the cap off and offered it to Jack.

Jack got a questioning look on his face and said, "What's this?"

Almost shouting he said, "Nectar of the gods, man!

Jack put the flask up to his nose and took a quick sniff, and recognition instantly appeared on his face. "Tequila! I'm not flying anymore today, so I don't mind if I do." He put the flask to his lips, tilted his is head back, and Rob watched as Jack's Adam's apple danced up and down. There was a steady stream of small bubbles shooting up from the throat of the flask, with a larger bubble here and there as he took one hell of a big swig. When he finally handed the flask back he said, "Now that stuff is more like it!"

Rob took the flask from him and thought that it felt considerably lighter than it had just a moment or two before. He put it up to his lips, and was taking a baby swig in comparison to what Jack had just done when the fox came walking out of the same section of pine trees as before. This time it sat down about eight feet in front of Jack. The staredown began again. Finally Jack broke down, reached into his pocket and brought out the rest of the dog biscuit pieces. Putting them all in the palm of his hand, he tossed the whole bunch over to the fox. His aim was not as good as before, and the fox had to take several rapid steps closer to Jack before reaching them. It ravenously gulped down the biscuit morsels with great gusto, not taking time to chew even one of the pieces.

Rob got a smile on his face and said, "I think that fox is a little short on table manners. What do you think, Jack?"

"Looks OK to me. Remember, I'm from a big family, and if you didn't eat fast, you didn't get seconds."

The fox finished his treat, and without looking at them it turned around and went back into the pine trees to their right. Turning to look at his long-time friend, Jack said, "He's probably going to take a nap now that he has a full belly. You ready to head back to camp Rob? I'd like to feel a lot more of your tequila burn its way down my throat." Pausing for a couple of moments like he was thinking something through, he continued, "That Southern Comfort's OK, but it's a long way from meaningful."

Jack's words provided the intended motivation. Rob quickly got up off his sled and put the flask of Tequila away, and as he did he said, "Sounds like a winner to me. See ya back at camp!"

* * *

Rob looked in his rearview mirrors as they headed down the first leg of the trail from the top of the mountain, and since he was not breaking any speed records he wasn't surprised to see Jack about twenty feet behind him. He was taking his time and enjoying the view of the distant mountains in New Hampshire and of the

Big and Little Kennebago Lakes below. The sun was sitting lower in the sky, casting red hues that gave the panoramic view an awesome appearance, making the snow look like it was on fire.

As they were approaching the Seven Gulpers camp, Rob saw that three snowmobiles had parked in front of it, and each of them had tag-along sled attached. He started wondering what they might be up to when he saw only two riders sitting on the sleds. The third rider was nowhere to be seen, and he quickly wondered if these guys were up to no good. He motioned to Jack that he was going to stop, and when he looked into his left rear view mirror, he saw him wave his acknowledgment.

They stopped their machines on the trail parallel to the two riders sitting on their sleds. Neither one of them made any attempt to greet them. In fact, he got the distinct impression that they were being ignored. Both of the snowmobile riders had their helmets on, and he saw the rider opposite him pull his face shield down. Rob thought that action was a conscious slap in the face, and it really annoyed him so he yelled, "Hey!"

Finally the rider furthest away from him slowly turned his head, and it seemed to Rob that he was considering whether or not he should bother to acknowledge him. At long last, the rider turned his head all the way around to face him. Rob was already on the defensive. He didn't like the guy's blatant display of *don't bother me* when he pulled down his face shield. The guy's next action really ticked Rob off; he simply sat there and gave him a half-hearted wave.

Rob felt his temper starting to soar, and he was trying very hard to maintain his composure when he noticed they both had darkly tinted face shields on their helmets. His mind kind of stopped short as he thought to himself, "This is really odd. I wonder why that guy found it necessary to pull his face shield down now, especially since there isn't a ray of sunlight to be seen anywhere on this part of the mountain. He started walking over toward them, and then it hit him right between the eyes. Each of the tag-along sleds were piled high with Have-A-Heart Traps! The mystery began to deepen as he wondered why they had so many of that type of trap with them. The whole scene in front of him was very much out of place. If anybody in this part of the country was carting that many traps around with them, and especially this time of year, they sure weren't going to be Have-A-Heart Traps.

Jack watched as Rob walked over toward the two riders and sensed that something was very strange. He got up off his sled and walked over toward where Rob was headed so that he could be close at hand if trouble started. He knew that Rob was talking to them, but he could not make out what was being said. At this point both of them were looking in the opposite direction from where Rob was standing, and Jack could plainly see that they were intentionally ignoring him. And that raised Jack's suspicion even further, so he made a greater effort to get closer to Rob as quickly as he could.

Rob was starting to get seriously agitated with their attitudes. The rider furthest away from him finally glanced at him again, from over his right shoulder, and rapidly turned completely around to face him when he saw how close Rob had gotten. Right at that moment Rob thought to himself, "Maybe I'm being oversensitive and these guys are just hard of hearing."

He walked right up to the guy that was looking at him and said, "A friend of mine owns this camp, is there something wrong here?" Then pointing to the rider-less snowmobile he continued, "And where is the person that's riding this sled?"

The rider said something to Rob, but he could not understand what it was because the guy's face-shield was still down, and the words were muffled. Rob put his hand up by his ear and shook his head side to side, letting the snowmobiler know that he couldn't hear what he had said.

Finally the guy raised his shield a couple of inches, but not enough so Rob could see his face, and said, "Our friend is out in the back of the camp using the outhouse."

That didn't make ANY sense to Rob at all. The guy would have had to dig down through about five feet of snow just to open the door. Besides, any guy that he knew would just step off the trail into the woods to take care of business. Just then he saw the door on the Seven Gulpers front porch open, and the missing rider started down the steps. He had something in his right hand, but Rob couldn't immediately make out what it was.

He motioned to Jack to come on over, and then put his nose right in the guy's face in front of him and yelled, "What the hell is going on around here!"

The guy stood up and raised his arms, intimating that he didn't know what he meant. That action really irritated Rob. Promptly deciding that it was time to employ a different tactic, he gave the jerk a forceful straight arm to the chest, just to get his attention. The snowmobiler stumbled a couple of steps backward before catching his balance, and then suddenly acting like a pacifist, he just stood there.

Then his friend took what Rob interpreted to be a threatening step toward him, and before the aggressor knew what hit him he was falling backwards. His head hit the snow with enough force that it flipped his face shield up, and Rob got a fast look at his eyes before the rider quickly flipped it back down. Those eyes were nothing like any eyes that he had ever seen. The guy that Rob had straight-armed was starting to move toward him and Jack grabbed him by the arm and spun him around, while at the same time taking his legs out from under him.

Rob turned his head just in time to see that the snowmobiler that had been coming down the porch steps was now running in his direction. A knowing smile spread across Rob's face as he bent over to pick up a board that was lying across the seat of the snowmobile right next to him. It resembled a 1 X 3, but not quite. It looked strikingly similar to the boards that were sticking out of the snow where the rabbit had been sucked into the circle of shimmering air. As the oncoming snowmobiler closed the distance, Rob wrapped both hands snugly around the 1 X 3, and patiently waited. When the guy came within striking distance Rob swung the board like a bat, hitting him in the left knee with all the force that he could muster. The board snapped like a twig, but it still had the desired affect. Face shield down or not, he clearly heard the guy's scream of agony.

Turning to see what was happening behind his back, he saw that Jack had the snowmobiler wrestled down to the snow, well under control. At that point Rob was pretty confident that the screamer wouldn't be causing too much trouble in the next couple of minutes, so he ran over to the other rider that was still laid out on his back. Even though he did not waste any time getting over to him, he remained cautious because he still wasn't one hundred percent convinced that the guy hadn't added some dramatics to his fall.

The mystery man started to get up as Rob approached, and in a flash he pinned the guy down with his knee. Then he reached down and popped his face shield open. One look at this guy's eyes, and he immediately knew that he hadn't been seeing things. His eyes were definitely different from any that he had ever seen before. The only thought that came to his mind at the time, was that they reminded him of a cartoon character's eyes that he had seen in a comic strip when he was a youngster. Only instead of being black ovals, they were gray, and they had a dull sheen to them.

Grabbing him by the collar of his coat, he pulled him a few inches up off the snow, stuck his nose in the guy's face and said, "Who the hell are you, and what the fuck are you doing here?"

"Let me up or ......"

He never finished his threat. Rob did not like what he was hearing and bounced his knee on the guy's chest with all his weight behind it, successfully knocking some of the wind out of him.

In a threatening voice Rob said, "Listen, pal. I'm an easygoing guy until someone does me wrong, and you've done me wrong by lying to me. If you don't give me some proper answers quick, I'm gonna rip that helmet off your head and get some satisfaction. Get my drift?

Suddenly the wimp started whining, "Please, please, we mean no harm. We're here on a scientific, humanitarian mission."

Rob's face rapidly developed a look of disbelief, and then he said in the best menacing voice that he could muster up, "Right! You're going to have to do much better than that pal! First things first! What's wrong with your eyes?"

His captive paused briefly before answering, "There is nothing wrong with my eyes. Where we are from, my eyes are normal."

"And just where are you from?"

More silence, and then he finally said, "We are scientists from a parallel dimension, and we have been conducting experiments to develop a means to help all human beings and other living creatures in your dimension."

Interrupting him Rob growled, "Help? How!?"

Now cowering somewhat to Rob's extremely aggressive behavior he said weakly, "To help them live a longer and healthier life." Then he quickly added, "Right now we are collecting small sick animals that we intend to heal by altering their DNA structure."

Still not believing a word that this guy was saying, Rob cut in, "I guess that sort of explains the Have-A-Heart Traps, but it doesn't explain why you felt it was necessary to lie to me, and why your buddy over there started getting aggressive."

"*You* are the reason Zen started to get hostile. Everything was fine until you found it necessary to shove me."

Rob had to think about that one, because when all was said and done, perhaps this guy was right. Maybe he *did* overreact to the lie. All at once he did not feel like he was in control of his emotions. He could not understand why he was suddenly becoming so soft, and then silently talking to himself he said, "Bullshit! I was right to react the way that I did." Right at that moment he felt like he was coming back to his old self and said under his breath, "Besides, this guy should not have gone down as hard as he did with the little push that I gave him." Taking a closer look at the rider he made up his mind that he was right, because the guy certainly did not look like a ninety-pound weakling.

Zen was still moaning and rolling around in the snow, all the while holding onto his left knee. Rob felt a tiny pang of compassion that he quickly brushed aside, but then decided that he would go check the guy's knee to see if he was really hurt as bad as it appeared. Looking down at his captive he said, "I'm going to take my knee off of you and go check your buddy, and you had best stay put! Understand?"

The wimp nodded his head yes and Rob turned to Jack saying, "Give me a yell if this guy starts moving while I've got my back turned to him."

Jack now had the third snowmobiler in a neck lock. And from the look on the rider's face, Rob thought that Jack was probably applying enough force to make the guy feel like his neck might pop, which probably accounted for the reason that he was being so docile.

Jack looked at Rob with a vicious sneer on his face and said, "No problem, man. And if you need a hand I'll just break this wimp's neck and be right with you."

Rob had to quickly turn his head away from the eyes of the other two snowmobilers. He did not want them to see him laughing as he continued on his way over to Zen. The moment that he was standing and glaring down at him, Zen stopped moaning and rolling on the snow. He stayed in one position on his back, now holding his left knee up in the air. Rob was about to lean down and feel the guy's knee to see how badly it might be swollen when the static sound started. However, it did not begin like the other times. Whenever the static hissing began before, it always started out at a low volume, and then increased in decibels as time went on, but not this time. These decibels began at the get-go with a higher pitch than any other time before.

Glancing over at Jack he saw that he was trying to look in all directions at once. Suddenly he saw Jack's arms fly open. It looked like he had decided to let his captive go, and simply flung his arms out to quickly get it over with. But Rob could tell by the surprised look on Jack's face that something else had happened.

As soon as that the rider was out of Jack's stranglehold, he ran over to his buddy that Rob had left lying on the ground. Rob grasped what was about to happen and yelled to the downed snowmobiler, "Hey pal! You had best stay put," and that is when he felt a tremendous force hit him right between the shoulder blades, and things instantly went black as he fell forward.

He quickly regained most of his faculties when his face hit the icy cold snow, and he was struggling to get his breath back as he raised his head. As his vision cleared and he was able to focus, he saw the snowmobilers standing alongside a fourth person dressed in a leisure suit. He would later remember thinking, "Where in the hell did that guy come from?" Suddenly, the decibels of the static noise increased to another level, and in the blink of an eye the four people, including their snowmobiles and tag-alongs were gone.

Rob looked over at Jack, and he could tell by the look on his face that he did not want to believe what had just happened. As he stood up he said, "What do you make of that one, Jack?"

He was silent for the better part of a half a minute and said, "I don't have the foggiest. I've got a lot of theories, but no answers."

"I'll settle for theories. What are you thinking?"

"Let's head back to camp and I'll give you my thoughts over some Corona and Jose Cuervo."

"I'll tell you what, Jack, why don't you get started and I'll catch up with you. I want to check the porch and make sure that everything's okay."

Without saying another word, Jack swung his leg over Eileen's machine and was gone.

Rob slowly walked up onto the Seven Gulper's porch, cautiously looking around for anything that seemed suspicious. Everything looked fine until he tried the front door. He turned the doorknob and the door opened easily, but he could not believe his eyes as he looked around the enclosure. Every square inch of the floor was littered with Have-A-Heart Traps, and each and every one of them had an animal in it. However, rodent is probably a better descriptive term. He took the time to look inside all the traps, and saw nothing but squirrels, mice, weasels, and a couple of other rodent type animals that he could not identify. All of them looked like they were as healthy as could be, which shot to hell the sick animal statement that he had been fed. He felt little compassion for the collection of rodents, but still he took the traps outside and let all of the little critters go.

* * *

Rob caught up to Jack by the beaver pond. He was parked on the bridge and it looked like he was looking back toward the place in the pine trees where the deer had come out onto the pond earlier. Rob shut off his machine, walked over to Jack and put his hand on his shoulder. Jack still did not acknowledge that he was there, and Rob started to get concerned. He yelled at Jack to get his attention, and the only response that he got back was a hand gesture that told him to be quiet, so he shut up and focused his attention to where it appeared that Jack was looking. He didn't see anything out of the ordinary, just the beaver pond with the pine trees as a backdrop. He did notice, however, that it was extremely quiet, which was not uncommon in the Maine woods when there was no wind. Besides, he did not think that the silence was threatening because he did not sense the vacuum-type feeling that always accompanied the hush. After about five minutes he couldn't take it any longer and said to Jack, "Just what in the hell are you so intent on?"

"Can't you feel it?"

"Feel what?"

"The quiet. Something's going to happen. I just feel it."

Rob stood there a couple of minutes longer trying to understand what Jack was feeling, but there was nothing except the quiet. Finally he said, "Jack, do you sense that the static noise is going to begin? Is that what you're waiting for?"

"Brilliant deduction, Einstein! When we were here earlier and it turned quiet like this, some serious shit happened, and if it's going to happen again, I want another look."

Giving back some of the sarcasm he had just received he said, "Listen, Dick Tracy, there's no vacuum feeling. Or don't you remember that the last time it became quiet like this, the vacuum feeling followed shortly thereafter?"

"Yeah, I remember that. But doesn't it seem interesting to you that in the eight to ten minutes we've been here, absorbing the quiet, we haven't heard one sound of any kind whatsoever, except the noise that we're making?"

That got Rob to thinking maybe Jack was onto something, and they sat in stone silence for another ten minutes when Rob finally said, "I think that this is just one of those weird times. I don't think anything is going to happen, because I still have no sense at all of a vacuum feeling. Do you?"

With that, Jack started up the Formula, and to Rob it sounded like he put the thumb throttle to the handlebar. When he looked up he saw him cutting a fast trail down the Harris Pasture Road. He did his best to catch up to him, but the only thing that he got close to was the dissipating cloud of snow that Jack had left behind. He finally laid eyes on him just as he was turning left onto Kennebago Settlement Road, and Rob, catching up, pulled alongside of him as he went by the front of the camp.

* * *

Gary Wilcox, a delivery driver with the Rangeley Building Supply Company was just pulling out of the driveway as they approached. When Gary looked to his left to see if there was any traffic heading his way, he saw Rob and Jack and waved to them. They waved back as he continued to make a right turn to head out to Route 16.

As soon as they had the sleds parked in front of the shed, Eileen and Nancy came bursting out of the camp, and the first thing that Rob and Jack noticed was the shotguns in their wives' hands. The next thing that they noticed was that neither one of them had a coat or boots on, and it was very obvious that they were extremely agitated, or excited, or both. Both of them were talking loudly, very fast, and at the same time. Neither Jack nor Rob could understand a word that either one of them was saying. Jack tried to tell them to slow down, but neither one could hear him because they were trying to out talk each other. Finally Jack yelled, "HOLD IT! Will the two of you please shut up!?" And they did. Then in a much calmer voice he said, "What's the matter, Nancy?"

"Jack!" She paused to take a breath and said, "It happened while you were gone, and it happened more than once!"

Rob said, "What happened, and why was Gary Wilcox just here?"

Eileen blurted out in an incredulous sounding voice, "Didn't you guys see the window when you rode past the camp!? I mean, come on! It sticks out like a sore thumb!"

Rob looked over at Jack, shrugged his shoulders as if to say, "Did you?"

Eileen was in no mood for his shenanigans and yelled, "The two of you are about as observant as a blind man. Look!"

Both Rob and Jack looked to where she was pointing and Jack was the first to speak. "How come he boarded up the front picture window?"

Eileen blurted out, "Because your wife blew the damn thing out when she tried to kill some weirdo pointing something that looked like a handgun at us through the window!"

Rob put his hand on Eileen's arm saying, "Come on. Cool down."

Nancy cut in saying, "Yeah, that about covers it, and Gary will be back tomorrow with a new window. He didn't have any windows already made up that could replace it, so he has to make one to specs, and he just didn't have time to get it done today."

Nancy hesitated just for a second and Eileen jumped back into the conversation saying, "That's right. So we had him board up the window to keep out the cold until tomorrow." Suddenly her teeth started chattering and Rob took her by the arm saying, "Why don't we go inside where it's nice and warm, and the two of you can tell us everything that happened."

Eileen and Nancy sat down at the kitchen table, taking the chairs closest to the picture window. They had been sitting there for a couple of minutes while the guys changed out of their snowmobile gear, when Nancy casually looked out the window and said, "Look at how that birdfeeder is swinging in and out from the window." Still looking out the window she lifted her glass to take a sip on her new margarita, and then she said, "I wonder why the birdfeeders that you've got hanging on the wire between the two birch trees aren't moving?"

Eileen kept her eye on the feeder, but chose not to make any comments. She could see that Nancy was getting ready to say something else, but Jack saved the day when he came into the kitchen and sat down at the table next to his wife. He was about ready to ask them what had happened while they were gone, when Rob came in and said, " Jack, you want that Corona and shot of Jose Cuervo Gold now?"

"Thought you'd never ask!" Then turning his attention back to Nancy he said, "So tell me, what went on here while we were gone?"

Rob was getting the Coronas, pieces of lime and shots of tequila as he listened to Nancy and Eileen tell Jack about everything that had happened. When it came to the part about the window, Eileen jumped in and told them all the details that she remembered, including her stunned reaction when Nancy blew out the front window, and the fact that they found nothing except broken glass in the driveway when they went outside to see if the stranger might be lying there in a pool of his own blood. Everyone remained quiet after she stopped talking, and it seemed like they were letting her story sink in. Finally Rob picked up his bottle of Corona, drank down the last couple of swallows, and as he was getting up from the table said, "Want another pair, Jack?"

"Sounds good to me. You know, I can understand why there was no blood on the ground when Nancy shot out the front window. The pellets probably lost all of their punch when they hit the glass, and at that close range they were probably in a pretty tight cluster. So unless Nancy was right on target with that stranger, the glass would have blown out and away from him. And it's useless for us to go out there now to try to figure out what happened, because with Gary walking around out there boarding up the window, coupled with these two pussy footing around in the same area, it would be a miracle if all of that guy's tracks weren't obliterated." He paused for a few seconds to see if anyone had anything to say, and when no one spoke up he continued, "What do you think, Rob, should we go out and take a look?"

"First of all, there's not enough light left to clearly see any tracks, and second of all, I think you're right about his tracks being obliterated, so it would be a big waste of time. What are your thoughts on what happened when they emptied their shotguns into that circle of air?"

"I haven't had enough time to think that one through yet, but I'll come up with something before we go to bed."

Rob set a Corona and a shot of tequila in front of Jack along with two pieces of lime. Jack picked up the saltshaker while he was licking the top of his left hand between his thumb and forefinger, shook some salt on his hand, grabbed the piece of lime, picked up his shot of tequila and said, "Good Health," and slowly sipped the tequila down.

Rob picked up his glass and said, "Yeah, I'll drink to that, as long as we don't ruin our health drinking to each other's *good* health." And then, like Jack, he slowly sipped his tequila down, savoring the taste and the burn. "Jack, there's something else that I need to tell you. Remember earlier when I was in the shed, and you came out and asked me to show you where the depressions in the snow were?"

"Sure."

"Well, shortly before you came out, something didn't seem quite right to me. I was standing near the window in the back of the shed when everything got very quiet. Then a few seconds went by and I started feeling the vacuum sensation, and low-and-behold, the static noise began just moments later. I turned around and walked to the front of the shed, opened both of the doors and stood between them looking all around to see if there was a circle of shimmering air around somewhere. All of a sudden I experienced a new feeling, actually a sense of weightlessness. I looked at my feet and I was a couple of inches off the floor. I don't recall how long I was like that, but when you came out and let the storm door slam shut, the static noise stopped and I dropped to the floor like a rock." He did not know why, but he did not share his feeling that he had been forcefully propelled to the floor.

Everybody sat there, very quiet, just looking at each other, and Jack recalled that Rob had told him about a tingling sensation that he had felt when Rudy disappeared from behind him. He got a pencil and a piece of scrap paper off of the counter behind him, and then he wrote down some notes to refer to later.

The silence was broken when they heard the storm door open, followed by the knocker banging on the inside door. No one moved until the knocker banged a second time. Rob was just starting to get up off his chair when the front door opened, and Thad stuck his head in saying, "Anybody home?" As soon as he saw the four of them sitting at the table, he opened the door all the way and Ginger forced her way through in front of him. He had a huge grin on his face as he walked up to Jack with his big hand out saying, "It's been a while, Jack! How're you doing?"

"I'm doing fine, Thad. How about you?"

"Better than nothing."

Getting up from the table Rob said, "Grab a chair, Thad, and I'll put some coffee on for you, or would you prefer some Crown Royal and water?"

He thought just for a second or two before saying, "Coffee's fine." Then he wrapped his huge hand around the top of the chair at the end of the table, sat down and made himself right at home.

As Rob was walking over to the cabinet to get the coffee and the percolator out, he said to Jack, "Why don't you start bringing him up to date with what's happened this afternoon?"

Jack looked over at Rob with a questioning look on his face, and Rob quickly knew what that was all about. "Yeah, everything, including what happened with those clowns up at the Seven Gulpers."

Jack nodded an "OK," looked at Thad as he picked up his bottle of Corona to take a swallow and said, "I think that you're goin' to find this mighty interestin'."

While he made the coffee, he listened to everything that Jack, Nancy and Eileen told Thad. Once all the details about the front window had been shared with Thad, Rob finally spoke up and said, "There's one more piece in the story that has to be told." He sat back down at the table, looked directly at Thad and took his time telling him about his experience when he went out to the shed to be alone for a few minutes. He intentionally left out the fact that he had *wanted* to be alone. When he finished, there was no more conversation. Except for the sound of the coffee pot in its final throes of perking, the house became very quiet. Everyone felt a sense of foreboding as to what they might be facing in the days to come.

Once the pot stopped perking, you could hear the sound of a pin drop in the camp for the better part of five minutes. But then the loud jangle of Ginger's dog tags as she scratched at a bothersome itch on her neck broke everyone's reverie. Slowly they all looked around the table at each other, perhaps to see if anyone had been watching them while they were in La La Land. Rob ended the silent inquiry when he got up from the table to get Thad his coffee, and as he was pouring it into a large mug, Eileen got up to get the half and half out of the fridge.

Thad was taking a third sip of his coffee when Jack came up with an idea, and looking across the table at him he said, "Rob told me that you had an EEG done on you yesterday."

Thad looked over at Rob as if to say, "Now what in the hell did you have to go and tell him that for?" But he kept quiet and looked back at Jack saying, "Yep! Sure did."

"I also understand that the doctor gave you a copy of it. Would you mind if I have a look at it?"

"Don't mind at all. Do you know how to read one?"

"I know how to read electricity, and an EEG is nothing more than a graph of the electrical charges emitted by your brain. Look, this is my main interest. I'm planning on conducting some tests tomorrow, and if I'm lucky enough to record the data that I need, then I want to make a comparison between your EEG and the graphs that I intend to generate from those tests."

That statement caught Thad's interest and he asked, "What kind of tests are you going to conduct?"

"I brought some electronic equipment with me that will measure the electrical pattern of the static that we've all been hearing. Of course that's assuming that I'm lucky enough to be in the right area at the right time to record it. Hopefully it will be there for more than just a minute or two. I need to lock onto it long enough to get a good reading on my instruments."

Thad took a sip of his coffee and said, "Well, just hold on for a minute or two, and I'll go out to my truck and get it."

While Thad was on his way out the door Rob said, "What've you got on your mind, Jack?"

"If we happen to be fortunate enough to be in an area tomorrow where this static phenomenon makes an appearance, we just might have enough luck on our side to see it trying to pull some unfortunate animal into it. I'd like to be able to record everything from A to Z. Ultimately, I would like to know if the electrical field in the circle of air changes from the time that it begins to focus on an animal to the time that it gets sucked in. What I'm trying to find out is whether or not the frequency remains constant from beginning to end. If it does, then I might have a handle on whether this circle of distorted air acts similarly to an electromagnet, to draw whatever it is targeting into it. The other theory I have, and I may still come up with more, is that perhaps the frequency of the circle of air does not change to match the brain wave, but perhaps something on the other side of the shimmering air is trying to lock onto the pattern of the electromagnetic radiation emanating from the animal's aura. I don't know that much about the magnetic field of an aura right now, but I do know that there is one, and I'm sure that given an hour or two, I can learn all that I need to know."

Rob had been listening very intently, and he had a lot of confidence in his friend's electronic knowledge, but he had a doubting look on his face and said, "That sounds like a serious reach to me, Jack."

"Well, how's this for a serious reach?" But he never got to continue with the statement because Thad came back into the camp in a dither.

Jack was the first to notice that he was very red in the face and said, "What's the problem Thad?"

"Somebody's been in my truck! Nothing's gone, but nothing's the way that I left it when Ginger and I came in here. And what's really strange is this EEG. It was all folded up nice and neat in this envelope, and I had the envelope in my center console. But when

I opened up the door to my truck, everything was out of the console, and my EEG was spread out across the seat."

Rob and Jack both looked at each other, and as if they had read each other's mind, they both said at the same time, "I'll bet one of our friendly leisure suit visitors is responsible for that."

By the look on Thad's face, Jack knew that he was not sure what they were talking about, and that was confirmed when he said, "What visitors are you talking about? The ones that Eileen and Nancy saw?"

Nancy piped in and said, "Yeah, you have the right ones."

"Why in the hell would they be interested in *my* EEG?"

Jack jumped back into the conversation and said, "Because if I'm right, Thad, they are locking onto the brain waves of the animal, person, or whatever they want to capture, and they're using that electrical pattern somehow to pull them into that circle of distorted air. That's just a theory, and I could be way out in left field. But hopefully I'll be lucky enough tomorrow to get some data that will help us understand more about this phenomenon."

While they were talking, Ginger got up off the living room rug, walked over to the front door and barked twice, which immediately got everybody's attention.

Thad started chuckling as he said, "Don't get yourselves all worked up, that's just her "I want to go out" bark. Anyway, I think it's time for me to mosey up the road. It's almost suppertime. Jack, you want me to leave that EEG with you?"

"I'd appreciate that, Thad. I'll give it back to you to tomorrow evening, okay?"

"That's fine, and if you don't give it back to me, that's fine too. I don't have any use for it. I could look at that thing until the cows come home, and I still wouldn't know what it's trying to tell me. See ya' all tomorrow."

* * *

As soon as Thad and Ginger had walked out the door, Rob went over to the coffee table, picked up his Sony digital camera and said to Jack, "I'm going to take a few minutes to download this into the computer. I'm kind of anxious to take a look at those pictures that we took at the beaver pond today. You gonna stay here with the women, or come with me?"

"First, I'm gonna help myself to another one of your Coronas, and then I'll be right with you."

"Sounds good to me. Why dontchya get me one also, and while you're at it you can bring me a shot of tequila too. I'm not in the mood for just *half* a drink."

By the time Jack walked into Rob's office with their drinks, Rob had already downloaded the pictures into the computer. As Jack set the drinks down, Rob was in the midst of selecting the first picture from the list.

As the picture loaded onto the screen he said, "Look at this, Jack! This is incredible!"

They both were staring at the last picture that Rob had taken of the deer at the beaver pond, just as it was being pulled into the circle of air. Only the last third of the deer was visible, and they could clearly see that the deer's rear legs were still positioned to stop its forward movement. The circle of distorted air was barely visible, but they could absolutely make out the outer perimeter.

Jack's mind was banging out one possible scenario after another to explain what he was seeing, and nothing made any sense to him. Frustrated he said, "I wonder why we can't see beyond the surface of the distorted air? It would seem to me that if you are at the correct angle, you should be able to see the deer going all the way through the wavering surface. It's not like we were at a 90° angle from the deer, we were almost at a 15° angle when it penetrated that ball of air, which should have given us a clear view of the entire animal. But you know, everything happened so fast, I couldn't tell you if I saw more of the deer as it went into it or not. However, the more that I think about it, your camera's probably telling the right story."

While listening to everything that Jack was saying, a thought came to his mind and he said, "Jack, let me ask you a question. Do you believe in extraterrestrials?"

"Do I believe in them? Yes." And then he paused for a few seconds before continuing, "In my heart I do. But in my mind? Well, that's another matter. In my field, if you can't prove that something exists, then most likely it doesn't. And I can't prove that they exist. Can you?"

Rob was on the verge of answering his question, and expanding the conversation to who knows where, but decided against it. Instead he said, "You missed your calling, Jack. You should have been a politician, because that's exactly the kind of an answer that you'd get from one of those people." He paused for a bit, trying to make up his mind if he should bring up exactly what he had been doing out in the shed earlier, and finally said, "You know that I have some psychic abilities, don't you?"

"Yeah, I know. I remember some of the things that you told me in the past that turned out to be right on the mark, and I also remember that at the time I thought that you were off your rocker. However, I've also seen you miss the mark by a mile!"

"Well, I go back to my opening statement, I have *some* psychic abilities, and I don't know if I can improve on them or not, but according to some books that I've read, it's something that you can consciously work on to improve. Maybe someday I'll do that, but for now just let me say that when I was in the shed earlier, just before that static noise phenomenon lifted me off my feet, I received a message that I was going to meet some people soon. And I was also told that they would make a statement that might make me believe that they are from the other side. Do you suppose when that guy that I had pinned down with my knee said that they were from another dimension, he was trying to con me into believing that he was from the other side?"

"I don't know what to think about that. But I have some other theories that I'm gonna run by you since the women aren't around. First, let me try to educate you a little bit. All material bodies, including gases, liquids, and solids have magnetic properties, but those properties are very weak in some of them. Many different phenomena regarding magnetic properties have been observed, and through many scientific experiments, today they are completely understood."

He paused to look at Rob to see if he had any questions, and when all he got back was a blank stare, he got a little facetious and said, "Now that you've obviously understood everything that I have said, I'll tell you this: I'm going to try to determine what physical phenomena these visitors are attempting to focus on before they pull an animal into the circle of shimmering air. An interesting point to consider is that animals are similar to people in this respect. No two people are alike when their electrical attributes are analyzed, and neither are animals. And think about this, the electrical pulse of either an animal or person's aura is as unique as a fingerprint, or even a voice pattern for that matter."

Rob cut in saying, "So how does all this knowledge actually help us in this situation?"

"Listen, Rob, for all I know, maybe the static sound is creating a gravitational field that is greater than the gravitational pull of the earth, then when the gravitational pull is strong enough, the animal that they are focusing on is pulled into the circle of distorted air. If I apply that same theory to the appearance of the strangers, they would lessen the gravitational pull from within the circle so that the earth's gravity would pull the stranger through the circle."

Rob leaned toward Jack a bit and said, "I understand the concept - not that I understand *how* they do it. You started to mention something about an animal's aura when Thad came back into the camp with his EEG. How about finishing that thought?"

"For years now, scientists have been studying the electro-magnetic radiation from an aura, and the frequency of the aura's ultraviolet light. Based upon what I have learned from those studies, I have another theory. Perhaps this circle of shimmering air is trying to match the electromagnetic radiation from the animal's aura, or maybe it's trying to match the frequency of the ultraviolet light coming from the aura. But if they're trying to match the frequency that's coming from the ultraviolet light of the aura, that can be extremely difficult because that frequency can change rapidly. For an example, the frequency of ultraviolet light emanating from an animal's aura could be in one range when it is not threatened. But the moment that it feels threatened, that frequency would change dramatically. So I don't think that it's the frequency of the ultraviolet light that they're trying to match, simply because it's way too difficult. So I'd have to go back to my other theories of either the gravitational pull or the magnetic radiation coming from the animal's aura."

"This is all very interesting, Jack, but how do you plan to try to prove which theory is correct?"

"Neither theory maybe correct. Be that as it may, I plan to set up some of my instruments on your tag-along sled to measure the frequency spectrum of the static sound that we hear coming from the circle of distorted air, and once we have determined the frequency, and assuming that it remains steady, I'll use directional receivers to determine if the static sound is actually coming from the circle of air. But the main factor that I want to prove to myself is that the circle of distorted air is an electrical field, as I suspect. If I am correct, then I need to know two other components of the shimmering air, its magnetic flux and magnetic flux density. With that information, I can set up a procedure for us to implement that will hopefully help us to develop a decent understanding of the phenomena that we've been seeing. Give me a pad of paper, Rob."

Rob handed him the pad and watched him as he wrote down the different phenomenon that was described to him along the left-hand side of the page: appearance of circle of air > quiet > vacuum feeling > static > appearance and disappearance of tracks > appearance and disappearance of people, animals or birds, etc. Then he wrote next to each of the phenomenon the events as he recalled them, and he did not care if they were in the proper order or not. One page was not enough, and he ended up with four pages side-by-side, which allowed him to get a complete mental image of everything that he wrote down. Being able to scan back and forth between the pages helped him develop a clearer picture.

Rob was beginning to get restless just sitting there watching him, and he broke Jack's concentration when he grabbed his empty beer bottle and shot glass. He didn't like the nasty look that Jack shot at him, but Rob still gave him an apologetic look and said, "I'll go get us another round while you think this through," and when there was no objection he headed for the kitchen.

The ladies were still sitting at the kitchen table, and it looked as if they had a fresh batch of margaritas going. Getting a grin on his face that went from ear to ear he said, "Hope you guys don't have any negative affects from those drinks tomorrow. I think you're way ahead of Jack and me."

The dazed, stupefied look they gave back to him told him that he was right on target, and he was pretty sure they were going to be making deals with God in the morning. Feeling the pangs of hunger, he went on to say, "I don't think it's a good idea to drive into town for something to eat. We've all been enjoying ourselves way too much. What do we have in the fridge that's easy to make up?"

Eileen tried to focus her glassy eyes on him as she said, "I've got hot dogs and buns in the freezer, and some B & M baked beans in the pantry. That'll do for tonight, right?"

"That's a winner for me. I'll fire up the grill in about 30 minutes. Would you thaw out the dogs and buns please?"

The girls went back to talking without acknowledging his request, and Rob continued pouring the second shot of tequila. As he was putting the bottle of Jose back into the liquor cabinet, he took another look at the women and was about to remind them to take the stuff out of the freezer, but then thought better of it. They had been sipping enough of those margaritas to cop an attitude if he brought it up again. Then he thought about doing it himself, but quickly discarded that idea when his male chauvinist side took over. Ultimately, he picked up the shots and brought them and the beers back to his office. He set the drinks on the desk near Jack and said, "I'll be right back. I want to put the TV on to see if there's anything in the evening news about this "phenomenon" business."

He did not really expect to hear anything about the sightings, since the closest TV news station is in Bangor, which as the crow flies, is more than 100 miles from Baldwin Plantation. He also knew that it was not likely anyone who had seen the circle of distorted air would have taken the risk to call the TV station to report it. He could just imagine what their rationalization process would be. Number one: Who in their right mind would believe their story? And number two: Public embarrassment when they were labeled by the news media as a nut case.

He turned on the TV, set the channel selector to two, and the moment that he could hear the newscaster's voice, he cranked the volume up loud enough so that he could clearly hear what was being said by the newsperson all the way in his office. His stomach was having a serious hunger conversation with him, and the tequilas and beers didn't help much, except to exacerbate the hunger pangs. And as he thought about the tequila and beer waiting for him in his office, he knew that he truly did not want any more, but he knew damn well that he could not bring himself to pour them down the sink either. He gave a longing look toward the kitchen before he grudgingly turned around to join Jack.

It was almost near the end of the newscast, and Jack was still slowly scanning the four sheets of paper, over and over again, waiting for the procedure to trigger something in his mind that would help him find the answer that he was looking for. Rob's mind went back to the TV as he heard an advertisement end and the news anchor person say, "And a closing story: While returning to Bangor from a business meeting that he had today in Lancaster, New Hampshire, a local pilot noticed what looked like a circle of shimmering air about 500 feet below him as he was flying over the Rangeley Lakes area. He said that in all his years of flying that route, he had never seen anything like it. He said that he circled around to go back to get a better look, and when he did he lost sight of it, and was unable to find it again. When asked if he thought it might have been a UFO, he declined to make any comment."

"Did you hear that, Jack?"

"Hear what?"

He told Jack what the news commentator had said, and Jack promptly inserted the information into the notes in front of him. He took a long pull on his beer, set it down and said, "Rob, now that I've taken the time to study these notes and let my mind digest the data, I have some thoughts. Number one, I'm leaning very heavily toward the idea that it is the aura that these strangers are focusing on. It is a good possibility that when you hear the static and feel the vacuum sensation, it is at that exact point in time that the manipulators of this phenomenon are using something like a directional antenna to locate and lock onto a specific aura. The only thing that makes sense to me right now with what I know is this; I think that these leisure suit people already know everything about their target that they need to know, and they got that information from previous encounters with it. Armed with that assumption, the rest is easy. When they are ready to take whatever their quarry is, to wherever, they simply feed the information that they have on its aura into a computer. At that point I think everything is automated. The computer is either tied into, or part of, the equipment that is employed to find the aura. Once it does, it maneuvers this circle of shimmering air to wherever the unlucky critter is."

Rob cut in saying, "I follow your thinking. That's why this circle of air is seen in different places."

"Right! And they've got to be using some kind of a device that allows them to control the effects of gravity. Somehow they must alter the earth's gravitational pull. Maybe it's as simple as using an electromagnet, or something like it, and that's how the object gets sucked into the circle, just like what happened to the deer at the beaver pond." He paused for a few seconds because something in his subconscious mind was nagging at him. He leaned closer to his notes, hoping that he might see something that would break it loose, and finally said, "Now that I think about it, Eileen and Nancy said that every time they heard the static noise and felt the static cling of their clothes and the static pull on their hair, that it got stronger each time. And let's add one more thing to that. I'm sure you remember telling me that when Rudy disappeared from behind you, that you felt a tingling sensation all over your body, right?"

"Sure, I remember that."

"Well I think that the tingling sensation you experienced was caused when these so-called visitors had locked onto Rudy's aura. Rudy was only a foot or so behind you, right?"

Rob thought about exactly where his tracks had ended behind him and said, "I think that it was less than a foot."

"Hmmm, then I'm certain that the tingling that you felt was caused by the gravitational beam that they used to snatch Rudy, or *whatever* it is that they're using to change gravity. Another thing, now that we saw the deer get snatched at the beaver pond, and watched the hawk get shot out of the circle of air, I'm positive that the 'whump' that you heard just before Ginger found Rudy, had to be the same kind of a deal. It takes no genius to see that Rudy doesn't have wings, so when he was ejected from the circle of air like the hawk was, he would have fallen into the snow, and there you have your 'whump'."

Jack paused to gather his thoughts and Rob cut in, "This all seems to make sense to me, Jack, but where are you headed with it?"

Looking at his notes he continued, "I'm not finished yet. I think the specific reason that the stranger showed up in your front yard was to use one of their hand-held instruments at close range. I say that because in my notes I noticed that the women made a statement that the stranger had something in his hand that he was pointing at them. I think that these schmucks were having a difficult time trying to get a good match on Nancy's aura from the circle of shimmering air, so they sent that guy to get a close-up reading."

Rob was staring at Jack with a questioning look on his face and said, "Why do you say just Nancy, why not Eileen too?"

"Because I'll bet you dollars-to-donuts that they've already got all the data that they need on her aura, and it's neatly stored in their computer. And why do I say that?" Without waiting for Rob to answer he said, "I'll tell you why. Because Eileen has had more than one visit by these characters, and more than one static cling session, and when you think about it, so have you!"

"You're forgetting somethin', Jack, according to my calculations, Nancy has also."

"Oh crap! Yeah, you're right." He thought about that for a bit and continued, "This shit really ain't no good, pal! Do we keep this info to ourselves, or do we dare share it? And keep this in mind, if we share it with our wives, we're never going to find an answer to what's been goin' on around here. I don't know about Eileen's reaction, but I'm positive that I know what Nancy's reaction will be, and I've had too much to drink to fly tonight."

Rob was quiet for a little while before saying, "If you're right, it's pretty damned scary. But we've got a few options, and telling the women right now isn't one of them. I'll tell you one thing for sure, we shouldn't even consider leaving them alone."

"You're absolutely right. We'll have to think about that one. Well, anyway, if we can get lucky and get near one of those circles of air again tomorrow, I'll be able to get a pretty good handle on whether or not I'm on the right track."

They both were quiet for several minutes, thinking about everything that had been discussed. Rob looked at Jack saying, "We don't have to leave the women alone tomorrow while we go out on the trail, but before we talk about my idea, I have a question. Why do you think the circle of air disappeared when they shot at it?"

He thought for a few moments before answering, and said, "I think that they disrupted the electrical field. Maybe it was set to have living matter pass through it, and if that's the case, maybe it couldn't handle the pellets flying through it. I really don't have a handle on that yet, but shooting it was an effective measure, and I think that we should keep that in mind for future use." He paused when he got an idea and then continued, "Rob, are you thinking of some kind of an errand for the women to do in Rangeley, or maybe even Farmington?" And once again without waiting for an answer he continued, "I kind of like the Farmington idea better, because it's further away, and it would take them a lot more time, which means that we would have more time out on the trail."

"That's a good idea, Jack, but I like this one better. I told you about Len, Bubba and Stormin. You know, the snowmobilers that I met in the Four Seasons yesterday. I also told you that Len offered their help when he called me this morning. Two of those guys would give Arnold Schwarzenegger second thoughts about tangling with them, and the third guy is an intimidator of a different kind." He intentionally paused for effect, and when he did he developed a smirk on his face as he said, "He's a lawyer, so his wits should make up for his lack of brawn. Besides, he seemed pretty sincere about offering their help. What do you think?"

"It's all right with me. At least we'll know where they're at. But make sure that you let these guys know about the effect that the shotgun pellets had on the circle of air."

Rob rolled out of bed at 04:55 hours and went directly to the kitchen to make the coffee. He was kind of surprised that Jack wasn't up and about, because he thought that he had heard him go into his office during the night. The coffee pot had started to perk when he leaned forward to look out the window over the kitchen sink. There was just enough light to let him see several deer standing in the birch trees, waiting for their morning feeding. He was turning around to go to the bathroom to brush his teeth and shave when he found himself nose to nose with Jack.

"Hey, Jack, good morning. A little close, aren't you?

He had no humor in his voice at all when he said, "I didn't expect you to move just yet. I was getting close enough to try to see what you were studying out there."

Rob took a closer look at his friend. His face looked very drawn, a sure telltale sign that he did not get any sleep last night, and then said, "I thought that you were up and about. Where the hell were you?"

"I was sitting on the couch over in the far corner of the living room, and you just walked right by me without even glancing my way when you came out of your bedroom."

"How come you were sittin' in the dark?"

"Sometimes I can think better in the dark, especially if there aren't any distractions."

"I don't need to ask you what you were thinking about. Get any answers?"

"I'm close, but not just yet."

"Well, I can see that you're backing away from me. It's that bad huh?"

Jack's face finally broke into something that could almost be interpreted as a smile and said, "Yeah! You've definitely got morning breath!"

Getting a smile of his own Rob said, " Well I've got news for you, dragon breath, you ain't no prize yourself. Tell you what, I'm going to brush my teeth and shave. The coffee will be done before I'm finished. Help yourself."

* * *

Jack was sitting at the kitchen table making some notes on a yellow pad, and his first cup of coffee was two thirds gone when Rob came back into the kitchen. He didn't move his head, he simply rolled his eyes up to lock onto Rob's and said, "I thought you got lost. I was just getting ready to send the Mounties after you."

"Yeah, Yeah. I decided to shave and then, what the hell! Are you writing a book or something?"

Jack let out a genuine laugh and said, "Hey, pal, I didn't ask *you* anything. What is this? You got a guilty conscience or something?"

Rob got a grin on his face, shot him the birdie and went to the kitchen counter to get his cup of coffee.

"By the way, Rob, I looked out into the birches a little while ago, and I must've seen a dozen deer out there looking back in at me. I think they're either begging, or giving you one real big hint."

He walked over to the window and said, "Yeah, there's a bunch of 'em out there all right." Then sitting down at the kitchen table with Jack he continued in a conversational tone, "Actually, I feel like I need a few sips of my coffee before I give them their feed." Picking up his cup, he took a long slow sip, and then looked over at Jack saying, "But then again, I may as well get it over with."

"You know something, Rob?"

"What's that?"

"You're acting more and more like a woman everyday."

* * *

In just a few minutes he was back upstairs with the bucket of feed in his left hand. He set it on the floor near the coat rack, grabbed his coat and slipped it on while he walked over to the kitchen table for one more sip of his coffee.

A short while later the storm door slammed with a resounding crash - an announcement to the deer that it was time for breakfast. Jack waited about a minute before looking out the kitchen picture window, and he nonchalantly sipped his coffee as he watched Rob's shadowy figure pour five small piles of feed, spacing them about four feet apart.

After a few minutes, Jack decided to get up from the table and walk closer to the window for a better look. As he stood there watching him pouring ten more piles of feed, he wished there was enough light for him to snap a couple of pictures. A few of the deer were getting so close to Rob that if he stepped back just one step, he would have bumped into them.

Ten minutes had elapsed by the time that he came back into the house. After pouring some more coffee into his mug to warm up the dregs, the two of them sat at the kitchen table quietly sipping their brew, absorbing the peace and tranquility as they watched the shadowy shape of the deer amicably devour the piles of Course 14 feed. Suddenly there was a blinding flash of light.

His body reacted to the blinding surprise, nearly knocking him out of the chair. Jack was trying to keep himself from falling over as he yelled, "What the heck was that!?"

"I don't know! But if I didn't know better I'd say that it was lightning. However, that doesn't make one bit of sense to me."

They both kept staring out the window to see if it would happen again, but there was nothing, and after about ten minutes they could see that the deer were gone. Looking back at his friend he said, "Jack, did you see the deer leave?"

"No. I was so blinded by that flash of light that I couldn't have seen a tank make its way through your back yard. It's my guess that the deer got spooked and ran off. But if you've got any feed left out there, I'll guarantee you that they'll be back. By the way, I need a few things from your cellar. Why don't you grab your cup of coffee and come on down with me. I want to take a look through all your stash. Maybe I'll get lucky and find everything that I need to secure my electronic equipment to your tag-along sled."

* * *

Rob's basement was loaded with a sundry of different gadgets and parts, but as many as he had down there, it was nothing compared to what Thad had lying around in his camp and shed. And there was another major difference. Everything in Rob's basement was well organized. If he could not see what was in a container without opening it, the container had a label on the outside detailing everything that was inside. In spite of the fact that everything was very well organized, they still spent the better part of an hour rummaging around before coming back upstairs for another cup of coffee.

As they sat back down at the kitchen table Jack said, "I think that you've got most of what I need to mount my electronic equipment onto your tag-along, and if not, I'm sure Thad does."

"Yeah, I'm sure he does. But finding what you need at his place may take more time than it's worth."

"Why's that?"

"For the simple reason that he doesn't organize his treasures very well. As a matter of fact, it's not organized at all, especially in the shed. I'm not kidding when I say that everything in the shed is in one big, massive pile, and if what you need happens to be in his shed, God help you. And I'll tell you why. Because there's no way of knowing where it will be in that mess. If luck isn't with you, it could end up being on the bottom of the pile, and you'll end up killing at least an hour, and maybe even more."

"You've got to be exaggerating big time! You've told me about this before, but it can't really be that bad! Can it?"

"Nope. It's worse!"

There was a momentary silence that was filled by the sound of Rudy's toenails clicking on the wood floor as he walked into the kitchen. Rob turned his head toward the sound and said, "Hey, Toot-man! How ya doing, buddy!"

Rudy walked over to his master and pushed his head between Rob's legs, which was his way of saying, "OK, OK, now you can scratch my back." Rob reached down to oblige his old friend for a couple of minutes while Jack filled their cups to the brim with steaming hot coffee. The moment that he stood up to take his coffee mug from Jack, Rudy went to the front door and stood there looking back at them.

"Hold on, Toot, I'll take you for a walk in a minute. Want to go with us, Jack?"

* * *

The sun was just coming up and it was a gorgeous Thursday morning. Steam billowed from Rob's mouth as he looked all around and said, "This is a ditto of Monday when Rudy and I took our walk, except then it was a little colder."

They walked down the Kennebago Settlement Road toward the open fields, and when they came to the Harris Pasture Road, all three of them automatically headed toward the beaver pond. The temperature was still well below zero, and Rudy took advantage of the thick crust that Mother Nature had provided on the snowy surface by wandering just about anywhere that he had a mind to.

They had walked about three hundred feet when they came to a logging road that cut off to the left, and suddenly Rudy stopped. Remaining frozen in the same position, he stretched his neck as much as possible to get his nose up as high as he could, and repeatedly sniffed the air all around him. Rob and Jack had stopped on the trail behind him, and neither one of them said a word. Normally Rob would have walked around Toot, and opted to leave him behind do his thing, but for some reason, this time he just stood there watching him. After about two minutes of this behavior, Rudy finally dropped his head and looked at a huge boulder that was about twenty-five feet off of the hard packed trail at their ten o'clock position.

Both of them were intrigued by Rudy's unusual behavior, and since the past few days had been anything but ordinary, Rob wanted to know what the big deal was. Leaning toward Jack he whispered, "Do you mind staying here a bit longer? I want to see what's so interesting to him!"

Jack shrugged his shoulders and said, "Why not?"

Several more minutes went by, and Rudy stayed rooted to the spot, looking at the boulder. Jack and Rob followed his gaze, but they failed to see anything that could hold his attention for so long. The wind was calm and the only sound that they could hear was a few chickadees calling out in the distance. Rob's mind was drifting along with the serenity, and he was just beginning to think that this is why he loved the Maine woods as much as he did, when all that tranquility ended abruptly.

Rob and Jack heard a low and threatening growl come from deep within Rudy's chest. Rob sensed that something bad was about to happen, and bent down to reach for Rudy's collar, but he was too late. Rudy bolted forward and Rob yelled for him to come back, but he knew that it was a futile effort. Toot was stretched right out, running as fast as he could over to the boulder.

Rob and Jack stayed where they were, and watched him with keen curiosity as he circled the boulder several times to the right. Jack's mouth dropped open in surprise when he saw him make almost the same number of revolutions going back to the left. He kept sniffing around the entire area much longer than he would have if it had been a rabbit track, and he did not show any sign that he was getting ready to give up.

After a while Jack got tired of waiting for him and said, "We're just wasting time here. You ready to leave yet?"

"Yeah, all right."

They started to continue on down the trail toward the beaver pond, but Rob was uneasy about leaving Rudy behind. Every few steps he would look back over his shoulder, hoping to see his furry friend running down the trail after them. The fifth time that he turned to look back, he saw Rudy starting to leave, and then go back, and then start to leave again, but then ultimately he stopped his movement altogether, and remained facing the boulder. He stood there motionless, and from a distance, it looked to Rob like he was staring at it.

His curiosity got the best of him and he said, "Hey, Jack, hold on a minute! I want to go back and see if I can figure out what the big attraction is."

He walked back up the trail, and as he left it to head over to Rudy, he estimated that the boulder was about twelve feet high, and he figured that it had about a twenty-foot girth. When he was about ten feet away from it he felt a sensation that put his survival instincts into high gear. Stopping dead in his tracks, he stood fast in one position, just like Rudy, and continually looked in all directions trying to identify what could have activated his sixth sense. After a bit he found himself concentrating very hard on the boulder, and wondered why. It certainly wasn't something he was doing consciously.

His mind came back to Rudy, and as he shifted his gaze to where he had last seen him, he happened to notice that the Tootman had walked out beyond the boulder. He was about twenty to twenty-five feet away at the 11:00 o'clock position. What disturbed Rob most about this whole scene was the fact that he could not remember seeing him move. Rudy was frozen in one position again, only this time he was looking at something up in the trees.

Rob looked up to where Rudy was facing, but all he could see were branches and tree trunks, and could not begin to imagine what would be of interest to Rudy up in a tree. He decided that the only way to find out was to go over and see for himself. He also made up his mind that this time he would not take his eyes off of his old friend. Concentrating one hundred percent on the Tootman, he shifted his weight forward just as Jack came up behind him without making a sound. He put his hand on Rob's left shoulder, which instantly broke his concentration, and scared the living daylights out of him to boot. He spun around on his heel with his heart in his throat. The moment that he laid his eyes on Jack, he instantly felt relief flow though his body. His first impulse was to give Jack a tirade of verbal abuse, but he thought better of it and said, "Thanks for the rush, Jack!"

For a change, Jack seemed very sincere when he said, "Sorry. I didn't realize that you were so engrossed in whatever you were fixating on."

Pointing to where Rudy was standing he said, "I've been watching him for the past three to five minutes, and he hasn't budged from that position. I was just going to see what he's found so fascinating when you took a year or two off of my life."

Still looking very serious Jack said, "Don't let me stop you. Have at it!"

Rudy was still standing in exactly the same position when they walked up alongside of him, Rob to the left and Jack to the right, and neither of them could understand why he did not turn to look at them as they approached. Almost as if on cue, they simultaneously looked up toward where Rudy was gazing. Rob was surprised to see a ledge that was about twenty feet high. He had never seen it before because the trees were hiding it. He scanned every foot of the ledge that he could see from where he was standing, but he couldn't see anything that he thought would be of interest to his furry friend. He reached down and started scratching Rudy's neck as he said, "What's so interestin' up there Toot?" And then turning his attention to Jack he said, "Do you see anything?"

"Nope, and I'm not real interested in walking up there without snowshoes to find out. I have a feeling that the further that we walk into these woods, the thinner the crust will be."

"Yeah, you're probably right. Come on, Toot-man, we've been here long enough." Rudy didn't move a muscle, and it was obvious that he was very reluctant to leave. At last, after a lot of coaxing from Rob and Jack, he followed them back out onto Harris Pasture Road.

As Rob stepped to his left to go around a huge pine tree he said, "Do you think we ought to take a look up on that ledge after breakfast Jack?"

"Yeah. It's probably a pretty good idea."

But neither one of them remembered that intention until much later in the day.

* * *

The three of them crested the hill above the beaver pond just as everything turned stone quiet. Jack quickly turned to Rob with a knowing look on his face and said, "I'm feeling the vacuum sensation. Something's gonna happen!"

He wasn't disappointed. The circle of distorted air appeared directly in front of them, almost at the surface of the pond. Their line of sight to the wavering air was at about a 15° downward angle, and Jack yelled in his loudest whisper, "Rob, I can see past the surface of the shimmering air. Look! Look at that bird in the circle!"

He no sooner got those words out of his mouth when Rudy started barking ferociously. The sound echoed throughout the entire valley, and Jack broke into a nervous laugh as he said, "So much for being quiet."

They never took their eyes off of the object in the circle. It had the physical appearance of a hawk, but there was something very different about it. Its features were far too angular, almost like it was made out of papier-mache, and when it moved its wings, it looked mechanical, like the owl in the "Clash of The Titans." It was visible for only a short period of time. But it was just long enough to distract both of them so they did not see the stranger clothed in a leisure suit, being snatched up into the circle of air out of the pine trees that bordered the left quadrant of the pond. It all happened so quickly that if a person looking at that section of the pond had blinked their eyes, they would have missed the entire event.

Just as their attention shifted from the papier-mache hawk, they noticed the wavering pattern of the air was starting to elongate, and they could see more objects forming in the circle. Slowly those objects materialized into hazy images of several buildings. They both stood there transfixed and amazed by what they were seeing. Amazement rapidly turned into excitement as they watched the scene in the distorted air dramatically change again. The frequency of the waves in the pattern continued to drop until they were about half of what they were before. Now the waves were so elongated that they could see the fuzzy outline of a whole city.

Jack turned to Rob and whispered, "You know what that reminds me of?"

Being just a little cynical Rob said, "Let me guess. It looks to me like the same type of view that we get on a very hazy summer day when we're making our approach to the Portland International Airport."

Jack looked over at Rob, as if he wanted to smack him for being so arrogant, and then said, "Yeah, that's right, smart ass."

They could see several buildings with the same architectural design as would be found in Portland, Maine, but what really had their attention was the gigantic pyramid in the middle of them. Then suddenly, as quickly as the phenomenon had started, it ended, and so did Rudy's murderous barking. The whole event lasted just short of fifteen seconds, but when Rob and Jack recounted the event to others, both of them said that it lasted at least a couple of minutes.

"Holy moly, Jack! Do you believe what we just saw! Did you see that friggin' pyramid?"

Jack gave him a curious look and said, "Yeah, I believe my eyes, but my mind is having a hard time accepting it. Actually, it's in its rationalization mode, it's trying to convince me that what I just saw was nothing more than an elaborate hologram."

"Jack, have you ever been up close to a pyramid?"

"Sure. Nancy and I went to Egypt on vacation about three years back. Why?

"Do you remember if the pyramid that you had seen was as big as the one we just saw?"

Jack thought for a little bit before answering and said, "Now that I think about it, I'd have to say no. The buildings surrounding it were very large structures, at least they appeared that way, and they were definitely dwarfed by the pyramid. Listen, I'd like to head back to camp ... right now! I want to get things ready so that we can get back out here ASAP. We need some meaningful data, otherwise we're never going to get a grip on what's happening around here."

Not yet ready to leave the subject at hand Rob said, "Jack, my instincts tell me that pyramid has something to do with what's going on around here. I don't know why I feel that way, but I feel like I'm one hundred percent on the mark."

Turning around to walk back up the trail Jack said, "I can't argue with what your instincts are telling you. There's been a lot written about the power of a pyramid."

"Yeah, there sure has. Jack, there's something else though. Did you notice that near the top of the distorted air, it had the shape of a ball?

"Yeah, I noticed that."

"Did you also see the partial outline of something that looked like the outer perimeter of a disk at the top?"

He stopped short in his tracks, and Jack stopped right along with him. Both of them just stood there looking each other directly in the eye. "Jack, Eileen and I had a clear view of the disk when we were above it in my Cessna. Actually, we saw the complete disk, and the shape of it reminded me of a dinner plate standing on its edge, and I remember that the concave side was facing the moose. I wonder why we only get to see this when we're looking down on it, and I wonder why we didn't see the whole disk just now?"

"I don't know, Rob. Based upon what you were saying, this thing had a different appearance from different angles when you were viewing it from above. And when you were at the same level, or below the circle of shimmering air, you only saw a shimmering surface that had no pronounced perimeter, but it didn't look like a ball either. You said it definitely looked like a flat surface."

"Yeah, you're right, Jack."

"But maybe that's just an optical illusion. Maybe this disk is in some kind of a force field, and that field is actually what we're seeing when we get a look at it from any place other than from above it. If that's the case, then the ball that we're seeing is actually the force field surrounding it. Anyway, it's a theory, but I just can't seem to come up with the logic to explain the dish, or disk, or whatever you want to call it."

Suddenly Rob blurted out, "That's it, Jack! The force field is the wavering air that we're seeing, and the disk is hidden inside of the shimmering air."

"Maybe. But I'm only saying maybe. I'm not totally convinced that we're on the right track."

Something was nagging at Rob from his subconscious mind, but he just couldn't bring it all the way to the surface. However he knew that it had something to do with the shimmering air.

* * *

Rob had forgotten about Rudy after he had stopped his barking, and took a moment to look around him to see if he was with them. The Toot-man was sitting right at his feet, and Rob was a little surprised to see him looking quizzically back up at him. A thin grin formed on his mouth as he reached down and gave his old friend a gentle pat on the head. He turned to Jack saying, "Hey, it looks like Toot's trying to figure things out too, or maybe he's remembering something and trying to find a way to communicate it to me. What do you think?"

"Hah! I think that you've watched way too many of those Lassie movies. That's what *I* think!"

Rob let that burst of sarcasm go by, and looking back down at his furry friend said, "What's the matter, Toot. Did that sight bring back some memories?"

But Rudy was no longer paying attention to him. He had wandered over to the side of the trail to check something out. As they turned around to head back to camp, Rob yelled, "Come, Toot!"

For a change, Rudy was quick to respond, and when Rob saw him loping up the trail toward him he turned his attention back to Jack. On the way back to camp they talked a lot about what they had seen, and a little about things that they *thought* they had seen. As they turned left onto the Kennebago Settlement Road Jack said, "How about that. We made it all the way out here without seeing anything else that could be classified as supernatural."

Rob was trying to figure out if he was being a little cynical, but finally responded, "Yeah."

What they didn't know was something supernatural *did* happen on the way out, and Rudy was the only one to have seen it. He finally stopped shaking after they had entered the camp driveway.

* * *

The women were still sleeping when they walked back into the camp at 07:45 hours. As Rob rinsed out the coffee cups he said to Jack, "I bet they're making deals with God. What do you think?"

"Well, they were pretty stressed yesterday, and I don't think they gave any consideration to the consequences that they'd probably be facing today. Bring my coffee to your office, would you?"

"Sure. What're you going to do?"

"The occurrence of this phenomenon is all too frequent, and I don't think that they're random. What's more, I'm convinced that there's a real purpose behind each one. On the way back to camp I decided that I should get on the Internet to make some inquiries. We need to know if anything like this is happening anywhere else. Think about this, we've been to the beaver pond three times since Nancy and I arrived, and shit happened twice. Don't you think that the odds of that are pretty astronomical?"

"Since you put it that way, yeah. What's your point?"

"My point is this. Ever since you heard the static and saw the circle of air on Monday, the development of these phenomena has stepped up. Of course the appearance of this phenomenon could have started before you got here, and it could have been happening just as frequently as it is now." He paused for a second and said, "Let me take that thought a step further. It also could be that we merely happen to be in the right place at the right time. But I'll give you my take on this right now. I don't think that's the case."

Rob cut in saying, "Listen, Jack, I don't have any problem with your gut feelings. As a matter of fact, I think that they're pretty damn good, and I've never seen you just jump to a false conclusion."

Jack looked at Rob for a few seconds to see if any hint of a smile or smirk started to surface at the corners of his mouth, and when none did he said, "Thanks for the vote of confidence. What I think is this; perhaps whomever is responsible for this phenomena is running out of time." He could see that Rob did not fully follow the direction of his thinking, so he continued, "Look, I think that they've got a short window of opportunity to create this phenomena, and that is the reason that they're in a big hurry to finish whatever it is that they're doing. What d'ya think about that theory?"

Rob thought for a few seconds before saying, "I don't know what to think about it, Jack. Actually, I think what you just said is so far out in the stratosphere, that I'd have to say you've been chewing on a big piece of peyote!"

Looking up at Rob, Jack said, "That's an interesting observation."

He did not clearly understand what Jack meant and said, "What observation?"

"Well you used the term stratosphere. Maybe the stratosphere is part of the equation in this whole matter."

Turning his attention back to the computer to begin his inquiries, he logged onto Google, one of his favorite search engines. Before he had finished, he used *all* of his favorite search engines. More relieved than disappointed, he found only one bit of news regarding the phenomenon, which happened to be the closing comment made by the WLBZ - TV newscaster on the Bangor station the previous night.

He sat back in his chair, and remained there for almost a minute, just staring at the computer screen while deep in thought. Finally he said, "I'm drawing a big fat zero here, Rob. I keep coming back to only one conclusion that makes any sense. This phenomena must be contained to this geographic area, and the big question is... Why? Why here, and why now?"

* * *

Rob started getting everything together to make pancakes, his breakfast specialty. Everyone that came to visit Rob and Eileen at camp who ended up staying over night usually were treated to a pancake breakfast the next morning. Almost always they raved about how delicious his pancakes were. As soon as the "Mmmmmmm, delicious" statements were over with, he never failed to say that Aunt Jemima pancake mix was his main reason for success. But he would also tell the visitors that he added a few of his own secret ingredients. Even on the occasions that he was coaxed to give up his complete recipe, he always declined.

The women were still sleeping, and Jack decided that they should bribe them to get up. He poured two cups of coffee, and made sure that the brews were prepared just the way that each of them liked it. Rob had just picked up Eileen's cup of coffee from the counter to take it to her, when she came around the corner saying, "That for me?"

Shaking his head from side to side with disbelief he said, "You never cease to amaze me. What makes you so sure that I was bringing this to you?"

With a very coy and knowing smile she said, "Women's intuition."

"I'll tell you what, you've been pulling this on me for years. I'm beginning to believe that your intuition is really that good!"

Looking him in the eye as she took the cup from his hand, she started laughing as she said, "Actually it's no secret at all. This is the cup that I always use, isn't it? And isn't this the cup that you automatically pour my coffee in each time? And you consider yourself to be so smart!"

Jack watched the big grin spread across Rob's face. He knew that he had been had. Jack picked up Nancy's cup of coffee, and as he was walking to the door to head upstairs said, "I'll leave you guys to your word games. Have fun!"

He could still hear them bantering back and forth as he took his time walking up the stairs. He had filled the cup almost to the brim and wasn't in any mood to mop up a mess. When he got to the bedroom, he turned off the hallway light before opening the door, simply because he did not want to blind Nancy with the sudden brightness. To say that he was pleasantly surprised when he walked through the doorway is an understatement. Nancy was on top of the covers in her birthday suit, casually lying there in a very sensual position. The scene that his eyes beheld had been the furthest thing from his mind. What he actually expected to see was a woman with a major hangover. The moment that he saw *that certain look* on her face, he felt his manhood come alive.

Mimicking Mae West she said, "I heard you coming up the stairs, big boy. Do you think that you might be ..." She never had a chance to finish her statement. He had already put down the cup of coffee and was in the process of quickly shedding his clothes.

Rob was mixing the pancake batter and Eileen was sipping her coffee while studying her puzzle, when they heard the unmistakable sounds of sexual pleasure coming from upstairs. They looked at each other, and without even saying a word Eileen picked up the TV remote control. She extended her left arm in Rob's direction, and crooked her index finger to let him know that she wanted his presence while at the same time she pressed the power button. Rob could hear voices coming from the TV as the picture tube warmed up, and without waiting to see what program was on, she cranked up the volume.

She set the remote on the coffee table and turned to face Rob. He felt all of his senses come to life the second that she began to untie the belt to her bathrobe. She had a mischievous look on her face as she slowly pulled it open. Sensual warmth immediately permeated his whole body when he saw that she was wearing nothing underneath. She never took her eyes off of his, and knew that she had his undivided attention. Raising her left leg she let her robe fall all the way open, and then gave him her best *come hither* look. A beaming smile exploded onto his face, and he instantly turned off the griddle. Breakfast had just been put on hold.

* * *

Rob was sitting at the kitchen table sipping his coffee and studying the notes that he and Jack had made last night. He heard the door to the upstairs open, and shortly thereafter Jack and Nancy came walking into the kitchen together. She still had that dreamy look on her face that women tend to get after making love. Looking up at her with a bit of a twinkle in his eye he said, "Good morning, sunshine!"

She replied, "Good morning, yourself. Guess your ever-lovin' must have just given you some sultry moments. You still look flushed."

If he wasn't flushed before, he was now. The bluff worked and the story was told. Looking at Jack he said, "I don't know which one of you guys initiated the throes of passion that we heard, but many thanks to whomever."

She gave him a big toothy grin and said, "You're welcome."

Jack sat down at the table next to him and started looking at the notes closest to him, and Rob said, I've been going over and over these notes to the point that I think I've got them imbedded in my mind, and I don't know any more now than I did last night."

Sliding them over to Jack he looked out the window just in time to see six deer returning to the piles of feed that he had put down earlier. He happened to glance down at the hooves of the lead deer as it walked up to a pile of feed that was only ten feet from the camp, and he was very surprised to see the deer spread its cloves each time it was about to set its hoof down on the snow. Talking to himself more than anything else he said, "So *that's* how they keep themselves from breaking through!"

Jack looked up from the notes and said, "You say somethin'?"

"Yeah. I think that I just learned why the deer don't break through the surface of their trails in the wintertime."

"I can tell that you want to tell me ... soooo?"

Pointing out the kitchen picture window at the deer that was feeding only ten feet from the house he said, "I just watched that deer as it walked up to where it's feeding, and just before firmly setting its hoof on the snow, it spread its cloves to form a web, a deer snowshoe! What d' ya think about that?"

Jack did not look very impressed. Rob's intuition proved to be right when he did not say a word, so he continued talking. "It looked to me like it kept three of its hooves on the snow at once to evenly distribute its weight over the surface."

Jack continued to sit there, just looking at him, and it did not seem like he was ready to make a comment. Rob suddenly felt like he had to defend his statement and said, "Look at it this way, Jack. The deer are simply using the same principal that you and I would use crossing thin ice. You know, to keep from breaking through, you lay down to evenly spread your weight out over the ice, then there are fewer pounds of force per square inch on the surface."

Jack was quiet for a while longer and it was driving Rob crazy.

Finally he said, "It's a good theory, but I'm not sure that I buy it."

"Consider this ... if you and I walk on those same trails after it's warmed up outside ... we break through, and they don't!"

Jack seemed to weigh that statement before saying, "You have a point. Could be you're right."

* * *

"Rob, do you remember when I told you yesterday about my theories regarding the use of gravitational pull and the possibility that they're using the aura as part of the equation?"

"Sure."

"I'm beginning to think that my theory about these people electronically synchronizing with the pattern of a person's aura to pull them into the circle of air is off base. However, I still think that the aura is a definite part of the equation. Do you remember my telling you that no two person's aura are the same, similar to the way everybody's fingerprint is unique?"

"Sure."

"I'm convinced that the signature of the aura is how they're readily able to find their target. What's more, I'm almost certain that they enter the data regarding a particular aura into a computer database, and I firmly believe that the computer operates some kind of a tracking device to locate a specific target, whenever they want it."

Rob cut in and said, "Let me see if I clearly understand what you just said, and I'm gonna use you as an example. I'm working on the assumption that these people were able to get all the data that they need on your aura, and that they have it entered into their computer. Now, let's say that on the third Wednesday of the fourth month of whatever year, they decide that they want to pick you up for interrogation. However, at that exact moment in time you happen to be in your Cherokee flying to Oshkosh, or wherever. Are you saying that they'd be able to find you, and snatch you out of your plane?"

"Yeah, that's pretty close to how I see it."

"Well then, that shoots our theory all full of holes!"

Jack was quiet for a little bit while he thought about that, and then said, "I don't remember saying that this circle of wavering air crap can happen just in this area. However, I do remember saying that it *seems* to be happening only here."

Rob thought about that for a few moments and said, "I guess you're right. But if we draw the conclusion that they can make this happen anywhere, then it won't matter if we vacate this area for greener pastures. When you come right down to it, there are no greener pastures."

"Right! And let me tell you this. I also think that different types of animals, mammals, birds, etc., each have a basic type of aura, but each one has its own characteristics. So if they're looking for a moose, they plug in certain basic data for the search, and if it's deer, it's different basic data. But when it comes to humans, I think that they already have certain people tagged for a trip to the Land of Oz. That's why, my fine friend, certain individuals have more encounters with this phenomenon than others."

"OK, Jack. So what you're telling me is that these motherless twits have just a certain amount of time when they approach an individual to get all the data that they need on his or her aura. Is that right?"

"Yes! But maybe it's not in the same way that you're thinking. Maybe they run out of time because of unexpected circumstances that their quarry creates, either on purpose or accidentally."

Rob looked out the window, and even though several deer were still feeding right in front of him, he did not really see them. Finally he turned to Jack saying, "It's certainly obvious that Eileen and Nancy have had more than their share of encounters, and because of that you seem to think that these schmucks have already gotten a good read on their aura."

"That's true, and if we expand that thinking, it seems that you and the women are the only ones that they appear to be focusing on."

"Why do you include me in that group?"

"If you recall, you told me that when you were checking the tracks left by the deer that Bubba and his friends had seen, you saw a stranger standing by your sled."

"Yeah. So?"

"You didn't let me finish. You told me that you got lightheaded. I'm convinced that when that happened, the stranger was probably pointing the same type of instrument at you that he had been pointing at the women."

Rob was quick to respond saying, "I think that you're way off base. I didn't see him pointing anything at me."

"I understand. But don't you recall telling me that you had to squint in order to see him clearly?" Rob seemed to be thinking about that one so Jack continued with his line of reasoning. "Maybe you just didn't see it, and if I'm right, he was attempting to, or maybe he even succeeded in getting all the data that he needed on your aura."

"If I'm reading you correctly, Nancy, Eileen and I are ripe for plucking, right?"

"Absolutely, if I'm right. But I'm not saying this just to activate your nervous system. What I am saying is that at least this theory gives me a direction to look in once we collect some data from this phenomenon. Of course, that's assuming that it appears near us again. And right now I don't think that getting next to this phenomenon is going to be a big problem."

"Yeah. If we consider what happened at the beaver pond yesterday and today, I have to agree with you on that point, and I think *that's* where we should start. But there's something else that's been bothering me. You remember our discussion earlier about the disk that Eileen and I saw when we were up in my Cessna?"

"Come on, Rob! Just when did you discover that I had signs of Alzheimer's setting in?"

Getting a big smile on his face because he knew that he had produced a *gottcha* on Jack, he said, "I haven't. Not *yet* anyway." He let that sink in only for a moment before saying, "When we were talking about the circle of air looking like a ball at the top, it triggered a memory, however it slipped away before I could get a grip on it. But now I remember."

Rob hesitated and Jack instantly got impatient and said, "Hey! How about spitting it out! What do you remember?"

"Do you recall what it was that you wanted me to show you yesterday?"

Jack thought for a bit and said, "Depressions in the snow." Recognition lit up on his face as he said, "Yeah! They were symmetrically perfect, circular concave depressions. Bingo!"

"Yeah, the force field had to make those depressions. That's how the Wiffle Ball depression was made. Now it's beginning to make sense."

Jack had a look of total concentration on his face and said, "We just have to figure out how that information can be of benefit to us. Why don't we shelve this for now and get that tag-along sled set to go?"

* * *

The women were cleaning up the breakfast dishes as the men headed out to the garage to start assembling the electronic equipment. The garage was nice and "roasty toasty" warm when they walked in and Jack said, "Glad you thought about firing up that propane space heater!"

Once they had all the equipment on the workbench assembled to Jack's satisfaction, they mounted it onto the tag-along sled in the exact same manner. As with any project, Murphy's Law always seems to rule and they were short a couple of items. Naturally, as the rule always goes, there were some items that Jack felt were absolutely necessary to make sure that his equipment was properly secured.

He turned to Rob saying, "Do you think Thad might have the parts that I need?"

Sounding very doubtful about the idea of going to get them at Thad's he said, "He might."

"Man, I sure hope that what I need isn't in the shed, and if it is, what's the probability of those items being on the bottom of the pile?"

Giving Jack a very serious look he said, "Better than average."

Getting his hopes up in spite of Rob's negative comments he said, "I think we should give it a try."

Rob walked over to the phone that was hanging on the wall in the garage and called Thad. As soon as he answered Rob said, "Hey there, Bigfoot, how ya doing this morning?"

"Better than nothing. You guys been out and about yet?"

He did not want to take the time to bring Thad up to date and simply said, "Yeah, we took a walk with Rudy earlier, and ever since we got back we've been mounting Jack's equipment onto my tag-along sled, which brings up the reason for my call. We're short a couple of parts to finish up the job, and we'd like to take a look around your place to see if you've got what we need. That okay with you?"

"Sure! You comin' up now?"

"Yeah, we'll be right up." He hung up the phone and almost as soon as he did, it rang. He quickly picked up the handset thinking that it was Thad calling right back and said, "Hello!" He was right.

He heard Thad chuckling as he said, "It's me. We haven't talked in a long time so I thought that I'd give a call."

Rob quickly shot back saying, "OK, Thad, what do you need?"

"I don't need anything. Listen, I've got a pot of coffee on the stove. Why don't you come into the camp and I'll treat you to a cup before you start rummaging around?"

"Sounds good to me, we'll see you in a short short." He turned to Jack as he was hanging up the phone and said, "How long has it been since you've been in Thad's camp?"

"At least a couple of years, why?"

"Because he's asked us in for a cup of coffee, and I probably should warn you, with all the stuff that he's collected from garage sales over the past couple of years, well, the inside of his camp kind of reminds me of the way he's piled up the paraphernalia in his shed. He has so much stuff heaped all over the inside of his camp that it's hard to find a place to sit, or for that matter, even a place to set something down. What's more, there's been several times that he wanted to show me an unusual tool that he picked up at a tag sale for hardly nothing. And the whole reason that he wanted to show it to me was to see if I could figure out what it had been used for. But when all was said and done, he couldn't find the tool after pawing through almost every pile of junk in his camp."

"So what you're telling me is that we're going to have to stand up while we drink our coffee, right?"

"Yeah. As long as we can find a place to stand!"

* * *

As they were turning into the driveway they saw a bright red pickup truck that had New York plates on it, parked by Thad's Arctic Cat. "You know who that is, Jack?"

He shook his head no and Rob said, "I think I'll park out on the road, this person may leave before we do."

They were walking alongside of the red pickup toward the front of Thad's camp when a short, round elderly gentleman came walking toward them. Rob smiled as he said, "Howdy! How ya doing?"

The gentleman also had a smile on his face, and was shaking his head from side to side as he walked right past them to the red pick up. He didn't say a word, and Rob looked at Jack as he shrugged his shoulders as if to say, "What's with him?"

It didn't take them long to find out the answer. They walked up the two steps and onto Thad's porch, and didn't even get a chance to knock on the door before it opened.

Looking Thad right in the eye Rob said, "Who's the guy that just left?"

"Have no idea at all. He came in looking for directions to Walter Champanga's camp in Rabbit Hollow, and after I told him how to get there, he asked me if I had just moved in." He paused as the beginning of a smile started to play at the corners of his mouth, and he said, "I told him no, this is the way I live."

"That's it?"

"That's it. Then the guy got this stupid grin on his face, turned around and left without saying another word."

Jack did not even try to hide the fact that he did not like the mess that he saw in Thad's camp. He abruptly cut into Thad's dissertation regarding the New York character and said, "Let's have that cup of coffee, Thad. Time's burning away and I need to find a couple of parts to finish mounting my equipment onto the sled."

Thad knew that Jack did not like being in his camp and instantly developed a pout on his wrinkled old face. Rob was sure that trouble was at hand, and was very surprised when Thad held his tongue and simply walked over to the wood cook stove to get the coffee pot.

Jack had actually given up on the idea of finding what he needed at Thad's, and just wanted to get the coffee over with. His decision was easy when he glanced around the camp and saw the massive amount of stuff stacked all over the place. He had thought that Rob was over exaggerating when he described the inside of the camp, and now he was in a hurry to go to the general store in Stratton.

Jack made a show of pretending to look through some of the piles of odds and ends that were closest to him. He did not want to hurt Thad's feelings anymore than he had already. Finally he turned to Rob saying, "I don't think that I'm going to find what I need." And that is as far as he got.

Thad walked up to him and stuck a cup of coffee in his hand as he said, "I'm sure that I've got what you need, you don't have to go all the way to town."

Jack was about to say something, but Thad never gave him a chance and said, "What's it you're looking for? Maybe I can put my hands right on it."

Jack did not say a word as he brought the cup up to his mouth and took a sip. Rob almost burst out laughing. The moment that the coffee assaulted Jack's taste buds, he saw Jack's face screw up into a look that said, "Now that's disgusting!"

Thad usually started brewing his coffee around the time that he got up, which was never later than dawn. That meant that this pot had been brewing for a few hours now, and to make matters worse, Thad served his coffee only one way. The way that *he* liked it, hot and black!

He quickly shot Rob a lost look and said, "Listen, Thad, first things first, this is *not* how I like my coffee."

Rob knew for sure that this time the words were going to fly, and was totally shocked when Thad said amicably, "How *do* you like it?"

"With cream or milk. I can't drink it black."

As Thad walked over to the refrigerator to get the milk, Jack described the three items that he needed.

The camp and the Cat House had been pretty well searched, and they each had a fresh steaming cup of coffee in their hand when they walked into Thad's shed. The moment that Jack laid his eyes on the mess inside he turned to Rob and said, "Oh, man! We've already lost too much time. I think we'd better head into town to get what we need."

* * *

More than an hour had gone by since they went up to Thad's, and the women were nowhere to be seen when they walked back into the camp. Rob went directly to the kitchen table and took the topographical maps down from their resting place on the wagon wheel chandelier. He rolled them out and taped down the corners to keep them in place. Jack came walking over and said, "What 'ya doing?"

"I thought that it would be a good idea to identify all of the open areas near the beaver pond. I'd hate like hell to get all your electronic equipment loaded onto the tag-along and run into a dead end because we didn't plan ahead. The concentration of the encounters has been within a one and a half mile radius of the beaver pond. So if we strike out at the pond, I'd like to be prepared to reconnoiter some of the other areas."

Jack was listening intently and said, "Yeah? Like where?"

"I like the easy questions that you give me. I think that we should concentrate in the open areas that are in a close proximity to the beaver pond. What do you think?"

"I think that makes sense. I'm sure that you know how to get to all of those open areas, but can we actually get to them with the tag-along sled?"

"That's why I took out these topographical maps." Then pointing to the map on the left he said, "It looks like we'll only need this topo, because as you can see, the beaver pond sits almost directly in the middle of it."

Jack looked at the map and said, "Yeah, I can see that, and I can also see that the heaviest concentration of the fixes for the sightings are not very far from the pond." Then almost talking out loud to himself he said, "I wonder what's so significant to these people about the beaver pond?"

Rob heard him and said, "That's the sixty-four thousand dollar question that I've been asking too. Why don't you finish securing your electronic equipment to the tag-along sled, and I'll mark on the map the location of all the clear areas that I can remember."

Without saying a word Jack left for the garage.

Rob got another cup of coffee, and then started marking each clearing on the map as he remembered it, including a rough sketch of the trail that they would need to use to get to it.

He was rinsing out his coffee cup when Jack came back into the camp, and as he walked by the phone it started to ring. He stopped mid step, leaned over to pick up the portable handset and handed it to Rob.

"Good morning, this morning! This must be Len to tell me that he's on his way over."

"Good guess, Rob, especially since it's late enough that it could be most anyone calling you. How goes it?"

Getting a little concerned that Len had changed his mind Rob said, "We're just fine thanks. How about you?"

Len could detect a change in Rob's voice and said in an encouraging tone, "We're leaving now, and we should be there in about forty-five minutes."

"You guys must be coming over on your snowmobiles if it's going to take you that long."

"Yeah, we figured that we would do some riding after you and your buddy get back."

"Sounds like a plan. I really appreciate your help, Len. See you in a while."

He could hear Dolly Parton and Kenny Rogers singing "Islands In The Stream" as he hung up the handset. He thought he had heard Jack come in, but when he looked up there was absolutely no one around. He yelled, "Jack! Where are you?"

"I'm down in the basement getting a couple of things that I need. I'll be right back up."

Rob walked over to the kitchen table to study the drawings that he had made on the topographical map, and in less than a minute Jack was standing next to him. Pointing to the map Rob said, "I've got six different open areas that basically complete a circle around the beaver pond, and I don't think that I've missed any."

"Do you think we can get to all of those locations?"

"Absolutely." Pointing at the map again he said, "Look here. These logging roads border all the open areas. Do you see the trails that I've drawn off of them that lead to the clear-cuts?"

"Yeah."

Pointing to two clearings located to the northeast of the pond he said, "But it might be somewhat difficult to locate and follow the skidder trails to these two."

"Sounds to me like we have a real good shot at getting stuck in some deep snow."

Developing a very somber tone Rob said, "Yeah, I agree. I think that we should bring a couple of come-a-longs, a small army trench shovel, and the snowshoes as a precaution. If we get stuck, or if the snow is getting too soft, we'll just have to break a trail with the snowshoes."

"If that's the case, then I suggest that we also pack some food and a thermos of coffee."

"Good idea! I'll get Eileen to get that together for us. That reminds me! Where are the women? I haven't seen them since we got back, have you?"

"I think that they're preparing their face for the day. You know how that goes. Within forty-five minutes or so, they go through a metamorphosis that takes them from something kind of scary to somebody that you recognize in the daylight."

Rob burst out with a deep belly laugh and said, "I'd like to see you say that in front of them! If you do, then I'd have to say that you've *really* got balls. As a matter of fact, I'd say that you'd have balls of pure steel!"

* * *

Jack was totally absorbed in making sure that his electronic equipment was securely fastened to the sled. He did not see or hear Rob come into the garage. The moment he knew that Jack had no clue that he was there, Rob walked very quietly over to an old RCA television set he had hooked up in the garage for watching ballgames when tinkering on his car, or snowmobiles, or some other toy that happened to get his attention for the day. He slid the volume control almost to its maximum, put the channel selector on a number that did not have a TV station, and turned on the TV. Loud static suddenly permeated the entire garage, and Rob was really disappointed when Jack didn't react the way that he expected. He flinched somewhat, but his body remained in the same position. Only his head moved, and it moved very slowly while he looked in all directions.

Rob was laughing inside so hard that he felt his stomach muscles start to ache, and then he thought that he might piss his pants when Jack's gaze finally fell on him. The initial look on his face when recognition fully registered in his mind finally brought an end to Rob's control. He burst out in the best roaring belly laugh that he had had in months. However, when he saw Jack's face turn beet red, he turned off the TV and quickly retreated from the garage. His instincts told him that he'd better let Jack cool down some before he went back in.

* * *

Rob was walking back to the house when the front door opened. Rudy trotted out onto the porch and as soon as he saw Rob, he came bounding over to him. The Toot-man put his wrinkled face between Rob's legs, letting him know that he was in the mood for attention. He knelt down and scratched his back and ears for the better part of five minutes before he stood up to walk back over to the garage. He opened the door, and as he did he expected a barrage of four letter words to come flying at him.

But instead Jack had a grin on his face and said, "Payback can be hell, and I guarantee you that yours *will* be."

"Well I suspect that you'll let this ride for awhile so that I won't be expecting it when you decide that it's time to get even. That's what I've always admired about you, Jack."

"Maybe, and maybe not. And just what in the heck is it that you admire about me?"

"I've never really seen you get openly mad at anyone for screwing with you, or over you for that matter, but I *have* seen you get even!"

Rob walked over to the tag-along sled and marveled at all the equipment Jack had mounted on it. It had two antennas that look like satellite dishes, several various types of meters, two scopes, several battery packs, and a small Honda generator. He started to open his mouth to ask a question when Jack said, "We better not go any faster than a groomer does when it's working on the trails, and if the trail is rough, then we'll need to go even slower. If we don't, we could screw up all the calibrating that I just finished doing on these instruments. And if we screw up the calibration, all of the information that we record will be absolutely worthless."

* * *

The women had packed the food they had asked for in the cooler, filled the Nissan stainless-steel thermos with coffee, and while they did those chores Rob topped off the Southern Comfort flask. Everything was completed, checked and rechecked to kill time while waiting for Len and company. They had been ready to leave for *over* forty-five minutes now, and Jack was getting very impatient.

Jack and Rob had decided to wait outside so that they'd be ready to leave the moment that Len and the crew arrived. Nancy and Eileen mutually agreed to join them. Sixty-five minutes had gone by since Len had called, and Nancy could see by the way that Jack was acting that he was rapidly running out of patience. She knew that he wanted to leave *now*. Finally she stood up and said, "Why don't you guys just go ahead and leave. Eileen and I'll go up stairs and get the shotguns and some ammunition. We'll be just fine." She saw Jack and Rob looking at her like she had lost her mind and she continued, "Besides, I'd love one of those lily-livered idiots to come around again while we have a loaded shotgun in our hands."

Jack didn't need any more encouragement and promptly walked over to Eileen's snowmobile. However, he did not lift his leg up high enough as he swung it over the seat, and ended up almost knocking the cooler right off of the rack. He heard Rob chortling while he was reaching for the ignition key, and shot him a birdie just as the machine roared to life.

Second thoughts started popping into his mind and Rob became very uncomfortable with the arrangement. Instead of starting his sled he yelled, "Hey, Jack! I'd rather wait until Len, Bubba, and Stormin get here."

Jack never heard him over the sound of the engine, and that was plain to Eileen, so she piped up and said, "Will you please leave? We'll be just fine. If you're that concerned, take your cellular phone, and if there's any trouble I'll call you. Just make sure that you have it on."

"All right. But remember, I don't get a cellular signal all the time. So if I happen to be out of range, leave a message. When I get a signal back, my phone will beep several times to let me know that you've called."

Since his was the only machine that had a hitch, Rob was pulling the tag-along sled behind him. It had been agreed that he would take the lead so Jack could keep an eye on his equipment as they went down the trail. As Rob drove his machine alongside of Jack he raised his shield and yelled, "We're going to the beaver pond first, right?"

The moment that he saw Jack shaking his head yes, he continued on out of the driveway.

* * *

Even with the tag-along sled, it only took them eight minutes to get to the pond. They spent the better part of one hour on the bridge, and they had a great time listening to the squirrels chattering, the woodpeckers pecking, and the occasional caw of a crow.

However, Jack had never been a very patient man, so when he felt that he had enough he said, "I've had it with this place! This is worse than fishing when the only things that are biting are the mosquitoes and black flies. Where shall we go from here, Rob?"

"I'm not sure that leaving is such a good idea, but if you're hell bent on moving, there's a clearing up ahead that we can reach from ITS 89. But it's my guess that we'll have to pack down the snow before we try to go over the snowbank left by the groomer." He could see that Jack was looking at him like he had two heads, so he explained, "Look, more than likely the snow is soft on the other side of the bank. If it is, and if the skis are pointed down as we come over the bank, just where do you think we'll end up?"

Jack was sitting on his machine, fidgeting like a four-year-old, and Rob was beginning to wonder if he had heard a word that he said. But since he missed a lot of what Jack had said yesterday when they were at the beaver pond, he decided to let it go and yelled, "Hey, you! Are you ready to leave or not?"

Finally Jack looked at him with a poker face and said, "Yeah, man. I've been ready."

When they reached the skidder trail that they were going to take off of ITS 89, Rob put his ski up against the snowbank on the right hand side and shut his machine down. Both he and Jack walked over to the opposite side and found themselves looking down the mouth of a skidder trail that emptied into a huge clearcut in the valley below. When they got to the edge of the bank Jack turned to Rob saying, "Is this the clearing that is northwest of the beaver pond that you had marked on the topo?"

"Yep. This is the one. Listen, Jack, I think that after we cut some of this snowbank down, we should put on the snowshoes and break a trail in there at least twenty feet, maybe more. But I'm pretty sure that twenty feet will be far enough to put us onto a real thick crust. That area down in there gets a lot of sun."

It was a good plan until they reached the clearing and started to make a U-turn putting them on a heading back out to ITS 89. Rob's sled started breaking through the crust as he slowed down to make the turn, but he had maintained enough speed to prevent him from sinking deep enough to lose traction. Unfortunately, Jack was not paying close attention to what was happening to Rob, and as he made his turn he followed Rob's track. That was a huge mistake. Especially since he had not kept his speed up enough to prevent him from sinking.

Rob continued moving forward until he was sure that he was on a good solid crust. The moment that he saw his skis riding easily on top of the snow, he stopped. However, when he turned around to see how Jack was doing, Rob's mood instantly changed. He was not a happy camper at all. He could see nothing but Jack's helmet sticking up above the snowline.

To be on the safe side, he put his snowshoes on before walking over to help his friend out of the mess he was in. When he stepped up to the stark white trench and looked in, he saw Jack just sitting on the machine with his head hanging down. Rob could not resist the temptation and said, "Hey, jerko! That submissive look ain't gonna work! Just when are you gonna finally learn how to ride a sled!?"

Jack took the time to slip off his mitten so that Rob would have no trouble at all understanding his sign language. Then he said, "You're the expert. How do I get out of this shit?"

"I'll tell you what, my friend, it ain't goin' to be easy."

They spent more than thirty minutes digging and pulling Eileen's machine out of its frosty quagmire, and when they finally pushed it back up onto the surface, sweat was profusely dripping from both of them, and steam was billowing up from their heads. They sat there long enough to eat a sandwich, drink some coffee, and get cooled down to the point that both of them were starting to feel a chill from the sweat-laden clothes they were wearing. Neither one of them heard or felt anything that would lead them to believe that a circle of shimmering air was getting ready to make an appearance.

When Jack started to shiver a little he said, "One of us should to go back to the camp to get some dry clothes. Otherwise we're gonna freeze our asses off before the day is done, and if our body temperature drops too much, we could be heading for one hell of a cold."

"That makes sense to me, Jack. Why don't we crank up the sleds and get back out onto ITS 89. You don't have the tag-along to slow you down, so once we hit the trail why don't you hightail it back to camp to get us some dry clothes?"

"That sounds OK to me. You gonna stay by the beaver pond?"

"I think that we should try someplace else. I'll tell you what, meet me at the turnoff by the big boulder, and we'll checkout the clearings that are to the southeast of the pond. How's that for a plan?"

"You're talking about the boulder that Rudy was real curious about this morning?"

"Yeah. I figure that by the time I get there, you'll probably be there waiting for me. In case you forgot, I can't go very fast with your precious toys behind me."

Jack flipped him the birdie and said, "Listen pal, it's not the toys that are so precious, it's all the frigging time that it took me to get them properly calibrated for the data that I want to collect."

Rob instantly got a grin from ear to ear and said, "I know that. I just wanted to get a rise out of you. I'd say that my mission was one hundred percent successful. What do you think?"

"I think that you must have been a female in a previous life, 'cause you have a serious penchant for busting balls. See you at the boulder."

Rob was about to take the lead going back out to ITS 89 when he heard Jack roar past him on the right. He could clearly hear the scream of Eileen's engine over the sound of his own as her machine went flying past him, and in what seemed like the blink of an eye, all Rob could see was a swirling cloud of snow.

* * *

As Rob approached the beaver pond bridge he coasted to a stop, and looked back at the equipment to make sure that everything was still riding fine. Raising his helmet face shield, he took a long casual look around the pond, taking in the entire surrounding area. Satisfied that there was nothing happening, or about to happen, he started up the trail.

As he rounded the last turn before the big boulder turnoff, he could see Jack parked on the right hand side of the trail waiting for him. As he pulled up alongside of him he noticed that he was holding a pile of clothes in his lap.

By the time that he stepped off of his machine, Jack was already standing next to him, patiently waiting to hand him his dry clothes. Neither one of them wasted any time at all getting out of their wet clothes. When Rob heard his teeth chattering, it immediately brought to mind the Southern Comfort sitting in the rear compartment of his sled. He took a quick look at Jack and said, "How come you didn't change at camp instead of freezing your ass off while changing out here?"

"I just asked myself that exact question! Back at your camp I thought that it wouldn't be fair to you, but as I think about it now, and that shit-biting stunt that you pulled on me in the garage, I don't think I should've cared!"

Rob paused just for a couple of seconds and said, smiling, "We both have our moments, don't we?" When Jack didn't answer he said, "You want a swig of antifreeze to help warm you?"

Jack immediately knew what the antifreeze was and said, "My mind says yes, but my common sense tells me no. God knows what we've got facing us, but I don't, and I think our minds best be razor sharp."

Rob did not have to think very long before saying, "Yeah, man. You've got that one right."

While he was answering Jack, he had been looking up the logging road, and his mind was trying to comprehend why there was such a well-packed trail running up the middle of it. His eyes followed the trail back to where he and Jack were sitting, and he could clearly see the tracks of several snowmobiles. Curiosity now had the best of him and he started walking toward the trail to test just how firm it really was.

He had taken only three steps when he heard Jack say, "Hey, Rob! What're ya doin' now?"

"This trail looks like its been pretty well used, and that seems mighty strange to me. It's a dead end, and unless there's been a major change since I was up there last, there's nothing worth seeing."

He raised his foot up as high as he could, and jammed his heel into the hard packed snow with all the force that he could muster. His leg was still vibrating from the impact as he pulled his heel away to inspect the damage. He was totally surprised when he saw only a tiny dent. Jack was watching him every step of the way, and when he saw the results of Rob's effort, he barked a sharp insinuating laugh and said, "That's about what I'd expect from a mealy mouthed wimp!"

Rob spun around, ready with a retort that would surely result in an all out verbal war, and stopped short when he saw Jack's victory written all over his face. He started laughing as he said, "Touché dickhead!" He paused a few seconds while looking Jack squarely in the eye and said, "This is another strange one, Jack. This trail has been traveled like it's Main Street."

Jack shrugged his shoulders and said, "Simple to explain. Somebody must have built a camp up there."

"That would certainly be a nice answer, Jack, but I'm almost certain that there's no camp anywhere up this road."

"So I wonder what's up this road that's so interestin'?"

"Like I already said, nothing! Unless you consider two huge clear-cuts and a humongous staging area interesting."

Jack thought about that while Rob was walking back to his sled and said, "Maybe it was just young kids riding their father's snowmobile up and down the road for enjoyment. You know, that could have been what he had told them to do, and he was probably thinking that at least they'd be out of the way of any riders on the main trail."

"I'm impressed with your analytical abilities, Jack, but there's a major problem with your thinking on this one."

"Yeah, what's that?"

"It snowed Sunday night, and all the weekend warrior flatlanders left Sunday afternoon. No one's been around since then 'cept Thad, Eileen and me, and now you and Nancy."

Jack was getting fed up with this useless bantering back and forth and said, "Hey! Enough of this crap! Let's get back to our mission."

Rob turned and looked back up the trail again. He was having a very hard time letting go of this puzzle and later he would understand why. Finally he said, "Yeah, you're right. We've got bigger fish to fry."

* * *

They rode up the logging road about four hundred feet before they came to a skidder trail on the right hand side. Rob stopped his machine and yelled back to Jack, "This trail leads to one of the clear-cuts that I have marked on the topo." He looked down toward the clearing for a few moments before turning back around to Jack saying, "This area doesn't get a lot of sun like the clear-cut that we were just in, and I think that we'd best break a trail all the way in there, that is unless you want another session just like the one we had in the last clear-cut?"

Jack was getting off of his machine as he said, "I've had enough of that kind of grief for one day!"

They strapped on their snowshoes and Rob took the lead. It was a quarter of a mile down the skidder trail to the clear-cut, and they switched the lead position twice so neither one of them would work up too much of a sweat. Whoever was number two still had work to do, but it was not as demanding as the lead position. The trail had to be wide enough to accommodate the width of the snowmobiles, which meant that the person in the number two spot had to step with his left snowshoe on the hump in the center of the trail left by the point person, and widen the trail by crushing the snow to the right side.

Once they finished stomping down the trail for the U-turn in the clearing, they started to head back out to the logging road, still breaking trail along the way to make it a little wider. They had gone only a short distance up the throat of the skidder trail when everything turned stone quiet. All the noise was sucked out of the immediate world around them, and neither one of them could hear even the sound of their snowshoes as they broke through the light crust.

Rob turned to Jack just as they both simultaneously felt the vacuum sensation, and he could see that "Uh, oh!" look on his face. He did not need a mirror to tell him that he had one too.

Their eye-lock was short-lived, and they broke into a trot back to the sleds. Rob looked over his shoulder and saw two deer coming into the clearing from the direction of the beaver pond, and instantly thought they were the focus of this event. However, when he ran the whole scene through his mind later to make a log entry, he would wonder why he had automatically assumed it was the two deer that were the targets, rather than the two of them.

* * *

They both had sweat pouring down their faces by the time they reached the sleds. Rob turned to Jack yelling, "You go first, and stop ahead of where you want your equipment. Just make sure that you plan enough room for my sled."

Jack had already gone around Rob by the time that he had gotten his sled started. As always, haste makes waste and he flooded his machine when he pumped the primer three times. He instantly regretted rushing things, because he'd known for years to pump it once if the snowmobile hadn't had time to get as cold as the ambient temperature. The only thing that made his mistake tolerable was the fact that he had electric start to solve the problem fairly quickly, but that still took more time than he wanted it to.

By the time they reached the spot where Jack had wanted to set up, the deer were gone, and so were all the signs of the circle of air. Everything was back to normal.

Both of them stood in one spot for several minutes, hoping that the quiet and the vacuum sensation would surface again. Finally Rob started walking to the back of his sled as he said, "Jack, I'm putting my snowshoes back on. I want to have a look at those deer tracks. I'll bet ya a tank of aviation fuel that I'll find a depression in the snow not very far from where the deer's tracks end."

"No bet! But I'm going with you."

* * *

It was a big surprise to both of them when they saw that the deer's tracks continued all the way across the clearing before disappearing into a thick growth of pine trees on the opposite side. And what they found even more surprising is that the deer did not break into a run at any time while crossing.

Turning to Jack, Rob said, "What do you suppose is so different about this encounter from the other times that it happened? I mean, all the other times it was very obvious that the animals were in a pure panic when the circle of distorted air was close by."

Jack did not reply right away, and for a moment there, Rob did not think that he was going to. Finally he said, "Now that I think about it, I didn't hear the static noise. Did you, Rob?"

"No, I didn't, and when I looked back I saw the deer slowly picking their way through the clearing. I remember the dead silence, and then the vacuum sensation, but I never heard the hissing sound."

Jack's eyes were still searching in every direction around the clearing as he said, "Yeah, it's kind of like they changed their mind before they really got things going, but I wonder why?"

"Jack, I have a suggestion. That thing just might return. In case it does, why don't you stay here with your equipment in the ready mode while I take Eileen's sled up to the next skidder trail?"

"I have no problem with that, but why?"

"I've got a hunch, but anyway, I'm pretty sure that the next clear-cut is going to be shaded also. If it is, I'll break the trail and come back for you when I'm done. OK?"

"Fine with me. Give me a sandwich and a cup of coffee before you go, though."

He reached into the cooler on the back of Eileen's sled and tossed Jack a sandwich. Then he reached into the knapsack for the thermos and while making his way over to Jack he said, "You can pour your own coffee."

As Jack was taking the coffee from him, Rob reached into his inside breast pocket and pulled out a Charter Arms Snub Nose .38. Taking a quick look to confirm that it was loaded he handed it to Jack saying, "If things get too hot, do like the women did."

"Thanks, man, but what about you?"

"My gut tells me that this is the area that they'll be in, so it's better that you have the .38."

"I don't know what makes you so sure you're right, but OK."

* * *

Rob had barely gone out of sight when everything turned dead quiet. As far as Jack was concerned, that should have been an impossibility. He thought, "How in the hell does one suddenly eliminate the sound of a snowmobile engine?" With that thought, he felt the vacuum sensation and heard the crackling noise. He set his sandwich on the snowmobile seat, and wasn't even aware that

Rob had barely gone out of sight when everything turned dead quiet. As far as Jack was concerned, that should have been an impossibility. He thought, "How in the hell does one suddenly eliminate the sound of a snowmobile engine?" With that thought, he felt the vacuum sensation and heard the crackling noise. He set his sandwich on the snowmobile seat, and wasn't even aware that he had spilled his cup of coffee as he turned around to look for the circle of shimmering air. There was nothing when he looked over his right shoulder. But when he turned his head to look back over his left shoulder, he saw the wavering air about seventy feet straight out from him, and it was about twenty feet above the surface of the snow. He quickly stepped off the sled, and after taking just two steps he was kneeling down next to his equipment. Being careful, but also trying to be quick about it, he flipped four switches to the "on" position, and as he flipped the last one, he felt a tingling sensation just as the intensity of the hissing sound increased dramatically.

He felt the tingling sensation progressively getting more intense as he was trying to locate where he had set the .38 down. He wished like hell that he had turned the equipment on as soon as Rob told him to. Human nature being what it is, he really didn't think that anything was going to happen, especially not so quickly. He didn't want to miss this opportunity and he was cursing the length of time that it took to boot up his systems, and that is when he felt himself getting a little lightheaded. And then he felt the hair rising on the back of his neck.

"Damn! They're honing in on me!" He felt himself starting to get lighter, like he was going to float off of his feet, and in a flash remembered what the women and Rob had told him about their experiences. All of his equipment finally came on line, and as it did, he immediately picked up his remote controls. His hands began to shake as he started to work the joysticks to point his directional transmitters and antennas at the circle of wavering air. He heard the crackling noise getting considerably louder, and at the same time he felt his body begin to lift off of the snow.

Even with all these distractions, he still had the good sense and ability to focus on his equipment, and he noticed that it was starting to register and record readings from the electrical patterns generated within the pulsating circle of air. Suddenly the word *pulsating* hit home and he looked back at the circle. It was not only pulsating, it was starting to move closer to him. He felt his knees go somewhat weak as this new stress surged into an already overloaded system. Frantically he searched for the .38, but still no luck. He was not ready to let these irritating obnoxious schmucks have their way. He had to do something!

Suddenly an idea popped into his mind, and he reached into his pocket for a third remote control, the one that operated the transmitters. Coordination was slipping away from him as the hissing sound got louder, and he wondered if he was going to be able to do it, but it happened. He did not remember doing it, but it happened. The output lever on both transmitters had been pushed to the max. He shifted his gaze to the gauges at the bottom right of the transmitters, and fought to focus all of his attention on them. The second that he saw needles pegging all the way to the right, he could swear that he heard something like a pop, and concurrent with the pop, the circle of air was gone. The world around him was still in a slow spin when he heard the sound of Eileen's snowmobile, and his first thought was that Rob was still working his way up to the other clearing. He was wrong.

* * *

Upon his return, as Rob rounded the bend into the clearing, he saw Jack down on one knee, and it looked like he was doing something to his equipment. Rob slowed down to a crawl and took a long sweeping look around the entire area to see if the circle of air had surfaced, but he could see nothing resembling it, and he didn't feel or hear any of the telltale signs.

He brought Eileen's sled to a stop directly behind the tag-along, and he somehow sensed that strange something had happened. He got off of the machine and Jack did not look up at him as he approached, nor did he acknowledge that Rob was standing there. Rob was hoping that it was because he was totally engrossed in whatever he was doing, and not because his mind was in La La Land. He stood there for a quarter of a minute before finally saying, "Hey, Jack, what're ya doing?"

Still not looking up at Rob he said, "Take a look at this scope."

Rob saw numerous lines waving all across the screen, and sometimes they looked to him like they were scrolling across the screen. Looking at Jack he said, "What's that all about?"

Jack told him about his wild encounter and said, "Right now I'm playing back some of the data that the equipment recorded."

"What do all those lines tell you?"

"Not much right now. I have to compile everything that's been recorded, and then I have to collate it to get a complete picture. But I do not have enough data yet. The sequence of events that I told you about happened very quickly, I doubt if I got more than thirty seconds worth. Most likely I can get by with fifteen minutes of data, but I would prefer to get twenty."

Then he stopped short and looked up at Rob saying, "How come you came back so quick? Did you feel the vacuum sensation, or see something?"

Rob looked at him like he was considering the peyote routine again, or something like it before saying, "Quick? I was busy breaking the trail in the other clearing. I didn't hear or see Jack Shit!"

As soon as he got those last words out of his mouth they heard snowmobile engines off in the distance.

Looking back over his shoulder toward the sound of the machines he said, "You know, Jack, it sounds like those snowmobiles are coming from the direction of the clearing where I just broke the trail." He paused for a moment to gather his thoughts and said, "I wonder who that could be? I didn't hear anyone go in there, did you?"

"Nope! But it's possible that they went up the trail after you turned off the logging road to come back down here, and we just didn't hear them over your machine."

"Yeah, that's possible, but not probable. I'll tell you why I think so. It would've taken them much longer to reach the skidder trail to the other clearing than the amount of time that it took me to travel the quarter of a mile down here. In case you didn't realize it, both of these clearings are in a huge valley. Any loud noises just resound off the sides of the surrounding mountains. And if that's the case, my friend, we should have heard them long after I shut my machine down."

While walking back to Eileen's sled he said, "I'm going to go out to the trail and have a look." He started up the Formula, and as soon as he got back on to the hard-packed trail that he and Jack had made into the clearing, he put the throttle to the handlebar and made short work of the quarter-mile back out to the logging road.

He looked to the right just as he approached the end of the skidder trail, and it was not long before he could see the headlights of three snowmobiles rounding a turn about two hundred feet away. He watched them as they were drawing near to him, one following the other, and he noticed that the middle snowmobile had a tag-along sled behind it. What *really* caught his attention was that it looked like it had Have-A-Heart traps piled on top of it.

Right then and there he decided that he wanted to talk with these people, and gave his snowmobile enough throttle to slowly move it forward until the tips of the skies were almost to the other side of the hard packed trail. Looking behind him he noted that he had the entire trail blocked, and while shutting down his machine he said to himself, "If these people don't want to stop and talk, they're just going to have to go out into the soft snow and make their own trail."

* * *

As the snowmobiles drew closer, Rob made it clear that he wanted them to stop. The sleds appeared to slow some as they approached him, and when they were about ten feet away they came to a complete stop.

The second that he heard them shut off their machines he started walking over to the lead rider. His mind was working feverishly to come up with the proper sequence of questions that he wanted to ask, and he never noticed that each of the snowmobilers had a tinted face shield on their helmet. It was not until he was almost on top of the lead rider that he finally noticed their face shields, and almost at the same time he knew for sure that the tag-along was loaded with Have-A-Heart Traps.

Without saying a word to the lead rider he continued on past him to the Have-A-Heart Traps. He had a burning desire to see if there were any rodents inside of them. As he walked up to the tag along he bent over slightly to take a quick look in each trap, and as he did, out of the corner of his right eye he saw the last rider lean over to his left. Without turning his head he used his peripheral vision to focus his attention on what the rider was doing. Uneasiness permeated every nerve in his body when he saw him come back up with a long object in his hand. Rob was no coward, but he was also no martial artist, and he worriedly thought to himself, "Oh boy! I'm in a heap of trouble now!"

His instincts took over and he dove at the lead rider, hitting him right between the shoulder blades with his left shoulder. The force was enough to topple him off of his sled, and as they were falling toward the snow he hooked his right arm around his guy's neck. The rider's face shield stopped his face from becoming a bloody mess as he crashed headfirst into the crusty snow. But it was a different story for other parts of his body when Rob landed right on top of him. The downed rider let out a very loud HMMMFFFF as the wind was knocked out of him.

Instantly rolling to his right side, Rob dragged the rider over with him, and used all of his strength to bring him up onto his chest. The moment that he had him centered, he squeezed his right forearm tighter against the guy's neck, and with his left hand he peeled back the snowmobiler's face shield. Moving as fast as he could, before the struggling rider could find a way to defend himself, Rob jammed his fingers into the guy's eyes. He made sure that the pressure was not enough to blind him, but he also made sure that he got the blood-curdling scream that he wanted.

As soon as the scream died away Rob yelled, "Hey bucko! Stop right there or your buddy is going to need a seeing eye dog for the rest of his life!"

It had the desired effect. The rider that had the long object in his hand stopped dead in his tracks, and the middle snowmobiler was frozen in a half standing and half sitting position on his sled. Turning his attention back to his captive Rob said in his best menacing voice, "Listen, friend, you tell your buddies to back off, and tell them if they don't, that I am going to make good on my threat."

When the snowmobiler said nothing Rob applied a little more pressure, which brought out another scream and a slew of words that he couldn't begin to understand. Out of the corner of his eye he saw the rider that was farthest away drop the long object that he had in his hand, and the squatter sat back down on his sled the moment that he heard it hit the snow.

Rob thought to himself, "Damn! Just what in the heck do I do now? Unless I come up with some brainy idea, all I've done is create a Mexican standoff."

No sooner had he completed that thought when he heard his "knight in shining armor" coming up the trail from the clearing below. Moving his head closer to his captive's open visor he said, "You just lay still, pal, otherwise you're gonna feel some *serious* pain, and by the way, what did you tell your buddies?"

There was no response, and the rider started to squirm for a better position, but he stopped as soon as he felt Rob apply more pressure to his eyes. Looking over at the snowmobiler's friends to make sure that they were not making any moves he said, "Now that's being a good boy, you just stay put." The other riders did not look like they were getting ready to do anything so Rob continued, "Now, butt head, one more time. What did you say to your buddies, and what friggin' language did you use?"

There was a very short silence before he said, "I spoke in our native tongue."

"Yeah? What native tongue is that?" But before he could answer Rob heard Jack's machine go silent, and he could hear the snow crunching as he walked in his direction. But all of a sudden his confidence went to hell in a hand basket as the spirit of doubt took over. Thinking silently to himself he said, "Holy moly! What if I'm wrong? What if this isn't Jack that just started walking over here?" His heart started to thud so loud in his chest that he could hear it in his ears, and he hoped like hell that the schmuck that he was holding wasn't hearing it too.

It only took Jack a few seconds to surmise what had gone on and he said, "Well, well, well, this looks like a repeat of yesterday. I'm gonna tell you guys something, if your buddies show up to rescue you again today, things just aren't going to work the same way. I'm ready for those bastards!" He took the time to glare at each one of them before continuing, "You guys aren't gonna just up and disappear on us this time. You're going to stick around to give us some answers."

Rob's curiosity got the best of him and he cut in saying, "I take it you have something that you think is a stopper."

"You bet your sweet bippy I do! As a matter of fact I have it on right now. These transmitters are beaming a dome around us that is about one hundred feet in diameter, kind of like a shield. That circle of air can be out there, but it can't do anything. And I'll tell you why. As soon as it tries to penetrate my shield, the frequency that I'm using will disrupt the static field of the circle, and shut it down, exactly the same way that I did it down in the clearing a little while ago."

The rider sitting on the middle machine said, "Your primitive devices are not even an annoyance to us."

Jack detected the smug tone in his voice and was considering whether he should take him down a peg or two when the rider suddenly started talking again.

"Your *toys* had absolutely no affect on what we were doing. We just chose to shut down so you couldn't get any more data than what you did."

Rob cut back in and said, "So what's the deal? Your friends were going to drop you guys off in the clearing where Jack was, and changed their mind when they saw him? Is that what you're saying?"

"Very good! You are only partially correct!" said the rider, with a "holier than thou" tone of voice.

Jack suddenly felt anger rushing through his body when the guy's insolent attitude hit him between the eyes, and he said, "Cut the crap, pal. You may *think* that you've got the upper hand, but you'd best not count your chickens before the eggs hatch!"

The rider flipped up his shield and gave Jack a look that implied he was nothing but a nuisance. Then looked back at Rob and said, "As I said, that's partially correct, Mr. Day, and we reestablished our link in the next clearing over, where you were so kind to break a trail for us."

It took a few seconds before what the rider had just said finally sank in, and he blurted out, "Hey, butt-head, how in the hell do you know my name?"

"There's no need to be so crude, Mr. Day. We know everything that we need to know about you," and almost as an after thought he added, "and several other people too."

Rob shot a quick glance at Jack that said, "So you ARE right!" and then quickly calmed down somewhat as he took control of his emotions. He did not want to be shown up by this idiot. That was the last thing that he wanted to happen right now. Feeling as though he was back in total control of his emotions he said, "And why do you need to know anything about anybody?"

There was total silence. None of the riders said anything. They did not move or even try to look at each other. Jack was watching the blabbermouth's eyes, and it looked to him like they glazed over for a couple of seconds, but that wasn't logical and he decided that he had imagined the whole thing.

Finally, the rider that Rob had in a chokehold said, "I told you the last time that we met that we are scientists from a parallel dimension, and that the only reason we are here is to help all living beings and creatures in your dimension."

Jack looked over at the guy and said, "That's a bunch of bullshit! If you people are really here to help everybody in this, in this *dimension*, you wouldn't be skulking around the way that you do here in the backwoods country. You'd be meeting with the mucky muck scientists at the universities and pharmaceutical companies that are working to find cures for cancer, heart disease, diabetes and whatever the hell else they're working on!"

The blabbermouth quickly shot back, "We don't want to work with the scientists because all of the scientists that we scanned did not have mankind in their best interests. They are more interested in fame and fortune, and they would end up taking all the credit for our work. What's more, we don't want to work with the pharmaceuticals either, because all they are interested in is the profits."

Rob let out a loud HA! and said, "Hey, Jack, you got any high top boots with you? The crap's really getting deep here!"

While Rob was talking, Jack began walking over to the tag-along sled with all the Have-A-Heart Traps. When he was only two steps from it he noticed a long object lying in the snow, and when he bent over to pick it up he saw that it was a piece of cast iron pipe. He was studying the pipe in his hands when he said, "Yeah, I agree." Then a vicious smile worked its way onto his face as he took a batter's stance and said, "Hey, Rob, do you think I could break this twit's neck with one good swing?"

The rider on the middle sled turned around and saw that he was the intended victim. Jack stood there for a couple of moments looking him in the eye before he feigned the beginning of a swing. Rob could not help himself and started laughing when the guy let out a squeal that sounded just like a piglet being castrated. The third rider started to make his move toward Jack, but he saw the guy's shadow coming in his direction, and without changing his position, swung the cast iron pipe back as hard as he could in a downward arc, hitting him in the right knee.

* * *

It was going on 11:00 hours and Nancy was getting bored just hanging around camp while waiting for Len and the gang to show up. "Eileen, I don't think these bozos are going to get here after all. Why don't we go for a walk up toward the fields?"

She thought a few seconds before answering and said, "I don't know about that, unless we bring the shotguns with us. That could be a problem though because they get pretty heavy after a while."

"Don't you have a toboggan in the garage?"

"Yes, we do! Outstanding idea!"

* * *

They both had a hand on the toboggan's towrope as they walked toward Harris Pasture Road, and the shotguns and extra ammo were securely lashed to the sled with bungee cords. They were about fifty feet from the turnoff to the beaver pond when they heard the sound of snowmobiles to the northwest of them. Nancy said, "That can't be the men, they don't sound like your machines."

"Yeah, you're right. Besides, it sounds like it's more than two sleds to me anyway, and I don't think that it's Len, Bubba and Stormin. After talking with those guys at the Four Seasons, I don't think that they know what slow means, and those sleds sound to me like they're going slow."

She had barely gotten the last words out of her mouth when the sound of the snowmobile engines suddenly stopped. They both stood there listening to see if the machines would start right back up, and after almost a minute passed by Eileen turned to Nancy saying, "Maybe they're taking a break."

Deciding that it was time to move on, Nancy took the first step forward, and Eileen quickly followed suit. They continued walking past the turn-off to the pond, and neither one bothered to look down the trail. They walked the better part of a mile when they came to an old deserted farmhouse. The house, barn and other outbuildings, including all the acreage had been sold to a couple from Rutland, Vermont several years ago.

Nancy looked at the house, and then at the barn and said, "Gee, they really fixed up the barn! It looks great! In fact it looks like it belongs in a Norman Rockwell painting."

While Nancy was talking, Eileen was staring at the farmhouse. She could never understand why so much time, money and effort was spent on the barn, and not one cent on the house. As far as she was concerned, the house was more of a historical landmark than the barn. And to add credence to that thought, some of the locals said that the materials used in constructing the house were consistent with those used during the 1700's. She let her gaze go up to the roof and said, "Did you notice that the house looks like it's ready to fall down?"

Nancy was shaking her head from side to side as she said, "You're probably right. It's a shame that the people that own this place are just letting it decay the way it is."

"I agree. I've got a hunch that if much more snow piles up on that roof this winter, it won't be standing come spring."

They stood there a while longer, just looking at the old house when Eileen said, "I knew the couple that used to own this place. You might remember Rob and me talking about them in the past. Their names are Emma and Floyd. As a matter of fact, we bought our camp from them."

"Nancy thought for a bit and said, Yeah, I remember the names."

Rob used to hunt with Floyd every now and then, and he really felt bad when he heard that Floyd had died."

Looking at Eileen, Nancy said, "Is that why the place was sold?"

"No, they sold it a few years before he died. Emma lives with one of their sons somewhere in southern Maine now. We still get to see her from time to time when she comes up here during good weather."

They silently stood there for a while longer, and Eileen broke the quiet when she said, "I remember coming here with Rob to visit with them. He really loved to hear Floyd's stories about the days when he used to hunt bobcat and bear with his dogs. We'd sit there for hours, and as far as I'm concerned, the stories never really changed. They were always about his hunting escapades.

You know the old saying, you go on one hunt you've been on them all."

Nancy started laughing and said, "Well I know that you're not into hunting, but I think that you've confused your saying with something else. So what did you do during the story telling, sit there like a bump on a log?"

Eileen giggled a little and said, "Absolutely not! While Floyd told all his hunting stories from days gone by, Emma and I would play cards to pass the time."

"Did they live in this house a long time?"

"All their married life. One night when we were playing cards I heard a thumping noise coming from one of the rooms on the second floor. I knew that Emma, Floyd, Rob and I were the only people in the house at the time, so I asked Emma what the noise was, 'cause I could see that she heard it too. She didn't say anything right away, and I think that she was considering whether she should tell me what was on her mind or not. Finally she let out a long sigh and told me that it was a poltergeist. She also told me that it had been doing that for years."

"You mean to tell me that she wasn't afraid of it?"

"Apparently not. She was very casual about the whole thing. The only other thing that I remember her telling me was that it never did anything but make those noises from time to time."

"Really! How did she come to the conclusion that it was a poltergeist?

Pointing at the second story window on the left backside of the house she said, "Emma told me that she saw a male ghost in that bedroom one night, and since then she would never sleep upstairs again. She only saw it that one time, but a couple of her children saw it several times. She claimed that it was a poltergeist because it made those banging noises. I'm not an expert, but that works for me. But she made a statement that I always found fascinating. She said she wasn't afraid of the ghost, only the darkness."

"No kidding! Well I'll tell you what, if that was me, I would've been scared out of my wits by the ghost."

"Me too, Nancy. But let me tell you what happened one night that Floyd was late coming home. She finished washing the supper dishes and had put the children to bed, and Floyd still wasn't home. She could count on one hand the number of times that he had missed supper since they had gotten married, and her mind started to convince her that something terrible had happened to him. Finally she couldn't take it anymore, and as much as she feared the dark, her fear that Floyd might be lying in the woods somewhere with a serious injury was even greater. Ultimately, she mustered up the courage to go look for him, and all the time she was hoping against hope that maybe he was at her sister's house."

"How far was that from here?"

"About two and a half miles back down the road. You remember where the river is?"

"Sure."

"Well, when you're coming up the camp road from Route 16, it's the farmhouse on the right just after you cross the river. Anyway, she told me that she lit up two lanterns to get as much light as possible for her walk down to the barn, and the moment that she went into it she put a match to every single lantern that she could find. She said that even after all the lanterns were burning brightly, she was still terrified because everywhere that she looked there were lots of dark, shadowy spots. And what made it even worse, every time she saw her shadow move, she'd think that something was coming to get her, and she said that she came very close to fainting several times."

"I'll tell you something, Eileen, Emma may have had a fear of the dark, but from what you're telling me, she had lots of courage."

"Yeah, I feel the same way. She told me that when she had made up her mind to find Floyd, she immediately started to work on her own thoughts. She knew that she had to convince herself to remain calm. The first things that she concentrated on were the sheep, cows and horses that were in the barn. She knew that they weren't afraid of the dark, so why should she be afraid. She basically became her own mentor, and just kept repeating to herself the whole time that she was in the barn, they're not afraid, so why should I be afraid?

" Unfortunately her fear soared to new heights when she opened the barn door and the darkness outside loomed in at her. And to make matters worse for her, at that time the fields weren't cleared all the way down to Harris Pasture Road like they are now.

Based upon what she told me, she had about two miles of woods to go through before getting to her sister's place."

Nancy looked over her left shoulder and tried to imagine almost a mile of the fields being covered by forest and said, "Do you know how long the fields have been like this?"

"No. But they've been this way for as long as Rob and I have been coming up here. But you know, I can still remember the look on Emma's face as she recalled that night. It was almost like she was reliving the event in her mind as she recounted it to me. Her eyes got much wider as she told me that she had become so terrified that she could hardly breath when she entered the wooded part of the road, and she couldn't stop shaking. The last thing that she remembered about that ride was that the horse started snorting just as she heard crashing in the trees to the right of her."

"What happened after that?"

"She didn't know. The next thing that she could remember was that someone was patting her on the face, saying kind and gentle words to her. Once she got the nerve to open up her eyes, she saw that she was in her own bed, and her sister was sitting beside her with a very concerned look on her face."

"Did she tell you how she ended up back in her own bed? Was it Floyd that was making the noise in the woods?"

"I don't think so. Emma told me that after she fainted the horse must have just kept going down the road until he got to her sister's house. She said that her sister was getting ready to go to bed when she and her husband heard the wagon pull up by the porch and stop. After a while, when no one came to knock on the door, her husband got a shotgun and they went outside to see what it was all about. According to Emma, as soon as her sister knew that she was okay, she immediately brought her home. She said that her sister was very concerned about the children being there by themselves."

"Was Floyd at her sister's?"

"No, he was out cat hunting with his brother and did not come home until the next morning. And Emma said she never let him live it down that he didn't tell her what he was up to."

* * *

Eileen had finished her story, and they were still standing at the back of the farmhouse when they heard a snowmobile coming toward them. Eileen looked at Nancy saying, "That's Thad on his Arctic Cat. I can tell the sound of that sled any day of the week."

"Sounds like he is going pretty fast. Let's move a little closer to the snowbank."

"Don't worry. It just sounds that way. If he's doing more than fifteen miles an hour, I'll eat your hat."

Sure enough, as the snowmobile came over the rise their eyes confirmed that it was Thad, and Nancy wondered if he was even doing fifteen miles an hour. It seemed to her that it was a lot slower than that.

* * *

As he brought his machine to a complete stop, he used his best imitation of Scottish brogue to say, "Good morning, my dear lassies, and how're the two of you this fine day?"

A big smile was beaming from Nancy's face as she said, "Good morning to you! We're just peachy! How about you?"

Thad couldn't be sure if that statement didn't hold just a touch of sarcasm, but decided to let it go. "I'm just goin' out for a ride around the loop. Thought I'd check my trails to make sure everything's all right. Are you ladies headin' ....."

Suddenly they all felt it and heard it at the same time. Eileen knew that something was going to happen fast because there wasn't the usual transition from the stone quiet, to the vacuum feeling, to the static noise. It all seemed to happen at once. Eileen instantly started running toward the toboggan to get the shotgun, and Nancy was in hot pursuit right behind her. The moment that they started running to get the shotguns they heard static noise step-up to an intensity that neither one of them had heard before. In an instant both of them felt a surge of adrenalin that gave them a shot of extra speed.

Thad was starting to get off his sled just as the women were about to pick up their weapons. Then in the blink of an eye, all three of them were simultaneously pulled into the shimmering air. It all happened so fast that if anyone had been there to witness the event, they'd have said that the people just seemed to vanish into thin air.

The snowmobiler went down with a shriek of agony, immediately grabbing his knee, as it instantly exploded in grievous pain. When the rider sitting on the middle snowmobile started wailing hysterically, the intruder that Rob had in a stranglehold said, "Please, no more. We are a peace-loving people. We are not used to such brutality."

"Now that's a bunch of malarkey if I ever heard one!"

"Please! Please stop! It is not necessary to use force and vulgarity. It's all so crude. I think that your kind must be Pagans. Don't you know what mercy is?"

"Hey, Rob, give him a quick demonstration of paganism ... pluck out his frigging eyes!"

"What'd ya think about that suggestion, pal? Personally, I think it's a *great* idea!" The rider started begging for mercy as Rob started to apply pressure to his eyes. He relaxed his fingers a little, releasing some of the pressure and said, "What's your name?"

"Guarl ... it's Guarl."

"Man! You *must* be from another dimension! Jack, you ever heard a name like that before?"

"Nope. Maybe it's alien for Billy-Joe-Jim-Bob, or something like that. What'd you think?"

"I think this guy's pulling my twinkie."

The rider cut in and said, "In your language, it's Carl."

Rob shot back, "How do you know so much about our language?"

"We've been studying everything in this dimension ever since the time that there were qulons roaming on this planet. We also understand and speak every language in this world, including all of the dialects."

"What in the hell are qulons?"

"Years ago when your scientists discovered their remains, they named them dinosaurs."

"You've been keeping tabs on this planet for that long? Why?"

"Please let me up so I can attend to Zen, and I'll tell you everything that you want to know."

"That's Zen huh? I guess he's got *two* bad knees now."

"No, he doesn't, just one. Please ... let me tend to him. Can't you hear how much he is suffering?"

"Yeah. But I kind of like the sound of it. It's a good reminder to you and that cry baby on the snowmobile over there that you shouldn't mess with us, or there's gonna be consequences."

"There'll be no more trouble from us. Do you hear that, Joua?"

"Why in the hell are you telling that to *him*. He's nothing but a pansy."

"Don't be so sure of that. He is a decorated patriot in our dimension."

Jack burst out laughing and said, "Really! That means that most everybody in your dimension must be a bigger pussy than him!"

Rob busted in and said, "But if you're a peace-loving people and are not used to brutality, how can that whuss be a decorated patriot?"

Totally ignoring Rob's question he said, "I see that Mr. King is just as crude as you are, Mr. Day. I'm beginning to believe that it is a normal practice with your species."

"First of all, dickhead, we're not members of the animal kingdom. We're members of the human race, and as such we're specifically referred to as being members of the Caucasian race. Breaking that down a little further, we're also referred to as Americans, and we're damn well proud of it."

"Well ... if you are a human and not an animal, please let me tend to my friend. And for your information, species is correct. Look it up, that is if you can remember to, and *that* is questionable.

But if your brain is functioning at least a fraction of its potential, and you do happen to remember, then you'll see that I am correct!"

"Listen, you little twerp, watch your tongue. You're in no position to be anything but contrite, you got that, pal?

Guarl looked at him, but did not say a word. Finally Rob said, "Let me ask you a question, pal. I thought that I hit Zen's left knee pretty damn hard yesterday. That knee should still be giving him a *lot* of grief. So how come you said that he's got only one bad knee?"

"Because when we went back to our dimension yesterday, our healers treated him and now his knee is back to normal."

Jack's body kind of twitched as that information sunk into his conscious mind and he said, "Let me get this straight, Carl. In the little bit of time that you were back to wherever it is that you claim you come from, they not only took care of all the swelling, they also removed all symptoms of the trauma. He feels no pain whatsoever?"

"That is correct. His knee is completely healed."

"Is that right! Hey, Zen! Drop your pants. I've got to see the miraculous job that they did on that bloody knee of yours."

"Mr. King! That is not about to happen. I forbid it!"

Making a show of getting ready to swing the pipe at the second rider, he said, "Yeah? Well I'll tell you what. I think you guys are up to no good, and all this crap that you're feeding us is just that ... crap! If this wimp doesn't want his scrawny neck shattered, then Zen had best show him some compassion real quick, and drop his pants!"

"All right! All right, Mr. King! I'll show you my knee if that's all it takes to make you stop this foolishness!" But instead of reaching up to open his coat to drop what Jack thought would be a typical pair of bib snowmobile pants, Zen reached down toward his left boot.

"Stop right there pal! That is unless you want your buddy's neck turned into mush!"

While grimacing from the pain in his right knee, Zen said through clenched teeth, "I'm just reaching down to pull my pant leg out of the boot so that you can see my knee."

"Yeah? Well let me tell you this pal ... if I see anything coming out of that boot except your hand and the bottom of a pant leg, kiss your buddy goodbye, and if I have time ... kiss *your* derriere goodbye too!"

Zen slowly pulled the pant leg up out of his boot and moved his index finger up along the inseam, and as he did the pant leg parted all the way up to just above his knee. Jack was trying to see what kind of a zipper it was that you could just point at and move it without touching it, when he heard Rob yell, "Look out, Jack!"

The entire show had been nothing more than a ploy to divert his attention away from the rider sitting on the middle snowmobile. They must have had a way to communicate that Jack and Rob had not seen. Jack turned just in time to see Joua rising up off of his snowmobile seat, and he was twisting back around to his left with something in his right hand that was obviously some kind of weapon. Jack dropped his left shoulder and the pipe started its trip around toward Joua's throat. However, his aim had been rushed and the pipe glanced off the guy's snowmobile helmet instead. When the pipe hit the helmet there was a resounding crack that echoed off of the valley's walls, right at the same time as Joua fired his weapon. Even though it was broad daylight, there was a dazzling flash of light that instantly blinded Rob and Jack.

Rob yelled, "Jack! You OK?"

Sounding very subdued he said, "I can't see anything, Rob ... nothing at all."

Rob knew that they needed to maintain control of the situation and instinctively started to exert more pressure on Guarl's eyes, and just as he did he felt a tremendous force rip his arms away from the subdued rider. He never experienced a sensation like that before in his life. He felt no pressure on any one particular part of his arms or hands. It was like something enveloped every square inch of his arms and hands and propelled them away from his captive. All he could equate the feeling to was the reverse effect of an elastic band being stretched to its maximum limits, then released. He could hear someone repeatedly calling him, but it was like being in a dream, not in a conscious state. It sounded hollow and very far away. But after a while the voice kept getting closer and closer, and when reality finally crept back into his consciousness he realized that it was Jack.

"Rob! Rob! Where are you? Rob!"

"Jack, I'm in the same spot where you last saw me holding Guarl. But he's gone now, and I can't see a damn thing! Are you OK?"

"Yeah, but I think these guys just did another disappearing act."

"That's what I think too. I'm starting to get some of my vision back. I can see some light, how about you?"

"Not yet."

"I can make out your silhouette, Jack, but I just can't seem to focus enough to be able to see all of you yet. But I think you're right. I think that they're gone for sure. I don't see *any* sign of them, or their sleds. The only things that I can see is an outline of you, and the outline of our sleds behind me."

"I'll tell you something, Rob. I'm absolutely one hundred percent convinced now."

"Convinced about what?"

"Remember when Joua said that my equipment was primitive, and that it wasn't even an annoyance to them?"

"Oh yeah!"

"Well, I believe him now."

* * *

By the time their vision returned completely, they were still reeling from the experience. They carefully checked the entire area around them for anything that could possibly be a threat. They found the boot prints made by the riders, and the tracks left by their snowmobiles, and also some shoe prints.

When Rob saw the shoe prints he pointed at them and said, "Hey Jack! I guess that's all the evidence that we need."

"All the evidence that we need for what?"

"Come on! You just reminded me about Joua telling you that your primitive device was nothing but an annoyance to them."

Sounding somewhat contrite he said, "Yeah, I see what you're saying."

"If I couple those shoe prints with the fact that those bastards are gone, I'd say that's excellent proof that he knew what he was talking about!"

While Jack thought that one through, Rob looked at his watch and noted that it was 12:00 hours. He tried to remember what time it was when he returned from the clearing below, but he had no recollection whatsoever, and he was not sure if they had lost any time once the bright flash had blinded them. "Hey Jack, what time was it when I left you down in the clearing to come out here?"

"I don't know. I haven't looked at my watch since we left camp. Why?"

"I was just wondering if we lost any time, but there's no way to tell."

"I don't think we did. But let me tell you something my friend. We've only got about five hours of daylight left, and I've got less than ten percent of the data that I need for my research." As he started to walk over to his equipment he asked Rob, "What strategy do you think we should use now? I mean, it's not like these guys aren't privy to what we want to do. If I were them, I'd be avoiding us like the plague!"

"Yeah, you've got a good point there, and I've been thinking about just that problem. Wasn't it Joua that said that they had stopped doing whatever they were doing down in the clearing because they didn't want you to get anymore data?"

"Now that you mention it, yeah, he did. So what's your point?"

"My point is this; if they knew what your intention was and pulled the plug, what makes you so sure that..."

"Hey, Rob! Come here! Quick!"

As he walked over he could see Jack making some adjustments to his equipment and said, "Don't tell me that you lost the little bit of data that you had."

"Not on your life! You're not going to believe this! We got REAL lucky, my friend!"

"Come on, Jack! Quit the crap will yah, and just tell me!"

Getting a smile on his face because he succeeded in getting Rob's goat he said, "Remember when you asked me if I had a stopper, and I said yes?"

"Come on, Jack! Quit bustin' them off on me!"

"You're getting awful touchy ... you know that?"

When Rob did not respond Jack finally said, "OK, OK ... remember when I had told you that I had my equipment on, and that it was creating a cocoon around us as a protective shield?"

"I don't remember the cocoon part, but I remember the shield."

"Well somehow they disabled the shield."

Rob cut in saying, "No shit, Dick Tracy?"

Ignoring his sarcasm Jack said, "I don't understand how this happened, but when they disabled the shield, they activated these receivers at the same time, and my equipment started recording data. I've got at least thirty minutes worth here."

Jack had gotten his undivided attention and he said, "How do you know that?"

"Because my data storage capacity is full, and when that happens the unit automatically shuts itself down."

"There's my answer."

"Answer to what?"

"We lost time! Think about this for a second. I can account for less than fifteen minutes from the time that the shit hit the fan and those guys vanished. What about you?"

Jack thought for a few seconds before saying, "I have to agree with you. It took three or four minutes at most to get our vision back, and about five minutes to look the area over, so yeah ... I'd say you're about right. So?"

"Jack ... you just told me that you have at least thirty minutes of data recorded. What the hell do you think happened during the extra time that your equipment was recording? Remember, you agreed that we can account for about ten minutes, what in the hell do you think we were doing during the other twenty?"

He thought for a minute and started shaking his head in disbelief as he said, "Man ... this shit is scary. I don't like it when I'm not in control, and when we lost time, what *were* we doing? We certainly weren't in control of whatever it was, that's for sure!"

Rob let that one settle into his subconscious as he said, "Let's head back to camp. I want to see what conclusions you can come up with from your data."

* * *

All the recorded data that had been captured by Jack's equipment was transferred to Rob's computer, and Jack had started to decipher it with a program that he had specifically designed for this purpose the night before. Rob watched everything that he was doing, and he did his best to comprehend what his eyes were transmitting to his brain. His facial expression must have been an open book, because when Jack saw the look on his face he said, "I can see that you clearly understand everything that's on this monitor."

"Stick it, you sarcastic, cynical, twit!"

Laughing out loud he said, "My, my. Still a bit touchy, aren't we?"

Feeling a little irritated with himself for being so sensitive, he said, "Probably a lot more than usual. I think that my self defense mechanism is on a high alert status because the women aren't here, and we don't have a clue as to where they are."

"You need to relax and have a little faith. You know that they don't like to just hang around camp. I'm sure that they've gone someplace with Len and the crew."

"Maybe you're right, but my gut feeling tells me that something's wrong. With all this crap that's been happening, it's real hard not to get some negative thoughts from time to time."

Almost as if he had ignored what Rob just stated he said, "Hand me Thad's EEG, would you? I want to compare it with some of this data that my equipment recorded for us."

As Rob went to get it he could hear the printer go into its warm-up mode, and when he got back with it, Jack already had the freshly printed pages laid out on the worktable.

"Let me see that EEG. I want to see if his brain wave pattern comes anywhere close to matching up with what we have recorded."

"What's the purpose of that, Jack?"

"Don't you remember? I have a theory that Thad's memory losses are somehow related to the appearance of the static in the circle of shimmering air, and that's why I asked for a copy of his EEG. Let's see if there's any match with what I printed out here." He laid Thad's EEG down next to each of the pages that he had printed out, and when he got to the next to the last page he found an exact match. "Holy moly! Look at this!"

Rob leaned further over Jack's shoulder, and when he got a glimpse of what Jack was looking at, he quickly stepped around him to where he could easily see the entire EEG and printout. The moment that he saw that the electrical waves on the printout were a mirror image of the EEG, a chill went shooting down his spine.

"Jack, just because there's a match, what makes you think that's the cause of Thad's fugues?"

"I don't know, Rob. Like I said, it's only a theory, and it could be just a coincidence that we have an exact match."

Rob paced quickly around in a circle, stopped short and blurted out, "I gotta call Thad ... right now!"

"Why? What's the big deal?"

"I'm not sure, Jack, but I've got a bad feeling ... a *real* bad feeling. It's like the sword of Damocles is hanging over my head ... ready to drop!"

Rob had to dial the number four times, because the faster that he punched the numbers the worse his accuracy became. Finally on the fourth try he deliberately made sure that he accurately and squarely pressed each number. The phone rang and rang. After about twenty rings Rob said, "I'm goin' up to Thad's. I'll be right back."

"What's the problem?"

"The women aren't here, and what if Thad isn't around? My instincts are telling me that all three of them are gone. Don't ask me why, because I don't know. I've just got that feelin'."

* * *

Rob's anxiety had transferred to Jack, and both of them were totally stressed out by the time they climbed into the Explorer. The front window defroster was blowing full blast, but due to their rapidly accelerating level of stress, both of them were breathing much faster than normal. That caused a problem which was more than the defroster could handle, and the moisture from their breath quickly fogged up the windows. By the time they were coming up to the old deserted farmhouse, the windows in the Explorer were almost totally fogged up.

Jack had kept saying that Rob's imagination was glancing off of the outer limits barrier. Yet. the closer that they got to Thad's, that little spirit of doubt that lurks in the back of everyone's mind was rapidly overshadowing his thinking. Just as they approached the old farmhouse, both of them simultaneously reached up to wipe some of the fog off of the windshield, and that is when they saw Thad's snowmobile alongside of the road. They could plainly see that no one was around, and Jack's mouth suddenly went dry. Instantly his little spirit of doubt shifted gears, slipping immediately into warp speed.

Rob wasn't going very fast since he could not see very well through the fogged up windshield, and as it worked out, he didn't even have to step on the break pedal to slow down. The moment that he had seen Thad's Arctic Cat he took his foot off of the accelerator, and he let the Explorer continue to roll up the slight incline. Just as the SUV rolled to a stop along side of Thad's sled, he stepped on the brake to keep it from rolling backwards. As soon as the vehicle stopped he heard Jack's door slam shut.

Rob continued to sit in the Explorer staring at Thad's sled, and he could almost feel his mind jump into a self-defense mode, fighting the growing feeling of dread that he felt in the pit of his stomach. All of a sudden a thought flashed into his mind, and he quickly pressed the button to get his window down, and his sense of urgency made him think that the window was going down much slower than it ever had before. As soon as it was low enough for him to stick his head out he yelled, "Jack, don't walk past the front of the truck! I want don't want to disturb anything until we can get a good look at what might have happened here." And as an afterthought he said, "Which I pray and hope is nothing."

"Yeah ... me too, Rob. I'm actually hoping that Thad broke down and went back to camp to get something to fix his machine." His mouth was saying hopeful things, but his mind was saying, "Oh, Shit!"

* * *

Rob slid to his right, getting as close to the center console as he could, and then lifted his body over it to the passenger seat. He didn't want to get out of his vehicle on the driver's side because he was afraid that he might mess up some tracks that could tell him something. After stepping out of the Ford he carefully shut the door and looked around the immediate area to see if Jack might have stepped on any of Thad's footprints as he got out. An unbeckoned thought came to his mind; maybe he should add Eileen and Nancy's footprints to that list.

As he stepped away from the SUV to check more of the area he said, "So far so good, Jack. There's no evidence of any tracks here except tire tracks and your footprints."

Satisfied with what he had seen at the front of his vehicle, he walked toward the rear, and as he rounded the back he saw his toboggan sitting alongside the snowbank with the two shotguns lashed to it. Right then and there he knew that the story had been told. He started to shake as his heart sank into the pit of his stomach, and his long time friend could hear the anguish in his voice as he said, "Oh my God! Jack, you'd better come back here!"

Jack felt a foreboding surge through his body as he quickly walked toward the rear of the Explorer saying, "What's wrong?" But in his heart he already knew, and he was dreading what he was about to see. When he saw the toboggan he immediately got a helpless feeling and said, "Aw, fuck! What are we going to do, Rob?"

Jack could feel the panic rising through his whole body. He wanted to run and do something fast. Anything, but what? Common sense started to regain control, and his terror subsided somewhat so he could begin to think this through. But as soon as that happened, his mind took over again and started screaming at him to do something quick. Unfortunately, it was just barking stupid commands at him! It wasn't giving him any logical objectives.

Rob felt a calming resolve enter his body as he started stepping back toward the center of the road. Jack nervously followed him. They stood in the middle of the road for a few seconds before Rob put his hand on his buddy's shoulder saying, "We need a plan to fix this, Jack. But first we've got to piece everything together that happened here."

"What do you mean ... a plan?"

Ignoring his question he said, "Let's take a real close look around here, but be careful not to walk on anything that doesn't look like a tire track." He began his investigation by first looking closely at the road where Jack and he had been walking, making sure that they had not inadvertently stepped on any of the tracks left by Eileen, Nancy or Thad. They had not covered very much ground since getting out of the Explorer, and it did not take him very long to determine that they had not disturbed any of the signs left behind.

Jack stayed right where he was as Rob went around to the back of the Explorer and looked along the road, beyond the driver's side of the SUV, right up to Thad's machine. Satisfied with what he saw, he backed up a couple of steps and looked under the rear of the Ford. As he stood back up he said, "Jack, stay where you are, I'm going to back up and angle it out to the center of the road to give us some maneuvering room. I think we got lucky. It doesn't look like we came close to stepping on any of their tracks."

He didn't bother starting the Explorer. Instead he just placed it in neutral to let it roll back. As soon as the SUV started moving he gently turned the steering wheel to the right to guide it out to the center of the road. By the time that he put the gearshift back into park, Jack was already standing where the Explorer had been, taking in everything that the tracks told him. There was'nt a whole lot to look at, and it didn't take them very long to get a clear picture of what had happened.

Watching where he placed his feet , Rob walked over to Thad's Arctic Cat, and Jack followed directly behind him. They could see where he stood straddling his machine, and it quickly became apparent that he never left it. When they walked up to it for a closer look, they could see that Thad must have twisted around to his right for some reason, because his boot tracks showed that they had slipped in a circular motion somewhat to the left. The story began to unfold when their eyes drifted over to the tracks left by Eileen and Nancy. According to the numerous footprints that they had left behind, it was obvious to Rob that they had been standing in this area for quite awhile, but he could not be sure if Thad had been there with them during the whole time or not. Then he found the tracks that clearly showed that they had turned around in a rush away from Thad, and as he followed them it was easy to see that they had been running toward the toboggan. The final piece of the story was told when their tracks abruptly ended one and three feet respectively from the front end of it. He turned to Jack and said in a subdued voice, "They never got a chance to defend themselves."

For a while neither one of them made a sound as they simply stood there, just staring at the telling evidence around them. Jack began to seethe with rage and was the first to break the silence when he said, "Why the hell don't I see any tracks left by your buddy, Len? Where the frig was he in this whole scenario!?"

Rob looked down at the road as he said, "I really thought that we could count on him, Jack. It just doesn't make any sense. Why would he have called me to say that he was on the way, when he wasn't? Does that make any sense to you?"

Jack did not need a lot of time to think about that one and said, "No, it doesn't. Maybe those guys ended up disappearing too." His eyes wandered along Nancy and Eileen's tracks as he said, "It looks like they definitely knew what was going to happen, because looking at those tracks it's real obvious to me that they were hustling to get to the shotguns."

"Yeah," was Rob's only remark, and then he said, "Jack, let's see if we can find a circular depression anywhere around."

Jack's head jerked quickly in Rob's direction as he said, "What the hell for? Unless you've recently become a total frigging idiot, it's very frigging obvious to me what happened. So why waste more time?"

Rob just stood in one spot looking at his friend for a few moments, and he could see that he was on the edge of losing it. He quickly made up his mind not to throw any fuel on the fire and decided that he needed to find a way to diffuse it. He had to have Jack thinking clearly, not flying off of the handle, so he said in a very calm voice, "All right, Jack, what do you want me to do?"

Jack did not say a word. He just stood there staring at Rob with this helpless look on his face. In all the years that he has known Jack, he had never once seen him come even close to being a defeatist. He always had a way of handling any adversity. However, this time was different. There was absolutely nothing that they could do to remedy the situation. Even though he was badly hurting inside himself, his heart still went out to his friend. "Listen, Jack. We've got to develop a plan to get our wives back, but first let's make absolutely sure that what we have assumed is correct. Doesn't that make sense to you? It's a long shot, I agree, but we could be jumping to the wrong conclusion."

In a much calmer voice Jack said, "Yeah, you're right. I just don't want to lose her, man. I've never been happier in my life than since I've been with her."

"I know, Jack, I know. You and I aren't quitters. We've always been able to find a solution to a problem before, no matter what it was, and we'll do the same this time ... right?"

Jack looked his friend square in the eye as he felt his resolve begin to strengthen and said, "Right!"

Jack, you check down the road, and I'll go up past Thad's machine. Give a yell if you see anything that'll help us out."

Each carefully examined the area around them as they walked along, and Rob finally found a spot up the road that looked like something circular had settled on it. He turned to look in Jack's direction and saw that he was about fifty feet past where the women's tracks had ended and yelled, "Hey Jack, if you haven't seen anything yet, I don't think that you're going to. I've never seen a depression that far from where tracks ended, or began, for that matter. Come up here, I think that I may have something."

Jack joined him and they carefully analyzed what looked like it could have been a circular impression on the right hand side of the road, but they could not be one hundred percent certain because several sets of tire tracks went right through it. Looking over at his buddy Rob said, "The game wardens must have been up here checking the deer herd, or something, that's the only thing that makes sense to me with this many tire tracks in the road. It's too early in the week for the weekend warriors to be up here."

"I've got an idea, Rob. Just for the hell of it, why don't we go check Thad's camp?"

"Yeah, that's a good idea. Besides, if we don't find Thad up there, and I really don't expect to, we should bring Ginger back with us. She and Rudy can keep each other company, which reminds me! I don't remember seeing Rudy when we were back at camp, do you?"

"Now that you mention it, no."

Rob felt a new nervousness begin to vibrate through his body while they walked back to his SUV. He did not see any of Rudy's tracks near the toboggan, or anywhere in the area for that matter, but why didn't he see him at camp? He was very anxious to get back to make sure that his furry friend was there.

The short ride up to Thad's was totally silent except for the sound of the Ford's engine and the blower motor defogging the windows. As they had expected, Thad was nowhere to be found, and Ginger was genuinely happy to see them. She didn't hesitate at all when Rob offered her a ride in his Explorer. It was like she knew that something significant was about to change in her life, and that she had to try to do something about it.

* * *

The moment that they walked into the camp Ginger promptly made her way over to Rudy's food dish, and as soon as she found that it was empty she made a beeline to the cabinet that contained her favorite goodies. Jack walked right past her on his way to his bedroom upstairs, he wanted to check out what Nancy had been wearing when she went out, although he was not sure how that information could be of any help in this whole ordeal.

Even before he had stepped all the way into the camp, Rob had started calling out to Rudy. He checked each and every room to see if he was sleeping in one of them, and he was absolutely crushed when he didn't find him. He was convinced that for some reason those bastards had grabbed him again. He was so deep in his vengeful thoughts that he did not see Ginger sitting in front of the cabinet when he walked into the kitchen.

She was undaunted by the lack of attention and let out a short but demanding soft woof. At first when he heard the muffled woof Rob's heart started to quicken with joy, but it quickly sank when he remembered that Ginger was with them. He saw her sitting in front of the goodies cabinet and automatically made his way over to her.

He had just put his hand on the cabinet door handle when he heard Rudy's unmistakable bark, and it sounded like he was outside in front of the camp. His mind started to jump to all kinds of positive conclusions, and he got very excited as he quickly went to the front door. By the time that he started to open it, he had convinced himself that in spite of all the evidence that he had seen at the farmhouse, he had misread it. He was certain that he would find Rudy standing there with Eileen and Nancy, and in his mind he could see them looking up at him with a big grin on their faces. However, the balloon burst when he opened the door, and most of his joy rapidly vanished into thin air when he found only Rudy standing there.

"Hey ... Toot-man!" He bent down to scratch his old friend behind the ears as he said, "How ya doing, buddy?"

But something was obviously *very* wrong because Rudy was not doing his normal happy act. He just lethargically stood in one place, showing no emotion whatsoever. Rob continued scratching him behind his ears, which always brought forth grunts of pleasure from him ... but not this time. Leaning closer to him he said, "What's the matter, Toot?" And that's when he saw tears welling out of Rudy's eyes. He never remembered seeing this before, and as he stood up he was trying to comprehend what was taking place. Stepping to the side and opening the door as wide as he could he said, "Come, Toot."

Before Rudy could move, Ginger came walking out onto the porch and stood nose to nose with him for the better part of a minute. Rob simply stood there watching them while the heat rapidly emptied out of the camp through the wide open door. It was like everything was suspended in time while the dogs communicated. Finally they both looked up at him with what looked like a sad and longing look in their eyes, and then they slowly walked into the camp.

Jack was sitting on the love seat by the phone as Rob walked into the living room. He noticed the dogs following him, and when he saw how they were walking he said, "Hey, Rob, what did you do to those dogs? I've never seen them look so dejected."

Rob looked at the dogs behind him and said, "Not a thing, Jack. I think they fully comprehend what went on around here today. I think they know that some people that are very important to them are no longer around."

Jack was not in the mood for any stupidity and said, "Like I said before, Rob, you've been watching too many of those Lassie movies."

Rob gave Jack a look that could have killed if it was armed, but did not say a word. He walked into the kitchen to get the Milk-Bone dog biscuits, and by the time that he had closed the cabinet door and walked back into the living room, Rudy was lying on his doggy bed. His back legs were stretched out behind him, and his head was resting on the bed between his front legs. As Rob walked across the living room from the kitchen, only Rudy's eyes moved as he followed his master's movement.

Jack was watching everything that was going on and said, "What's with him, Rob? He doesn't look like he's very interested in that dog biscuit."

Rob looked at Jack for a few seconds, trying to make up his mind if he should answer him or not. Finally he said, "I wish I could tell you what went on between Ginger and him out on the front porch." And instantly he regretted his last statement. He was absolutely certain that Jack was going to jump on the Lassie thing again.

Jack looked quizzically back at him and said, "Well, now that you've got me hooked, you'd better at least tell me what you saw."

Letting out a long sigh he said, "The two of them stood face-to-face, nose to nose for the better part of a minute, and neither one of them was wagging their tail. I don't know about you, but I've never seen two dogs that are as close to each other as these two are, not wag their tail and use some kind of body language to show their genuine pleasure to be with their friend again."

When Jack had seen Rob's reaction to his Lassie quip, he instantly regretted making the statement, even though that was the way that he actually felt. So now he resigned himself to indulge this stupid line of conversation and said, "I don't know nearly as much about dogs as you do, but as far as I'm concerned, you're making a mountain out of a molehill. I think that they're just stressed out like you and me."

Rob just stood in one place for a few moments and considered what his buddy had just said. Then turning to Ginger he laid a biscuit in front of her nose as he said, "I agree with your statement that they are probably stressed out like you and me, but I do not believe that accounts for their behavior. I think that there's much more to it, and that's why I said that I wish I could tell you what went on between them. I firmly believe that these two dogs were telepathically communicating, and yeah, I know what you're thinking."

"And just what do you think I'm thinking?"

"That I've seen too many Lassie movies. Right?"

"Right!"

* * *

Rob had been staring out the kitchen picture window trying to gather his thoughts when he looked up at the clock on the wall and saw that it was 13:05 hours. He looked over at his friend and saw him leaning his elbow on the kitchen table with his chin in his hand, and he was staring at a spinning pencil that he continuously twirled the moment that it slowed down. "Penny for your thoughts, Jack."

He looked up at him and Rob saw that he had tears in his eyes. "Hey, buddy, I know where your mind has been and that ain't doin' nobody any good."

Without taking his chin out of his hand, Jack nodded his agreement and said, "You know, Rudy has not been acting like himself ever since we took our walk this morning. Perhaps it started when his attention was captivated by whatever it was that made him stare up at that ridge by the big boulder." He paused to gather his thoughts and said, "We need to start doing something right now. I can't continue to just sit here feeling sorry for myself. Why don't you go check out whatever is up on that ledge, and let me continue to see if I can get some answers from the data that we collected this morning."

Rob remained standing by the kitchen table, again staring out the picture window, but not really focusing on anything in particular. Without turning around he said, "It's a place to start. Unless I come up with some surprises, it'll probably take me about twenty minutes to check that area over. Does that give you enough time to study your data?"

"Probably not. I figure that I'll need the better part of an hour."

"Okay, see ya in an hour then."

* * *

He parked his Formula in front of the big boulder, put on his snowshoes and started walking into the woods at a forty-five degree angle to the trail that Rudy, Jack, and he had left that morning. He knew that he could not climb the ledge from where they had stood looking up at it, but he remembered seeing that it sloped somewhat downward when he looked off to the right. After walking the better part of two hundred feet he found the way up that he was looking for. The ledge sloped down into a miniature horseshoe-type valley, making it a very easy climb for him.

He stayed about three feet in from the edge of the ledge, and had walked about fifty feet up the incline when the terrain in front of him dramatically changed. Suddenly he found himself looking up a steep rise, and as he climbed to the top of it, it started to give way very easily. He stopped and looked to his left and right, and as far as he was able to see, the rise came to a very defined edge in both directions. Actually, when he thought about it, the crest of the rise looked very similar to the edge of a knife.

He started to take another step, and the snowbank instantly began to crumble. He was unprepared for such a sudden change and almost lost his balance. Completely stopping his movement, he looked down into what reminded him of a crater, and momentarily wondered how Mother Nature created this strange formation. But that thought was only momentary, and then he began to draw some other conclusions.

Looking all around the immediate area, he decided to check just how firm the snow was that he was standing on. He bounced up and down on his snowshoes several times, bouncing a little harder each time. Finally when he reached the point that he was sure he was not sinking any further, he looked down at his snowshoes and could easily see that they were only another inch or so deeper in the snow. Now confident that he would not be venturing into a snowy quagmire, he walked approximately fifteen feet down into the crater below. As soon as he was on the flat surface he casually took a few steps out from the snowbank. Before going any further he took a careful look along the perimeter that he could see to the left and right of him. He let everything that he had seen while up on top of the snowbank settle into his mind a bit, along with what he could see from where he was standing. He finally had to admit that this valley reminded him somewhat of the various depressions that he had seen over the past few days. The major exception being the fact that the walls of this depression curved downward for about fifteen feet, and then it flattened out. Whereas the other depressions had been symmetrically concave.

The snow that he was standing on was very hard-packed, as a matter of fact it was so hard-packed that his snowshoes barely broke through the surface, so he decided to take them off. While he was unbuckling the straps he turned his head to the right and saw numerous boot and shoe tracks. They were everywhere that he looked. Talking out loud he said, "Holy moly! It looks like there was a frigging convention here!"

Once he had his snowshoes off he tried to jam their tails into the flat surface right next to him, only all they did was bounce off of the hard packed snow. He bent over to get a closer look at the impressions that the tails had left in the snow, only there was not much of an imprint. The two depressions were only about a half an inch deep, and it looked like soft snow was puffed up all around the perimeter. Slipping off his right glove he brushed the snow aside and immediately ran into a layer of ice.

Slowly standing up, he could not grasp the reason for the ice lying just under the snow. It appeared that something very hot had been on the surface, making all the snow under it liquefy. But what could it have been? If it was the circle of air that had touched down here, why isn't the depression concave like all of the rest?

Dozens of questions were running through his head, and not one logical answer came to mind. Finally he stuck the tails of his snowshoes into the soft snow near the bottom of the snowbank that he had just walked down. Once he was satisfied that they would not topple over, making it more difficult for him to find them later, he turned around, and with his back to the snowbank looked in both directions along the bottom perimeter of the icy crater. Deciding that his first mission was going to be to locate the spot where he, Rudy, and Jack had stood while looking up here, he worked his way to his left.

He followed the bottom edge of the snowbank until he came to the location that he believed would allow him to see the area where they had been standing below the ledge this morning. But in order to confirm that belief, he had to climb up the slope to get a better look. He began to get a little nervous as he approached the upper edge of the incline. The snow was becoming much softer, just like the snowbank that he climbed to get in here. The higher he climbed, the easier the snow seemed to give way, and visions of falling over the edge of the ledge flashed before his eyes. He tried to convince himself that it was his mind playing tricks on him, but then he began to wonder if a warning was actually being sent to him.

Ultimately, he decided to follow his instincts, and edged back down the slope. Talking to himself once again he said, "I think I'll continue following the bottom of this slope and see if it brings me back to where I left my snowshoes."

As he walked along the entire perimeter of this newly created valley, he continually performed a thorough scan as far as he could see in all directions around him. He had to marvel at all the boot and shoe tracks in the soft thin layer of snow that covered the entire icy surface – they were everywhere that he looked. And they were not going in any particular direction, they looked random, like the people that had made them were just walking around in a stupor.

He looked at his watch to see how much time he had left, and was mildly surprised to see that he still had more than twenty-five minutes to go. A smile worked its way onto his face as he said, "It's just like when I was in history class in junior high school. Every time I looked at the clock on the wall, it seemed like time was moving in slow motion. But then again, maybe I just want the time to move quick because I think that this exercise is a waste of time in the overall picture."

As he stepped around a particularly large pine tree near the side of the snowbank, he could see his snowshoes about fifty feet up ahead of him, and he picked up his pace to get to them. He had just pulled them out of the snow and was about to walk back toward the point where he thought that Jack, Rudy, and he had been looking up at the ledge, when he heard a noise that sounded like water gurgling down the throat of a toilet during the last phase of a flush. He turned and looked in the direction that he thought the sound had come from, but it was gone as fast as it had made itself known. Rob shook his head from side to side, wondering if he was conjuring up some of these things in his own mind. A couple more moments went by before he started back to the point in the ledge that he had wanted to check out, just to confirm that it was in fact the same spot that they had been looking up at.

When he got to the place in the snowbank that he had started to climb and had ultimately chickened out, he strapped on his snowshoes. However, instead of starting up the bank right away, he turned around and looked in the direction that he thought that he had heard the gurgling sound. He stood in the same position for the better part of a half a minute before turning back around to side step up the incline. He had only taken four steps when he started chuckling to himself, and again talking out loud for no other reason than to hear himself talk he said, "I guess I was just trying to see if my mind would create that gurgling sound again."

As he neared the upper edge of the incline, he started to sink in deeper than he had expected to with his snowshoes on. Slowing his pace he began to take more care with each step, and finally decided to gingerly lie down to look over the edge of the bank when he was about four feet from the top. He was very concerned that the snow would not support him, and falling off of the ledge was definitely not at the top of his list of priorities. Once he was fully stretched out on the snowbank, and reasonably sure that the snow was going to support his weight, he looked over the ledge to confirm that he was above where he had stood with Rudy and Jack that morning.

He could hardly believe what his eyes were telling him, but stopped short of rubbing them although he thought that they could be playing tricks on him. He did not want to lose sight of the object in front of him. He was also concerned that something might happen during that brief moment of time when he lost visual contact with the object he was looking at.

Right over the exact same spot where Jack, Rudy and he had been standing early this morning, there was a translucent sphere hovering about three feet above the snow. He could not bring himself to do anything more than stare at it while he tried to make up his mind if it was actually a figment of his imagination. As he continued to stare at the sphere, he saw something begin to take a shape inside. His mouth dropped wide open as it developed into what looked like the figure of a human being. It did not have any recognizable features other than the rough human shape. As the form fully developed he could see variations of color, almost as though he were looking at an aura, except it did not have the blazing fire-like outline. After about two minutes passed, he could distinctly make out the shape of a human, but then he thought that human was not really an accurate description.

A few more seconds went by and he thought about the movie, The Predator, and how the alien creature saw the human form in various shades of color. For the life of him he didn't understand why, but he tried to remember why the alien could see life forms as various shades of reds, blues, and greens. He was still wrestling with that thought when he saw the form's head start to move, and it moved in such a manner that it was obviously checking out its surroundings. He held his breath because he did not want a cloud of puffy steam to give away his presence, and he remained rock still while he intently watched the thing examine its surroundings. He felt a warm sensation fill the crotch of his pants when the form's head suddenly jerked to look directly up at him. He couldn't see its eyes, but he felt the eye contact just the same, and as soon as he did, the sphere instantly vanished.

His mind was in a turmoil and he could not focus on anything for a few moments. Finally he said to himself, "What the hell *is* goin' on here." He looked back down to where the sphere had been, hoping that he would see it again, but then he quickly thought that maybe he was checking to make sure that it was still gone ... and it was.

When it became obvious to him that the event was over, he started to put pressure on his elbow to lift himself to a standing position. Suddenly he felt the bank starting to give way. His body automatically reacted, and he immediately started to roll over to his left side, while doing his best to bring himself parallel to the upper edge of the incline. The last thing that he wanted to do was fall twenty some odd feet to the surface below. It would be one thing if he landed in a deep cushion of snow, but it would be another if he landed on a pointed object buried underneath it. However, as he began to roll down the incline he wondered if the fall would not have been a better option. Each time that he made a full revolution, he felt like his ankles were going to snap before the snowshoes finally broke loose and followed as he tumbled down the bank. When he landed at the bottom and looked up to the top of the snowbank, he saw that a large section of the rim was missing.

While he was taking off his snowshoes he said to himself, "Maybe that gurgling sound that I heard before wasn't a figment of my imagination after all. Perhaps I should take a look around to see if I can locate where that sound had come from. If I find it, maybe it'll give me some more pieces to this puzzle."

He had just placed his snowshoes on his shoulder and started to take a step toward the interior of the depression when he heard three shots ring out that were spaced about one second apart, and they came from the direction of Camp Stress-A-Rest. His first thought was that Jack had a problem and needed him back there quick, but then it occurred to him that maybe he had been gone longer than an hour, and looked at his watch. However, it was only 13:40 hours. Then a very happy thought took over his mind as he imagined that the women had come back to camp. The mission to check out the gurgling sound was completely forgotten, and he decided that it didn't matter why Jack wanted him back at camp. He resolved to get his butt in gear, and rush back there.

* * *

When Rob walked into the camp he found Rudy lying in the exact same position that he had last seen him before he went to check things out up on the ledge. He watched his eyes follow him as he walked over to pet him on the head. "What's the matter, Toot? I hope that you're okay ol' buddy." Just before standing up, he gave him an affectionate scratch behind the ears then headed off toward his office where he could hear Jack rapidly typing on the computer keyboard. Setting his helmet and gloves on the humidifier next to the office door, he went into the bedroom to put on some dry underwear and dungarees. He had made up his mind that he would leave out the part about pissing in his pants when he told Jack about the sphere.

As soon as he had changed, he walked into his office to see what his buddy was doing. Ginger was lying at Jack's feet, and he barely acknowledged that Rob was standing alongside of him.

He could see his rifle leaning up against his desk as he said, "How come you fired the signal shots for me to come back?"

"I've got a plan," and then he shut up.

Rob stood alongside of Jack for more than a minute, and since he was being ignored he assumed that Jack was typing up the details of the plan. Because of the glare on the screen he could not make out a single word of the text, and for a change *he* was the one getting fidgety. Actually he was beginning to get pissed that Jack was ignoring him, especially after making the opening statement that he had. However he finally rationalized that he must have a good reason for not saying anything more at this time, and maybe it was because he did not want to break his concentration until he finished typing. Unwilling to just stand there any longer he finally said, "I'm going to grab a beer, Jack, do you want one?"

Jack looked up at Rob with a totally unreadable poker face and said, "Beer's out of the question for me, but don't let that stop you from having one."

That statement got Rob's attention and he said, "Forget the beer. I'd just like to know what you've got on your mind?"

"I've been studying this data that my equipment recorded, and I've been through it three times now. I think I have a pretty good handle on some of the answers that we have been looking for, but now is not the time to discuss them with you. It's 14:05 hours and we're burning daylight. The way I see it, the only way that we're going to be able to help Nancy, Eileen and Thad is to find a way to get into that circle of air. Of course there's a short fall to that statement ... first we need to figure out how."

"I agree, and that's just what I've been thinking about."

Jack looked up at him and said, "Did you come up with any ideas?"

"Oh yeah, lots of them. But not one of them makes any sense."

Jack sat there shaking his head up and down in agreement and said, "We need to find a way to help our wives and Thad, and to do that we need to be where they are."

"I've been thinking along those same lines, Jack, I just haven't come up with the how, have you?"

"Not yet. The only idea that keeps jumping out at me is this, we need more information on this circle of wavering air."

"What kind of information, Jack? I mean, wasn't the thirty some odd minutes of information that you recorded today enough to understand what makes that circle of air tick?"

"Not even close. It helped me to understand more about some of the attributes of this phenomenon, but there sure wasn't anything solid that would help us in our mission to find our wives. I do have a place to start, though."

"Yeah, well put that thought on hold for a minute. There's something that I need to tell you about what happened while I was up on the ledge, and it might end up changing whatever you've got planned. By the time that Rob finished telling him about the icy crater, the shoe and boot prints running every which way everywhere that he looked, the sound of a toilet flushing and the sphere, Jack was up and pacing the room like a caged lion. Finally he stopped right in front of Rob, looked him in the eye and said in a conversational tone, "We're in way over our heads, and what's worse, we've got no one to turn to without risking being put into a psychiatric ward at some hospital while they try to figure out what we did with our wives' bodies."

"I agree. We're between a rock and a hard place. Listen, I interrupted you before when you said that you had a place to start. If what I've just told you hasn't changed your mind, then I'm all ears, Jack. What do you have in mind?"

Almost relieved that the subject was changed he said, "We need more visual information about what is on the other side of that shimmering air, and we need it now, not in a day or so. This is my plan: I think that if I go up in my Cherokee to act as a spotter to find the circle of air, and direct you to it on the ground, that should speed things up in a big way. The way that I see it, this plan of attack will dramatically magnify our ability to gather data more expeditiously. What do you think?"

Rob could feel excitement begin to flow through his body as he said, "I agree. It's a great idea! We've absolutely *got* to have a better handle on what to expect on the other side of that shimmering air. I'll put some new batteries in my hand-held NAV/COM and gas up my sled. By the way, do you want to use the Rangeley Airport Unicom channel to communicate, or some other channel?"

"I think that using the Rangeley Unicom will broadcast to the world what we're doing, and I don't think that's a good idea right now. So let's use a different channel."

Rob thought about that for only a second and said, "Yeah, I agree. Good thinking, Jack. I'll give Larry Williams a call and ask him to warm up the engine on your Cherokee."

Jack got a sheepish grin on his face as he turned to Rob and said, "Thanks for that one. I should of thought of that myself."

Not wanting to let the upper hand go just yet, Rob said, "You didn't fuel up your bird when you landed yesterday. Just thought I'd remind you of that in case you need to load some on."

With an Ellen Barkin-like sneer developing at the corner of his mouth he said, "Thanks again. I just know that statement came from your heart, and not from your open pit of sarcastic remarks."

10

It was 14:20 hours and Jack was on his way to the Rangeley Airport. Rob checked on the dogs before he filled up Rudy's water dish and also filled his stainless steel bowl with IAMS. He still couldn't get a rise out of him, even when he put a dog biscuit in front of his nose. He gave Rudy a scratch behind his ears and a pat on the head and said, "I'll just leave this biscuit right here for you, Toot." Looking over at Ginger as he was standing up, he saw that she had already eaten the biggest part of the biscuit that he had just given to her. As soon as she saw that he was getting ready to leave, she scrambled to get up and trotted immediately over to him. The moment that she was alongside of him she gave him a firm nudge in his right thigh with her nose, and he had no trouble figuring out what that was all about. She was letting him know in no uncertain terms that one biscuit was simply not enough. "Okay. Okay, fatso, I'll get you one more, but you're going to have to jog one mile tonight to work off the extra calories." As soon as he said it he knew that it would most likely never happen.

Talking to himself, he said, "At best, Jack won't get up into the air until 15:00 hours, and the last thing that I want to do is hang around here for the better part of an hour. I think I'll take a slow ride up and down Harris Pasture Road and see how lucky I get." He mounted the hand-held NAV/COM speaker and voice activated microphone in his helmet, and then he tucked the NAV/COM in the inside breast pocket of his snowmobile coat. Just before walking out the front door he gave one last concerned look at the Toot-man.

* * *

He had just passed the turnoff by the huge boulder on Harris Pasture Road when he began to methodically think through everything that Eileen and Nancy could have experienced during the phenomenons, hoping to find a clue that would help him develop a strategy to get the women back. He reflected upon the conversation in which Eileen had told him everything she could recall about the first appearance of the stranger in front of the camp, and remembered that she had said, "It was like someone popped a flash card into my mind, and I remembered that you had a shotgun and ammo upstairs." Rob muttered to himself, "I wonder if her Guardian Angel had anything to do with that?" The more he thought about it, the clearer it became that indeed it was probable that her Guardian Spirit had helped her.

He had just barely completed that thought when another memory came to mind. He remembered a dream that he had had recently. It happened as he was coming out of his deep sleep phase for the night, and it had been so vivid, that for a while he was convinced that it had actually happened. Even now he could clearly see himself sitting forward on the living room couch in their home in Cape Elizabeth, suddenly feeling a gentle pressure on the backside of his legs, right above the knees, and also under each armpit. As the pressure increased, he had felt himself being lifted off of the couch. For a second or two he was suspended in the air, sort of hovering about six inches above the sofa. Then he felt himself moving slowly forward, and as the forward movement accelerated, he rose higher and higher off of the floor until he was about three feet above it. Even though he did not understand what was happening to him, and what's more he had absolutely no control over it, he had no fear. In fact he was awestruck, and his sense of well-being amplified one hundred fold as he continued to rise even further off of the floor during his forward movement. During the time that he was circling around the entire room, he seemed to be moving in slow motion.

He vowed that he'd always remember the feeling of elation that he had, and he heard himself calling upstairs to Eileen to "come and take a look." By the time that the first revolution around the room had been completed, he had been elevated about another two feet above the floor, and made yet another complete revolution around the room. He had wondered why he had no fear whatsoever, because in the past whenever he climbed a ladder, he would get very nervous as soon as he stepped as high as the third rung. But in this case, being air born was not only comfortable but he realized that he was totally at peace.

As the third revolution began and he felt himself rise up about another three feet, his wife had appeared at the railing upstairs and said, "Oh my God!"

It was then that, he felt himself descending, gradually angling toward the couch, then the circling stopped and he was gently lowered back onto it. Rob woke up at that point, and immediately wrote down every detail while it was fresh in his mind. As he put the pad and pencil back into his nightstand drawer, he felt a pang of disappointment that it was only a dream. But then he thought, since it seemed so real, maybe there was more to it than just a dream.

Rob came out of his reverie as he found himself crossing the bridge by the beaver pond. The moment that he realized where he was, he gently squeezed the brake handle, bringing the snowmobile to a complete stop before reaching the opposite side of the bridge. He shut off the machine and slowly looked around the whole area. After a few minutes he said to himself, "Nothing out of the ordinary, but then again, maybe I shouldn't say that because these strange happenings are becoming quite ordinary."

* * *

Larry Williams was still warming up the engine on the Cherokee when Jack King climbed up onto the wing and unlocked the cockpit door. Larry hadn't realized that he was there because of the noise that the blower motor was making, and he spun around in surprise when Jack tapped him on his right shoulder. "How much longer, Larry?"

"About five minutes. What's the matter, don't you say hello to your friends anymore?"

"Sorry, Larry, I'm just preoccupied. You know I'm not a stuffed shirt."

"Yeah, I know that. Is Rob okay? He didn't seem like himself when he called me before."

"I guess you could say that both of us are preoccupied today. By the way, would you mind fueling my plane for me while I make a phone call?"

"Sure. Be happy to."

Jack handed Larry the keys to the Cherokee and walked over to the office to use the payphone. On the way over to the airport he had made up his mind that he had better call some pilot friends and alert them to the fact that Rob and he might need some help on Friday. He did not have a clue as to what kind of help that might be, and to make things worse, he wasn't quite sure how he was going to approach the topic during each conversation. He made seven phone calls in all, and was fortunate enough to be able to talk to five pilots. He felt especially lucky when four of them said that they would keep the date open in case he needed their help.

Larry was just taxiing the Cherokee over to its parking place as Jack came out of the Flight Base Operations (FBO) office. He caught Larry's eye and motioned for him to turn the plane around, and at the same time he signaled to him that he was going to depart right away. Larry promptly increased the RPMs and turned the aircraft around. He had intended to shut the Cherokee down because he wanted Jack to tell him why he and Rob were so preoccupied today. But just as he was reaching for the throttle and fuel shut off, Jack opened the door and said, "Just set the handbrake and I'll hop right in."

Larry shook his head no and said, "I'm not going to do that, Jack, it's too dangerous without chocks." Jack held up his hand, signaling to Larry to hold tight, and without another word he jumped off the wing, grabbed a pair of chocks and put them in place.

He climbed back up on the wing just as Larry opened the cabin door and began yelling over the sound of the engine, "I really want to talk to you, Jack! You promise me that when you get back you'll give me a call?"

Jack gave him a thumb's up and said, "You got it, pal!"

As Larry closed the cockpit door he said, "Call me at home. I'm not going anywhere at all today."

Jack nodded his acknowledgment as he locked the door.

When he felt the aircraft rise up slightly as Larry stepped off the wing, he keyed the mike and said, "This is Cherokee Two Five One Whiskey Papa at the Rangeley Airport taxiing to the active runway three two." As he pushed the throttle forward and started rolling, he looked over his left shoulder and saw Larry standing by the FBO watching him. He waved and Larry waved back just as the Cherokee rolled past the corner of the hanger and out of sight.

As soon as he reached 1000 feet AGL he immediately set his course to take him to the beaver pond. "Rob Day, this is Cherokee Two Five One Whiskey Papa. Do you read me?"

* * *

Rob had been sitting on the bridge at the beaver pond for less than five minutes before he decided to take a ride up to Harris Pasture. He had no idea what motivated him to go up there except for the fact that the view of Flagstaff Lake from Dave Spencer's front porch was spectacular, and he had nothing better to do just now. When he got up there, he saw a depression that was almost in the middle of the clearing below Dave's camp, and noticed there were several sets of animal tracks that seemed to end within ten to fifteen feet of it. He said to himself, "I'll be... It looks like the frigging schmucks have been busy here too. I wonder if Spence has been up here to see any of this."

With that, he shut off his machine and took a walk to the back of the camp, and when he rounded the corner he found the answer to his question. Two snowmobiles were parked there. He knew Dave didn't leave his machines at camp when he wasn't around. Then he thought, "Well, that's funny, because I don't remember seeing his pickup truck and snowmobile trailer parked out on the Kennebago Settlement Road." He walked up to the camp's back door and tried to push it in as he turned the doorknob. The door opened easily and he stepped inside yelling loudly, "Dave! Leona! Are you guys here?"

He walked through the whole place and it seemed obvious to him that Dave and Leona would be somewhere around. Except for being as cold inside as it was outside, the camp looked lived in. When he looked in the bedroom he saw that the covers were turned aside from both sides of the double bed, as though both of them had quickly gotten out of bed to do something, and evidently with all intentions of getting more sleep. As he was walking back out into the living room he heard Jack calling him on his hand-held NAV/COM. He pulled the radio out of the inside breast pocket of his snowmobile coat and said, "Cherokee Whiskey Papa, this is Rob. I read you, loud and clear."

"Rob, I'm about two and a half miles southwest of the beaver pond, both tanks full of fuel."

"10-4 on the full fuel. Do you see anything developing up there?"

"Negative. But if recent history holds true, it won't be long before something does."

"I agree with that statement! I'm up in Harris Pasture in Dave Spencer's camp. I've got some interesting things to tell you when you're back on the ground."

"How interesting?"

Rob thought for a moment and said, "I think that Dave and Leona might have taken a walk with Nancy and Eileen."

Jack didn't say the words that had been forming on his lips, which were "Holy moly!" He took control of his knee jerk reaction because he felt that is was absolutely necessary to do everything by the book to prevent suspicious minds from being activated. He quickly responded by saying, "You've got to be joking!"

"I wish I was." He had just keyed his mike to add another bit of wisdom, but Rob never got to hear it.

* * *

"Rob, I think this is way over our heads. We need to come up with a logical way to get some help." As soon as Jack let his thumb off of the transmit button, static started blaring in his earphones. He quickly turned the volume control way down to get rid of the raucous noise that was screaming in his head, but the damage was already done and he had a loud ringing in his ears. He concluded that his radio transmission to Rob had been jammed, and began to methodically scan the entire area, looking for a circle of shimmering air. He suddenly found what he was looking for when he looked up toward the clearing on the top of East Kennebago Mountain. However the thrill of success was short lived as wave after wave of chills ran through his body the moment that he spotted it. As he tried to focus on it, he thought that he could see radio waves emanating from it that were actually visible to the naked eye. What's more, it looked like they were coming in his direction! Only these radio waves were far different than anything that he had ever seen in a textbook. Instead of starting out small and increasing in size as they got further from the transmitting tower, these waves seemed to be radiating from the outer perimeter of the circle of shimmering air, and got smaller as they came toward him. Jack blinked his eyes several times to make sure that he wasn't hallucinating, and when he looked again the waves were gone.

Now convinced that he had been imagining things, he reached for the volume control on the radio, only to find that when he turned it up, the static was still there. He tried different frequencies, but every single channel was the same. He needed to find a way to communicate with Rob. He had to let him know that the circle of distorted air had appeared up on the Kennebago! His mind was scrambling for an answer, and as each second ticked by he became more and more frustrated with himself. He was stymied for the moment. But then a thought that made some sense to him began to take shape in his mind, and he quickly built a plan around it. When his strategy was complete, he said out loud, "Well, I'll just play the role of Lassie."

Dropping the nose of his Cherokee, he banked left to come back around on a heading to Harris Pasture, and as he approached 500 feet AGL, he eased the nose back up for level flight. As he drew nearer to Rob's location the terrain below him started to climb, and so did he, enough to maintain 500 feet AGL. Reaching for the throttle, he pulled it back and reduced power as he crested the rise just before Harris Pasture. The instant he went over it, he spotted Dave Spencer's camp and Rob's snowmobile, but there was no sight of Rob.

* * *

When Rob could get nothing but static noise on his NAV/ COM, he walked out onto the front porch to see if he could find a circle of shimmering air. He had been standing there scanning the entire area around Harris Pasture for the better part of three minutes when he heard the sound of an airplane directly over the camp. Stepping off of the porch he looked up and saw Jack's plane in a climb. Rob ran over to his snowmobile, keeping an eye on Jack as he made that wide turn that would bring him over Tim Pass.

He sat down on his machine, turned the key to start it, and upon hearing the pleasing sound of that Bombardier engine humming smoothly, he stood up on the tunnel rails. Rob watched as Jack completed his 180-degree turn and came about on a heading that would bring him directly above him. Reaching up as high as he could, he started waving his arms to get Jack's attention.

Jack completed his turn over Tim Pass and lowered the Cherokee's nose so he could get a quick look around Spencer's camp and see if he could spot Rob. As soon as he saw him waving his arms, he pulled the nose back up and made a climbing right turn to come back around one more time. As he completed his turn this time, he lined up his angle of descent so that it would bring him directly over Rob, but he also wanted it to line up with the trail that went from Dave's camp on down to ITS 89. As he approached Rob, he started to rock the plane, wagging his wing tips up and down, and continued doing so as he passed over him and continued on down the mountain.

* * *

While maneuvering his machine out into a clearing in order to turn around and follow Jack, he yelled out, "I got the hint, buddy!" The snow seemed to be good and firm as Rob picked up speed, so he squeezed the throttle harder and he leaned hard into the turn. As he came out of it and accelerated toward the snowmobile trail in front of Spence's camp, he lifted his butt off of the seat because he knew that he would be grabbing some air. The moment that the sled was airborne he leaned forward and stood up a little further, and by the time that he had gone another twenty-five feet after touching back down on the snow, he was doing sixty-five mph, which was *way* too fast for this narrow trail. The only thing that he had going for him in the realm of safety was the fact that the trail was fairly straight almost all of the way to ITS 89.

* * *

Jack saw the beaver pond straight ahead and started pulling back on the yoke to make a climbing turn to the left, with the intention of leveling off at 1000 feet AGL. Once he completed a 270-degree turn he had a clear view of the top of East Kennebago Mountain. The circle of air was still there, and once again he had the visual sensation that translucent radio waves were coming from it, kind of like bubbles coming up out of water. Once again he felt chills running through his body when he saw that they were coming right at him. But he knew that he had a remedy to quell his fears and blinked his eyes several times, totally confident that the vision would be gone. However, it did not work this time, and he felt his fear jumpstart a sick feeling in the pit of his stomach. The waves were still coming at him.

As they rapidly approached, the waves suddenly appeared like they were shrinking in diameter, and as they did, it looked more like a black dot that was shooting towards him. Terror began to paralyze his mind, and he was totally convinced that it was going to impact him head-on. He jammed the yoke forward and put his Cherokee into a steep descending left turn. Abruptly, the tail of his plane also started coming around to the left so he immediately stepped on the right rudder pedal to correct that nerve rattling development. The rudder pedal was almost to the firewall and it wasn't making any difference at all. The turn was rapidly developing into an uncontrolled skid, and stress sweat was starting to bead up on his forehead. His mind couldn't think fast enough for him to come up with a solution at this low of an altitude. He was so close to the ground that he thought he could see the individual pine needles on the trees below. Instinctively, he grabbed the throttle handle and pushed it forward as far as it would go to get all the thrust that his power plant could deliver to him. Relief started to move through his body as he began to regain control of his aircraft once again. The tail quickly came back around, and as it did, he automatically pulled the yoke back to gain some precious altitude. His heart was still pounding in his chest as he leveled off at 2000 feet AGL, on a southeasterly heading that left the tail of his Cherokee looking back at East Kennebago Mountain. Jack was no coward, but he was no fool either. He needed to let Rob know where the circle of air was; yet he also wanted some time to think things through before he headed back toward ITS 89.

* * *

Rob covered the one half mile to ITS 89 in record time. He slowed down as he approached the intersection, and as his speed dropped off he scanned the sky above him to see if he could spot Jack. He didn't see the Cherokee until he had come to a complete stop and had stood up on his tunnel rails. The moment that he laid eyes on Jack's plane, he was horrified by what he was seeing. It looked like Jack had lost control of his Piper, and Rob was sure that he was going to crash into the trees below. Just as he took off his helmet, he heard Jack increase the power, and he could feel his concern wane as he watched the airplane begin to recover. But as he was watching, he thought that he had seen something else – something he was not able to comprehend, therefore it was quickly forgotten. He continued to watch Jack as he flew his plane on a direct heading toward the Bigelow Mountain range, and he knew that he would soon be out of sight.

Rob reached into the breast pocket of his snowmobile coat, pulled out his hand-held NAV/COM and turned up the volume to see if the static was gone. When he knew that he had clear air he keyed the transmit button and said, "Cherokee Whiskey Papa, this is Rob Day, do you read me?" After fifteen seconds went by he made the call again, but still no reply. He stood there trying to understand what was going on when he heard the sound of Jack's plane coming back. Still standing on the tunnel rails he started waving his arms back and forth, and in a few seconds he knew that Jack had seen him because he started to rock the wings on his Cherokee. Then he saw Jack go into a steep descent, and when he flew over him he was about seventy-five feet over his head. Quickly turning his head to the right he watched the Cherokee as it flew west along ITS 89, wings rocking up and down all the way.

Picking his helmet up off of the handlebars he said, "I guess he turned his volume down on his radio, and he probably doesn't realize that we have clear air." By that time he had his helmet on and was rapidly accelerating up the trail in the same direction as the Cherokee.

* * *

The last thing that Jack wanted to happen when he was flying at such a low altitude was to see those translucent waves coming right at him again. He still had no clue what defense he should employ to defeat them, and briefly wondered if there was any defense that would be effective. For now, the best plan that he could come up with on short notice was to fly low and close to the side of the mountain. He reasoned that by doing so he would be below the angle of sight from the circle of distorted air, and he had to couple that thought with a high degree of hope that it would not suddenly appear in another clearing directly in front of him. When he had traveled halfway across the face of the mountain, he dropped his left wing and followed the slope down to the valley below. As he approached its surface he turned left again and headed back toward the beaver pond, all the while looking over his left shoulder to see if he could spot Rob on ITS 89.

Once he had crossed over the beaver pond he made a climbing one-hundred-eighty-degree-right-hand turn, which put him on a heading that would take him back over it. It was not until he was at the highest point of his turn that he dared to take a look back at the top of East Kennebago Mountain. He actually felt a wave of relief rush through him when he saw nothing except clear air. But that euphoric feeling was short-lived when his logical side kicked in and said, "Okay, then where is it *now!*"

His defenses were already on red alert and his eyes tried to take in every direction at once to see where it could possibly be. But fortunately, common sense took control, telling him to slow down and proceed cautiously. He hugged the side of the mountain while flying along the right hand side of ITS 89, and he made sure that he kept his left wing low enough to give him a clear view of the trail. He had to find Rob.

He finally spotted him at almost the same location on the mountain where he had decided to bank left and drop down into the valley below. Shaking his head side to side he said, "Wow, that boy is moving!" This time he dropped down to about one hundred feet above the surface and changed his course until he was flying directly over ITS 89, but was reluctant to go any lower because of the rolling terrain and the varying height of the trees.

* * *

Every single inch of his torso was dripping with sweat as Rob fought to keep his machine on the trail. The groomers had not been out since Monday and it was worse than a washboard. His body and sled were taking a beating, and the muscles in his neck were starting to tighten up like banjo strings because he was constantly looking up in the sky above him trying to locate Jack. Finally he saw him come from behind, almost directly over the trail. He was still rocking his wings up and down, but this time the rocking was slower than before.

Rob felt a wave of momentary fear rip through his body as he almost lost control of his sled. Like a fool, he broke a cardinal safety rule by taking his eyes off of the trail longer than three seconds while watching Jack change his course to head for the summit of East Kennebago Mountain. However, as his mind settled down somewhat after the adrenalin rush, he realized why he had been so stupid. He had fixated on Jack's Cherokee as the wings began to increase from almost a lazy rock to a very fast one as Jack approached the summit of the mountain.

The fear disappeared and he began to concentrate one hundred percent on the trail, now fully aware of where he had to go. Even though he was pretty sure what the mission was, he still was thinking of different reasons that might have made Jack direct him to the top of the mountain. Just as he decided it had to be one of two reasons, he almost lost control of his snowmobile again. His speed was way too fast for the trail conditions, and this was no time to think about anything except making sure his sled didn't have a close encounter with a tree. Nevertheless, he decided that his objective was to find either Guarl and his buddies, or the circle of air.

* * *

Jack definitely wanted to make sure that Rob would understand that he was directing him to go to the top of the Kennebago. After considering his options, he decided that his best approach would be to follow ITS 89 and make a low pass directly over him, and then as soon as he did, quickly change his course to the top of the mountain. The moment that he saw ITS 89, he began to look along the trail over the nose of his Cherokee. Once he spotted Rob, he began to slowly rock his wings, and the moment that he passed over him he banked to the right and started his climb up along the side of the mountain. As he approached the crown of the Kennebago he started to rock his wings more rapidly. Just then, he felt his heart beating faster and faster as his fear enveloped him. He didn't want to die! Not yet! Not this way!

He continued to climb after he flew past the summit, and he was disappointed and relieved at the same time. Disappointed because the target wasn't there, but relieved because he could feel the tremendous amount of stress that he had bottled up inside of him begin to drain from the upper part of his body. He leveled out at 3500 feet AGL and made a left turn to fly up the north face of the mountain, and as the west end of it passed by below him, he dropped his port wing to make a descending left turn around it. By the time he was flying parallel to the south face of the mountain, he had dropped down to 700 feet AGL, and he started to look for

Rob on ITS 89. When he finally spotted him on the trail he estimated that he was about a half a mile from the Seven Gulpers.

As he flew over him he muttered to himself, "Since the circle of air is gone, I wonder if we have clear air for transmitting again." He leaned toward the radio and turned up the volume. Expecting to hear static he was pleasantly surprised when he heard a Bonanza pilot radioing that he was inbound, ten miles southwest of the Rangeley Airport, and was asking for the active runway. Jack did not remember changing his radio frequency to the Rangeley Unicom, and before changing it back to the other frequency, he keyed the mike and said, "Bonanza driver, this is Cherokee Two Five One Whiskey Papa, the active runway is three two."

"Bonanza Seven Eight Four Lima Foxtrot, the active is three two. Thanks for the feedback."

"Cherokee Whiskey Papa, have a good day." He barely got those words out of his mouth when he spotted something fuzzy on the horizon, and as he concentrated on it, it began to take on the shape of a circle of shimmering air. His reflexes took over before he saw anything else and he found himself in a very steep descending right turn. Taking a quick look in the valley up ahead he saw the old deserted farmhouse through his spinning propeller. Then he totally surprised himself when he found that he was looking at Thad's Arctic Cat, and surprise went quickly to absolute amazement when he heard himself laughing maniacally.

He leveled out at 250 feet AGL and made a right turn that brought him on a heading toward Brochu's Landing. He still didn't know what he was doing. He only knew that he was reacting, and hopefully his actions would keep him out of trouble. When he reached the Landing he turned right and dropped his altitude by another 75 feet. He still was not aware of what he was doing and without thinking he pointed the nose of his aircraft right at the south face of East Kennebago Mountain. He kept scanning the horizon and the sky above him for any sign of the circle of disfigured air, while at the same time wondering why he changed the description of his quarry. He carefully scanned and rescanned everything within his field of vision, and after going the whole length of East Kennebago Mountain, he finally accepted the fact that there was no threat at hand and said to himself, "Sometimes I do get lucky!"

The threat was gone and he quickly planned his next move. Stepping on the starboard rudder pedal, he made a 180-degree right turn to come back over the beaver pond, and then promptly set his course to take him directly over the Seven Gulpers.

He keyed the transmit button and said, "This is Cherokee Whiskey Papa, do you read me, Rob?"

"Cherokee Whiskey Papa, this is Rob and I read you loud and clear. What's your 10-20?"

Dropping all radio protocol he said, " I just passed over the Seven Gulpers and I'm headed toward the Big and Little Kennebago Lakes. What's your 20?"

"I'm almost to the summit. I thought that's where you wanted me to go."

"Yeah, I did. But the item that we're looking for is no longer there, and right now I don't think that this approach is going to work for us. I recommend that we both go back to home base and develop another strategy. What do you say?"

"I'm sure that you've got your reasons. See you back at camp."

* * *

Rob was headed back down the mountain, and as he approached the Seven Gulpers he decided to stop to take a look around. He didn't know why he was doing it because he had checked it out only the day before. When it came right down to it, the only justification that he could come up with was the fact that he had developed a neighborly habit. He took a walk around the entire camp in the same tracks that he had already used two times this week, and he was happy to find that nothing was different. When he pulled the front porch door open, he noticed that all the Have-A-Heart traps that he had emptied and stacked back in there were gone. It must have been his feline curiosity that prompted him to carefully examine everything around him. Now his curiosity was accelerating as he walked down the steps to head over to his snowmobile. Being careful sometimes has its rewards, and as he walked out to the trail where his snowmobile was parked, he happened to pick up on something that he had not noticed before, and wondered how in the heck he could have missed it.

There were boot and shoe tracks everywhere in the trail, and all of them funneled into two narrowing directions. One set of tracks were going to and from the side of the trail farthest from the Seven Gulpers, and the other set was going to and from the front porch. Rob walked closer to the far side of the trail and saw a large depression in the snow. As a matter of fact it was the largest depression that he had seen. Pacing it off from one side to the other while walking along the trail, he estimated that it was about 40 feet in diameter. He stood there for almost ten minutes, scrutinizing every square inch of the open area around the circle to see if there was anything else that could tell him more of the story that had unfolded here. Unfortunately the only evidence that he was able to find was a repeat of what he has seen several times before. All the tracks going in the direction of the depression ended about fifteen feet in front it. Thinking out loud he said, "I've got to learn how these people do this. It would sure make things a lot easier at times."

* * *

The ride down the mountain was slow and uneventful, and that was a good thing because his mind was not on the trail. He did not have any situational awareness at all, and if a moose or a deer had jumped out onto the trail in front of him, there is no doubt that he would have hit it.

Falling darkness was the catalyst that finally brought his mind back to present-time reality, and it took him at least a minute to recognize where he was. When he finally pieced everything together, he realized that he was halfway through Brochu's Landing, and what bothered him most was the fact that he still did not have an answer to any of the questions that he had been asking himself all of the way down the mountain. "How do we get Eileen, Nancy, and Thad back? Do we wait to hear a 'whump', and then run to check it out, hoping to find them standing in a daze near a depression in the snow? Do I accept Jack's theory that the leisure suit strangers had abducted Rudy, and when they were finished with him they simply dumped him in the clearing behind the camp? Can we really count on the fact that even one of these theories is a good hypothesis? And what about the wild animals and rodents that are taken by these aliens, are all of them returned? Wow! Now that's a statement! These people are *aliens*!"

Lots of these questions rolled around and around revealing the obvious one new thought. "These people are aliens!"

* * *

It was 17:55 hours when Rob walked back into the camp, and both Rudy and Ginger came to the front door to greet him. As far as Rob was concerned, Rudy was acting like his old self again. He was wagging his tail so hard that his whole torso was waggling from side to side along with it. When he tried to walk away from the front door and into the living room, the dogs stood to their ground to left and right of him, and it was obvious that they had no intention of moving until they were forced to. He squatted down between them and began to scratch each one behind an ear while he said, "Hey, Toot-man! Boy, am I glad to see that you're acting like your old self," and with that Rudy rested his head against his master's left leg, grunting with pleasure as Rob continued to scratch him behind the ear. It quickly became apparent that Ginger did not want to be left out of the act, because the next thing that he knew, she was resting her head against his other leg. She was not grunting and groaning with pleasure like Rudy was, but when Rob looked down at her, he could see a look of pure contentment on her furry face.

As he was standing up, his peripheral vision registered a flashing light, and he looked over at the Caller ID unit sitting on the end table next to the loveseat. His heart quickened as he desperately hoped there would be a message waiting for him from Eileen and Nancy. He was in such a rush to get to the answering machine in his office that he almost tripped over the ottoman as he hustled across the living room, and his excitement increased when he saw the message light blinking. Without hesitation he pressed the play button, and his excitement grew as he listened to the tape rewind. However, it seemed to be taking much longer than usual, and his impatience began anew as he continued to stand there watching the machine do its work. After a while he began to develop the illusion that things were going in slow motion, and finally he started to urge the machine on saying, "Come on! Come on! Hurry up!

The message indicator on the machine said that there was only one message, but it seemed like it was taking forever to rewind. Finally he said, "Man! She must be giving me a blow-by-blow description of everything that went on." He had just gotten the word "description" out of his mouth when the tape finally stopped rewinding, and the machine began to play the message. As soon as he heard the sound of Len Purdy's voice, his heart sank. He listened to the full length of the five-minute message hoping that he would get some information regarding Eileen and Nancy, or maybe even Thad, but no such luck. The whole message was about Bubba's sled breaking down, and it also included a bunch of unnecessary information regarding all the grief that they went through trying to fix it. The story finally concluded with a statement that they ended up having to tow the sled back to camp. Mixed in with all of the explanations were profuse apologies for not showing up as he had promised.

As he was walking back into the living room he saw the lights of his Explorer pulling into the driveway. He was really looking forward to talking with Jack. Rudy and Ginger trotted over to the front door and expectantly stood there, wagging their tails the whole time. As the door opened Rob yelled, "Rudy! Ginger! Come! Let the poor guy get through the door." Almost as if on cue, both of them turned around and dropped their heads and ears in unison, in an open display of their disappointment as they slowly walked over to him.

Jack closed the door and turned around to face Rob, and Rob got the immediate impression that Jack had aged. Brushing the thought aside he quickly decided to try to boost his moral and cheerfully said, "I didn't expect to see you for another thirty minutes!"

Jack's look didn't change as he said, "Larry was standing near the hanger as I taxied over to my tie down spot, so I asked him if he'd do me a favor and button up my plane for me. I'd have to say that he got more than just a little miffed at me. He asked me what was going on, and I put him off by promising that I would tell him tomorrow."

"I'm not surprised at that! Between yesterday and today he's seen both of us doing things that we've never done before. I'm surprised that he was willing to take care of the Cherokee for you without some kind of blackmail."

"Don't be so sure there wasn't any blackmail involved. Why do you think he finally agreed to take care of the plane and let me get going?"

Staring at Jack with a questioning look on his face he said, "So, what'd you agree to? I know money wasn't involved, that wouldn't do the trick with that guy."

Even though he didn't feel like smiling, one still played at the corners of his mouth as he said, "You know that he's always wanted to fly your Cessna, so I made a promise to him that before we left, that you'd let him take it up for a few hours."

Rob couldn't believe his ears. He never let anyone fly his plane! As far as he was concerned his Cessna was as sacrosanct as his marriage, and there was no hiding the animosity in his voice as he said, "Thanks, friend. I'll return the favor some time."

Getting a very serious look on his face, Jack said, "I had no idea that you would get so upset. You and I both know how Larry babies his planes, and you know as well as I do that he'll treat your baby just like it was his own."

"Yeah, you're right. Sorry. It was just a knee-jerk reaction. I'm glad you did it so that you could get back here sooner."

* * *

After they briefed each other with the details of everything that they had seen and done that afternoon, they continued sitting at the kitchen table while sipping on a Corona. Both of them were simply staring out into the darkness of the backyard when Jack finally broke the silence by saying, "I have some more theories about the reason why you, Eileen, and I have lost time during one or more appearances of this phenomena, and why Thad's brain, as you so aptly put it, went into neutral."

Rob quickly jerked his head around to look at Jack and said, "You've got my undivided attention, my friend."

"First let's consider the loss of time. I think that it is directly related to the loss of memory. We know that these visitors from wherever, are much more scientifically advanced than we are. Just suppose that they know how to manipulate your brain waves, you know, kind of like forcing them into to a flat pattern, even though you're not dead. I know that sounds far-fetched, but hear me out. If they have developed a way to somehow control your brain waves by first matching the pulsations, then somehow creating a magnetic field that would influence them in any manner that they wished, just think about the implications! I feel fairly certain that if an individual's brain waves are flattened, that they would be the next thing to comatose, and if that is the case, they would have no memory of what transpired during that period of time."

Rob held up his hand and said, "Whoa! Wait just a second here! What would be the purpose of blocking a person's memory?"

Shaking his head in disbelief Jack said, "Well just expand your imagination a little bit and consider this. Just suppose that they don't want you to see or remember what's going on around you at a particular point in time. And maybe their reason is that they are doing something to you that they don't want you to remember. How about this for an idea? Maybe you're being programmed to do something at some point in the future."

Rob had a questioning look on his face when he said, "You mean like brainwashing a person with some type of an electronic device instead of subliminal suggestions?"

"Now you're getting my drift. Of course, I've got another theory regarding the question of memory loss. Suppose they create a match to your brain waves by manipulating a magnetic field, and also suppose that the moment that they make a corresponding wave pattern, they just push a button and pull your electrical essence into their dimension. Now they've got you, and there's nothing that you can do about it. They've got all the uninterrupted time that they need to perform whatever type of scientific manipulations that they had planned to do on you all along. The rest is simple. Once they're finished working on your electrical essence, they just reverse the magnetic field and repel it back into your body. If they can do that, I'm certain that you'd have no clue as to what went on. When your conscious mind took over again, your memory would just pick up where it had left off. You'd be none the wiser until you looked at your watch, but only if you did so immediately after the event."

"So tell me, Jack, let's assume that your theory is correct, and they can zap my electrical essence into their dimension. Just what in the hell am I while they have my electrical essence in limbo?"

A big grin started to spread across his face as he said, "How's zombie strike you?"

"Not cool at all! So what you're saying is, that you think Thad's electrical essence was someplace else when his brain took a hike into neutral?"

"I don't know what I *truly* think. But it's one explanation. Since you're looking for explanations, here's another one. We found one exact match while I was comparing Thad's EEG readout to the data that my equipment recorded, but there were also several instances when his brain waves closely matched. His fugues could be just a fluke, or they could be tied to the static's electrical pattern. There's another thing to take into consideration. It could also be that because of his age, he is more susceptible when the electrical pattern is close to his. You did tell me that he has signs of dementia, right?"

"Yeah. But what's that got to do with it?"

"I don't really know, maybe nothing, but it could be what makes him more susceptible than you and me. If you want a definite answer, you'd better check with someone in the medical field with expertise in this area. But think about this before you start dialing for answers. How do you explain the reason behind your question?" He saw that Rob did not follow his thought pattern so he said, "You had best be prepared for that line of questioning, because if someone approached me with a query like that, I'd want to know why."

Rob was silent for almost a minute before saying, "Yeah, well I hope none of your explanations hold water, especially the crap about taking a person's electrical essence into another dimension."

"Yeah, I have no trouble going along with you on that."

"I'll tell you what, Jack, these theories are all well and good, but what we really need is a sensible plan for getting Eileen and Nancy back. What theories do you have in that area?"

"I didn't come up with a single idea yet that I haven't been able to punch a million holes into. By the way, I forgot to tell you that I made some phone calls to a few of our pilot buddies while I had Larry fuel up my Cherokee. If we need their help, Al Carroll, Mel Marshall, Jimmy Matthew, and Art Bell all committed time to us on Friday. The key question is, What good can they be to us?"

Rob stared at him with an empty look on his face and said, "Without a plan, none. But what did you tell them?"

"I kept it simple. I told them that some cross country skiers were missing, and if they're not found today, we could use their help tomorrow to try to spot them from the air."

"Nice white lie! I'll tell you what, I know how busy those guys are, and I'm really impressed that they agreed to give you their time."

"Yeah. Me too. But I'll tell you this, when I made that call, I didn't realize how dangerous these people are that manipulate that circle of shimmering air. As far as I'm concerned, I don't want any part of putting our friends in harm's way. When I called them I had it in the back of my mind that they could be helpful as spotters, but only if I couldn't get the job done by myself today. However, after what I went through, I think that scenario is most likely out."

When Jack finished speaking, Rob remained sitting at the kitchen table and just stared out the picture window, almost as if he was looking into outer space and said, "Jack, would you like another Corona?"

He never changed his focus from his hands folded on the kitchen table as he said, "I'll tell you what, ol' buddy, a Corona sounds real good, but if I don't get something to eat real soon I'm gonna end up with a splitting headache."

Shifting his gaze from outside to Jack, Rob said, "I'm not in the mood to cook, not even anything simple. Why don't we go to the White Wolf and get something to eat?"

"That sounds good to me, but should we?"

"Why not?"

"What happens if Nancy, Eileen, and Thad come knocking on the door while we're gone? If that happens, I don't want to be at the White Wolf, I want to be right here!"

"I hear what you're saying loud and clear, Jack. But let's be realistic. I don't think there's a chance in a million that's going to happen, and if it does, we'll just leave the door unlocked. And if it'll make you feel any better, we can leave a big note on the kitchen table telling them to call us at the White Wolf."

"What if they're hurt and need our help?"

"Damn Jack! Now you're getting frigging ridiculous! We can do 'what ifs' all night, and that makes absolutely no sense to me. I think that we need a change of pace. You know, sometimes when you walk away from a problem and get a fresh outlook, most often you come up with a solution. We're getting utterly nowhere sitting here talking shit, and that is exactly what this is!"

Jack, feeling beaten, was forced to agree and said, "Okay, Rob, let's go."

* * *

Heat was blowing over the windshield and through the floor vents by the time they turned off of Kennebago Settlement Road onto Route 16, headed toward Stratton. There was no conversation, which was highly unusual during the two and a half mile ride out to the Stratton/Rangeley road. Normally they would have some kind of discussion going, that is unless they were on one of their favorite ponds, fly-fishing from Rob's canoe. For a change, Rob was not deep in thought. As a matter of fact he found that he was unable to concentrate at all, and he decided that the reason must be that his brain was finally fried.

Just as they were approaching the bridge that crosses over Dyer Stream, Jack looked up into the sky to his right and saw a string of lights that looked like they were suspended over the forest, about a half a mile in from the road. They almost looked like Christmas decorations because the group of lights formed a crescent. The lowest light appeared to be right at treetop level, and the highest light seemed to be about two hundred fifty feet above it. As he was staring at the lights, they began a flowing movement from the top to the bottom, and it gave him the impression that something was either being fueled up or charged up. He did not understand why he got that impression, and was about to tell Rob to take a look when he felt the Explorer braking and turning hard to the left. He turned his head to look out the front windshield just in time to see a moose flashing by him on the right side, and he yelled, "Holy moly! That was too close for comfort, Rob!"

His heart was beating like that of a racehorse in the fifth, and his eyes were wide as he said, "Sorry, Jack! I was looking at some lights in the sky and wasn't paying any attention to the road. For all I know that fucking moose could have been standing there all along."

Turning his head to look back up at the lights, Jack said, "I was looking at those lights as well. Hey! They're gone! I'll tell you what, I'm glad that you saw them too, otherwise I'd be convinced that I was hallucinating."

This was the catalyst that Rob needed to get his mind working again. He couldn't stop thinking about the crescent shaped string of lights suspended over the forest. Something was trying to surface from his subconscious to his conscious mind. He almost had it several times, and just as they were entering downtown Stratton, he finally had it.

The crescent shaped string of lights helped to spark a memory about a Bible passage that he had read one morning while having his coffee. Without fail, every weekday he watched the early financial news in the family room as he sipped his brew. On this particular morning he decided that it was more than strange when he found the family Bible sitting on top of the coffee table, open. It's never open, and it's never on top. Rob thought that maybe Eileen had left it open for him to read a particular passage, and went over to see what it was. The Bible was opened to the Old Testament: Ecclesiastes; and a pencil was lying on the right hand page pointing to 12:6-7. To this day he clearly remembers the passage that he read, which stated: "Before the silver cord is snapped, or the bowl is broken, or the pitcher is broken at the fountain, or the wheel broken at the cistern, and the dust returns to the earth as it was, and the spirit returns to God who gave it."

There is a very good reason that the passage was instilled into his mind. The moment that Eileen had walked into the kitchen that morning to get her coffee, he had imediately asked her why she wanted him to read that particular passage. She claimed that she had no idea what he was talking about. He always knew when she was trying to pull a fast one on him, because when questioned, she, like he did, would show signs of a smile developing at the corners of her mouth while hiding all or part of the truth. Not even a hint of a small smile surfaced on her face that day. How the Bible got onto the top of the table, opened to that particular page, with a pencil pointing to that particular passage, remained a mystery for quite some time. When the answer finally came, it was a major revelation to Rob. It was during his early attempts to learn how to communicate with his Guardian Angel that the answer came to him. It was not until then that he fully understood the meaning of the passage.

* * *

The White Wolf is a favorite spot of Rob's, and he and Jack have been going there for many years. The menu is unusual for the area, and the food is always delicious. Over time, Rob had gotten to know Sandy Socobeson, the owner of the restaurant, fairly well, mostly because of the fuss that he made over her companion, a White Wolf that she always has with her. Sandy is a Passamaquoddy Indian, and she and her family are members of the Bear Clan. Her given name was Thitiyas, phonetically pronounced Ditias, which means Blue Jay. However, whenever she told a person her name, she was usually asked to repeat it, so after a while she just started telling people that her name was Sandy.

Whenever Rob was in the White Wolf and business happened to be slow, he would always take advantage of that off time to chat with her. A small part of him is North American Indian, and he had a strong desire to know more about his heritage, so he would never miss an opportunity to get her talking about her culture. During one of their conversations she told him that her father was from the Maliseet Tribe in St. Mary's, Canada, and that same day he had learned how she was named. In her culture a name is not just arbitrarily picked, and she told him that her uncle, who was a Pipe Carrier, gave her the name after it had come to him during a meditation in a tribal sweat lodge.

That particular conversation lasted a long time, and it was at that time he also learned that tribal ceremonies, tribal customs, dances, and beliefs are still passed down by story telling, from generation to generation. However, one custom that he learned about during that same conversation answered one of several questions that he had pondered for many years about the North American Indian culture. Long before a Medicine Man passes away, he chooses and grooms a tribal member to carry on in his place. It is a position of trust and honor, and the person chosen would have already demonstrated through their acts and deeds, not only their ability to learn, but also their desire to help other tribal members.

* * *

Rob and Jack could easily see that it was not an off-night at the White Wolf when they walked into the front dining room. As a matter of fact, they were very fortunate to walk in just ahead of two other people because they got the only empty table left. Once they were seated, Rob took a quick look around and saw Sandy standing alongside the table right next to the "menu of the day" board. Looking over at Jack he said, "She must be shorthanded since she's taking an order from that large group sitting there."

Jack nodded his head in agreement and said, "Looks like it could be a family get-together."

Rob looked back over at the table and saw that one of the young ladies was holding a baby, and he guessed that it was no more than six to eight weeks old. When he took a second look at the proud mother, he recognized her as one of the waitresses from the White Wolf, which explained why Sandy was waiting on the table. Behind and over the young mother's head was a pink and white banner suspended across the top of the menu board that had tiny little babies printed along the edge of its border, and the banner simply said, "Welcome, Elizabeth Jane. We Love You!!!!"

As people came into the front dining room, they would carefully work their way through the labyrinth of tables to see the baby, and of course there was the usual fuss made over the newly arrived bundle of joy, especially by the women that Rob assumed were the doting aunts and cousins. As each one came over to see her, Elizabeth Jane would calmly look up at them with wonder in her eyes. Almost without fail, every one of the well-wishers seemed to have their own opinion as to whom they thought the infant resembled most. Rob was amused when he saw that if any one person spent too much time in front of Elizabeth, her arms and legs would slowly develop a movement that looked similar to a back stroke, like perhaps she was trying to get away from them.

While waiting for a waitress to come to take their order, both Jack and Rob kept themselves occupied by watching all of the activities at the table. But they paid especially close attention to an obviously mentally challenged man as he walked over to the baby. He appeared to be in his mid-50s, and unlike everyone else he did not make a fuss over Elizabeth Jane. He cordially greeted the baby's mother, and then simply bent over to give Elizabeth a gentle kiss on the cheek. But her reaction to this man was remarkable when compared to her response to all of the other people. It was like someone flipped a switch, and her personality instantly changed from passive to joyous, and a *huge* smile spread across her face that seemed to convey that he was someone special to her.

The mentally challenged man was still standing near Elizabeth Jane, listening to the conversation that was going on around the table, when the waitress finally came up to take Rob and Jack's order. When Rob looked up and saw who it was he said, "Hi, Denise! Longtime, no see!"

"Yeah, Sandy's real shorthanded, and asked me if I would come in and help out."

"Well, it's good to see you again. How's Gene doing?"

"He's doing just fine. But I wish he would find a job and go to work. He's driving me crazy hanging around the house all day."

"Aw, give the guy a break. He's worked his butt off all these years, can't you let him enjoy his retirement?"

"Yeah, I have to agree, he did work hard, and provided real good for me and the kids, and I do want him to enjoy his retirement, but I also want him to stop being a pain in my derriere!"

"Sounds like you guys need some time away from each other. By the way, do you know who that guy is that's standing next to the baby?"

She turned to look over in the direction of the table, and after a few seconds said, "Nope. Haven't seen him before. They've got a family gathering here tonight, and some of them came in from out-of-town for the baby's baptism on Sunday. He must be one of the out of town family members. Sandy might know, some of them are staying in the rooms upstairs."

Denise wrote down their order, and as she was walking away Jack said, "If she's right about him being from out of town, then it's my guess that the baby's never seen that guy before. I wonder why she appeared to be so happy when she saw him? He certainly didn't seem to be overly happy to see her."

"Jack, I'm sure that you've heard the age-old statement that mentally challenged people are God's special children?"

"Sure, I've heard that before."

"Well you've been coming up with a bunch of theories this evening, let me give you one that I personally don't believe is a theory. Various people, religions, and organizations have written much about reincarnation over the years. And it has been said by some spiritual mediums that during a casual conversation with a young child, if it is nonchalantly asked who they were in their former life, that it is very likely that they will come back with a matter of fact answer, and tell you who they were."

"Yeah, right! And you said that my theory was far fetched!"

"Now hold on, Jack, and let me finish. Maybe baby Elizabeth already knew that man from a former life, or even from the other side, and the moment that she recognized him that huge smile started to beam from her little face, or maybe she just recognized him as one of God's special children."

As he was finishing the last sentence his peripheral vision caught a movement near the ceiling, and when he looked up he saw that a leaf was gracefully floating down from it. He looked back at the ceiling to try to figure out where it had come from. There was not one single heating and air conditioning vent nearby, and when he focused his attention back on the leaf, what he saw next was even more unexplainable than the leaf's origin.

The last booth in the dining room borders the bar area, and a large dream catcher hangs in an archway right above the rear seat. The leaf stopped its downward motion when it reached the same level as the dream catcher, and it kind of hovered in one position for a couple of seconds. Rob was looking around to see where the draft could be coming from that stopped the leaf's descent, and looked back just in time to see it rapidly shoot forward. His mouth dropped open as he watched it go straight through the center of the dream catcher to the bar area on the other side.

Rob scrambled up out of his seat and walked quickly into the bar to pick up the leaf. There was a foliage display on the far wall near the entrance to the kitchen that had leaves in it, and he wanted to see if the leaf was real or imitation. If it was imitation, it could possibly provide an answer, but he really thought that was a serious reach. First of all, a breeze needed to rip the leaf off of the display and push it up about two feet to the ceiling, and then it would have to carry it along the ceiling for about another twelve feet to reach the spot that Rob had first seen it. But still, if the leaf matched those in the display. The mystery would be solved.

The dining room may have been full, but the bar was another story. Not one person was sitting on any of the stools, and no one occupied any of the booths, which is a scene that Rob has seldom seen at the White Wolf. He looked everywhere for the leaf, but it was nowhere to be found. Determined to find it, he got down on his hands and knees to look in every nook and cranny. After a while Jack got tired of sitting by himself and finally went into the bar looking for him. When he walked in he found Rob crawling around on the floor and said, "What in the hell are *you* doing?"

Not quite ready to tell him what he had seen he said, "I thought I saw a quarter roll in here, and thought that if I found it I'd give it to the mother for the baby's piggy bank."

Jack rolled his eyes because he didn't believe a word that he heard and said, "You are an unadulterated twit after all. Look, if it'll make you feel any better, here's a stupid quarter. Go and give it to her and get your butt back to the table. I'm thirsty, and Denise just brought our beers."

Rob stood there glaring at Jack for a few moments, trying to decide if he should tell him to go take a long walk on a short pier, but ultimately decided to let it go. The beers sounded good.

They walked side-by-side back to the dining room, and Rob looked at every square inch of the bar room floor that he could see on the way out. But there still was no sign of the leaf.

They sat at the table in silence while sipping their beer, and Rob saw Denise looking at him as she went by with food for the table alongside of them. She had seen that Rob was occasionally looking over at the mentally challenged man still standing right near the baby, and decided that she would ask around to find out his name. Diverting somewhat to his table so she wouldn't have to yell she said, "His name is Gary Davis."

* * *

Occasionally Rob's eyes would drift over to the dream catcher because he still could not get the leaf event out of his mind. Something about it was gnawing at him. After a while he let it go and said to Jack, "We've got to come up with a feasible plan to get through that circle of air to rescue our wives," and almost as an afterthought he added, "and Thad."

Without really meaning it Jack cavalierly said, "That's easy, why don't we just fly our planes into it?"

"That's it!"

A look of disbelief quickly spread across Jack's face as he said, "Whoa! I was just kidding. Have you already forgotten what I went through this afternoon?"

"Not for a New York minute! But both you and I have always said that there's more than one way to skin a cat. This is no different. We just have to find that way."

"Yeah? Well we also have to make sure that we don't become the cat! Besides, what makes you so sure that flying into the circle of distorted air is what we should do?"

Rob gave Jack all the details about the leaf and why he was in the bar for so long, and he intentionally held back the information that he thought was most important of all.

Jack gave him an incredulous look and said, "And the leaf buzzing through that hoop is what makes you so sure that we should fly into the circle of air?"

"Yeah, that, and I just happen to feel very strongly that it was a message from my Guardian Angel." When Jack did not immediately respond Rob felt that it was necessary to defend his statement and said, "How else would that leaf do what it did?"

Jack looked down at the table while he twisted his beer glass around and around and said, "I know that you and Eileen strongly believe in that spirit stuff, and if you keep this up you're liable to convince me too. There's just one major problem among many small ones."

"I'm glad to hear there's just one major problem. What is it?"

"Based on what I experienced today, it's an obvious fact that those people have the ability to thwart anything that we try. We don't even have to be close to them before they can start wreaking havoc on us."

"No problem. We can overcome that little inconvenience. All we need is a diversion. What are the small problems?"

"I don't know, but we'd damn sure be fools to assume that there's not going to be any. It's all going to depend on what we experience as we go through the circle of shimmering air, and what problems we run into on the other side. What I find to be of major concern is that maybe they won't be small problems. Maybe we'll find out that we've bit off more than we can chew, and there'll be five of us missing instead of three!"

* * *

They spent the next hour talking about and closely examining every option they could think of to penetrate the circle of air. Some of the ideas were really bad, but once they had exhausted every possibility that came to mind, they made an outline of each good one on paper. However, both of them were fairly well convinced that they already knew which plan they would be using tomorrow.

Rob motioned for Denise to come over to the table with their check, and as soon as she laid it down, Jack and he both argued that it was their turn to pay the tab. The debate was going nowhere fast, and as the argument got louder they soon had quite a few of the other patrons looking at them. When Jack paused to look around the dining room, he saw a lot of eyes on them, so he finally said, "Listen, why don't we just split it, OK?

The battle was finished, the check was paid, and as they were walking out the door Rob said, "Jack, when we get back to camp, I just thought of another item that we need to take care of."

"Yeah, what's that?"

"We've already accepted the fact that these people are more sophisticated and scientifically advanced than we are, and to me that means that we've got to be extra careful. We've got to dot every i and cross every t, at least twice."

"Yeah, I agree. In this mission there's no such thing as being too careful."

Rob was quiet for several moments before saying, "I've been thinking, and I'm convinced that we've got to assume that those bastards have a database that contains replicas of our topographical maps. If they do, then we can't use the coordinates as detailed on the map. We'll have to develop a code of our own."

"Fine! While you're doing that I'll get a hold of Al, Mel, Jimmy, and Art, and let them know what time and where to meet us tomorrow morning."

Rob thought for a few seconds and said, "You know, Jack, I think that you'd best plan enough time when you call them to give them the whole story."

"There's no question about that. I've been wrestling with how I'm going to overcome the white lie that I told them to begin with."

Getting a bit of a smile on his face Rob said, "I have a solution in case you don't come up with one that you like on your own."

11

It was during the wee hours of Friday morning when a heavy gust of wind roared its way through the trees that surrounded Camp Stress-A-Rest. The racket that it made was so loud that it woke Rob out of a very badly needed deep, sound sleep. He had spent most of the night wide-awake with his mind in high gear, working through the plan that they had carefully structured to get their wives back, plus all the possible problems that his vivid imagination could conjure up. The grogginess brought on by his deep sleep was still hanging on as he automatically rolled to his left, seeking the heat of his wife's warm body. He was brutally brought back to reality when all he felt next to him were the cold sheets. He fought back the rising lump in his throat and immediately assumed that it was the lack of sleep that allowed this strong emotion through. He knew full well that absolutely nothing but having a positive attitude was going to make this situation any better. He rolled to his right side, looked at the clock on his nightstand and saw that it was only 04:15 hours. His mind quickly slipped back into high gear and he readily grasped the fact that sleep was at an end for today. Mentally motivating himself to a positive state of mind he said out loud, "It's coffee time!"

As soon as he opened up the bedroom door the aroma of freshly brewed coffee filled his nose. He bypassed the bathroom and headed directly to the kitchen to get a cup before answering nature's call. There was no doubt in his mind that the need for coffee was more urgent. As he rounded the corner he saw Jack sitting at the table with his head resting in his right hand, and he was holding a cup of coffee in his left hand. It looked like he was in a trance, just staring at the notes that they had made the night before. Rob walked over to Jack and saw that he was holding an empty cup – as empty as the look on his face. "Morning Jack. How're you feeling?"

"I'm feeling like I didn't sleep at all last night, and I wish that frigging coffee would get done."

Acting more lighthearted than he felt he said, "Well pardon me if I bust your bubble, but it looks to me like the coffee *is* done. Want me to fill your cup?"

"Sure."

Rob filled both cups and added the half and half. However, he was amazed that when he had poured in more than the normal amount of half and half, that the coffee still looked extremely dark, and said, "Say, Jack? Did you kind of slip with the coffee?"

"Nope. I just like my coffee a little strong."

"Well, I'll tell you what ol' buddy, you take a sip of this coffee and your eyes will be wired wide open for the rest of the day!"

He walked over and set Jack's cup down in front of him, and then immediately proceeded over to the sink. As he poured a third of his coffee down the drain he grabbed a paper towel to wipe the drippings off of the side of the cup. Then as he filled his cup back up with tap water, he leaned over the sink to take a quick look out the window to see if the deer were gathering, but it was early, and he did not see any long-legged silhouettes.

Turning to his right he walked toward the microwave to warm his coffee, and as he did he took a sip before saying, "Now that's more like it!"

As soon as those words came out of his mouth he heard Jack's kitchen chair sliding back from the table. He stood there and watched as Jack poured part of his coffee down the drain and he said, "Hey, Jack! I thought that you liked your coffee a little strong!"

"Yeah, I do, but this is way too strong, even for me."

"Oh, boy! That admission really had to hurt." There was no rebuttal; he just gave Rob a murderous look that was usually reserved for people that he was about to pound on.

Rudy and Ginger actually saved the day when they came walking into the kitchen. But when you come right down to it, moping into the kitchen was a more accurate description. Taking advantage of the interruption to change the subject at hand Rob said, "Well, it looks like you guys didn't get much sleep last night either."

With perfect timing, Ginger gave a low guttural doggy grunt, which gave Rob the impression that she agreed, and then turning around she promptly started toward the front door. Rudy took a look at Rob, looked back at Ginger, then looked back at Rob again, and finally made up his mind that he was going to follow Ginger's lead. Rob looked out the kitchen window at the thermometer to see how cold it was, and when he saw that it was ten below zero, he decided that it wasn't too cold to go for a walk. Looking back at the dogs he said, "All right, you guys, hold your horses for a minute and I'll go with you."

Both dogs just stood expectantly at the front door, patiently waiting for him to open it. It was obvious to Rob that neither one of them had understood a word he had said. He blew on his coffee to cool it off a little before taking a long sip, and just as he was setting the cup down on the counter, Ginger let out a soft but demanding woof.

While he walked toward the closet to get his coat, hat, and gloves, he made enough noise to get the dogs to look in his direction. The moment that he opened up the closet door they understood the game plan, and came trotting over to him with their tails wagging. "Well you guys don't seem to understand everything I say, but you sure don't have a problem understanding what I'm doing, do you?"

He got his answer when he saw the dogs start to wag their tails even harder, and almost instantly a real happy look developed on their furry faces.

* * *

Rob and the dogs had just barely walked out the front door when the phone started to ring. Jack said to himself, "Holy mackerel! Who in the hell is calling at this hour?" But he quickly changed his mind as his excitement rapidly accelerated to a euphoric high, and he yelled out, "YES! It's got to be Nancy and Eileen!"

He raced over to the phone and picked up the receiver, and he didn't even get a chance to say hello when the person on the other end of the line started saying, "Hey, Rob! Sorry to call you so early, but I wanted to tell you that I'm sorry that we did not ..."

His euphoric high instantly sank to the pit of his stomach where it was over powered by the despair that he had been trying to conquer all night. "This isn't Rob. Who's calling?"

"My name's Len. Are you Jack?"

"That's me. What can I do for you?"

"Is Rob there?"

"No, he's out walking with the dogs, but he should be back in a few minutes."

"Oh. Would you do me a favor please, Jack? Would you please ask Rob to give me a call as soon as he gets back in, and tell him not to worry about waking anybody, everyone's already up!"

"I'll be happy to give him the message. By the way, Len, what happened to you guys yesterday?" And with an unmistakable sarcastic tone in his voice he said, "We kind of expected that you'd be here to keep an eye on our wives yesterday morning!"

"That's why I'm calling. We ran into a problem, and if you'll just have Rob give me a call, I'll explain everything to him."

As he was hanging up the phone he said, "Yeah, like I said, I'll give Rob the message as soon as he gets in."

* * *

Jack had just sat back down at the kitchen table when the front door opened, and both Rudy and Ginger were struggling to get through the partially opened door at the same time. The first thought that went through Jack's mind was an image of the Three Stooges doing exactly the same thing. Even though his mood was very dark, he still broke a thin smile.

It was no surprise when the dogs went straight for their food dishes. When one quick sniff told them that they were empty, they took a fast look at each other and headed directly to the cabinet where the IAMS dog food and Milk-Bone biscuits were kept. Rob had just closed the front door, only to turn around and see that the dogs were giving him a clear message. They kept a vigilant eye on him as he went over to the kitchen counter and grabbed his cup of coffee. Out of the corner of his eye he saw Jack staring at him as he was taking a sip. He turned toward him and said, "What?"

"Listen, I really couldn't care less if you want to drink cold coffee or not, especially when there's hot java in the thermos, but

I do have to tell you that Len called while you were out, and he'd like you to give him a call back."

"Did he say why they didn't show up yesterday?"

"He said that they ran into a problem, and that he'd explain everything to you when you called." Jack did not bother telling him that Len might have told him more than he did if he hadn't been so sarcastic and cynical with him.

"I'll give him a call in a little bit. I need to get myself into the right frame of mind before I get him on the line. He just might have a good reason why they did not show up yesterday, and I don't want to make a jerk out of myself by prematurely flying off the handle. By the way, I saw you studying your notes when I came into the kitchen before. Do you have any new ideas for our game plan, or is everything that we put on paper status quo?"

"Everything's the same. I just like to keep hammering at the plan to see if any new ideas pop into my mind, but nothing new seems to surface."

"Well, I thought of something while walking the dogs. We haven't actually decided if we're going to use your Cherokee or the Hawk XP, but when all is said and done, I think we should use the Hawk. It has a better climb rate than the Cherokee, a little more speed and a bigger payload. If some of those small unknown problems that we had talked about come up when we are least expecting them, each of those factors could prove to be very important. And another thing that I thought of while walking the dogs; we should bring them with us. They might turn out to be very useful in helping us to find Eileen, Nancy and Thad."

Jack walked over to the counter by the double kitchen sink, grabbed the thermos and poured himself another cup of coffee as he said, "Everything you said makes sense to me. We just have to make sure that our pilot friends from Portland are in sync with our plan. I think that I should give each one of them another call just to make sure, and let them know that we are going to be in the Hawk. Which brings up another point. If we're goin' to be in your XP, then the lead diversion plane in Plan C should be Art Bell, because his Cessna 206 closely resembles your Hawk. That, in itself, may be enough to throw our alien friends off kilter."

"You're planning on calling them now?" Rob said, incredulously.

"Yeah. They won't like it much, but at least I'll be sure to get them before they leave home."

As Rob walked over to the thermos to get more coffee he said, "Fine. You use the phone in here, and I'll use the fax line in the office to call Len."

* * *

The phone only rang a half a ring when he heard Len say, "Hello, Rob."

Still acting in a lighter mood than he actually felt he said, "Given the early hour, and since you asked me to return your call, I guess it's a no-brainer as to who was calling." Doing his best to maintain a friendly attitude he said, "How's everybody doing, Len?"

Ignoring his question Len said, "I wanted to personally apologize to you for the fact that we did not show up yesterday morning as I had promised. Bubba's sled broke down on the way over there, and we couldn't get it going no matter what we did. So Bubba doubled up with his wife on her sled and we continued on. But as luck would have it, her sled broke down after going only a half a mile. I guess that the suspension on her sled couldn't handle their combined weight and we ended up towing both sleds back to camp. How's everything going?"

Rob had constructed a clear image in his mind of their poor snowmobile getting crushed under about five hundred and seventy-five pounds of riding fury, and almost burst out laughing. However, when the information he was wanting to tell Len came to the forefront of his mind, it was a sobering reality, which quickly vanquished the urge. He took his time and shared with him everything that Jack and he had done yesterday morning, which included the encounter with the snowmobile riders. He found it more difficult than he had imagined when it came to telling Len about the women's disappearance. Once he had finished describing their plan for today, Len said, "What can we do to help?"

"Well, I'll tell yah, if you really want to help, then maybe you could keep an eye on the camp in case we get lucky and those bastards decide to ship Eileen and Nancy back while we're gone."

"No problem, we'd be happy to do that."

Rob thought for a second and said, "Thanks, Len, and there's something else that I think would be a good idea. I think you should keep a log of any appearances of that circle of distorted air. Oh yeah, and another thing, if we're not back in seventy-two hours from the time that we penetrate the circle of shimmering air, notify the authorities that we're missing. But I recommend that you don't tell them how it happened."

"I guess I don't have to ask you why on that one! They'd probably cuff us and take us to the men in the white coats."

When he heard Len's statement, in spite of the seriousness of the conversation, Rob got a smile on his face and said, "Exactly my thought! You should check with Mel Marshall sometime this afternoon. I'll give you his phone number, and he can tell you what time we penetrated the circle."

"How's he going to know that, Rob?"

He decided that he'd better explain their plan in more detail, and when he was finished Len immediately volunteered to go with Mel.

Rob thought for a moment and said, "You just gave me an idea. Do Bubba and Stormin have any guns and ammo at camp?"

"You bet they do! As a matter of fact, if people knew what they have there in the way of arms and ammunition, they'd probably think that they're Militia members, but I assure you that they're not. Why, what do you have in mind?"

"I don't remember if I told you this or not, Len, but when Nancy and Eileen had the circle of distorted air directly in front of them, Nancy fired several rounds from my shotgun at it, and the circle disappeared. I'm betting that when the pellets pierced the surface, something was disrupted in the electrical field and that's why it disappeared." Rob went on to explain exactly what he wanted Bubba, Stormin and him to do, and Len vehemently agreed, stating that they wouldn't let him down this time, come hell or high water!

"I really appreciate your willingness to help. Make sure that you stop by the camp before we leave for the airport at 06:15 hours, and I'll give you a hand-held NAV/COM so that we can direct you guys to where the circle of air is. Remember, if the circle of shimmering air starts shooting those translucent radio waves at any of the planes, unleash hell!"

* * *

Rob came walking back into the living room just as Jack was hanging up the phone. "Did you get to talk with all of them?"

"Yep! I reached every one of them. I briefed them on the mission, and I also told them what had happened when those translucent reverse radio-type waves came at me from the circle of shimmering air. I also told them that it would probably happen again, and I emphasized that when you take that into consideration along with all of the other potential problems that could surface, this mission is extremely dangerous."

Rob was shaking his head from side to side and said, "Yeah, there's no question about that."

"Yeah, that's for sure, but I offered each one of them an opportunity to opt out. I told them that we would understand if they did, but each and every one of them was even more resolved to help. Oh, and another thing, Art Bell knows what his mission is going to be if we have to implement Plan C."

"Good! Jack, did you tell them to be over Phillips by 09:00 hours, and also the fact that we're going to email a topo to them with the sector names?"

"Don't be such a worrywart. You're starting to sound like you lack confidence in me!"

"No, I have plenty of confidence in you, Jack. It's got to be the stress, that's all. By the way, I have some news for you!"

He told Jack about his conversation with Len and when he was finished Jack said, "That's a brilliant idea!" And trying to act happier than he felt, he said, "Every now and then you surprise the hell out of me! I didn't know you had it in ya!"

"Yeah, yeah, yeah. Everybody loves a smart ass! And since I'm on a roll I'll share another idea with you regarding the game plan that we put together last night. After I assigned code names to the different sectors on the map, it kind of hit me right between the eyes that if we use code names that are radically different from what the aliens probably have in their database, we could send up a red flag, unintentionally letting them know that something's up."

"That's a good point Rob, but let me ask you a question. Why are you calling them aliens at this point in time, when you'd been referring to them as strangers all along?"

"Because I now feel that *alien* is more appropriate than stranger, and maybe I've just copped a different attitude. Anyway, let me complete my thought. All the snowmobile trails have signs on them that identify each rescue zone, along with a mile marker. If a rider is in an accident, the people with him can easily identify the location when they call emergency rescue. We'll use rescue zones on our map, but we'll change the letters and numbers so that the rescue zone is actually reversed with another distant location. Get my drift?"

"Sure, we transmit a rescue zone location that is maybe near Pittsburgh, New Hampshire, when actually we're directing everyone to the beaver pond. I think that's a great idea!"

"By the way, Jack, what did Larry have to say when you called him this morning?"

"Damn! I didn't call him yet. I truly forgot! Maybe it was my subconscious mind blocking my memory. When you get down to brass tacks, I really don't want to call him to apologize for not calling when I was supposed to, and as soon as I get done apologizing, ask him for a favor. If it were me, and I was receiving that phone call, I'd think that the only reason that I got the call and the apology was because the person really wanted something else from me."

"Jack, knowing how these mountain people think, your assessment is probably not far off the mark. But you'd better get past it real quick and take what ever abuse you've got coming, because we really need Larry's help on this one. Just keep this in mind, Larry may be ticked at you, but he'd be even more pissed if you didn't ask him to help."

Jack picked up the phone and started dialing Larry's number just as Rob said, "While you're bringing him up to date I'm going to put together a list of everything that we need to take with us."

Jack gave Rob a thumb's up just as he heard Larry's sleepy voice come on the phone saying, "This better be good!"

"Larry, this is Jack."

"You really picked a lousy time to finally make good on a promise to call. I'll just mark this down in my Get Even Book. I'll call you back in two hours. You at Rob's?"

"Larry, please don't hang up, this is real important."

Larry paused and then said, "Sorry, Jack. But I'm more than just a little pissed that you didn't call me when you said you would. You've known me long enough to know how I feel about a person that does not do what they say they're going to do! I guess that I've beat you up enough for now. What's up?"

He brought Larry up to date with everything that had happened the day before and said, "Rob and I are going after our wives and Thad today," and after a short pause said, "We need your help."

"No need to say anymore. What do you need?"

"We have three different plans, Larry. Plan A, which is basically a straight approach. Try to get into the circle of distorted air without involving any of the other pilots. The situation that developed with those translucent reverse radio type waves was scary as hell, and we don't want to expose them to that crap. All of them have a wife and kids. Sure, we have a strategy to defeat those radio waves if the aliens use them again, but if our strategy doesn't work, it could get extremely dangerous. If Plan A doesn't work, then we'll implement Plan B, which involves Mel Marshall flying a diversion maneuver, and Plan C involves all pilots. Mel Marshall, whom I'm sure you know, will be flying his Skymaster, and he'll be the second diversion plane in Plan C. Art Bell will be the primary diversion aircraft. Mel will approach the circle from behind at maximum speed while you and Rob fly a direct approach. The idea behind employing that tactic is to divert attention from the planes that are approaching the circle head on. When Mel suddenly flashes by from behind, we expect that in the confusion the aliens will temporarily forget about transmitting those reverse radio wave-like signals that I told you about, and that'll give us enough time to penetrate the circle. But we want to give Plan B our best shot before we even think about implementing Plan C. If at all possible, we want to avoid involving the other pilots. We really don't want to expose them to the risk involved. Any questions so far?"

"Not so far, and when you're finished briefing me, if I think you've left out something of importance to me, I'll ask."

"Fair enough. Also, would you call Steve Savage and ask him to act as a reconnaissance plane for us?"

"Sure."

"Steve's Tri-Pacer is the slowest plane in the group. Tell him that when we take off from the airport, that he'll depart first, and tell him to climb to 2500 feet AGL. Also tell him to circle in an area that will give him a clear view of the Seven Gulpers and the beaver pond. If he can see those two landmarks, he'll be able to see all of the locations where we've most often spotted the circle of distorted air. And another thing that I forgot to mention; let Steve know that you'll be 1000 feet above him to give him a hand with reconnaissance until you need to rendezvous with us. By the way, you know all of our pilot buddies from Portland. I'll fill you in on those details when we get to the airport. Two more things: First, I'd like you to use your Chieftain; and second, I'd like you to get a hold of Tommy Yorks. Ask him if he'd be willing to ride shotgun with you. And, oh, I lied, there's three, ask him to bring some of his heavy artillery with him."

"I have no problem with anything that you've said so far, but what do you have in mind?"

"Well, first of all, you and Tommy are old friends and we trust you. Second of all, Tommy is one hell of a marksman and that could come in very handy. And last but not least, we need you to follow us through the circle of air because Rob can't dump enough fuel to compensate for Eileen, Nancy and Thad's weight, and be able to fly safely back through."

"Now I understand why I have to rendezvous with you. That was going to be my question. There's still one thing I have to say about you, Jack, when you ask, you always ask big. But I'll tell you what, no problem. You've got my commitment, and I'm sure you'll get Tommy's also!"

"Thanks, buddy. We owe you big time!" Jack looked over at the kitchen table and saw that Rob was still working on the list of things to bring, so he filled Larry in on the rest of the details. "Remember, Larry, we do not want to call in the other pilots unless Plan A and Plan B fail, and then only after we have given them one hell of a college try. Plan C is just so damned dangerous."

"I agree. But these guys have lots of hours in the air, and hopefully that will reduce the risk."

* * *

Jack came over to the Explorer after Rob had almost all of the items loaded in the back and asked, "Do you have room to bring along some electronic equipment that I think may come in handy?"

"No problem with having enough room, but it could be a different issue on the return trip. It's a strong probability that any equipment that you bring along will have to be left behind. Any problem with that?"

"None! I can easily replace everything. Isn't your buddy, Len, supposed to be here by now?"

Rob looked at his watch and saw that it was almost 06:15 hours and thought to himself, "So much for not letting me down this time, come hell or high water!" He looked over at Jack and when he saw that he was staring at him, all Rob could think of to do was to shrug his shoulders. Then he promptly turned around to head back into the camp to get the rest of the gear that they needed. Just as he was opening up the storm door he could hear snowmobiles in the distance. He stopped in mid step, and with a big grin on his face; he looked back over his shoulder at Jack with an expression that said, "Are you happy now?"

* * *

Len, Bubba, and Stormin were pulling up alongside the Explorer as he came out of the camp with the last of the items in his arms, and Rudy and Ginger were close behind. As soon as the last machine was shut down Rob said, "Hey, guys, nothing like showing up as the last curtain is coming down!"

With his head hanging contritely down Bubba said, "It's my fault. My frigging sled broke down again and we had to go back to camp so I could get another ride. I left that piece of junk sitting on the side of the trail, and if I'm lucky somebody'll steal the friggin' thing."

And Len added, "Yeah! He even left the key in the ignition switch to give them encouragement." Little did he know that call would be very close to the truth.

Rob cut in, "We're in kind of a hurry, guys, so I'll go get the NAV/COM and be right back out." In less than 30 seconds he was standing in front of Len and he quickly briefed him on how to use it. He also gave him an abbreviated tour on proper radio protocol, and just before he turned away to get into the Explorer he said, "Hey, Len! I almost forgot. Here's Mel Marshall's phone number."

It was 06:30 hours by the time they finally left for the airport. The ride was quiet the whole way, with both Rob and Jack deep in thought, continuously reworking in their minds the plan that they had put together. Both were trying to find any crack in the plans that they might have missed. As they drove up to where the Hawk was tied down, both dogs started prancing back and forth across the back seat, whining with excitement. Jack said, "Do you suppose that they know what's goin' on?"

"It sure seems that way. Rudy's never acted this excited before when we've come to the airport." Rob looked over at his Hawk XP and said, "Larry's already got the heater blowing warm air into the engine compartment."

* * *

Jack was closing the passenger door to the Explorer when he saw Larry walking over to them. There was no cheerfulness in his voice as he said, "Hi, Larry. How long's the heater been cranking?"

"Only about five minutes. Need some help loading your stuff into the plane?" And without waiting for an answer, he walked over to the tailgate and opened it. Both dogs came bounding out and Larry jumped back in surprise, blurting out, "What the hell? You guys ain't bringin' them dogs with ye, are ya?

Rob was quick to respond and said; "I think that their noses will be a big help while we're trying to find Eileen, Nancy and Thad!"

Larry thought about that one for a couple of seconds, nodded his head in agreement and turned his attention back to the rear inside of the Explorer. Once he got a good look at everything piled there he said, "I'm impressed! It looks like you guys are fully prepared for whatever grief may pour down on ya."

The three of them were quiet as they each made trips back and forth from the Explorer to the Hawk XP. Once everything was loaded inside, Jack turned to Larry and said, "Is Steve Savage here yet?"

"Yeah, he's over in the hanger working on the King Air."

"I'll see you guys back here in a couple of minutes. I want to go talk with Steve."

Steve Savage is the only rated Airframe & Power Plant (A&P) mechanic at the airport, and as such, frequently puts in many twelve to eighteen hour days. He had his head stuck in the cowling of the right turbine on the King Air as Jack came walking into the hanger. He didn't hear the hanger personnel door open or close, he only heard Jack's footsteps, but he didn't bother to stop what he was doing until he heard Jack say, "Hey, Steve, I know you can hear me, even though I'm pussyfooting to sneak up on you."

Without taking his head out from the cowling he said, "What makes you so sure that I heard you?"

"Cause the first time that my shoe squeaked on the floor I saw your knees jerk, very slightly, but they jerked."

"You always were an observant twit. Sorry to hear about Nancy and Eileen. You gonna give me more details about what's goin' on? 'Cause all that I know right now is that I'm going to be doing some reconnaissance."

Jack briefed Steve with all the same information that he gave the Portland pilots earlier that morning and finished up by saying, "Here's a copy of the topo — and thanks, Steve. You don't know how much this means to Rob and me."

* * *

At 08:30 hours several local residents saw Rob and Jack in the Cessna Hawk XP, Larry Williams and Tommy Yorks in Larry's Piper Chieftain, and Steve Savage in his Piper Tri-Pacer as they taxied out to runway 32 for departure. Anyone near the Rangeley Airport at 08:30 hours was apt to notice what was going on because it is highly unusual for three aircraft to be going through their run-up procedures all at the same time. That airport just didn't get that much traffic.

Steve was the first to take off, followed by Larry and then Rob. Larry's Chieftain is much faster than Steve's Tri-Pacer, and Rob and Jack knew that he would be circling at 3500 feet AGL a full three minutes before Steve got to altitude. And that had an advantage. Tommy and Larry would be able to start reconnaissance sooner than Steve, plus at 3500 feet AGL, they would be able to see a greater distance. But Rob and Jack didn't really think that the greater distance was going to be a factor since the circles of air seldom showed up anywhere other than the areas right near, or in between the Seven Gulpers and the beaver pond.

Larry leveled out at 3500 feet AGL just as he was approaching the area that he felt would be the best position to see both the Seven Gulpers and the beaver pond. As soon as Tommy confirmed that he could see both locations, Larry entered a right hand holding pattern and said, "Tommy, I'll keep an eye on Steve while you look for the circle of distorted air."

Then Larry turned his attention to locating Steve. As soon as he spotted him he took a look at his Directional Guide (a mechanical compass) to determine what heading to give to Steve, and without even thinking about it, he pressed his microphone key and said, "Tri-Pacer Two Zero Two Five Sierra, this is Two Three Niner Lima Romeo, come about to three six zero degrees. I'll let you know when you're right under me. I think that this is the best location for you to maintain a visual on both the Seven Gulpers and the beaver pond."

* * *

Jack looked back over his right shoulder at the Rangeley Airport, and when Rob glanced over at him, he could have sworn that Jack's demeanor said, "I'm never gonna see this airport again."

Jack checked the harnesses on the dogs to make sure that they were tight and secure before he turned his head to look out the front window of the aircraft. The first thing he saw was the sun glaring off the tip of the peaks on Bigelow Mountain straight ahead. He wondered what Sector Rescue Zone the mountain was in, and scanned the topographical map on his lap until he found that they had designated Bigelow Mountain as Rescue B14. When they were about three miles from Rescue B14, Rob pulled slightly back on the yoke, initiating a climb to 2500 feet AGL, which was the altitude they were going to use while maintaining a holding pattern over the Bigelow's most eastern peak. Looking over at Jack he said, "Now all we need is cooperation from the circle of shimmering air."

Twenty minutes had gone by without a word from either Steve or Larry and both Rob and Jack were getting edgy. He was just about ready to key the mike when he heard Steve on the Rangeley Unicom saying, "Cessna Seven Five Eight Mike Yankee, this is Tri-Pacer Two Zero Two Five Sierra. The bogey's in Rescue A4."

Rob looked over at Jack and said, "That's the beaver pond, right?"

"Good memory! Let's get going!"

Rob quickly dropped his left wing to tighten the circle so that he could get to the beaver pond heading as quickly as possible. Just as they were within five degrees of the heading, Rob started to bring the wings back to level, and simultaneous to that they heard Steve on the Unicom again. "Cessna Seven Five Eight Mike Yankee, this is Tri-Pacer Two Zero Two Five Sierra. There are snowmobilers in the immediate vicinity of the circle of distorted air, and I just gotta say this: from the position that I'm in right now, that circle of air looks like a disk standing on its edge. Weird, huh?"

Rob acknowledged Steve's radio transmission and immediately called Len on hand-held NAV/COM. "Ground Support, this is Cessna Seven Five Eight Mike Yankee, do you read me?"

"Cessna Seven Five Eight Mike Yankee, this is Ground Support. We read you loud and clear."

"What's your 20?"

"We're about a half-mile away from Rescue A4. We anticipated that A4 would be the first place that the bogey would surface."

"Ground Support, be advised that there are other snowmobilers in the immediate area, and I have a feeling that they could be the enemy. It could be possible that they're flatlanders getting an early start on their weekend riding, but my instincts tell me that they're the bad guys. We'll hang back until you check them out."

* * *

"Cessna Seven Five Eight Mike Yankee, this is Ground Support. We have the snowmobilers in sight."

"Ground Support, describe the riders to me."

"They're riding Polaris machines and they all have darkly tinted face shields on their snowmobile helmets."

Rob looked over at Jack and saw him vehemently shaking his head yes. He keyed his mike and said, "Ground Support, we're convinced they would be the enemy."

While listening to the conversation back and forth between Rob and Len, Steve decided to drop down to get a closer look at the circle of distorted air from the backside. The moment that he had a clear view of it he forgot all proper radio protocol and blurted out, "Man! This circle of air looks much different on the backside.

It doesn't look anything like the way it was described to me. It looks like a mirror because it's so smooth, but the only difference is that there's no reflection of what's behind it. And I'll tell you something else; at this position it *really* looks like a disk standing on edge. From what I see, I don't think you'll have to worry about any translucent reverse radio-type waves coming from the back side of it." As Steve dropped lower he could see that one of the snowmobiles had a tag-along sled behind it, and promptly relayed that information to Rob.

"Cessna Seven Five Eight Mike Yankee, this is Chieftain Two Three Niner Lima Romeo. Tommy just told me that the tag-along sled is loaded with Have-A-Heart Traps, and it looks to him like all the traps have one or more animals in them."

"Ground Support, this is Cessna Seven Five Eight Mike Yankee. It's my guess that the circle of distorted air is going to pick up those riders and their equipment."

Len, Bubba, and Stormin were just getting in position at Rescue A4 and didn't hear Rob's transmission. Only a few seconds went by when Jack and Rob heard Steve say, "Cessna Seven Five Eight Mike Yankee, you hit the nail right on the head. All riders and equipment are gone. It looked like they were just sucked right into the circle."

* * *

The airwaves were silent for a minute and a half before Steve broke the silence by saying, "This is Tri-Pacer Sierra. The bogey's still there."

Fewer than ten more seconds went by when Rob and Jack heard Len on the Rangeley Unicom. "Cessna Seven Five Eight Mike Yankee, we're in position and have the bogey in our sights."

Rob looked over at Jack, a little surprised to see a grin on his face, and said, "Showtime, ol' buddy."

Jack's grin noticeably grew as he said, "Let the fun begin!"

* * *

"This is Tri-Pacer Two Zero Two Five Sierra. I'll go into a holding pattern over Rescue A6 and remain in position on the backside of the circle of air."

Jack looked at the topo and said, "He's going to hold over Harris Pasture."

"This is Chieftain Two Three Niner Lima Romeo on a heading to Rescue B14."

"This is Cessna Seven Five Eight Mike Yankee. Let me know when you have visual contact and I'll do same."

"Lima Romeo, roger that!"

While scanning the sky to the northwest Rob said to Jack, "Got a visual on him yet?"

"I think I see him. As soon as you're on a heading toward the beaver pond, look at the 12 o'clock position, and up about fifteen degrees."

"Got him!" He was just about to key the mike to transmit to Larry when he heard, "Seven Five Eight Mike Yankee, have you in sight."

"Lima Romeo, take a position on my port side!"

* * *

The Hawk XP was passing over the northernmost peak of Bigelow Mountain and the dogs were fully alert as Rob announced, "This is Seven Five Eight Mike Yankee ... I'm going to begin a descent that will bring me to tree top level by the time that I am within one mile of the beaver pond. By the time that he realized what he was saying he tried to cut his statement short, but it was too late. As soon as he got the last words out of his mouth he screamed, "Damn! That wasn't very smart!"

Jack jerked his head toward Rob and said, "You got *that* right! Hopefully they didn't hear you. If they didn't, we should have a low enough profile to stop them from getting a quick lock on us like they did when I tried this crap."

* * *

As soon as Rob's radio transmission had stopped Steve noticed that the circle of air started changing its position, and it became obvious as Rob and Jack got closer to the beaver pond that it was making a slow and deliberate turn to face them square on. The moment that Steve keyed his mike to warn Rob that the circle of air was positioning to face him, he saw the translucent reverse radio type waves that Jack had cautioned him about. Even though he had been warned about them, his mind still went into a total state of confusion. At the same time, the radio waves began to appear, all that everyone heard in their headsets was static because Steve forgot to release the mike button.

* * *

Jack and Rob's nerves were vibrating intensely as they watched the face of the circle of air slowly rotate in their direction. Emotions skyrocketed as the dogs started barking furiously the second that it was facing directly at them. A major bolt of fear shot through their bodies as the radio waves started to rapidly telescope out at them. Without thinking Jack blurted out, "Holy moly! Now we don't have to wonder *if* they heard you!"

With the roar of the Hawk's engine, the raucous barking of the dogs, and the static in his headset, Rob never heard a word of what Jack said. Even if all that noise wasn't suffocating his hearing at that particular moment, it wouldn't have mattered. His mind was whirling in high gear, trying to determine a defense if Len, Bubba, and Stormin weren't following his instructions.

* * *

Len saw the circle starting to pulsate, and as soon as radio waves started to emanate from it he yelled, "Bubba, Stormin, hit that mother now!" But before he completed his statement they had already started to unleash a barrage of firepower that sounded like World War III had just begun. All three of them had semiautomatic weapons, and in less than ten seconds the radio waves drew back into the circle of air, and the circle disappeared. Bubba and Stormin looked over at Len with huge grins on their face, all of them were giving each other the thumb's up.

* * *

A flood of relief surged through both Jack and Rob as soon as the radio waves and the circle of air disappeared and the dogs stopped their barking. Rob keyed his mike button and said, "Lima Romeo, this is Mike Yankee. Execute a climbing left turn now." He looked slightly to the left to affirm that Larry was following his command as he pulled back the yoke and set his course to return to Bigelow Mountain.

"This is Mike Yankee, Lima Romeo we're heading to Rescue B14."

Rob wanted to privately discuss what had just happened with Jack so he turned the radio switch to intercom. He wanted to make sure that if either one of them accidentally hit the mike button, nothing would be transmitted. "Jack, I have the distinct feeling that we're both right and that our radio transmissions are being monitored, how else would the aliens know to turn and face our direction?"

Jack thought for a moment and then looked over at Rob and said, "Why don't you let Larry know that we're having a conversation?"

Rob looked out his window and saw Tommy Yorks staring back at him. He gave Tommy some sign language that he hoped he would understand, and evidently he did because he nodded okay. Then he turned back to Jack with an expectant look on his face.

"I think we have to maintain radio silence and hope that the other guys pick up on why we're not responding to their calls."

"I agree, Jack. Let's see what happens when the circle of shimmering air shows up again."

* * *

They had just agreed to this strategy when they heard a very excited voice on the radio. "Seven Five Eight Mike Yankee, this is Two Zero Two Five Sierra. I have the bogey in sight. It's in Rescue A8, and there's nothing around it. It's facing your direction and it just seems like it's waiting there. I'm holding at 2500 feet AGL over Rescue A21.

Jack looked down at the topographical map on his lap and said to Rob, "The bogey's at the Seven Gulpers, and he's over the Little Kennebago."

* * *

Tommy Yorks looked over at Larry Williams and said, "It appears to me that Rob and Jack are maintaining radio silence. I think that they need to know how high that circle of air is above the snow, 'cause if they approach it from the wrong altitude, they could run into a hornet's nest of them translucent radio waves."

Larry was rubbing the beard stubble on his chin when he said, "You've got a point. I wonder if those aliens are smart enough to be monitoring all of our radio transmissions, or if they're just focusing on Rob's." He rubbed the beard stubble on his chin with more vigor, looked over at Tommy and said, "There's only one way to find out!" With that he keyed his mike and said, "Two Zero

Two Five Sierra, this is Lima Romeo. How high it is that bugger off the snow?"

"Lima Romeo, it's about seventy-five feet above the snow."

Tommy saw that Rob heard Steve's radio transmission because he was waving a big thumb's up at him. Larry had been leaning forward, looking past Tommy to see what Rob's reaction would be, and when he saw that he was getting the thumb's up signal, he said to Tommy, "Give him the sign to get going."

Tommy gave him the sign to get going and was totally dumbfounded when he saw Rob shake his head no. Tommy put his hands up in the air to either side of him, palms up, asking what's up?

Rob held up his finger signaling for him to wait just a minute. "Jack, get the pad out of the side pocket on the door and write a note saying that we have to wait for Len to get into position." As soon as Jack handed him the note he put it up in the window and it only took a moment for Tommy to grab his binoculars to read it. And then it took only two more seconds till Tommy nodded his head okay.

* * *

Len had heard Steve's radio transmission to Rob and took a quick look at his topographical map. As soon as he located Rescue A8 he yelled to Bubba and Stormin, "Let's hit the trail, guys! The circle's at the Seven Gulpers!"

Len was in the lead, and as soon as they hit ITS 89 he knew it would be a quick trip. The groomer must have just gone by in the past hour or so because there were only a few snowmobile tracks on the trail.

In just over five minutes Len slowed down and motioned to Bubba and Stormin that he was going to stop. They were almost to the top of a steep rise in the trail when he finally saw what he was looking for. Still hidden from the view of the Seven Gulpers, he pulled as far as he could to the right side of ITS 89, and came to a complete stop when he was in front of a narrow trail that led to the back of the camp.

They shut off their machines and put on their snowshoes before they left the snowmobile trail to circle around to the backside of the Seven Gulpers. They had agreed among themselves that they would be able to get a good line of fire from that position. Even though Bubba was carrying a lot of extra beef on his frame, he still was in the best physical shape, and he took the lead to break the trail. When they finally came out of the woods right behind the Seven Gulpers outhouse, Bubba leaned out around the corner to see if he could get a good visual on the circle of air. However, he quickly pulled his head back when he thought that he had seen someone standing right in front of the shimmering air looking in his direction. He squatted down into a lower position while taking off his snowmobile helmet, and leaned cautiously around the corner of the outhouse for another look. Either he had been hallucinating, or the person had left. He turned around and let Len and Stormin know that it was all clear.

Len immediately keyed the NAV/COM and quietly said, "Ground Support in position."

* * *

While Len and his crew were on the way to the Seven Gulpers, Jack said to Rob, "I'm convinced that those aliens have been listening to all of our radio transmissions, and it's obvious that they're expecting us to come from the same direction again. And what makes me so sure that I'm correct is that the circle of air is faced directly at our current location. I have a suggestion. While Len, Bubba and Stormin are on their way over to the Seven Gulpers, why don't we head over to Rescue A30?"

With a questioning look on his face Rob said, "Good idea! Maybe. But since I don't have a photographic memory, where the hell is Rescue A30?"

A big grin spread across his face as he said, "Rob, you're slipping! It's Saddleback Mountain. Just do like you did before, drop down low and skim the trees."

Rob looked out his window at Tommy Yorks, held up his hand and rapidly moved it in a circular motion, letting him know that they were departing. Tommy acknowledged and turned to Larry saying, " I don't know what's up. But follow Rob!"

They were just entering a holding pattern over Saddleback Mountain when they heard Len on the Unicom, "Mike Yankee, Ground Support is in position." As soon as Len's transmission ended they heard Steve say, "The bogey's still facing niner zero."

"Jack, I have an idea. Grab the pad and write this down ... Larry, contact me on my home base frequency!"

As soon as Jack had written down the message he handed it over, and Rob put it in the window for Tommy Yorks to see. The moment that he saw the paper in the window he picked up his binoculars and read the message to Larry. Larry immediately switched his frequency to 120.9 and said, "This is Lima Romeo. Do you read me, Mike Yankee?"

"This is Mike Yankee. Larry, tell Tommy to let everyone know to change to the home base frequency. The aliens shouldn't recognize his voice at this point in time."

"Roger that."

* * *

"Jack, set NAV/COM 2 to the Rangeley Unicom. I want to confuse the shit out of those bastards!" Then he keyed his mike and said, "Tri-Pacer Sierra, do you read me?"

"This is Tri-Pacer Sierra, I read you loud and clear."

"Tri-Pacer Sierra, go to the Rangeley Unicom."

Steve pressed the mike button and said, "Tri-Pacer Sierra switching to the Rangeley Unicom."

Rob placed the intercom switch to NAV/COM 2 and said, "Two Zero Two Five Sierra, what's your 20?"

"Still holding over Rescue A21."

"10-4. Scan Sector Rescue A30"

Steve started a scan over toward the Saddleback Mountain. When he saw two aircraft, he picked up his binoculars and as soon as he found his target he pressed the mike key and said, "Two Zero Two Five Sierra, finished my scan and understand. Changing to home base frequency."

"10-4, Tri-Pacer Sierra. Will advise when we are beginning our descent from Bigelow."

Rob switched back to NAV/COM 1 and said, "Lima Romeo, we're going to hold here while Jack and I have a pow-wow." Rob looked over at Jack and said, "Steve seems to think that circle is sitting there waiting for something, and that could be true, but it could be *us* that it's waiting for, and there's another thing to consider ... we don't know how long it's going to wait. Whatever decision we make, we gotta make it quick! How do you think we should make the approach?"

"I think that we should approach it from the southwest. Go in low and keep hugging the mountain as it slopes up, and when we've crested the top of the Kennebago, reverse direction and reduce your air speed to the low side of maneuvering speed. Then all we need to do is get back down to tree top-level while approaching the Seven Gulpers at approximately a forty-five degree angle. At maneuvering speed, if the circle of air changes the direction that it's facing from niner zero, we'll have time to maneuver to a different position to still approach it at a forty-five degree angle."

"I don't like flying the low side of maneuvering speed at that low altitude, but other than that, the plan makes sense to me." Rob keyed the mike and told Larry the game plan. Larry acknowledged that he understood, and declared that he would break right with Rob from the holding pattern. The second his transmission ended, they broke from the holding pattern over Saddleback Mountain into a descending turn toward the Seven Gulpers as Rob switched back to NAV/COM 2 and said, "This is Mike Yankee. I'm beginnin' a slow descent from Bigelow Mountain on a direct heading of two two five degrees to the Seven Gulpers. "

* * *

As they crested the top of the Kennebago Rob keyed his mike button saying, "Lima Romeo, execute left descending turn."

"Mike Yankee, Lima Romeo executing left descending turn now." Right at that moment Larry pulled back a little on his throttles, while at the same time pressing the microphone button and said, "Mike Yankee, my maneuvering speed is a little bit higher than yours. Just keep that in mind."

"Lima Romeo, thanks for that. We both neglected to take that into consideration. Two Zero Two Five Sierra, is the bogey still at niner zero?"

"Mike Yankee, that's a big 10-4."

Ginger let out a low growl just as Jack said, "I can see Steve over the little Kennebago, and I can also see Fred Power's Camp. We're right on course."

"Keep a sharp eye out, Jack, we should see that circle any time now."

"I see the circle, Rob! We're almost on a ninety-degree angle to it. You've got to head up the mountain some to get a better angle!"

Rob instantly pressed the microphone button and said, "Lima Romeo, breaking left to head up the mountain to get a better angle of attack!"

Rob turned the yoke to the left as he looked out his window to determine Larry's exact position when he heard Larry say, "Mike Yankee, two steps ahead of you!"

"Lima Romeo, so you are. Once we have a good approach angle, I'm going to set my course for the lower right quadrant."

"10-4, Mike Yankee. I'll be aiming at the top left quadrant."

The moment that Rob and Larry altered their course and increased their speed to head back down the mountain at a forty-five degree angle to the circle, it started turning to face them square on again. It was acting the same way as it did the last time, and both Rob and Jack noted that its speed of rotation in their direction was very slow. Their nerves were already on edge, and when both Rudy and Ginger started barking ferociously, the tension in their bodies rapidly accelerated to a level that neither one of them had ever experienced before. As the circle rotated to a more direct heading toward them, Rob and Jack expected that any second the translucent radio waves would begin erupting from the outer perimeter. Both knew that that would be a major problem. They were just way too close to do anything about it. Precisely when Rob thought that they were going to succeed in penetrating the circle, it moved. In fact it moved so fast that at first they thought it had simply disappeared, but then it reappeared seventy-five feet to the right. Rob and Larry flew right by it and as they did, Jack got a good look at the circle through his side window, and a big frown formed on his face. He thought that he had seen the pyramid, but he wasn't sure, so he decided to keep his mouth shut.

The dogs had stopped their barking about the time Rob had pulled back on the yoke to maintain level flight. He looked out his window to make sure Larry was still in the same position. "Lima Romeo, let's maintain altitude and make a left turn to head east along the South face of the East Kennebago Mountain. I need to have another pow-wow with Jack." He looked over at Jack and said, "Did you see that? When the circle turned to face us, it turned real slow, just like it did the last time!"

"Yeah, I saw that. But that son of a gun sure could move fast to the right!"

Before Rob could respond they heard Len on the intercom saying, "Two Zero Two Five Sierra, this is Ground Support. We lost sight of the bogey when it went below our line of sight. Can you see it?"

"Ground Support, the bogey's still here. It looks like it is slowly moving to the left, back to its original position. Maybe it *was* waiting for something, and that's why it has to get back to that same position."

Rob looked back at Jack again and said, "Why do you suppose it's moving so slow to the left, when it moved so fast to the right?"

Jack stared at Rob with a blank look on his face and said, "Don't ask me why I am saying this, because I don't know. But I have this real strong feeling that it just *can't* move fast to the left."

Rob and Larry were almost directly over the beaver pond when they heard Steve say, "This is Two Zero Two Five Sierra. The bogey's back in the original position, and it's still facing niner zero."

"What are your ideas for an approach this time, Jack?"

"Well, you know that clearing that's northeast of the Seven Gulpers camp?"

"Yeah. What've you got on your mind?"

"Why don't we make our approach over that clearing?"

Rob thought for a couple of seconds and said, "I don't want to have to repeat this to Larry. Let's transmit this conversation to him."

Jack pressed the microphone button and said, "Lima Romeo, we've got a plan that we're going to run by you. Let us know what you think. We're going to go back around the mountain and come up over the north side, and then immediately get on a direct heading to the clearing northeast of the Seven Gulpers, and just as soon as we have the correct heading established, we'll descend the south face at treetop level. I know that'll put us on a tight approach to the circle, but we need all the edge that we can get. This is my thinking, I figure that we'll be making our approach at about a fifteen degree angle, and I really think that's a good idea, especially since it will take the circle a lot longer to turn to face us square on, and that, my friend, lessens the chance of encountering those radio waves."

There was dead air for about ten seconds until Larry came back and said, "Sounds good! Lead the way."

"Lima Romeo, we're going to make the approach targeting the same quadrant, 10-4?"

"10-4, Mike Yankee."

"Lima Romeo, this time I'm going to use maximum cruise speed as we approach the circle. Hopefully that will give it less time to get a lock on us to transmit those radio waves, and less time to move from our flight path."

While they were approaching the clearing to the northeast of the Seven Gulpers, they saw the top of the circle of air. Both of them immediately dropped the nose of their aircraft a little bit to establish a descent path that would penetrate the same quadrants as before. Rob pressed the mike button and said, "Lima Romeo, if that circle turned slow to face us the last two times, perhaps it simply can't rotate very fast. If we are lucky and that is the case, our approach will be a surprise, and just maybe it won't be able to square off to us, and if that assumption is correct, then we won't have to worry about those translucent reverse radio type waves.

When he released the microphone button, he looked over at Jack and said, "And at maximum speed I think that I could avoid those radio waves if Len's artillery doesn't stop them."

As they were crossing over the clearing just to the northeast of the Seven Gulpers, Rob noted that his Air Speed Indicator was almost in the red ark. He took a quick look over at Larry, and then back at Jack before focusing his attention on the circle of shimmering air, only to catch a glimpse of it doing its disappearing act to the right again. Like before, Rob pulled back on the yoke to bring the nose of his Hawk level with the horizon, and then followed the same flight path east along the South face of the mountain. He was thinking that something was different this time, and it didn't dawn on him what in the heck it was until Jack said, "I wonder why the dogs didn't bark this time?"

* * *

Jack turned his head to Rob and said, "You know, that's the second time that the circle of air has avoided us by moving to the right. I think that there's a pattern developing here. What do you think?"

"I think you're right, but let's make another run at it and see if recent history repeats itself. But something's bothering me, Jack, why do you suppose they haven't tried to jam our radio transmissions today?"

"Good question! Haven't even thought about it!"

Their conversation was interrupted when Len came back on the airwaves and said, "Two Zero Two Five Sierra, I don't see the circle of air, is it still there?"

"Negative, Ground Support, it's gone."

Abruptly Jack yells, "I think I see it at the one o'clock position." He picked up his binoculars, and after adjusting the focus he saw that the circle of air was about seventy-five feet above ITS 89. He quickly scanned the surrounding area and said, "I think it's in Rescue Zone A5.5." He looked down at the topo on his lap and said, "Yep, that's right. It's one half mile west of Harris Pasture Road and ITS 89 intersection."

He looked back down at the circle of distorted air, and when he caught movement in his peripheral vision he looked further down the snowmobile trail. He saw four sleds following one after the other, doing what he estimated to be about forty miles per hour. They were heading west across the mountain, directly toward the shimmering air. It flashed into his mind that the circle was probably focusing its attention on those riders, and almost as if it wanted to confirm that he was right, it started to pulsate. There was not even a momentary delay in his reaction time. It was immediate and he yelled, "Rob! That circle of air is beginning to pulsate! I think it's goin' to try to snatch those riders headin' in its direction!"

By this time the circle of air was at their four o'clock position, and Rob immediately reacted, dropping his right wing as he started a steep descending tight right turn toward the circle.

"Rob! What the hell are you doing!?!"

"I'm going to buzz it! I'm pretty sure that'll distract those bastards from the snowmobilers, and hopefully at the same time those rider's will get the hint to get the heck out of this area." Then as an after thought he said, "Or maybe at least they'll figure out that something isn't right up ahead."

He had leveled out and was flying at a thirty degree angle directly at the circle when Jack yelled, "Damn, Rob, we don't have any backup in place! I don't think that this is such a great idea!"

"Hey! I'm in this plane too! Listen, I think that we're going to be just fine, I'm closing fast and we already know that it can't rotate that quickly. Besides, it's concentrating on something other than us, and to boot, it doesn't even know that we're in the area."

Jack put his hands on the dash as he said, "What makes you so sure that they don't know..."

They had their answer. The aliens absolutely knew that they were in the vicinity. They were still about the length of two football fields away when the circle of air stopped pulsating. Then almost immediately it started to move in short, quick, jerking motions to its right side. The way that it was moving made Rob think that it couldn't make up its mind if it wanted to keep pursuing the riders, or if it wanted to move to avoid them. Then it disappeared.

Jack was the first to react, yelling, "No way!"

Rob turned the yoke and started a climbing turn to the right, and then remembered Larry and started looking for him everywhere at the same time. He had totally forgotten about him while he was trying to divert the alien's attention away from the snowmobilers, and now he may have put both of them into jeopardy when he made his decision to turn to the right. But Larry was nowhere to be seen. Rob depressed the microphone button and said, "Lima Romeo, what's your 20?"

"Mike Yankee, we saw what you were trying to do and decided to get out of your way. We've been keeping tabs on you, and I'm to the northeast about 1000 feet above you."

As the flood of stressful fear receded from his body he said, "Lima Romeo, thanks for that one!"

Jack tapped Rob on the shoulder to get his attention and said, "I was just thinking, why do you suppose the aliens haven't been using the radio waves on us?"

"I thought about that before, and I think it's because Len's been there with his artillery, and every time we've approached the circle today, with the exception of just now, the circle of air was not pulsating. Maybe when it's not pulsating, it can't transmit those translucent radio waves. Did you notice if it was pulsating when it sent the radio waves at you yesterday?"

"I was shitting in my pants. I couldn't tell you if it was doing flips." With that, Jack keyed the mike and said, "Ground Support, this is Mike Yankee. Was the circle of air pulsating this morning when it began transmitting those radio waves?"

"Mike Yankee, that's affirmative."

Rob looked over at Jack and said, "I think the only reason it hasn't been sending out the radio waves is because something happened when Len, Bubba, and Stormin gave it a good dose of lead poisoning."

"You could be one hundred percent right. But let's not take *that* to the bank! However, I think something's up. They've just been way too persistent. "

"Yeah, I agree. Pressing the mike key he said, "Lima Romeo, hang loose for a couple of minutes. Two Zero Two Five Sierra, please do the same."

* * *

Rob stared out the front windshield for the better part of a minute, wondering why nothing was working and why Rudy and Ginger hadn't been barking. He looked over at Jack and said, "We're getting nowhere fast. We've got to come up with a plan to bring all this crap to a screeching halt. Do you have any suggestions?"

"Yeah. We need to find a way to get this circle of air to stick around long enough so that we can develop a way to trick it. That's the only way that I can see that we'll get a chance to try to penetrate it. Suppose we just go back to Rescue A30 and go into a holding pattern until the circle of air appears again. Once it appears, we'll wait until Len gets into position, but we need to tell him not to get trigger-happy. We don't need him shooting the circle the second it starts emitting the radio waves."

"Well, that's a big change since our first encounter with it this morning. Did you suddenly get more moxie, Jack, or have you lost your mind?"

"Neither. When the radio waves hit me, I was in big trouble, and I was scared shitless. But I wasn't out of the ballgame, and I did manage to get out of harm's way. You told Len that as soon as he saw the radio waves starting to project from the circle of air to start shooting. All I'm saying is that he doesn't have to act so fast. I'm positive that we've got time to react."

"So, what've you got on your mind?"

"Once Len's in position, tell him not to fire until he sees that we can't break loose from its control. I want you to keep making runs at this thing until we find a weakness. Look, if we keep making passes at it, and the circle of air keeps avoiding us, it just might build the confidence of whomever is operating that thing, and they'll stick around long enough to make a mistake."

* * *

Rob got on the radio and briefed everyone as to what the plan was. Steve said that he would start circling once more in the area where he could see both the Seven Gulpers and the beaver pond, and it was not very long before the circle of shimmering air appeared again. But every time it appeared, it disappeared as soon as Rob and Larry started making their run at it. However, it was acting differently than it had before when they made the two approaches at it while it was in front of the Seven Gulpers. Instead of moving seventy-five feet to the right, it would disappear, and then reappear in a totally different location, although it was always a place that they had previously seen it in.

Finally Rob said, "It's like this thing is playing hopscotch. It makes an appearance so that we can make a pass at it, only it doesn't let us get nearly as close as it did before. I think that they know that we're waiting for Len to get into position. What's more, I think that they're monitoring all the radio chatter on both the home base frequency and the Rangeley Unicom. But I also think that they're missing some of what is being said, because I don't think that their scanner can listen to two channels at the same time, and another thing, maybe their scanner is just missing a small portion of our radio transmissions between the two channels."

"Maybe, Rob, but I smell a rat. I think they're setting us up for something, just like we're trying to do to them."

* * *

After fifteen minutes of circling over Harris Pasture, and with their friends from Portland still in a holding pattern over Phillips, Jack saw a circle of shimmering air hovering over ITS 89 again. It was almost in the exact same spot where it was setting up to snatch the four snowmobilers earlier that morning. He tapped Rob on the shoulder and said, "There she is! She's hovering about at seventy-five feet above the snow again."

"It's time to implement Plan B! What's the Sector, Jack?"

"Rescue A5 is close enough."

Rob pressed the button on his microphone and said, "Skymaster Five Two One Eight Tango, this is Seven Five Eight Mike Yankee. Plan B is a go. I repeat, Plan B is a go. The bogey's in Sector Rescue A5 facing four zero degrees. Announce when you are two and a half miles from the bogey."

"Mike Yankee, will announce two and a half miles from the bogey."

"Lima Romeo, you gonna join up with me on the port side?"

"Mike Yankee, Lima Romeo on the way."

Rob continued holding over Harris Pasture until they heard Mel Marshall say, "This is Skymaster Tango, two and a half miles on a heading of four zero at 3500."

"Skymaster Tango, slow down and execute some big S turns and announce two miles. We'll tell you when to begin your descent at max speed. Once you begin descent, level out at 500 feet AGL until you have a visual on the bogey, then drop down so that you blow by it to the right, about one hundred feet out, and somewhere near its equator. As soon as you make the pass, perform a climbing 180-degree right turn. Do you copy that, Tango?"

"Tango copy."

Rob and Larry broke their holding pattern, and headed directly toward Flagstaff Lake. Once they were two miles from the circle of air, he made a 180-degree left turn. As soon as he was on a heading of two three zero degrees he leveled his wings and lowered the Hawk's nose, and now he was descending on a heading that was directly opposite that of Mel Marshall's. Since Mel's plane had a higher max cruise speed, Rob estimated that he needed to be at maximum cruise by the time that he was within two miles of the circle of shimmering air. They actually hit maximum cruise speed about five hundred feet before the two-mile parameter, and that was when they heard Mel Marshall announce that he was at the two-mile marker. Rob keyed the mike and said, "Skymaster Tango, begin descent at max speed!"

As he eased the throttles all the way to their stops Mel said, "Skymaster Tango beginning descent."

And Rob muttered under his breath, "May God be with us all."

* * *

At the same time that Rob broke his holding pattern to head for Flagstaff Lake, Steve Savage flew his Tri-Pacer to the Harris Pasture Road and ITS 89 intersection, and entered a holding pattern at 2500 feet AGL. When he heard Mel Marshall's transmission back to Rob, he said, "Tri-Pacer Sierra, that bogey's still in the same position."

"This is Mike Yankee, 10-4, Sierra."

* * *

Rob was concentrating on flying the airplane and Jack was keeping his eye on Mel Marshall. When they were a half-mile from the circle Jack yelled to Rob, "I don't think you calculated this right because Mel's gonna get to that circle before you do!"

"How long before me?"

"Maybe three to five seconds."

"This is Skymaster Tango passing the bogey and executing a climbing turn to the right."

Jack yelled, "Only half a football field to go!" But when they were only one hundred feet from the circle of air it suddenly moved to the right, and for the second time that morning Jack got a good look inside it. But this time he had a much clearer view of the pyramid, and for some reason it looked a hell of a lot bigger than it did the last time. Looking back over his right shoulder he said, "Rob, the circle of distorted air moved about seventy-five feet to the right, and when it moved I got to see inside again."

Rob had made a climbing right turn in the opposite direction from Mel when he said, "What'd you see?"

"I saw the pyramid again."

"Did you see anything else?"

"No, only the pyramid!"

Rob thought about that for a moment and wondered why Jack didn't see the other buildings along with it, like they did when they got a look inside at the beaver pond Thursday morning. Suddenly his mind changed gears, almost like somebody else took control of it, and he said, "Something just flashed in my mind about this seventy-five feet business. Whenever we've seen the circle of air today, it's been hovering about seventy-five feet above the snow, and when we've tried to penetrate it, each and every time it's moved about seventy-five feet to the right. I wonder why seventy-five seems to be the magic number today?"

"I don't know, but if I have to guess I'd say that whatever alien is operating that circle of air today is not the same one that's been doing it in the past. This one seems to have definite habit patterns."

"I agree. Although I'm not sure that I agree that it's a different alien doing the operating, but I agree that there are definite habit patterns today. I have an idea that Plan C is going to work, and if that circle of air stays put at the Harris Pasture Road and ITS 89 intersection, we'll kick the plan into gear right now." Just as he crested the eastern peak of East Kennebago Mountain he pressed the microphone key and said, "Tri-Pacer Sierra, this is Mike Yankee. Is the bogey going back into position or has it left?"

"Mike Yankee, it looks like the bogey's going back to its original ... check that! It's gone. Two Zero Two Five Sierra is heading back to its holding position to be able to monitor Sectors Rescue A4 and A8. Will advise as soon as I have a new contact."

Rob turned to Jack and said, "Shit! Then keyed his mike and said, "Roger that, Tri-Pacer Sierra."

"Rob, why don't we tell Mel and the guys holding over Phillips that we're going to implement Plan C as soon as the circle of air reappears?"

Rob was pressing the mike button as he said, "Good idea Jack! Ground Support, this is Mike Yankee. What's your 20?"

"Mike Yankee, Ground Support. Thought you guys forgot about us. We're on high ground and had a good view of the circle of air just before it disappeared."

Rob looked over at Jack, shaking his head from side to side and said, "Good thing *he's* on the ball. Ground Support, you're right, we did forget. Why don't you get down onto the main trail so that when the circle of air appears again, you're ready to boogie?"

"You got it! And don't worry about us. We'll be there!"

"Roger that, Ground Support. Skymaster Tango, this is Mike Yankee. Do me a favor and have all the guys holding over Phillips meet you in a holding pattern over Sector Rescue A30. Do you understand?"

"Mike Yankee, Tango understands and will do."

Then he turned to Jack saying, "What d' ya think, should we hold over Bigelow?"

"Makes sense to me. If the bogey appears in any of the places that Steve can see, it will be just about in between Mel and the guys, and us."

* * *

More than thirty minutes went by and there was still no sign of the circle of air. Rob and Jack were getting nervous because this was not part of today's pattern. Mel and the other pilots from Portland had been in a holding pattern over the Saddleback Mountain for the past fifteen minutes. Rob looked at his watch and saw that it was 10:30 hours. They'd been up for over two hours now, and if something didn't happen soon they'd have to go back to Rangeley for fuel. It would be too dangerous to try to penetrate the circle of distorted air without enough fuel to return. Rob looked over at Jack and said, "Do you think that they've shut down for the day?"

"Not likely. But I hope that they show up again soon, because if we have to land for fuel we're liable to lose some of our support crew. I don't know how much time they've got on their hands before they have to leave."

"Well hopefully Art ...."

Rob never got to finish his statement: "This is Two Zero Two Five Sierra. Heads up! The bogey is back in Sector Rescue A3. It's approximately seventy-five feet off the snow and its facing one six zero degrees."

"Roger that, Sierra! Where's Rescue A3, Jack?"

"It's the last clearing that you broke a trail in yesterday."

"Outstanding! There's lots of open space there." He pressed the microphone button and said, "Cessna Niner One Zero Foxtrot Golf, this is Mike Yankee. Do you have the bogey's coordinates?"

"Foxtrot Golf has the coordinates."

"Foxtrot Golf, go to Sector Rescue B1 and go into a holding pattern at 2500 feet AGL. Advise when in position."

"Roger that, Mike Yankee. Will advise." Art Bell looked at the topographical map on his lap and saw that Rescue B1 was Black Nubble Mountain, which is located halfway between Bigelow and Saddleback Mountains.

"Ground Support ... This is Mike Yankee. Do you read me?" There was nothing except dead air. Rob keyed the mike again and said, "Ground Support, this is Mike Yankee. Do you read me?"

Jack cut in and said, "I wouldn't worry about it, Rob. Len told you that as soon as they have the coordinates that they'd be on their way."

"Yeah, I know. But since we forgot about him last time, well, I just thought it would be bad karma to do it again." He keyed the mike and said, "Skymaster Tango, this is Mike Yankee. Everybody ready?"

"10-4, everybody knows what has to be done. Just give us a one minute warning so we can be in the right position to start our descent."

"Roger that, Tango."

Jack cut in again saying, "Rob, I see Art and he's almost..."

"Mike Yankee, this is Niner One Zero Foxtrot Golf. I'm at Rescue B1."

"Foxtrot Golf, set your timer for sixty seconds, and at the forty-five second mark I want you to go to the Rangeley Unicom. Using my call sign, make an announcement that you're over Black Nubble, and then tell the world that you're going to make a descent straight at the circle of shimmering air, and one more thing, set your course to make it look like you want to penetrate it in the upper left hand quadrant. By the way, Art, after you make that announcement I want you to come back to this frequency, and don't forget to start your descent on the sixty second mark!"

"Will do, Mike Yankee."

"Lima Romeo and Skymaster Tango, did you copy that?" Both acknowledged and Rob said, "OK, will begin descent on the sixty second mark. All pilots, start marking time on one. Three, two, one! Tri-Pacer Sierra, hold your position and advise if the bogey makes any changes."

"This is Tri-Pacer Sierra, 10-4."

Rob reached over and gave his friend a tap on the shoulder and said, "I'm going down to tree top level and set my course for the lower right quadrant."

"You're the boss! Forty seconds to starting our descent!"

* * *

Steve Savage had his timer mounted on the shaft of his yoke, and as soon as it started beeping he keyed his mike and said, "The bogey is stable!" While he was making his announcement he was looking in the direction of Saddleback Mountain and saw three planes beginning their descent. He picked up his binoculars and quickly determined that Skymaster Tango was in the lead, followed by Jimmy Mathew in his Piper Dakota and Al Carroll in his Piper Arrow. At first he could not distinguish who was number two, but then saw that the number three plane had its landing gear retracted, so he knew that plane had to be Al Carroll.

He figured that this time the diversion should absolutely work even if the timing for the diversion planes coming in from the rear was off somewhat. If the first plane didn't get the job done, certainly either Jimmy or Al should hit the mark with Rob. As a smile began to form on his face he said, "Those aliens won't know what hit them with Art coming in high, Rob and Larry coming in low, while Mel, Jimmy, and Al are buzzing them from behind. It should work!"

* * *

Mel could see both Rob and Art making their approach, and his intuition was telling him that the timing was going to be "right on." He was getting ready to key the mike to tell Jimmy and Al to remember to bank to the right and stay low after they pass the bogey, and that's when he heard Len say, "Ground Support is in position and ready."

* * *

Rob had set his course to make his approach at a 45-degree angle to the right side of the circle of shimmering air. He was at tree top level and took a quick look at his Air Speed Indicator, 133 KIAS. He keyed his mike and said, "Foxtrot Golf, remember, once past the bogey execute a climbing right turn!"

"Roger that, Mike Yankee. Good luck!"

* * *

"Air Support. This is Ground Support. Heads up. The bogey's beginning to pulsate!"

Len turned and said, "Keep it cool, Bubba. You too, Stormin. Don't squeeze those triggers unless you see a plane in BIG trouble!" He turned to look back at the circle of air and saw that it was rotating its position to the left. He stood up to get a better look over toward Bigelow Mountain and went cold when he saw that it was turning in Rob and Larry's direction. He looked at Stormin and Bubba and knew from the strained looks on their faces that they were very worried, but he also knew that they were very ready.

* * *

Mel was close enough that he had seen that the bogey was turning left from its one six zero position, and started getting very concerned about the approach and exit that they had planned. If anybody changed course to compensate for the bogey's new position, they'd all better change or there was going to be a lot of bent metal on the ground. He pressed his mike button and said, "This is Skymaster Tango. The bogey's rotated to the left! Maintain your original course! Repeat; do not change your course! Maintain original plan! If we have to make another run at this thing, we'll do it!"

* * *

Larry Williams took a quick look at Tommy Yorks and saw that most of the color had drained from his face. He was surprised. He always thought that *nothing* fazed Tommy. But when he turned to look out the windshield he saw something that sent a chill down his spine. The translucent radio type waves that Jack had told him about were coming from the circle, and it looked like they were headed right at him. He yelled, "Tommy, where's Rob! I don't see him!"

"He's about fifty feet below us to the right, at the two o'clock position!"

"Is he...."

The radio waves made contact with the Chieftain and it didn't make any difference what Larry did with the ailerons, rudder, or elevator; nothing would alter the plane's current course. It was like the radio waves had wrapped his plane in a force field, slowing its forward speed. When he looked at his altimeter he yelled out, "They're pushing us to the ground!" If he didn't do something quick he and Tommy were going to be the subject of a NTSB investigation. Pure panic began to writhe in his guts when he saw the trees, which were close enough to begin with, look like they were getting ready to tickle the belly of his Chieftain. Just when he thought that the props were going to start chopping up the tops of the pine trees below, he had control of his plane again. He heard Tommy yell, "Yes!"

* * *

When Mel Marshall saw the circle of air starting to emit the translucent radio type waves that Jack had told him about, he knew that Rob or Larry or both were going to be in *big* trouble soon. Common sense told him that something was about to happen, and he momentarily forgot about Len and his buddies on the ground. Instincts to help his friends took over, and he put his throttles to the firewall, getting as much speed as he could. His instructions were to pass the circle of shimmering air on its right side, and he was supposed to maintain about one hundred feet separation. But he changed his mind when he saw the radio waves lock onto Larry's Chieftain. He turned his yoke to the left and set his course so that one or two feet of his left wing would slice through the outer edge of the circle. When he looked back at Larry's plane he saw that it was just about ready to make contact with the pine trees below it. He looked back at the circle of air just in time to see his left wing slice through the outer edge of it, and then instantly wondered what in the hell was going to happen to him and his airplane, he really hadn't thought about that in the heat of things.

* * *

Rob saw the radio waves shoot past him to his upper left and knew that Larry was going to be in a shit storm. He pushed his throttle to the stop, but didn't get any noticeable additional speed. He started rocking forward like he was trying to physically push some more speed out of the Hawk, knowing all the time that the effort would be futile, but he *had* to do something!

He was about the length of a football field from the circle of distorted air when he saw Mel's Skymaster flash into view as it buzzed it. But he knew immediately that Mel had not just buzzed it, because he clearly saw that part of Mel's wing had penetrated the outer edge. His mind quickly winked an image to his consciousness of the Skymaster doing cartwheels in the snow below.

Jack broke his thought pattern when he yelled, "The circle's gone! It's gone!"

Rob's reflexes kicked in as his mind screamed the exit plan to him. He pulled the yoke almost all the way back into the pit of his stomach while banking the Hawk for a right turn. The steep climb almost immediately began to burn off some of the kinetic energy that they had built up in their run at the circle. They were just breaking through 1700 feet AGL when they heard Steve Savage say,

"The bogey's back already! It's in the exact same position as before."

Jack looked over at Rob and, said, "They're toying with us!"

Rob looked out his left window to see if Larry was still with him, and as soon as he caught sight of him in his peripheral vision he turned to Jack and said, "I'm tired of playing this game! All that matters is that we penetrate that circle of shimmering air."

As he continued climbing to 2500 feet AGL he pressed the microphone button and said, "Lima Romeo, this is Mike Yankee. At 2500 feet AGL I'm gonna break right, go into a dive and I'm not holdin' back on the speed. They might not be expectin' us to try anything this quick. Every time they've pulled this disappearing act today we've regrouped, and they just might be expecting us to repeat recent history. If we're going fast enough on the approach, we just might get lucky."

Larry keyed his mike and said, "Lead the way, Mike Yankee!"

Rob shouted back, "I'm probably going to red line this mother, but we're going in!"

Both dogs began barking in a frenzy the moment that Jack started pounding the dash and yelling, "DO IT! DO IT! DO IT!"

Rob jammed the throttle all the way home as he rolled to the right and put his plane into a dive.

* * *

Art Bell was listening to the conversation between Larry Williams and Rob Day, and when they had finished he keyed his mike and said, "This is Foxtrot Golf. I'm at 1500 feet AGL and I'm heading directly at the circle from Black Nubble. I'm going to drop down to about fifty feet above tree level and head for the lower left quadrant. My plan is to fly straight ahead and make a climbing left-hand turn after passing the circle. Acknowledge, Mike Yankee and Lima Romeo."

* * *

Both Rob and Larry acknowledged Art Bell's radio transmission. Rob yelled, "Perfect, Jack. I'm going to set my heading to a target seventy-five feet to the right of the circle. When they see Art Bell heading at them, they'll surely think it's me coming from that direction again, and move quickly to the right. The way it looks to me right now, we should just about be at the target the moment that it moves."

Jack was wide-eyed and had a big grin on his face as he said, "I think you're right!"

They were only half the distance to the circle of shimmering air when Rob noticed that his Air Speed Indicator had already gone into the never exceed territory. Suddenly, Steve Savage was on the radio saying, "It looks like there are some bad guys trying to get near the circle. Maybe they are going in for another pickup."

* * *

Focusing all his attention on the target that he established seventy-five feet to the right of the circle of air, Rob quickly said, "With all this going on, the operators of that distorted air must have their hands full. Jack, I think that we're gonna make it this time!"

Jack was rapidly nodding and said, "Yeah! Yeah we are! We're gonna make it this time!"

Rob guessed that they were about three-quarters of the way to the circle of air. He didn't bother looking over to see where Larry was. He knew that with his fighter pilot training, that he'd be right with him.

* * *

Jack yelled, "Less than three hundred yards to target!"

Rob didn't even bother to look at his air speed indicator again because he knew that it was probably pegged by now. He had never been this scared before in his life. So much was riding on success. He didn't even want to think about the excessive stress on the airframe, because if it let loose, *everything* would be lost: his life, Jack's life, and Eileen, Nancy, and Thad's chance to come home.

Jack yelled out again, "Two hundred feet to target!"

Rob saw Art Bell out of the corner of his eye, and he was only a short distance from the circle. Just as he expected, the circle disappeared and reappeared right in front of them. Suddenly they hit turbulence that was so violent that it shook the earphones off of their heads. Immediately the dogs stopped their barking. Rob looked at Jack and yelled, "I sure hope this ol' girl hangs together!"

Jack yelled back, "She will! She will! I know she will! We're going in!"

12

The moment that the translucent reverse radio type waves shot out at the Piper Chieftain, Stormin turned around and brought his Remington 30-06 rifle up to his shoulder. He had instantly made up his mind that he was going to be ready to shoot the shit out of that circle of air the second that Len gave the command. Len and Bubba, on the other hand, continued to watch in horror as those radio waves locked onto Larry William's plane. When it became obvious to Len that the plane was going to be forced into the tops of the pine trees below it, he started to yell a command to Bubba and Stormin to begin shooting. But he stopped short when a very loud thud came from the direction of the circle of air, and when he turned around to see what had caused it, his eyes immediately locked onto a plane that was wobbling in a funny way, and a thought flashed into his mind that the pilot was going to lose control. Unfortunately, the moment that unwished-for thought popped into his mind the aircraft began to rapidly drop down into the clearing below, the same clearing where the circle of air had been, and things instantly jumped from bad to unspeakable when he saw the left wing of the plane suddenly drop off. A feeling of despair and helplessness permeated his whole body as he watched the plane make a 90° roll to the right, and for a couple of moments he thought that the Piper would continue all the way around to an inverted position. But that never happened, and it stayed at a 90° angle to the surface below, quickly losing its remaining altitude. He did not have a complete view of the airplane when it hit the snow, but he did see enough of it to know that it had made several cartwheels before coming to a stop.

The clamor caused by Mel's crashing plane almost totally suffocated the sound of Len's voice as he screamed out, "OH, NO ! Let's hustle! We've got to see if we can help that guy!"

* * *

The moment that Al Carroll and Jimmy Matthew saw the translucent reverse radio-type waves, they simultaneously keyed their microphones to warn Rob and Larry. However there was nothing but static as the voice transmissions were melded into an electronic mishmash. By the time that Al and Jimmy realized that they were both transmitting at the same time, it was too late.

Jimmy was the first to notice that Mel Marshall had changed his direction of flight, and he could clearly see that the Skymaster was headed directly at the circle of shimmering air. Neither he nor Al had to guess what Mel was attempting to do, and a feeling of dread went through each one of them. Just as Mel's left wing sliced through the right outer perimeter of the bogey, Jimmy pressed his microphone key, and dropping all proper radio protocol said, "Al, execute a climbing right turn now!"

Al immediately pulled back on his yoke, and simultaneously turned it to the right as he pressed his microphone button and said, "Roger that, Jimmy, executing climbing right turn now."

Jimmy looked out of his left window to see if Mel had made it past the circle of air OK, and he cursed out loud when all he could see was the left wing of his Dakota. He owns two aircraft, a low wing Piper Dakota as well as a high wing Cessna, and in the heat of the moment he had momentarily forgotten that he was flying his low wing Dakota. He quickly keyed his mike and said, "Al, this is Jimmy. I couldn't see if Mel made it OK or not, did you see what happened?"

"That's a negative, Jimmy. When I banked my plane to the right to make the turn, I lost sight of him just as his wing was about to penetrate the circle of air."

Al could hear the anguish and frustration in Jimmy's voice as he said, "Yeah, same with me. Listen, let's continue this turn until we come around a full one hundred and eighty degrees, and I think that we ought to keep climbing until we reach 2500 feet AGL. That should keep us out of everybody's way until we know what's going on."

The second that Jimmy released his mike button, Al pressed his, and once again using proper radio protocol he said, "Skymaster Tango, this is Piper Arrow Hotel, what is your 10-20?" There was no response, and after about ten seconds he repeated the call again.

Another ten seconds went by and he was ready to make the call the third time when he heard Steve Savage on the Unicom saying, "Piper Arrow Hotel, this is Tri-Pacer Sierra, Mel has gone down in the clearing where the circle of air was, and I can see that Ground Support is on the way to help him."

Jimmy's hand was shaking as he keyed his mike and said, "Is Mel OK, Steve?"

"I don't know, Jimmy. Part of his left wing was sheared off when it hit the outer perimeter of that circle of air, and he lost control of his plane almost immediately. I think I saw the rest of his wing fall off before he hit the ground, but I'll tell you, it looked to me like he hit the surface pretty doggone hard. We'll just have to wait for a report from the Ground Support guys."

Al Carroll was fighting back the lump in his throat as he pressed his mike button and said, "In the meantime, I think we all should say a prayer for him and his family."

Jimmy was just getting ready to tell Al that his suggestion was a good one when he heard Steve Savage come back on the Unicom saying, "The bogey's back already!"

Both Al and Jimmy hesitated to make a radio transmission to Rob Day to request new instructions. Neither one of them wanted a repeat of what happened a little while ago when they had tried to warn Rob and Larry about the translucent radio waves coming at them. Besides, they had automatically made the assumption that he would change the diversionary tactics since Mel was out of the picture. As it turned out, they did not have to wait long to hear his voice on the Rangeley Airport Unicom, but both of them were somewhat dismayed when all they heard him say was, "Lima Romeo, this is Mike Yankee. At 2500 feet AGL, I'm gonna break right, go into a dive and I'm not holdin' back on the speed."

Right after Rob's radio transmission ended, Steve, Al, and Jimmy heard Art Bell on the Unicom telling Rob and Larry that he was flying his same diversionary tactic from Black Nubble. Steve immediately felt a tremendous amount of admiration for his fellow pilot, especially in view of what had just happened to Mel Marshall.

His eyes got a little teary as he listened to the very calm and matter of fact tone in Art's voice. Steve tried to quickly think of a way that he could help. He desperately wanted to do something more than be just a spotter for the operation. He wanted to fly some type of a maneuver that would provide some extra diversionary assistance now that Mel was out of the picture. But as soon as he came up with a possible option, he would promptly discard it as foolhardy, especially when he took his plane's capabilities into consideration. His frustration was rapidly mounting when he heard Al say to Jimmy, "Piper Dakota Romeo, this is Piper Arrow Hotel. Are you up to making another diversionary run at those schmucks from behind?"

He had barely released the mike button when he heard Jimmy say, "You bet your sweet ass I am! Lead the way!"

* * *

If Rob and Larry had heard Al and Jimmy telling the world that they were going to make another run at the circle of distorted air from behind, neither one acknowledged, and Steve started to get very concerned that once the pass at the circle of shimmering air was completed, that somebody might climb and turn in the wrong direction. He started to key his mike to make sure that everyone was singing the same tune when static started blasting in his headset.

* * *

Larry was nodding his head up and down as he listened to Art Bell say that he was going to make his approach from Black Nubble again, and as soon as he heard Al and Jimmy state their intentions that they were going to make a pass at the circle of air from behind, he said, "Tommy, I don't like this, we're not coordinated like we were the last time, everyone is acting independently. You keep an eye on Art and let me know his distance from the circle of air in half mile increments, and I'll keep track of the other guys"

Tommy reluctantly diverted his attention from what he inwardly thought was his oncoming nemesis, and when he finally spotted Art he said, "It looks to me like he's about a mile from the bogey, and he's about to blow the snow off of the top of those pine tress below him!"

Larry quickly calculated that Art and he were at almost exactly the same distance from the circle of shimmering air, and if that was the case, they were on a collision course. He took a quick look to see if he was right. There was no time to think about where he should look, he only had time to react, and he quickly prayed that he would make the right decision. He looked out to his left, and when he did not see the Cessna 206 he rapidly scanned forward. His instinctive reaction was right on the mark. He was on a collision course with Art! Survival instincts automatically took over as his mind went from takeoff speed to Mach 3 in a flash. His right hand shot over to the Chieftain's throttles and he eased them back a little, while at the same time his left hand pulled gently back on the yoke to raise the Piper's nose up a couple of degrees. His airspeed quickly bled off, and the threat of collision with the Cessna 206 was no longer imminent. However, a new nervousness took over at that point. He was a lot farther behind Rob than he was supposed to be. Without taking into consideration the possible damage to his power plants, he rammed the throttles forward and dropped the Chieftain's nose, hoping to quickly close the gap. The words were forming on his lips to tell Tommy that they were way too far behind Rob, but they caught in his throat. The circle of air had moved, and his eyes did not register the complete movement. He had the feeling that one moment it was in one position, and in the next moment it was seventy-five feet to the right. Then he heard Tommy yelling, "Did you see that! That frigging circle of air just jumped right in front of Rob!"

He was in the midst of trying to figure out how to get more speed out of his Chieftain when he heard Tommy Yorks yell out, "Holy Mother of God, Larry, look at how badly Rob's plane is bouncing around. Do you think they're gonna make it?"

Larry knew instantaneously that Rob was going to make it in this time, and he quickly positioned himself in his seat to get ready for the turbulence that Rob had already encountered, but his jaw dropped open in total surprise when he saw the Hawk and the circle of air simultaneously disappear. Then he heard himself blurt out, "Did you see that? Houdini has got to be coaching those schmucks!"

* * *

Art's nerves were stretched almost to the snapping point as he rapidly closed the distance to the circle of wavering air. He instinctively knew that Rob, Larry and he were on a collision course, and his mind was screaming at him to pull back on the yoke to get the hell out of the way. But he also knew that if he did that too soon, it could screw up the mission. Suddenly he saw the circle of air move to the right, and it happened to be at exactly the same moment in time that Rob came into his line of sight. It was right then and there he knew that his long time friend would make it in. He shouted out, "Way to do it, guys!"

As he was saying the words of cheer he pulled back on the yoke to begin a climbing turn to the left, but he got a jolt of surprise when he saw the Cessna Hawk XP and the circle of shimmering air disappeared at the same time. Then his heart skipped a beat when the Chieftain, Arrow, and Dakota simultaneously appeared in his windshield. At first he did not know what to do. Then he quickly began to say a short prayer that everyone had heard him announce that he was going to make a climbing turn to the left. As the nose of his Cessna came up and his plane rapidly gained altitude, he lost sight of the aircraft in front of him. Trying to calm himself he said out loud, "Lord, my fate is in your hands."

* * *

Larry's mind instantly adjusted to his new set of circumstances and he executed a climbing turn to the right, not once taking into consideration the possibility that one of the other pilots might deviate from the original program. But then his rational mind began to make itself known, and an uneasy feeling crept into the pit of his stomach as he looked nervously into the airspace around him. The moment his adrenalin rush began to settle down, he keyed his mike saying, "Tri-Pacer Sierra, this is Piper Chieftain Lima Romeo, do you have a visual on everyone?"

"Chieftain Lima Romeo, this is Tri-Pacer Sierra. Al Carroll and Jimmy Mathew are south of your position, and they are headed in a southeasterly direction away from you. Art Bell is east of you, and it looks like he's also flying in a southerly direction. Mel Marshall crashed into the clearing where the circle of air was, and we don't have any information regarding his condition yet, but Ground Support is on the way to him, as a matter of fact it looks like they're pulling up to his Skymaster now. I called Portland Air Rescue and they have a chopper on the way."

Larry and Tommy were both trying to locate Mel's plane, but they were facing the wrong direction. Larry pressed his microphone button, and while trying to keep his emotions under control he said with a wavering voice, "That's a 10 – 4 Tri-Pacer Sierra, we're doing a 180 to get a look. Let me know when Ground Support gets to him."

"Roger that, Lima Romeo, Ground Support is parked alongside of Mel's plane now, and it looks like one of those guys is already trying to get the cockpit door open."

* * *

Not one of them could see the pilot as they rode up to the mangled Cessna. Both wings had been torn off of the plane and the tail section was grotesquely bent to the right. Even though the Skymaster had finally come to a stop right side up, they could not tell if there was a door on the left side or not. And even if there was, the damage to that side was so extensive that it would have been impossible to open it anyway. Bubba was the first one to react, and he literally sprang off of his sled to head over to the wrecked plane. He may have been a big boy with more than his share of beef, but Len was really impressed as he watched him hustle over to the airplane.

The moment that he had his hand on the door handle, he could see that the pilot's head was all bloody. He knew that the pilot had to be unconscious, because even with the raucous noise that he was creating while trying to get the cabin door open, the pilot did not move at all. The door was jammed and he needed some help to get it open. Hoping that he could arouse the pilot, he pounded with all of his might on the side of the aircraft, but after only a few seconds he quit. When all was said and done, he had only succeeded in putting more dents in the metal, and much to his dismay the pilot did not even flinch.

By the time that Len and Stormin had made their way over to the aircraft, Bubba was already struggling to get the cockpit door open, and they instantly knew that he was putting his all into the effort. His face was beet red and the veins in his neck were bulging out.

When Mel did not react to the deafening noise that he made as he pounded on the side of the aircraft, Bubba's concern for the injured pilot grew in leaps and bounds, and that was a good thing. It was the catalyst that he needed to erase the excruciating pain from his mind that surged through his hands and fingers as he pulled harder and harder on the door handle. The door was not budging. Determined that he was going to get that god forsaken thing open, he set his jaw, braced his foot against the Skymaster, and then he pulled with every ounce of strength that he could muster, and for a second or two he imagined himself as the Incredible Hulk.

The door handle was the only thing to hold onto to try to force it open, and Bubba's huge hands covered it entirely. Len and Stormin could only watch as Bubba struggled with the obstinate piece of metal, and when they saw that he was starting to make a little bit of headway, they began to cheer him on. Finally, it opened enough to see a tiny bit of the doorjamb, and the moment that Bubba felt it give way, he gave a great heave hoping that it would break free. There was the sound of metal grinding and crunching as the stubborn cabin door grudgingly opened up a little more. Without releasing any pressure on his grip, he leaned toward the opening and saw that he had pulled it out about an inch and a half. His hands were killing him and he desperately wanted to shift his grip from the handle to the outer edge of the door, but he was afraid that if he let go with either hand, he'd lose everything that he had gained. Len could almost read Bubba's mind and started to run back to his machine as he yelled, "Hold onto that door, Bubba! I still have that screwdriver in my sled that we used to try to fix the track on your machine yesterday. That sucker's big enough to use as a pry bar."

He stopped when he heard Stormin yell out, "Bubba! Move over to your right and give me some room to get alongside of you! I'll wedge my hands in that opening and keep the door from closing, but don't waste any time getting a grip in there with me!"

As Len was turning back around, he heard the sound of scrunching metal echo throughout the entire clearing. The door had slipped open somewhat further, and when it ripped free there was an ear shattering POP. Bubba lost his balance and fell backwards into the soft snow behind him, and as he was clambering to get back up on his feet, Stormin forced the door open enough to stick his head in the cockpit. He couldn't tell whether or not the traumatized pilot was breathing. He was carefully backing his head out of the plane when Bubba came up next to him, and in no uncertain terms said, "Move!"

He quickly stepped aside and Bubba took his place. While putting both of his hands on the jamb, he leaned his shoulder tightly up against the inside edge of the door. Once the position felt right to him, he pushed against it several times as hard as he could. His frustration jumped to a new level when the door just continued to spring back and forth, so he decided to try another approach. Keeping his shoulder in place, he angled his feet out to his left side and wedged them into the snow. The moment that he had a good solid footing, he rammed his shoulder up against the end of the cabin door with every ounce of thrust that he could get from his weary arms and legs. This time it sprang all the way open, and once again he found himself falling helplessly into the snow below. Len instantly became very concerned when he saw Bubba's head bounce off of the door's armrest as he fell to the snow. He heard a loud thump, and he knew that his head had hit it very hard.

By the time Len had gotten to Bubba's side, Stormin was already leaning across the passenger seat to feel Mel's neck for a pulse. He placed his index and middle fingers on the pilot's carotid artery, and at first, he felt nothing. Thinking that he might have had his fingers in the wrong place, he kept shifting them slightly to different positions to find the telltale sign of life. A feeling of dread started to swell up inside of him, and pity for the man was rapidly becoming a prominent part of his thinking. He had developed a deep respect for this pilot when he saw him change his flight path to head directly at the circle of air. He knew that he had intentionally sacrificed himself to help Larry Williams.

Just when he was about ready to give the pilot up for dead, he felt a small pulse and immediately shouted out, "He's alive! Len, get Steve Savage on the radio and get some help out here! Quick!"

Len's hand shot to the inside breast pocket of his coat, and he quickly pulled out the hand-held NAV/COM. It was still on the way to his lips when he pressed the transmit button and said, "Tri-

Pacer Sierra, this is Ground Support. The pilot is alive but unconscious, I repeat, the pilot is alive but unconscious. We need medical help, fast!"

"Ground Support, this is Tri-Pacer Sierra. I have already contacted Portland Air Rescue. A chopper is on the way."

Len yelled to Stormin, "There's a chopper on the way!"

Stormin had not taken his finger away from Mel's neck, and by now he knew that the pulse was very weak and he said, "I hope it gets here soon. I don't know how long this guy can hang on."

By now Bubba's dizziness had mostly subsided and he was standing next to Stormin, doing his best to see inside of the aircraft. Shifting his position to get a better angle, he leaned in around his cousin as far as he could and said, "Do you see anything in there that we can use to try to keep him warm? He's got to be in shock, and I've heard that if a person is in shock that you should try to keep them as warm as possible."

"Yeah, I've heard something like that too. I don't see anything up here, and if there isn't anything in the back, there's an emergency blanket in the back compartment of my sled. It won't be as good as a nice warm blanket, but it's a lot better than nothin'."

Bubba quickly rummaged through everything that was in the back of the plane, and when he found nothing that could be of help he started to pull off his coat as he yelled out to Len, "Hey, Barrister, hurry up and get the emergency blanket out of the back of Stormin's sled!"

* * *

Larry was shaken up when he heard that Mel was unconscious, but he was thankful that at least he was still alive. He keyed his mike and said, "Tri-Pacer Sierra, this is Piper Lima Romeo, what's your 20?"

"Lima Romeo, this is Tri-Pacer Sierra. I'm in between the Seven Gulpers and the beaver pond at 2500 feet AGL."

"Tri-Pacer Sierra, keep an eye peeled for that bogey. Is that a 10-4?

"Lima Romeo, that's a BIG 10-4!"

A knowing smile spread across his face as he pressed the mike button and said, "Thanks, Steve, I'm headed back to Rescue B14, and I'm sure that you guessed what I'm up to. Let me know when that circle of air surfaces again." Without waiting for his reply he pressed the microphone button again and said, "Cessna Mike Yankee, this is Piper Lima Romeo. Do you read me?"

He did not expect an answer during the whole time that he kept repeating the call, but that did not prevent him from being extremely disappointed when he didn't get one, especially since there was not even a hint of static noise, which would have indicated that Rob was trying to respond. After more than ten minutes went by without any positive results, he took the microphone boom away from his mouth, dropped his head and said a short silent prayer. He had finally accepted the fact that for the time being he had lost all contact with Rob and Jack.

The short prayer helped him regain some of his composure and he turned to Tommy saying, "We've got to get through that circle of air to help Rob and Jack! If we don't, I don't even want to think about the possibilities. But without us there to help, he's going to have to leave somebody behind when he makes the trip back, and I don't want *anybody* left behind."

Tommy just sat motionless in his seat while staring out the front windshield at nothing in particular, and after a few moments he finally said in a very subdued voice, "Whatever you want to do, Larry, I'm with you."

Larry put a reassuring hand on his friend's shoulder and said, "Thanks, Tommy. I know that it took a lot of courage for you to say that, especially when I think about what we just went through. I'm getting low on fuel, and before we start getting back into our positions to make another attempt at penetrating that circle of air, I'm going to top off my tanks. I'll tell you what, if you want to change your mind once we're on the ground, it's really OK with me. There'll be no hard feelings. OK?"

When he looked over at Larry, he had a determined look in his eyes as he said, "That's not going to happen, my friend. We started this together, and we're going to finish it together."

A smile quickly engulfed Larry's entire face as he clapped his buddy on the shoulder in a warm manifestation of his appreciation. Then he keyed his mike saying, "This is Piper Chieftain Lima Romeo. Listen up, Air and Ground Support. I'm executing a right turn to come about on a westerly heading. I need fuel, and I'd like to have a meeting with everyone in my office. Tommy and I can't give up on this mission, and I'd appreciate it if you gentlemen would stick around to give us a hand. But if you can't, well, I understand."

Larry released the mike button and held his breath while he waited for their replies.

Art Bell was the first on the Unicom saying, "This is Foxtrot Golf, I'll see you on the ground."

One by one, each and every pilot followed suit, and for the first time since he was a young child Larry was on the verge of tears. When the translucent radio type waves had telescoped out at the Chieftain and locked onto it, stress had immediately electrified Larry's feelings, and it was still lurking in every cell of his body. The combination of the unabated tension, Mel's heroic sacrifice, and the steadfast commitment from each and every one of the pilots to stay on to the end, had basically left him emotionally defenseless. Larry is a man's man, and he prided himself on always keeping his thoughts and feelings under control. As he listened to the pilots that he now considered to be his closest friends, and he heard them essentially state the same words of affirmation that Art had, he could no longer control himself. Unwanted tears flooded out of the corners of his eyes. He averted his gaze away from Tommy to prevent him from seeing this sudden weakness, and he had to wait a little bit to get the lump out of his throat before he triggered the microphone. Once he was certain that his voice would not betray him he said, "Gentlemen, I can't begin to tell you what this means to me. Thank you is totally inadequate, but for now it'll have to do. I'll see you on the ground!"

The airwaves went silent. Each pilot was deep in his own thoughts. And if there were a way to record what each of them was thinking, all of the tapes would have been similar. Without exception, each man was deeply concerned about Rob and Jack, their wives, and Thad, and, without exception, not one of them had given a thought to the additional risk that they were taking upon themselves. Art Bell was the first to break the radio silence when he said, "This is Cessna Foxtrot Golf. I'm five miles southeast of the Rangeley Airport at 2500 feet. Is the active runway still three two?"

Larry was about to press the mike button to call out his position and state his intentions when he heard Steve Savage say, "Piper

Lima Romeo, this is Tri-Pacer Sierra. I'm gonna stick around out here until the rescue chopper gets here. 10-4?"

Still having a difficult time with his emotions he hesitated before keying his mike to say, "Roger that, Steve. See yah when you get there. Keep us posted if you hear anything from Len Purdy."

* * *

All of the planes in the group had landed, were refueled, and each one of them had been parked near the same twelve-foot high snowbank where Jack's Cherokee was still tied down. It was an impressive sight to see all of the planes parked side by side. It brought a fond memory to Larry's mind of F14 fighters lined up on the alert pad, ready for departure at a moment's notice.

Steve Savage was still circling above the Skymaster as the group of pilots walked towards the hangar where the King Air is kept. Larry looked back over his shoulder several times at Jack's Piper sitting amongst the other aircraft, and he found himself wondering if Jack was ever going to sit in that left seat again. He knew that thinking like that was the wrong thing to do, and he hustled the rest of the way to the hangar to take his mind off of the subject.

Al Carroll noticed an empty Mr. Coffee carafe sitting on top of the coffee maker as they were all walking into the Rangeley Airport's multipurpose room. The room is situated in the rear of the hangar, and it serves as a pilot lounge, trip-planning room, as well a classroom to teach various levels of ground school. The Mr. Coffee machine acted upon Al like a magnet, and he stopped directly in front of the mesmerizing pot and yelled, "Hey, Larry, how about some coffee?"

"I didn't make any coffee this morning, and if I did, it would be mud by now anyway. Coffee's in the cabinet underneath the coffeemaker, and the water is in the john."

Al was about to shoot some sarcastic wisdom back at Larry, but stopped short when Jimmy yelled out, "Hey, Larry, that water's not yellow, is it?"

His mood was too dark for the humor, and he did not even cast a glance back at Jimmy as he walked up to a twelve-foot long whiteboard in the back of the room. He picked an erasable marker and a crumpled up cloth that was used to wipe the board clean.

The board took up almost the entire wall, and without saying a word he started to draw some objects that ended up covering the whole length of it. In just over a minute he had depicted several nondescript items in various locations on the board's surface, and then he proceeded to label each one of them. Once he was finished he walked to the far left side of the white board, wrote the word "OPTIONS" at the top, underlined it several times, and before turning around to face everyone in the room, he wrote the number "one" with a colon after it under the caption.

By the time that he turned around, everyone in the group was sitting in a chair at the table closest to him, and their attention was riveted on his creative rendition. He is not much of an artist, and not one of the objects that he had drawn on the board came even slightly close to resembling the description printed next to it. But at least the geographic location of each object in respect to the others was pretty much on target. He had drawn several squiggly ovals, some larger than others, each representing a mountain, clearing, lake or pond.

Larry stood back from the board for several minutes to let his friends get acquainted with the impromptu topographical map that he had just constructed. But for some reason that he could not understand, during the silence he began to develop the feeling that these guys might change their mind about helping. As soon as he felt satisfied that they had enough time to get a handle on what he had put up on the wall he said, "Gentlemen, I don't know if Jack and Rob briefed you on why I was also supposed to penetrate that circle of air right along with them, but the fact of the matter is this, his Hawk doesn't have the room nor the weight capacity to bring everyone back, and he doesn't want to leave anyone behind. And there's another thing that just entered my mind. Suppose that there's more people there than just the three people that we know about, which happens to be Eileen Day, Nancy King, and Thad Cook."

He paused for a couple of seconds to let that information settle into their minds. He heard the sound of a chair scraping across the floor. His heart sank a little as Art Bell stood up, and he thought that he was going to leave. Art was a key component in the plan that he had in mind. He held his breath as Art stood there, shifting his gaze between the other two pilots, and he could swear that he felt his heart skip a beat when Art began to talk. "Larry, I've known Al and Jimmy for most of my adult life, and I think I can safely say that you've got a commitment from each and every one of us to help you with whatever plan is devised in the next few minutes, or however long it takes."

As he was sitting back down both Al and Jimmy looked at Larry, and without saying a word, each nodded their head in agreement. The second he knew that he definitely had their help, the tension began to melt like sweat out of every pore in his body, and he said, "I know what I have to do to penetrate that circle of air, but we're going to need a better plan of attack." He hesitated for a couple of moments to gather his thoughts, and said, "As far as I'm concerned, we shot our wad this morning, and we need a new approach if we're going to succeed. We need to do something that those bastards won't be expecting. It doesn't take a rocket scientist to figure out that they've got to be wise to our diversionary tactics by now. We've GOT to be a lot more cagey than we were before."

Larry walked over to the table where everyone was sitting, and as he pulled out a chair to join them he said, "Gentlemen, I know that you savvy what I have on the board up there, and I need some ideas from you. What can we do different from what we did this morning?"

There was nothing but silence after he asked his question, and as the time dragged on, the hush became as nerve wracking to Larry as the gut wrenching moments that he had experienced when the translucent radio waves locked onto his Chieftain, but he also realized that he'd best not say anything which would interrupt their thought process. The ticking of the classroom wall clock seemed to become more and more thunderous as the time marched on. He was so damn anxious to get back out to the area where the circle of air had been making its appearances, that his impatience was rapidly reaching the point of no return. Steve Savage came walking into the training room just as Art Bell said, "Larry, if we want to surprise these people, then we'd best not go into visible holding patterns like we did before."

Larry desperately wanted to know what Art had in mind, but he was also extremely anxious for information concerning Mel, especially if it was good news. The look on Steve's face didn't even come close to giving him a hint as to what the report may be.

* * *

Steve immediately felt the tension pervading the atmosphere in the room when he pulled the door open. Larry was the only person facing him, but the second that the heavy metal door closed and the spring loaded bolt made its metallic clicking sound as it sprang home into the strike plate, four heads turned in unison to see what had caused it. Each of the men had an expectant look on their face, and he knew what they were waiting for. Because he also knew that it was not the news they wanted to hear, his eyes automatically averted from theirs as he said, "The rescue chopper is on the way to the Maine Medical Center ER, and according to the EMT on board, Mel is stable." He glanced back up and could see by the look on their faces that he had given them only a half a loaf, so he continued, "I'm sorry, guys, but that's all that he could tell me."

Jimmy reached behind him and pulled another chair over to the table as he said, "Well, that's about the best news we can expect for now. I've got a friend that works in that ER. I'll call her after a while and see what I can find out. But I'll say this, if that EMT said that he was stable, that means to me that his vital signs are OK."

As soon as Jimmy had picked up the slack, Steve felt some relief flow through his body, and he briefly wondered why he had felt like the proverbial messenger of doom. "Yeah, I agree with you, Jimmy. I just wish I had some solid good news to share with you guys."

Larry jumped into the conversation because he was anxious to hear what Art had to say, and he quickly briefed Steve on all that they had discussed before he entered the room. During the whole time that he was apprising Steve, he could see that he was thinking about something else, and when he finished he said, "Any comment?"

"Yes, as a matter of fact I do have something that I'd like to add to that. Len, Bubba and Stormin are humpin' their way over here right now. After the chopper left I told them that everyone was back here to make a new plan. As soon as I finished talking, Len told me that he wanted to be in the meeting, and he also said that they saw something today that will probably be of interest to everyone here, and he thought that it may be important in your decision making process. He sounded real serious to me, and I suggest that we get their input before we make a final decision on the game plan."

Old habits die hard, and sometimes they never go away at all. Larry was rubbing the stubble on his chin as he was listening intently to Steve. He could see a lot of precious minutes being wasted before they got under way again, and the instant that he stopped talking, Larry said, "Steve, I have no problem with that. We need all the edge that we can get. How long do you figure it will be before they get here?"

"I don't think it'll be too much longer, maybe five or ten minutes. By the time that I made my turn to head back to the airport they were already on their way, and I mean to tell you, they were flat hauling ass!"

A thin smile appeared on Larry's face as he looked over at Art and said, "So, tell me what you were going to say before. I think it was something about not going into visible holding patterns."

"Well, I was thinking that if these buttheads that operate this circle of air are wise to us, then we can't broadcast to them that we're in the vicinity, and if we go into the same holding patterns as before, that's exactly what we'd be doing."

Larry had already thought about that fact and quickly shot back at him, "Then we'll just go into holding patterns in different locations."

"In my humble opinion that won't work either. I've heard you say before that if something acts like a duck, then it's a duck, and to me, if I'm flying a holding pattern at one thousand feet AGL over mountain A, and I simply do the same thing over mountain B, I'm still acting like that duck."

Larry shook his head from side to side in dismay, and his frustration was clearly rearing its ugly head when he said, "Damn, Art! I'm beginning to feel like a dentist the way that I have to pull these frigging answers out of you! Would you please just spit out what you have in mind?"

If Art was taken aback by Larry's barrage he did not show it, and he simply said, "I think that all we have to do is go into our holding patterns behind the mountains instead of over them. Instead of making Steve do his reconnaissance from a holding pattern between the Seven Gulpers and the beaver pond, have him traverse the area like a passing aircraft, and he should alternate his altitudes, maybe from 2500 feet to 5000 feet AGL. That way those aliens shouldn't get suspicious."

Al Carroll cut in saying, "I'm not sure that's such a good idea. The wind was picking up when we came back here to land. Steve's got a light plane and if the winds are blowing across those mountains, he's going to have his hands full."

"You're right, and I've already thought about that. We need somebody with a high powered pair of binoculars to go up with him to act as a spotter."

Steve had been leaning back in his chair, and as he was listening to Art's suggestion he thought of just the person that should go with him. When Art finished he said, "Listen, I like what you're saying, and I think that Len Purdy could be a good choice. From what I understand about his physical makeup, my Tri-Pacer can handle his weight, and from what I've already seen, he's a pretty doggone resourceful guy."

Jimmy leaned forward and put his elbows on the table as he said, "I know that weight is a consideration in your Tri-Pacer, but you said something extremely important, Len is a very capable person. I think that his talent would be more useful to the mission if he's on the ground." He saw the looks that he was getting and said, "Hey, listen. I'm not trying to say that Stormin and Bubba aren't as capable as he is, but I don't think that they have the leadership ability that he has."

Al finally decided to put in his two cents and said, "I have to agree with Jimmy, but I have a suggestion. How about asking Sandy Socobeson to help out? She's as gutsy as they come, and I saw her out by the hangar before. She may still be around."

Larry literally bolted from his chair and ran to the door, and he was gone before anyone could say anything else. Steve, Al, Jimmy and Tommy sat there for a couple of moments just looking at each other when Jimmy said, "I think I'll try to reach my friend in the ER to see if she can give me any news on Mel. I'll be back in a couple of minutes."

* * *

Len, Bubba and Stormin were just pulling up alongside of the hangar when Larry came running out. The second that he laid his eyes on them, he guessed who they were and sprinted in their direction. As he came up to Stormin he stuck his hand out to greet him and said, "My name is Larry Williams, are you Len Purdy?"

Motioning behind him, he said, "Nope, he's on the sled furthest away. That's Bubba right behind me, and I'm Stormin."

He grabbed Stormin's hand and pumped it up and down a few times as he said, "Did you see a woman anywhere around as you drove into the parking lot?"

"Stormin thought for a second and said, "I'm not sure if either one was a woman, but I saw two people in snowmobile gear walking toward the back of that big building over there."

Larry looked to where he was pointing and said, "That building's called a hangar. Thanks!"

Stormin had never been to an airport before, and he did not hear the word thanks. His mind had shut that out as he was trying to figure out why the building was called a hanger.

* * *

Sandy Socobeson was thirty-six years old, and she did not always have the nice things in life that she does now. She grew up in poverty on a Passamaquoddy Indian Reservation in Princeton, Maine. Prior to 1975, not many members of her tribe had an opportunity for higher education. But thanks to the determination and resourcefulness of an attorney who began his legal career in Calais, Maine in 1969, many opportunities rightfully opened up for her and every other member of the tribe. She met her best friend, Kathy Crafts, while attending one of her classes at the University of Maine in Orono, and their lasting friendship developed almost overnight. The two of them were just getting onto their snowmobiles to make the trip back to Stratton when Larry came running breathlessly around the corner of the hangar.

He was yelling as loud as he could for them to wait, and neither one of them heard him over the sound of their engines. Sandy was in the lead, and just as she was about to press her thumb throttle, Larry grabbed her left arm. That was a big mistake. Sandy instantly thought that she was being attacked. She jerked her arm free and in the same fluid motion pivoted around in the opposite direction from her attacker. As she did, her right arm came around like a Samurai's sword, catching him squarely on his right cheekbone. His head snapped to the left and he crumpled down onto his knees before he even had a chance to bring his hand up to comfort the explosive pain that he felt on the side of his face.

Sandy's momentum brought her the rest of the way around to her right, and she virtually leapt off of her machine to continue the attack. Fortunately for Larry, the second she was standing over him to deliver the next blow, she recognized who he was. Her adrenalin was still rapidly coursing though her body, and she was more than just a little confused. She had known Larry as long as she had owned the White Wolf, and he was one of her regular customers.

He was still reeling from the blow that she had just delivered, and he could feel the swelling begin to surface on the side of his face. When Larry looked up at Sandy, he had a dazed look in his eyes, and she knew right then and there that he had not meant her any harm. Just as she reached down to take a hold of his arm to help him up, Kathy came up alongside of her and grasped him by the other arm. In his current position he was nothing but dead weight, and even with the two of them lifting, they still could not get him all the way up. He gathered his legs under him to get back into a kneeling position, and as they held on to steady him, he struggled to stand the rest of the way up. His head was pounding, and he knew that an excruciating headache was going to blossom any moment, and that was REALLY bad because he needed all his faculties functioning perfectly when he went back up in his Chieftain.

When Sandy's eyes locked onto Larry's, she could tell that something was troubling him, and she did not think it was because she had just clobbered him. She leaned closer to him and said, "I'm sorry, Larry. You surprised me and I guess that I overreacted."

Larry was not sure what to say, but he decided that trying to get verbal revenge at this juncture was pointless. "Sandy, we need your help, and I've got to find a way to stop this headache that's coming on like an express train to Tim Buc Tu."

Looking at Kathy she said, "Keep a good hold on him while I get something out of my sled."

As Sandy was walking over to her machine, Larry tried to lighten the mood by saying, "Does your girlfriend always react like that?"

"Not usually, but we've seen some real strange things between here and Stratton over the past couple of days, and she's a lot more on guard than she normally is. As a matter of fact, I am too. If you pulled the same thing on me that you did to her, I would have reacted the same way, but it would have ended differently." Larry started to get a questioning look on his face, so she kept on talking. "I wouldn't have stopped until you were unconscious."

Larry looked her hard in the eye, and it did not take him very long to believe that she was telling him the unadulterated truth. He was getting ready to tell Kathy that she was a hard woman when Sandy walked up and said, "Put this powder in some warm water and drink it right away, and your pain will be gone in minutes."

Larry looked at the powder with a jaundiced eye and said, "Thanks, but no thanks. I've got to fly pretty soon, and I need all my wits about me."

Sandy put a stern look on her face as she said, "Put a sock in it, Larry. This won't do anything to your mind, and it won't affect your coordination either. It's an all natural mixture that I've put together from what Mother Nature has given to us."

Larry took it from her and said, "Listen, Sandy, I need to ask you a favor, would you mind coming into the hangar with me for a few minutes?"

She took a quick look at Kathy, and her friend did not waste any time to let her know that it was OK with her. Looking back at Larry she said, "Sure, I'll go with you, and Kathy's gonna come too. It makes absolutely no sense to me for her stand out here in the freezing cold."

Larry looked a little sheepish as he said, "Yeah, no problem. I should've asked her already."

As the three of them walked toward the doorway near the front of the hangar, Larry began to tell Sandy about all the things that happened that morning.

* * *

Jimmy Mathew was just hanging up the phone when Larry, Sandy, and Kathy walked into the multipurpose room. One look at

Larry brought a parade of questions to his mind, but he decided to hold his tongue when he realized that Larry was briefing the two women with him. He did not move from the desk until the three of them had walked by, and then he went back to his chair at the table.

Al, Steve, and Art were in a serious quandary. They wanted to know what Jimmy had found out, but they did not want to interrupt Larry. Finally Art decided that they should take a walk with Jimmy out into the hangar while Larry talked to the women. He had silently gotten his idea across to his friends, and they were just getting ready to walk out of the room when Larry said, "Hold on, you guys, I want to know what you found out, Jimmy."

Larry asked Sandy and Kathy to take a seat at the second table back while the men sat back down. As soon as everyone was situated in their seat, Larry looked at Jimmy and said, "Well?"

"Well, the news isn't all that bad. According to Marnie, Mel's conscious, but he has three broken ribs, a slight concussion, and a bunch of bruises, but other than that he's OK."

There were murmurings around the room, mostly focused on how relieved they felt, and how happy they were for Mel. Art suggested that they all chip in to get something sent to his room to cheer him up, and it did not take very long for all of them to agree upon a gift certificate to DiMillo's Restaurant. DiMillo's was a long-standing favorite of Mel's that was located in the Old Port section of Portland. Sandy and Kathy adamantly stuck to their guns that they wanted to be included as part of the gift givers, and the second that everything had been accepted by everyone, Larry looked directly at Sandy and said, "So tell me, can we count on you to help out as a spotter?"

"You already knew from the get-go that I wouldn't refuse to help you, Larry, but Kathy just told me that she also wants to do something to help out."

Larry looked to the four guys sitting at the table in front of him, which said that he was looking for their suggestions. However, Al Deyoe disrupted the moment when he stuck his head in the door saying, "Hey, Larry! There's three guys that have been hanging around outside, and they tell me that they're here to see *you*."

"Holy smokes! I forgot that they were out there." Al Deyoe, the airport maintenance man, was standing near the door. Larry looked at him and said, "Would you show them in, Al?"

Getting up from the table Steve said, "No sweat, Larry, I'll go get them."

* * *

Larry looked over his shoulder at the clock on the wall and was dismayed to see that it was already 12:05. The day was rapidly getting away from him and he still had too much to do. When Len, Bubba, and Stormin walked through the door, he knew immediately that whatever they had to say was going to take more time than he was willing to give up. They looked *totally* beat. And well they should be. Of everybody in the group, their task was the most physically demanding. They had covered some serious territory since early that morning while racing back and forth across the face of East Kennebago Mountain.

Deciding to take the bull by the horns, Larry walked up to Len and said, "We haven't met, but Stormin pointed you out to me in the parking lot. I know that you want to talk with me, and I can see that you're really tired, but I'm running out of time. Why don't you guys grab some coffee while we finish up our plan? I've got to get back up in the air as soon as possible. Rob needs my help, and I don't want to miss an opportunity to penetrate that circle of air today. If the planning doesn't take too long, then we can have our talk, fair enough?"

Larry was already turning around, convinced that he had handled the situation rather well, when he felt a firm hand on his shoulder. The first thought that entered his mind was that Len was trying to stop him, but when he turned back around and found his nose stuck in the middle of Bubba's massive chest, he knew that he had been wrong. When Bubba started to talk, for some reason Larry was reminded of the gentle giant that played Hoss Cartwright in the Bonanza series. Bubba looked down at him, stared him squarely in the eyes and calmly said, "I don't think that you should be in such a big rush, mister."

Larry quickly glanced at Len, hoping that an explanation was cursorily forthcoming, and his hopes instantly diminished when he heard Len say, "Mr. Williams, I think that what we have to say will have a direct bearing on the planning session that you're about to have. I'd love some coffee, and I'm sure that these two guys would also, but if you're in such an all fired hurry, the coffee can wait."

Kathy found a way to help out and said, "Neither the coffee nor the conversation has to wait. I'll get the java for you guys. Just tell me how you like it."

* * *

There was a resounding bang when the door slammed home, and that seemed to be the signal that simultaneously shifted everyone's gaze to Len. He could almost feel the intensity of everyone's stare as he said, "Gentlemen, let me begin by refreshing your memories. I'm sure that you all remember where the bogey was when the plane crashed. But do you also remember that Steve Savage had said that he thought maybe they were making a pickup of some bad guys that were nearby?"

Everyone except Jimmy remembered the radio transmission, and Steve started to explain what he had seen to Jimmy when Len cut in saying, "That's not really necessary, Steve, because when you answer my question, he'll know everything anyway. Do you remember how many of those suckers were being picked up?"

Steve mentally recreated the scene in the clearing and finally said, "I don't really know how many people were there, but now that I think about it, I think it was a fairly large group, maybe ten to fifteen people."

Bubba stood up and walked over to the white board and wrote the number nineteen in the middle of Larry's drawings, circled it for effect, and as he was walking back to his chair Len said, "We've been debating among the three of us what the number is. Stormin is convinced that it was twenty-two people, and I feel that it was more. There were just so many tracks everywhere that in all probability, there is no way to tell for sure."

Just as Kathy was walking back through the door balancing three cups of coffee on a makeshift tray, Larry jumped up from his chair and started to pace around the room. Kathy set the steaming coffee down on the table in front of each of the guys, and as she was making her way back to her chair Larry calmly said, "So tell me, Len, what's the point of all of this?"

"There's more to tell. While I was doing my best to keep the pilot that crashed warm....."

Art Bell cut in and said, "His name is Mel Marshall."

Len looked over at Art and said, "Thanks for that. We tried to determine who he was." He stopped short, looked down at the floor and said, "Let me correct that, who he is. But we couldn't find anything in the plane to give us any clue. By the way, does anyone know how he is?"

Larry was becoming more and more impatient ... he wanted to get this over with so he could get back up in the air, and he yelled out, "He's just fine! Would you please get to the point!? I'm losing precious time!"

Len felt his anger begin to rise to the surface, but easily brought it under control, which is something that he had to do it in court all the time. He gave Larry a smile and nodded his acknowledgment as he continued, "Anyway, there wasn't much room in that airplane, and while I was trying to keep Mel warm, Bubba and Stormin decided to go check out the area where the people had been standing just before they were picked up."

Bubba stood back up and cut in saying, "And it's a good thing that we did, because when we found more tracks than we could count, me and Stormin decided to follow the trail that they had made to the clearing from the woods."

Taking over the story Len said, "Yeah, and as they followed the trail back, it crossed another clearing that was closer to Harris Pasture Road, and then it went up a steep incline into the woods again."

Then Stormin decided that it was time for him to get his two cents in and said, "That's right, and it ended in what we finally determined was a huge concave depression up on the top of this plateau, and there was more friggin' tracks up there than you could shake a stick at. They went everywhere. It was like the people that made them were just walking around to get some exercise, because it sure didn't look like they had anywhere to go."

Anxious to be the storyteller again, Bubba cut in saying, "That made me and Stormin real curious, so we decided to check out the entire area until we heard the sound of the chopper coming to get Mel. First we walked along the edge of this big...." He paused, trying to think of what word would accurately describe it, and then blurted out, "...*depression*, to see where it would take us, and after maybe five or ten minutes we came back to the same spot where we had started. And everywhere that we had walked the snow was loaded with all kinds of boot and shoe tracks. I ain't never seen nothin' like it."

Stepping back into the conversation, Stormin said, "When we got back to where we had started, I told Bubba that we must be in one of those circular depressions that Rob Day had told us about, so I told him that we should separate and check out what was in the middle. We decided that he'd stay put while I walked to the opposite side of the depression, which I calculated should take me five minutes. So Bubba checked his watch, and when the five minutes was up he was going to start walking slowly in a straight line into the woods, assuming all the time that I'd be doing the same from the other side, and we were fairly certain that we'd meet somewhere in the middle."

"That's right, and while I was waitin' for Stormin to get to the other side I hear this sound like a toilet flushing, and then the ground all around me started to shake, and then I hear this loud rumbling noise that lasted for a long time."

"I heard the exact same thing, and the first thing that I thought was who in the hell put a flush toilet out in the friggin' woods, and how come it ain't frozen!? But I stopped thinking about all that crap when the ground started shakin' under me," Stormin added.

Larry was intrigued by the Ground Support team's story, but he knew that time was waiting for no one, and he desperately wanted to get back to structuring a strategy that everyone would be comfortable with. He interrupted Bubba and said, "So what did you two see that could affect our planning session?"

Len took over the conversation and said, "The long and short of it is this. We think that whoever these people are, they're gone. We think that they finished whatever they were doing here, and now they've vacated the premises. I personally don't think they'll be back."

Larry's patience had reached an end and he said, "Just how in the hell did you come to THAT brilliant conclusion?"

"It wasn't very difficult. Bubba, tell him what you and Stormin found."

"As soon as the ground stopped shaking around me, I started to run straight into the woods, just like Stormin and I had planned, only I didn't run too far before I had to stop real quick, 'cause if I didn't I would have fallen into this huge crater."

Stormin wanted tell his own story about what had happened to him and said, "The same thing happened to me, only when I tried to stop real quick my feet slipped out from under me and I didn't stop sliding until my feet were hanging over the edge of that crater. When I stood up, I saw Bubba standing almost opposite me on the other side."

"I'll tell you what, when I saw Stormin fall and keep slidin' toward the edge of that hole, I thought he was a goner. The bottom of that thing was about seventy-five feet down, and there were all kinds of jagged stuff sticking up everywhere. If he fell down in there, it would have been like falling into a pit of spears. I'll bet you that he'd have probably gotten skewered by at least two of those mothers."

The room went silent for several seconds before Stormin picked up the story again and said, "In among all those things sticking up, I could see different things that looked like busted up furniture, and other stuff that looked like maybe they had been cabinets, or something like that. I'm not sure. I ain't never seen nothing quite like that stuff before."

Stormin looked down at the floor, almost like he was looking for the answer there, and Len took advantage of the pause to take over. Larry, the point is this; I think we made things too uncomfortable for them around here, and they left in a hurry. Since they destroyed whatever it was on top of that plateau, or in the bowels of it, it tells me loud and clear that they don't intend to come back."

Steve Savage got up out of his chair and said, "Maybe we should find out what is down in that hole. Maybe that could give us some answers, and then we'd know what to do."

Larry had enough and he was almost shouting when he said, "Steve! For crying out loud! We don't have time for that crap right now. I've got to find a way to get to where Rob is, and I've got to do it quick! Looking in that stupid hole isn't going to do anything but waste more time that I don't have!"

Len suddenly yelled loud enough to get everyone's attention. "GENTLEMEN! I see no point in going down into that hole, and the reason is simple. As Bubba and Stormin stood at the edge looking down into it, everything disintegrated right before their eyes. There's nothing left except an empty hole. Not even the spears, or whatever they were, could be seen. It's like it was nothing but an empty hole from the very beginning."

* * *

In spite of Len's convincing argument that they would be wasting their time, Larry managed to get everyone's attention back on the mission that he wanted to implement as soon as possible. They decided on the locations where they would maintain a low altitude holding pattern while Steve and Sandy would crisscross the area at different altitudes in the Tri-Pacer. Steve was to be the first to take off, then followed by Art, Al, Jimmy and Larry respectively.

The plan that they had ultimately decided upon was not very different from the strategy that they had used when Rob and Jack successfully penetrated the circle of air. But they did find a use for Kathy. She would ride with Art Bell to act as a safety pilot while he was making his diversionary run at the circle of air. The main reason for that decision was a statement made earlier by Art. He had told everyone that he sure could have used another set of eyes to watch what the other aircraft were doing as he was diving at the circle of air.

Larry had filled each and every one of his fuel tanks that are in and on the Chieftain to the max. He wanted to make sure that if it was more than two hours before the circle of air surfaced again, that he would not have to worry about landing to take on more fuel. As it turned out, Len had been correct in his assumption that the invaders were gone, at least for the rest of that day. When the daylight began to fade, and most of the aircrafts were about out of fuel, Larry glanced over at Tommy with a forlorn look in his eyes as he said, "As much as I hate to say it, I think we have to pack it in for the day."

Tommy did not say a word; he only shook his head in agreement. Larry keyed his mike and said, "This is Piper Chieftain Lima Romeo. Listen up, everyone. I know that you're low on fuel, and besides, we're running out of daylight." Frustration brought on emotions that were rapidly overpowering his normally calm demeanor. He was being forced to quit, and his mind would not accept the inevitable. He had to stop for a second to swallow the lump that was forming in his throat, and then continued, "It's time to hang it up. You guys that flew up from Portland probably don't have enough fuel to safely make it back to your home base. I'd appreciate it if you'd join me in the meeting room for a few minutes. I won't take any more of your time than that, I promise, and your fuel is on me."

Each of the pilots radioed back his appreciation to Larry for his kind offer. They all agreed to meet with him, but not one of them would let him pay for their fuel.

Len heard Larry's radio transmission, and it was obvious to him that he sounded like a beaten man. He did not have any spunk left in his voice. Len turned to Stormin and Bubba and said, "I'm sure that you guys heard what he had to say, do you want to head back to camp, or do you want to go to that meeting?"

Bubba did not say a word. He simply sat down on his machine, started it up and pointed it in the direction of the Rangeley Airport.

* * *

There was not a sound in the room when Larry Williams hung up the phone. All eyes were on him as he slowly walked up to the white board, and when he turned around to look at everyone sitting at the tables in front of him he said, "Mel's doing really well. As a matter of fact, the nurse that I was talking with said that he'd probably go home in the morning."

That statement brought a round of applause from everyone just as Len, Stormin and Bubba walked into the room. Larry knew that none of them understood what the cheering was all about, and after sharing the good news with them he said, "Thanks for coming, guys. I really appreciate it. The reason I asked everyone to come in here is that I want all of you to know that I'm not giving up. I'm going to keep checking the area until I find where that circle of air is surfacing again. I probably know more about what's been going on around here this week than any of the rest of you, and I'm not one hundred percent convinced that these people have given up in this area."

Len cut in saying, "I hope and pray that you're right, and that I'm totally wrong, but I feel pretty certain that they won't show up around here again. Maybe somewhere else, but not here."

Larry stared at him for several seconds and he could see the conviction in his eyes that he was sure that he was right. He stood back from the table as he said, "Whether it's here or someplace else, when I locate where those bastards have surfaced again, I'd like to know that I can count on everyone here for their help."

Everyone except Len absolutely guaranteed their help. When it came to his turn he said, "I'm totally committed to helping out, and to boot, I feel somewhat responsible that Nancy King, Eileen Day, and Thad Cook are missing. The only thing that I can tell you is this: If I'm not buried in the middle of a court trial, you can count on me too, is that fair enough?"

Tears of gratefulness were flooding Larry's eyes as he said in a wavering voice, "I'm proud to know each and everyone one of you. Thank you."

Steve stood up and walked to the front of the room, and when he was standing alongside of Larry he said, "I know Jack and Rob as well as anyone in this room, and I know this in my own heart as well as I know my own name. Whether we can get Larry through that circle of air to help them or not, as sure as I'm standing here in front of you, those guys will find a way to bring everybody back.

Steve sat down and not one person in the room moved a muscle to get up to leave. Whether they knew it or not, the events of the past couple of days had bonded them together. It was a bond of deep friendship that is usually only shared between men and women that were in combat together. Everyone was deep in their own thoughts, especially Len. Before getting up to leave the room he made up his mind that trial or not, he was going to be there to help if and when Larry was lucky enough to find the shimmering air again.

* * *

Before Steve sat down, Larry was already diligently structuring a PURSUIT in his own mind.

To be continued...................